A New History of Torments

A New
History of Torments

Zulfikar Ghose

Holt, Rinehart and Winston
New York

Copyright © 1982 by Zulfikar Ghose

All rights reserved, including the right to reproduce this
book or portions thereof in any form.

First published in the United States in 1982 by
Holt, Rinehart and Winston, 383 Madison Avenue,
New York, New York 10017.

Published simultaneously in Canada by Holt, Rinehart and
Winston of Canada, Limited.

Library of Congress Cataloging in Publication Data
Ghose, Zulfikar, 1935–
A new history of torments.

I. Title.
PS3557.H63N4   813'.54   82-6093
AACR2

ISBN 0 – 03 – 061949 – 1

First American Edition

Printed in the United States of America

1 3 5 7 9 10 8 6 4 2

ISBN 0-03-061949-1

To Alfredo Pareja Diezcanseco

AUTHOR'S NOTE

The title of this novel was suggested by the line, "en esta historia de martirios" in Pablo Neruda's poem "Vienen por las Islas (1493)". The titles of the two parts of this book are the two phrases in the penultimate line in the following quotation from Neruda's poem "Rapa Nui":

Sólo la eternidad en las arenas
conocen las palabras:
la luz sellada, el laberinto muerto,
las llaves de la copa sumergida.

PART 1

The Sealed Light

Who then devised the torment? Love.
Love is the unfamiliar Name
Behind the hands that wove
The intolerable shirt of flame
Which human power cannot remove.

T. S. Eliot, *Four Quartets*

1

Jorge Rojas Jiménez ascended the stone steps and emerged on the rooftop terrace for the habitual stroll he took before lunch, walking unhurriedly among the rows of rosebushes growing with a profusion of flowers in large wooden tubs. He walked to each of the four corners of the terrace where the brick wall came up to the height of his chest and looked across at his eight thousand hectares of land, enjoying best the view from the southeast corner that showed at a distance of some thirty kilometers, one of the peaks of the Andes which was always capped with snow and which, at this hour, stood clear against a blue sky. He breathed in the cool, fresh breeze which, coming through a forest of eucalyptus trees, was finely scented, and walked diagonally across the terrace to the northwest corner from where he could see the pastures sweetened by the three narrow rivers that, coming through a plantation of pine trees, became one on the eastern edge of his ranch and finally, some hundreds of kilometers away, joined the Amazon. He walked back across the brown tiles of the terrace and came to the thick blue line he had had painted from east to west. This is where the Equator ran, and at the age of forty-seven it gave Rojas a boyish sort of pleasure to walk along this line with a foot in each of the two hemispheres. He was slim and proportioned sufficiently elegantly to make the awkwardness of walking with one's legs wide apart a graceful, even a natural act. He knew that this act, which he performed only when alone, was meaningless because cartographical divisions had no bearing on human destiny but he derived from it a profound satisfaction—as if by possessing a little of each of two worlds he had effected their unification and thus secured for the earth an essential and a fructifying harmony.

Reverting to his natural walk, he went and stood from where he could look across his land at some of the objects of his industry. There, far to his left, was the slaughterhouse and to the right of that, closer to the house, the refrigerated warehouse where the beef was stored until the trucks from the distributor in the city came to transport it away. In fact, there were the two trucks, right then, driving to the warehouse. In another direction, he could see the corral and next to it the building that housed the dairy plant making butter and cheese. The land was still under the noonday sun with its mild, but growing, heat; but little details—a peasant on a mule emerging from a pine plantation where he must have spent the morning tending to the seedlings; Emilio, the general foreman, riding his motorcycle toward the beef warehouse to attend to the transportation—showed Rojas that the work was going on and that the order he had imposed upon his land was fruitful and harmonious.

"Are you still here?"

He turned around from where he had again been looking at the peak of the Andes where clouds had begun to gather and a haze had permeated the blue sky, and saw his wife standing beside the wooden tub from which the branches of a climbing rose had been trained to form an arch in front of the entrance to the terrace.

"It's you, Manuela!" he said, surprised.

"How long do you plan to keep us waiting?" she asked in a sharp voice.

He was walking toward her and stopped. He narrowed his eyes and his lips twitched involuntarily at the right corner, producing a momentary dimple on the cheek. He turned away, saying, "I'll be down in a moment."

"In a moment!" she said, the tone of her voice making his phrase sound ridiculous.

"I said I'll be down, all right!" He could not restrain a touch of anger in his voice.

"When the soup is frozen," she said, going away.

He saw the back of her heavy, small figure, and felt deeply irritated. He walked quickly to the southwest corner and looked across the rows of eucalyptus trees as if he could see the city a hundred and fifty kilometers away. The breeze had freshened, for the leaves were shimmering and rustling. All he could see beyond the trees was a valley, but what his mind saw was the highway curving around the sides of the valleys, rising to just below the snowline of the mountains, making descents and loops, cutting through villages where the Indians in their ponchos and felt hats cultivated corn on small tracts of sloping land, and entering the city.

Suddenly, he longed for the city. Manuela had only come to call him to the lunch that was getting cold. But her voice and fat little body filled him with a strong impulse to do something violently wrong to her.

Married to her for twenty-two years, he had never desired to be estranged from her; their quarrels had been brief, like a quick afternoon thunderstorm which left one refreshed. The land had been his passion and he had rarely—only twice before, in fact—needed the distraction of infidelity to reinforce the sense of his own virility. But the voice that he had just heard imbued him with a despair at his condition; it had taken him by surprise and jolted him into a recognition of complex emotions. He looked in the direction of the city as if he could see Margarita Aparicio from a hundred and fifty kilometers away.

When he went down from the terrace and entered the dining room, he saw Manuela sitting silently in her chair at the table, her hands clasped on the bulging curve of her stomach: an image of quiet rebuke that increased his irritation. Their two grown-up children, Rafael and Violeta, were next to her, opposite each other. Rojas, avoiding Manuela's cold stare as he walked to his place at the table, glanced at Violeta's profile and sucked in his breath: an awareness of his daughter's loveliness evoked a memory of Margarita's beauty, coming to him in that moment as a particular odor, a female fragrance which he breathed in, inhaling her sex. He paused by his chair, suppressing a sigh, momentarily

13

consumed by a surging sensation within his chest.

"There you are at last," Rafael said. "Thought you'd never come."

Rojas looked at his son as he took his chair. The young man was smiling; he had a frank, open manner, and what he had just said was not meant as a rebuke but rather as a joke to relieve the tension built up by the mother's silence. Normally, Rojas would have joked back but his wife's words on the terrace had triggered an emotion within him which he felt as an unidentified pain. Across the table, Manuela began to serve the soup and passed the first plate to Violeta who placed it in front of Rojas, saying, "Creamed potatoes, your favorite."

Rojas was struck by the girl's long fingers, and he remarked to himself that there was little resemblance between his daughter who, at nineteen, was slender and beautifully featured, and her mother who, at forty-five, resembled the squat little round-faced women who sold ponchos at the market.

The other three had begun to eat when Rojas took his napkin from its silver ring and placed it across his lap, and he was picking up his spoon when he heard Rafael say, "It's gone cold."

Manuela, chewing a piece of bread, jerked her head up as she swallowed a spoonful of soup, and, her mouth full and the corners of her lips wet, said, "What do you expect when no one respects time?"

Rojas put his spoon down and stared at his wife. Some of the soup had trickled down her chin and she was rapidly swallowing more, bending her head down to her plate and then jerking it back as she raised the spoon to her mouth. Her uncouth manner did not offend Rojas so much as the words she had spoken. He rose from the table, pushing his chair back, seeing just then his wife's small dark eyes dart up at him.

"What's the matter?" Violeta asked, a touch of alarm in her voice as if an instinct informed her that the moment was charged with an obscure passion.

Rojas began to walk out of the room. He had reached the door when he heard the ringing sound of a spoon being dropped in an empty plate and then the voice of his wife saying, "Finish your soup, Violeta. I've had enough."

"But Father . . . " Violeta began.

"Don't worry about him," Manuela said. "He will learn to repent."

Rojas was already out of the room and did not hear his wife's concluding words. He went to his bedroom and changed into a lightweight woolen suit and, checking to see that he had his wallet and checkbook on him, walked out of the house. He drove down the avenue of eucalyptus trees in his green Passat, heading for the highway, but before he could be out of the property he was overtaken by Emilio on his motorcycle. He stopped and asked through the window, "What is it, Emilio?"

"The beef warehouse," Emilio said, out of breath as if he had been running. "The refrigeration broke down. Must have broken down Friday. It stinks real bad in there. There are a hundred and twenty carcasses in there. The trucks just came to take the shipment and when I unlocked the door I was thrown back by the smell."

He ought to go and see. The loss was enormous and was more than the price of the hundred and twenty cattle. The trucks' futile journey would have to be paid for; the slaughtering of the next lot of beef would have to be delayed, which would thin out the pastures that were already suffering from lack of rain; the refrigeration plant would have to be repaired; workers would have to be diverted from their normal jobs in order to dispose of the hundred and twenty carcasses . . . he did not want to think about it.

"Get Rafael to deal with it," he said to Emilio.

"The stink is incredible," Emilio said, sniffing the air around him. "I can smell it even here."

Rojas drove away. Leaving his ranch, he joined the highway and turned south. The city was only ninety minutes away, and yet in the past he rarely went to it except for the necessary reason of attending to business with his bank or his accountant, and occasionally when he needed to see his doctor. He was too attached to his land and the view of the world from his rooftop terrace was so vast and so wonderful, and so filled with

15

a sense of freedom, that he found any narrower perspective oppressive. He felt stifled by the city and until two months ago had always tried to finish his business there as quickly as he could and return to his land.

He had gone to see his doctor about an abdominal pain, which was not so severe but had been naggingly there for a week, long enough for him to feel concerned, and had used the occasion to have his car serviced. The doctor prescribed some antibiotics for the pain which, he diagnosed, was due to an inflammation in the colon. Rojas used the doctor's phone to call the garage and found that his car, promised for three o'clock, was not going to be ready before five. Having time to kill, Rojas wandered into some boutiques, hoping to find something to take back to Violeta. It was in one of these shops that he met Margarita Aparicio. She was tall and slim with straight black hair and dark-brown eyes.

"Can I help you to find something?" she asked, seeing in him the well-dressed middle-aged man looking for a present to take to his mistress.

The voice was soft but flat, a music without melody. There was a glass case of silver jewelry beside where they stood, and he saw her light-brown hands lift up the lid, the fingers long and straight with the nails cultivated to a curving point. As she bent down toward the case, her slender neck defined a beautiful curve.

"This necklace, for example?" she said, turning her face to him and smiling.

"No," he said. "No jewelry."

She closed the case and stood erect, facing him. "Well, why don't you look around," she said, "and see if there's something you like. For the young lady," she added almost out of malice for his failure to buy something at once.

"There's no young lady," he said, "not the kind you mean, but I will look around."

She walked away to attend to a woman who had come out of a changing room holding three dresses from their hangers. Rojas walked about the shop, looking at nothing, but now seeing the young woman from behind stacked-up dresses and now in a mirror as she filled out the charge card for the other woman's purchases. The latter left with her parcel, and he was again the only customer in the shop. He walked up to the counter behind which she stood and said, "You have a beautiful shop but I'm completely lost as to what to buy."

"The shop's not mine, but thank you," she said, closing a drawer where she had put the tickets torn from the recent sale. She looked up a moment later, expecting him to be on his way out of the shop but he was still standing there, staring at her.

"If someone came in here to buy a present for you," he asked, "what would give you the most pleasure to receive?"

"Why, what a funny question," she said, and laughed. Then, casting a serious glance around the shop, she said, "It's difficult. Everything here's so well known to me, it wouldn't give me any surprise to receive anything."

He was amusing, she thought.

"Would you like to be surprised?" he asked.

She did not know what to make of the question. He seemed too cultivated and gentle to be making a vulgar proposition. She wished that another customer would come in. No one did and he was still looking at her. "I don't know what you mean," she said.

There was the Hotel Nuevo Mundo down the street, two blocks away. He would be in the Christopher Columbus bar with a surprise for her.

"It will be a long wait," she said, laughing as if dismissing his proposal. "I don't finish here till seven."

"My name is Jorge Rojas Jiménez," he said.

"And mine is Carmen Miranda." This time there was scorn in her laughter.

"The name is not important," he said, smiling at her. "I just mentioned mine in case you needed to ask for me."

"You have no idea how insulting your words are," she said, sniffing and looking away from him.

"I'm sorry that you think so." She looked back at him with a surprising intensity, and he added, "Come to the Christopher Columbus bar at seven and I will prove my sincerity. Why, I think I'll even give you a name. I will call you Margarita."

17

"That *is* my name!" she cried out animatedly in spite of her resolution to be rid of this man who was trying to pick her up. "Margarita Aparicio."

A loud, piercing sound of a horn jolted him out of his reverie and he looked at the rearview mirror. At first, for a fraction of a second, he was blinded by what appeared to be an intense golden light and then he saw that a large car had driven right up to his rear bumper and that its driver was eager to overtake him. The golden light was the sun reflecting from the car's roof and hood, he saw as he accelerated. The road was ascending in wide, looping curves, and the other car hung back for a few kilometers. Shifting down and going fast into curves, Rojas increased the distance between the two cars and at one point he was on an upper tier of the road from where he could see the large car below him going in the opposite direction before it could reach the horseshoe curve in the road. Painted a metallic gold, it was a large American car of a make that he had never seen before. After a wide curve, the road straightened through a pine forest. Although Rojas was driving at a hundred and fifty kilometers an hour, the American car flashed by him in a dazzling golden streak.

He had bought a gold watch and waited in the dim light of the Christopher Columbus bar. She had come twenty minutes late, having changed from the slacks she wore in the shop to a dove-gray woolen skirt.

And now he was going to see her for the seventh time. A casual encounter had become a passion. He was dimly aware of the chaos he was going to bring to his family, but any upheaval, he felt, was a small price to pay to prevent the chaos within himself that threatened a deeper disintegration.

Nearly halfway to the city, he came to a town and, remembering that he had not eaten lunch, he drove to a café on the main square. The large golden car was parked outside it. Leaving his own car some distance away, for there was nowhere else to park, Rojas walked up to the American car. The word *Continental* could be seen on its rear from a distance. A red-faced white-haired man wearing a white open-neck shirt came out of the café and seeing Rojas staring at the car with what he assumed was admiration, said, "A beauty, isn't it?"

Rojas was not so sure. It seemed garish and vulgarly ostentatious to him, but he smiled at the man and nodded his head.

"To me," the man said, unlocking the door, "it's worth more than its weight in gold." He entered the car and just before he closed the door, added, "and it weighs two tons!" He was laughing as he drove away.

Rojas entered the café and was greeted by its proprietor, Sergio, whom he knew from previous visits.

"That man was a charmer," Sergio said. "See what he made me do!"

He was holding a piece of paper in his hand.

"He came in, asked for a glass of ice water—not even a beer, mind you!—and then talked me into cashing this traveler's check. Said he needed to buy gasoline. I've never done this before. How do I know it isn't fake?"

"Let me see it," Rojas said and Sergio gave him the check, saying, "Thos. Cook, doesn't even sound like a bank."

Rojas saw the signature: Mark Kessel. The check looked genuine enough and he returned it to Sergio, saying, "It's all right. You'll get your money. It's only twenty dollars anyway, and my guess is you made a few centavos by giving him a rotten rate of exchange. Listen, I'm hungry."

Rojas tried to phone Margarita from the café to tell her that he agreed with what she had said the last time. He was not interested in an occasional tryst either. She was right. But he could not give her up. She must come and live with him. It was intolerable when one's real life had to remain a secret. He was finished with Manuela and did not want to hear her voice again. He would get his lawyer to work something out. No, it was not an idle dream, not an aberration. He wasn't going to play with her emotions. The land, if she came to live on it, would be hers. He was quite clear in his mind that this was what he was going to tell her. But he could not get a line to the city. The operator said there was a two-hour wait. He put the phone down. Ridiculous how modern technology gave you a convenience and then let you down.

Successive peaks of the Andes were ranged on the horizon to his right, their slopes of sheer ice streaked with bluish lines. A cold breeze blew into the car through the open windows. There, in the hollow among the mountains, below him ten kilometers away down the winding road, was the city.

2

The entrance to the cold-storage warehouse as well as the wide doors beside its loading bay were left open so that the smell of the decaying beef could decrease sufficiently for the men to go in to haul the carcasses out. But now, instead of being confined inside the building, the smell was picked up by the breeze and carried across the land. It entered the plantations of pine and eucalyptus. It swept across the pastures and some of the cattle grazing near the river looked up, held their nostrils to the air and made a loud moaning sound. Manuela heard the cattle when she went to close the window of her bedroom, for the breeze was carrying the smell to her pillow. Her husband had not returned from wherever he had gone. She guessed it must be to the city. To see a woman: for what else put a man into these terrible moods? Let him go to her, spend his money and his passion, she thought, hearing footsteps in the corridor. She had done her duty, raised two beautiful children. Let him go and appease the desires of his middle age. It was terrible, but that was how it had to be. A man's lust returned to him when his children were of age to have children. She thought, at least she hoped, that the injustice was in nature. Her poor Jorge would need to spend his lust, it was like needing surgery to get rid of a malignant growth before one could be whole again; poor Jorge would need to pour out his superfluous semen before he was healthy enough to resume his duties as a father. He would return, for this was his land, his house, his family.

She opened the door and saw it was Rafael who was going about the house closing the windows.

"What have you done, Rafael?"

"I didn't think the smell would come this far," he said. "It stinks everywhere. Even the cattle are going crazy."

They heard a hissing sound. Violeta was coming up the stairs in a white nightgown, spraying the air, her arm waving a can above her head and creating a misty cloud above her. Rafael laughed and the mother smiled. The light on the half-landing behind Violeta made her nightgown appear nearly transparent, and showed the outline of her hips and thighs.

"Save some for my room," the mother said.

"There's plenty," Violeta said, smiling at her mother and going into her bedroom which she sprayed until the bed seemed damp with the perfumed moisture.

"I hope to be asleep before the scent wears off," the mother said, closing the door.

Violeta went in and out of the other rooms, spraying them lightly. "You've made a terrible mess," she said to Rafael who followed her.

"It wasn't my fault the refrigeration broke down."

"Where do you think Father went?"

"I don't know."

"Oh, yes, you do," she said. "What's wrong with him, Rafael?"

"I didn't notice anything. Maybe he's just annoyed with Mother."

"Why should that be? Mother's an angel. No one, but no one can be annoyed with her."

"She's our mother, not his."

Violeta looked at him, shaking the can in her hand, and said, "We must not let him harm Mother."

"We must not."

He walked after her to the next room.

"Rafael, why are you following me around like a dog?" she asked, entering her own bedroom.

"Just keeping you company," he said. "But I'll go to bed now. Hope you sprayed my room sufficiently."

She nodded her head, putting the can on the floor near the door.

"What have you got there?" he asked with amazement, looking at her bed.

She ran the few paces to her bed, flung herself upon it, turned on her back and, throwing up her arms, said, "A bed of roses!"

"Violeta, you're crazy!"

He walked up to her bed and saw that it was covered with rose petals—some of which floated up in the air when Violeta jumped into the bed.

"I got them from the terrace, a basketful of them, and crushed them with my own hands. Father's favorite roses, all of them! It's his punishment for going away."

She held a hand to her nose and then stretching out her arm toward Rafael, said, "It still smells beautiful from crushing all those roses."

He bent his head toward it and brought up his own hand to hold hers.

"Beautiful," he said, sitting next to her. He picked up a handful of rose petals, crushed them in his hand and let them fall on her lap. "It's a good idea, to sink into a perfumed bed."

"I will have a bed of roses on my wedding night," she said as if forming a resolution, throwing her arms up and beating her heels on the mattress in a quick, theatrical gesture of longing, so that some of the rose petals lifted and fell. "And also with every new lover," she added as an afterthought and laughed with exaggerated delight.

The image passed through Rafael's mind of two bodies making love and he shuddered when he realized that the bodies he had imagined had been Violeta's and his own.

"I'll be glad when the vacation ends," she said. "I long to start college and meet lots of people."

"Lots of boys, you mean?"

"Of course. Why don't you go to college, too, Rafael?"

"You're the one with the brains in this family. And the looks, too. I prefer to be on the land."

"But don't you want to be where you can meet girls?"

"Don't worry about me," he said, smiling and standing up. "I'd better go to sleep. Have to be up early."

*

23

A field of dead brush had been cleared and on the next morning the men, wearing handkerchiefs across their noses, carted the trunks of dead pines and placed them in the field to make a vast square of ignitable timber. The sound of their chainsaws filled the air as a number of large trees were cut down and their limbs sawed into logs. It took the men all morning to form a large pyramid of trunks and logs and dried brush. Then six men, their heads covered with homemade hoods, rubber gloves on their hands, and wearing gum boots, entered the warehouse. Blue-green flies covered the carcasses and their buzzing noise on top of the nauseating stench created a terrifying atmosphere. Rafael had offered the men a week's vacation with double pay for the work and they grimly proceeded with their horrible task of bringing the carcasses out into the sun and throwing them on the heap of firewood. Several times during the trips, they stopped to suck at a lime or to spray their clothes with an insect repellent. One of them collapsed after two hours of hauling carcasses, but stood up, tearing the hood off his head, staggered to a pump, and drenched his head in cold water, and then went back to his task. It was nearly sunset before the warehouse was empty. Two hundred liters of gasoline, which had been brought in on a truck, in four drums, were emptied on the heap.

Rafael stood on a pickup truck holding a lit kerosene lantern. He told the man at the wheel to drive away from the heap and to accelerate when he gave the signal. When he was about twenty meters from the heap, he shouted, "Now!" and threw the lantern into the air toward the carcasses. The driver, with the engine still in first gear, pressed hard on the accelerator. Rafael fell forward but stopped his fall by holding on to the tailgate of the truck. Nothing seemed to happen. "Slow down," he called to the driver. A little flame could be discerned in the firewood, and then another. Suddenly, there was a muffled explosion, a ball of fire burst out and then contracted.

The entire heap lit up, flames began to soar into the sky. The firewood shifted and settled and the pyramid sank down a little. Rafael told some men to keep watch over the flames.

There was a good distance between the nearest trees and the conflagration, but one never knew, a fire could get out of hand. He ordered some men to hose down the inside of the warehouse and to scrub its floors and walls with disinfectant. "I want the place to be smelling like a hospital by tomorrow morning," he said.

He drove back to the house and walked straight to the bathroom to take a shower. Then he went up the stone steps to the terrace on the roof where he found his mother and Violeta standing in the darkness that had fallen, watching the fire in the distance. When he joined them, his mother asked, "Rafael, are you sure that was the right thing to do?"

"It smells worse now," Violeta said. "I wish it would rain."

"It was the only thing to do," he said. "The smell will stay with us for some days, I'm afraid. But we'll get used to it and won't even know it when it has gone. It will be good to get some rain. It would clean the air. Besides, the pastures are beginning to be parched."

3

Five days had passed and Rojas had not returned. Manuela rose early in the morning and asked a servant to fetch her a mule from the stables. She put some fruit in a basket and, when the mule was brought to the courtyard, rode to the southeast, going past a eucalyptus plantation and entering a pine forest. It was dark under the tall trees but the track was clearly visible, meandering around the trees and going downhill. About an hour later, she emerged from the forest and came to a clearing which had in a corner an old stone structure: four columns stood some ten meters from one another on the four points of a square floor made of slabs of granite. The columns were three meters high and looked as if they had once supported a roof; remnants of the crossbeams could be seen where the timber had originally been cemented into the stone. Creepers grew around the columns and weeds sprouted from the gaps in the granite floor.

Alighting from the mule, Manuela climbed up the three steps, surprised at the calm that prevailed within her. She stood on the floor with her basket and cast a glance around the clearing and at the trees on the edge of the forest. She could see no one. A granite slab formed a low table in front of her and she knelt down to place the basket on it. She brought out four oranges and a bunch of small bananas and placed them on the table. She looked up: in the distance, but closer here than seen from the terrace on the roof of her house, was the peak of the Andes rising to a perfect point in the clear dark-blue sky.

She stood up and turned around, and faced the forest. "Missú," she called in a loud voice, and again, "Missú!"

A thin, short man, completely bald and slightly stooped under a heavy poncho, appeared and walked slowly toward her. Even from a distance, his dark eyes stood out as the only lively organs on an otherwise emaciated and wrinkled body. He came up to the floor and seeing the fruit on the table, picked up the bananas, snatched and peeled one and ate it rapidly. He devoured two more, and then picked up an orange. He bit into its skin, pulling a part of it away, and then tore at it with his fingers and began to stuff his mouth with the fruit. He chewed with a quick movement of his jaw, his lips smacking loudly, the juice trickling down his chin. She went and stood against a column, looking up at the mountain peak and wondered if Missú could reveal anything to her. He was such an old man now.

Missú came from an Indian tribe which had flourished in some distant valley beside a river which flowed east. He could never tell where, or how far away, it was but when asked only pointed to the peak in the southeast, thrusting his arm up and making his hand with the pointing finger rise up and go down to indicate that he meant a region beyond the peak. He would not say what calamity had struck the tribe, only that he was its only surviving member. It was over thirty years now since he had come to this region, driven by some terror to discover a distant and safe habitation for himself. Once, he had been able to live with the Indians native to this region who had for many generations adopted the language and the habits of the people who had conquered the country, and he had learned to speak the tongue and to use the tools with which they cut the earth. But the memory of his own tribe that appeared to him in his dreams filled his mind during his waking hours with images with which there was no correspondence in the world around him. He had lost the words of his native ceremonies and forgotten the prescriptions of his tribe's rituals, but the images existed as demons within him. He came away to live in the only tribe he could belong to, solitude, here in the forest, leaving it periodically when he could find no fish in the streams or when the people who came to him from time to time, bringing him fruit and asking him to look into their future, did not come.

27

Manuela had heard of him from a woman who had worked in her kitchen. It was twenty years earlier, soon after Rafael had been born and Manuela had discovered that Rojas was keeping a mistress in the city. "Go to Missú," the woman had said, divining the source of Manuela's unhappiness. He had looked at her idly when she talked, his lively eyes darting now at her bosom and now at her hands, and then, as if completely bored, he stared around him at the open air, and snatching a butterfly which had happened to be fluttering by, killed it between forefinger and thumb, and began to examine it with a gleeful sort of interest. Suddenly, he put the butterfly into his mouth, chewed it and spat it out, and then told her what she must do. *You must give him your own blood.* How? In what quantity? But he had turned from her questions and run away into the forest. She had interpreted his prescription in her own way, and watched Rojas eat the calf's liver in its bloody sauce.

He looked away from her now when she began to tell her story, and picked up an orange and began to play with it, throwing it from one hand to the other. Occasionally, he looked at her. She was embarrassed that twenty years later she had the same story to tell. His black eyes stared at her moving mouth and then looked above and beyond her shoulder at the mountain peak in the distance. *What can I do?*

The question, she realized, was not as desperate as it had been twenty years earlier, not being touched by the anguish of desire. It came from another darkness, a deeper source of torment. Her husband's absence from her bed caused her no pain now. It was a sense of a larger loss that did. As if the husband had become blind and did not know that he was leading his family into that desert where, could he but see, the scattered bones of former travelers who had mistaken their vanity for bravery would show him his error. She feared a loss of order, the snapping of a taut tension which held her world together.

Missú had gone and sat on the edge of the floor and was staring at the mountain peak. The voice behind him stopped its flow of troubled words, and he looked down at his feet where ants had crawled up between his toes. He raised his feet one at a time and brushed the ants away. He stood up and looked at the woman.

"The daughter's blood," he began, but looked away sadly, pained that these were the words he had to use.

"What are you saying, Missú?"

"If she has the body of a virgin." He was almost talking to himself, pondering a thought.

"Missú!"

He saw the ants near his feet scurrying into a crevice.

"What are you *saying*?" she asked. "What blood?"

He looked at her. His eyes had gone still. "The daughter's," he said, turning and beginning to walk away. "The daughter's," he repeated quietly to himself. "The daughter's."

"Missú!" she called after him. "Missú!" And then, seeing that he was not going to turn back, "Missú!"

She could have been screaming at a horror that she alone had witnessed.

4

A flamboyant tree in the garden of the hotel threw its flaming branches of orange-red flowers over the wall and the light, coming through the tree and then penetrating the arching branches of the tall hibiscus bushes whose pink flowers hung above the small pool, gave a rosy hue to the blue water as if the pool were that fragment of the sky just above the horizon which at sunset gave up its transparent blue for a murky, but spectacular, violet. Five meters long, the pool fitted snugly in the small enclosed yard at the back of the bedroom whose walls were decorated with pictures of legendary lovers. From over the walls on either side came the low voices of men and the laughter of women and the sounds of splashing.

The rosy light, touching Margarita's bare shoulders as she sat on the edge of the pool with her legs in the water, gave the light-brown skin of her back a pink translucency, while her face and breasts on which the shifting violet of the circulating water threw its revolving light glowed with a striking vividness, as if touched by a throbbing passion. Her black hair, wet from a recent immersion in the pool, hung straight to her shoulders and below them to her back. There was a serenity about her face where the cheeks, glowing in the reflected light, expressed the contentment of one who has known only the happiness of a deeply satisfying sexual love, an idea suggested also by the full lips held open in a lingering smile and by the brown eyes which, while emphasizing their dreamy acquaintance with pleasure, possessed that brightness which is the outer light of a memory of an intense joy.

She was looking at Rojas, who, submerged to his neck in the water, was swimming toward her. During moments when there was a pause in the laughter among the lovers in the back gardens, the ocean could be heard in the distance, its swells rising up as waves and crashing loudly before being spent with a sigh on the white sand.

Rojas stood up in the pool in front of Margarita. Putting his arms around her, he touched her forehead with his own and ran his tongue down the line of her nose and said, with his mouth at her lips, "Happy?"

"Yes, very," she said, clasping his head as he lowered it to her bosom. "Very," she repeated—as if she needed to reassure herself.

He ran his tongue along the hollow around her navel and hearing laughter, said, "This is a funny hotel, isn't it? With all the honeymoon couples hysterical with love."

"It's beautiful," she answered and then, trapping his head between her thighs, said, "They're not all honeymoon couples. Don't tell me you never came here before!"

"Swear to God, I did not!"

"Then where did you take your women?" She was running her fingers through his hair.

"There were no women to take anywhere. I've told you my life. I loved my land more than I did any woman. Until I met you."

She parted her thighs to release his head and drew it up, her hands at his cheeks, and kissed him. "You are a delicious liar," she said and laughed softly.

"Is that why I insisted we see a lawyer?"

She kissed him again and said, "You are so thoughtful and I love you."

She had been surprised when he had turned up late in the afternoon at the boutique and had thought at first that he had come to the city on some business and was merely dropping in to say hello. But when the customer she had been waiting on had gone, he told her why he had come. To take her away, to give her everything he had. His life. She could not leave the shop till the evening, and they met again at the nearby hotel.

He was proposing an immediate and a permanent change in their association, asking her to leave everything at once and to come away with him. There were hesitations, reservations; the terror of too sudden and too irrevocable a commitment to a new life. No, he had told her, it was not the romantic foolishness of his middle age, not the common desire to recover one's youth through a liaison with a beautiful young woman. His feeling was profounder. He wanted her, but more than that, he wanted her to be his with the secure knowledge that she could depend upon the depth of his love; to prove that, he offered her a firm material foundation, a legal contract which would give her the proportional rights to his property which would have been hers if he could have married her. What could she give him to prove *her* seriousness? she had asked. Only yourself, he had answered.

His lawyer had spoken to him privately. "Jorge, you and I are about the same age, so I can be candid with you . . . No, no, let me finish. I know that you know what I'm about to say, but I have to say it nevertheless. You are not the first man to find such happiness in a young mistress that he is convinced that he has at last discovered a real, a true love. All a man needs to do in such a situation is to buy the young lady a diamond brooch and to enjoy her until the delusion of love has passed."

"Francisco, you do not know how offensive your words are."

"Please, let me finish, even if I'm insulting you. I owe a duty to your family even if you think that you yourself do not. What you are proposing is madness. You brought two children into the world and now you are saying they have only diminished rights in your house. You don't seem to understand the tragedy you are about to bring to your house."

"Francisco, if you don't stop talking like a priest, I'll go and find myself a new lawyer."

The lawyer became silent and then agreed to draw up the document, for it occurred to him that any other lawyer, not knowing Rojas and his family, would do for a fee whatever he was asked whereas he himself, being familiar with the

32

circumstances and an old friend of the family, could at least insert some ambiguous language into the articles and thus provide the heirs grounds for contesting the contract.

The proposal both dazzled and shocked Margarita. At their previous meetings, she herself had wanted to end the association. He was sweet-tempered, charming, generous; but she was disgusted with herself for being available to him whenever he visited the city. At the same time, when he had left her the last time, she was terrified that he would never return. She was not certain what her emotions really needed. He represented a form of excitement in her life, which was otherwise dull and monotonous.

Margarita was a stranger to the city, having come to it as a refugee from her own country when her parents and brothers were lost in the revolution that replaced a democracy with a military junta. Her father had been a professor of economics whose views were poison to the junta; and her two brothers were even more extreme in their views. She had survived the terrible slaughter of her people only because she was too young to be at the university and was at a fashionable girls' school in a distant province. Years of privation and suffering had followed and she experienced the horror of losing her family, which she had not witnessed, each day of her life. Finally, she left her country and came to a foreign city where the only thing she had in common with the people was the language. Although rarely without a customer to talk to during the hours she was at the boutique, she lived a lonely life, burdened by the painful memories of her past. Rojas did not know it, but he was offering her a chance to break with a situation which could only become increasingly intolerable. But vague fears came to her, for she knew nothing of the world she was being invited to enter. Obscurely, she saw the outlines of a disruption, the scattering of Rojas's family, the breaking up of an order, and the collapse of his family's habits of twenty years. But she saw nothing else for herself, no future other than the one that chance had brought to her. However beautiful she was, the fact of being a penniless foreigner excluded her from the class of society she had belonged to in her own country. She would be consigning herself to a mediocre existence if she refused. His enthusiasm thrilled her when she accepted his proposal. He was so *young*, really! He wanted to go away on a honeymoon, to a hotel overlooking the ocean where only lovers went. He wanted to take her to Miami to buy her clothes. He wanted to fly to Paris so that they could dine at a famous restaurant. She settled for the honeymoon, and he liked to hear her say that he had swept her off her feet.

She took her lips away from his mouth and, laughing, pushed him back into the water; his hands were at her shoulders and since he was still holding her when she pushed him, she fell into the water with him, so that they stood there in an embrace after finding their balance.

Later, dressed for the evening, they walked past the pool and went out of the small yard to the larger garden of the hotel where the wide lawn was broken by flower beds and scattered trees and at the far end walled in by a magnificent row of royal palms: beyond the palms, below a short stone wall, a rugged cliffside sloped down for some twenty meters and then fell sheer to where the Pacific crashed against it, and receded, leaving a narrow sandy beach. The sun had just set and the pink which still suffused the western horizon was gradually fading. Several couples, the young women in long cotton dresses leaning against the men whose arms they held, strolled about the lawn. Some stood by the stone wall under the palms where they had been watching the sunset, arms thrown around waists. The sound of low voices filled the air—the deep murmuring of the males, the sing-song melody of the voices of young women, soft sounds coming from different directions of the garden and casting a spell on the evening—and it seemed that the air was charged with currents of pleasure. Even the little bursts of laughter from the young women were filling the air with perfume.

Rojas and Margarita sat down at a table where a waiter brought them drinks.

"The flight back is early, at six in the morning," he said.

"Good," she said, smiling, her eyes catching a distant light which had just come on. "Then we don't have to sleep. We can make love all night!"

"It is enchanting here."

"But five days is enough? Is that what you mean?"

"I've never been happier in my life."

"Tell me the truth, Jorge. Do you not feel guilty? When you are silent, are you not thinking of your family then?"

"Whatever I think, I don't want you to think about it. But no. I have no guilt. Why should I?"

"Jorge, I'm not simply your mistress in the bedroom. You've made me mistress of your land, too."

"But that is how I want you, with your freedom secure."

She leaned toward him and said in a whisper, "Your family does not know what it has lost."

He might have been alarmed had her whispering voice not appeared to his ears as forcefully erotic.

5

As if she saw the portents in a dream, Manuela's premonition grew that when her husband returned he would not be alone. She stayed in her bed for three days, thinking. Meals were brought to her but she scarcely touched the food. Violeta came and sat by her bed several times, expressing her concern and asking her questions, for she thought that her mother was ill. But Manuela gave her no clear answers. What had Missú meant? Manuela kept wondering when Violeta was in her room. *The daughter's blood.* She could not interpret the words in any way that made sense.

Rafael, too, came and sat by her in the evening when he had finished work. The refrigeration plant had to be repaired, he told her. It was the biggest single loss the ranch had ever suffered. He just hoped the price of beef would go up so that they could make up the loss. He knew she was not listening but talked on nevertheless. It was better than sitting there saying nothing. He sensed that the source of his mother's illness was not some organic disorder but a grief which was simple and profound. And when he went away, Manuela wondered what would happen to him and Violeta when the father returned with a young mistress.

Her own unhappiness did not cause her so much pain as the fear that the children would become outcasts from their own land. The longer she remained in bed the more clearly she foresaw the unfolding of a tragedy. Her memories were filled with a history of errors—how a moment's lust in a man brought down a house, how a fierce violence was aroused because a man's eye was struck by the curve of a young girl's cheek. She knew the passions of her race that led to tribal disruptions and, therefore, she suffered no despair; for it was inevitable that men commit those wrongs that dried up rivers and burned the crops under a ferocious sun, so impossible it was for them to suppress the impulse to draw a terrible curse upon themselves and their land.

What she suffered from was the torment the knowledge produced in her. She lay thinking of her own past, the twenty-two years of her married life, remembering how her young husband used to dote upon her. The children were such a pleasure in those early years! Tears came to her eyes when she remembered that happy time. No, it had not been entirely happy. A lot of anxiety had attended Violeta's birth, for her blood pressure had been dangerously high. And there had been illnesses when she had sat awake at night, not daring to look away from the child lying in the cot with a high fever for fear the child might die when it was not watched. But, in retrospect, all that anxiety seemed a kind of happiness; it was a natural thing, the mother suffering because the child could scarcely breathe. Her poor Jorge was blind and did not know what he was doing to his children.

When Rafael came to see his mother on the third evening, she suffered a sharp pain in her chest: what had he done, her poor innocent boy, that the passions of people in the Old World thousands of years ago were his inheritance and should bring him grief through the unthinking actions of his father?

But he sat down beside her without seeing her concern and began to talk about the work he had been doing. "At last the electrical engineer from the town came to look at the refrigeration plant. These men are so hard to get nowadays, it's almost as if they're doing you a favor by coming. And they charge the earth just to take a look at what needs to be done. Seems we need a whole lot of new parts," Rafael went on, seeing his mother turn her eyes from the window to his face, "including a transformer. That's going to cost a bundle. Plus, the spare parts might have to be specially ordered from the city, and if they don't have them there they might well have to be ordered from the United States. On top of all this, there should be a herd ready for slaughter in another month. We're going to have a big problem if the refrigeration remains out of order for that long. Father's going to get a shock when he returns."

He stopped himself, realizing that he should not have mentioned his father. In order to divert her attention, he added, "At least that terrible smell has gone. But you know something, I asked the men to scrub the walls and floor with disinfectant, they poured so much disinfectant on the floor the place now smells like a chemical factory."

He did not succeed in amusing his mother who looked at him with tired eyes and said, "Rafael, you will have to go away. You will have to take Violeta with you and go away. I pray to God that no harm will come to you and that you will be able to return soon to your land."

"What are you talking about, Mother?" Rafael was startled by what his mother had said and the idea occurred to him that while he and his sister had not seen any evidence on her body of a physical illness these last three days, neither of them had thought of the possibility that what might have become infected was her mind.

"Can you make the sacrifice?" she asked. "I myself will leave the house tomorrow. There is a cottage on the land where Julio Reyes used to live. Remember him, that wonderful forester? His widow lives alone there now, and I will go and live with her."

"You do not know what you are saying, Mother. Please don't talk like this. If Violeta could hear you, she would cry."

"No, you must both be strong and go. Go to some other country for some months. Or years. For however long it is necessary. The time will pass, and you will come back to your land."

Rafael held her hand in both of his and leaned close to his mother's face. "Mother, this *is* my land. I am my father's son."

She looked away from his eyes and said coldly, "But I am no longer your father's wife."

"Mother, stop it!" he said in a loud, exasperated voice. "Stop tormenting yourself for nothing."

"Listen to me, Rafael," she said in a hard, dispassionate voice, staring at him unblinkingly. "In a day or in a week, your father will return. With a young woman, a beautiful young woman. It is useless for me to fight his passion. He will not find me here and therefore will not need to make ugly scenes in the house and will not need to disgrace me with a legal separation. I will be safe from the fires which are consuming him. But *you?* The young woman is beautiful, close to your age. Think what that means. What would happen if you fell in love with her? How could you sit at the breakfast table next to her knowing that your father had discharged his semen in *her* body during the night? And if she fell in love with you, would she not *need to despise* you for being younger and handsomer than your father? And when she bears a son of her own, will she not despise you even more for being the man she would have preferred in her bed and for being at the same time the man with rights superior to the child which not you but your father gave her? No, my son. I see nothing but trouble whichever way I look. It will be better for you to go away, for they cannot take away your life in your absence. Let the storm in your father's loins pass. Your flesh does not need to be touched by the fire consuming him."

"But Violeta," Rafael said as if agreeing with his mother's rehearsal of the future events, "she need not be involved."

"You are too young to understand these things, Rafael! Remember that your sister is exceptionally beautiful and that she is only nineteen. No young woman, coming to a house to be its mistress, could tolerate that. Rafael, you cannot know the power of an unconscious jealousy. This is not a world in which people know their real thoughts. A young woman who creates a life out of her body surrenders her own life. She may think she still is an individual, but really she is only a mother. Someone who has played her part in nature. And nature is quite cruel to women, Rafael. You can have no idea what few resources women really do have with which to fight for themselves. Try to imagine, then, what curse your father's young woman will not want to fall on Violeta's head. Take Violeta away with you, Rafael. Do not let her suffer."

"One thing, Mother. You have not seen this woman, have you?"

"No."

"And you do not really know if Father has not gone to meet some business acquaintance in the city?"

"No, I do not know that."

"So, how do you arrive at your ideas?"

"Look out of that window, Rafael."

He walked to the window and looked out of it while she remained in bed from where she could, if she looked out of the window, see only a patch of graying sky.

"You can see, what I cannot see from here, the pastures that lead to the river," she said, having closed her eyes. "That is the view from the window. Usually, at this time of the evening, the cattle are there, some still munching on the grass and some lying down. I have not looked down from that window for some days but I can tell you that there is not a single cow in the pastures right now. Why? Because there cannot be. The smells in the air have disturbed them. Something is wrong in the world they were accustomed to. If you go down, you will find them huddled beneath the trees, where it is dark."

Rafael was looking out of the window, and she added, "Well, do you see any cattle in the pastures?"

"No," he said, turning back to her, understanding her larger meaning.

Rafael spent a disturbed night, waking up several times and thinking again of his mother's words. Were they only the ravings of a mind which suffered from an invented jealousy, or had she, through some extraordinary perception that saw more than the given facts, arrived at some indisputable truth? Did she possess a magical sixth sense that made her prescient? Or was she simply mad? He was afraid of the knowledge women possessed without there being any immediate evidence to warrant it.

In the morning, an event occurred which took his mind away from the troubled thoughts of the night. He had just risen from breakfast when he saw from a window a car enter the courtyard. It was painted a metallic gold. The door at the driver's side opened and a white-haired man wearing a white open-neck shirt and brown corduroy trousers came out. Rafael had never seen him or that car before.

6

Mark Kessel had been driving north on the highway from the city and the road zigzagged into a valley, curved in a wide loop, and then began to ascend a mountain in a series of tight bends, before it reached the plateau near the Equator. When he began to take the sharp corners to climb up the mountain, Kessel noticed the truck which he had overtaken some ten minutes earlier: it was just beginning to negotiate the horse-shoe curves across the mountain down which he had descended some minutes ago. He was glad not to be ·stuck behind the truck. But then he noticed the car which was: it had a red light upon its roof. It was a bright yellow Volkswagen and from that distance he could see the blue markings of the Federal Police insignia on the door. From the jerky movement of the car—accelerating in spurts, braking hard, swerving out—it was obvious that the driver was trying desperately to overtake the truck. But the road was narrow, with one horseshoe curve after another and unless the truck came to a complete halt, there was no way the car could overtake it. Fortunately, there was no traffic ahead of him, and Kessel drove up the mountain as fast as he could take the Lincoln around the bends and reaching the long straight stretch on the plateau, pressed forward with all the enormous power at his command. But he knew that no amount of speed could help, for if the yellow Volkswagen did not catch up with him on the highway, it would merely radio ahead and have him stopped at the next village.

Who could have tipped off the police, he wondered while he looked for a way of anticipating being stopped. He had come

41

into the country as a tourist and was now leaving it. It had been a bold idea to come in a conspicuously flashy car when his mission had been a covert one. Many people saw him but no one really knew who he was, seeing him only as a wealthy tourist; and those to whom he introduced himself understood that he was a fanatic collector whose obsession was to find a rare piece of Inca jewelry which only he seemed to know about and which, he indicated, he was desperate to discover in order to complete his collection. He had spent an entire morning with the curator of the National Museum and an afternoon with the keeper of the Gold Museum. Those, he assured the curator and the keeper with many a joke, were the last places where he hoped to find the missing piece, which he described as a tiara, showing them a sketch he had with him made from information in an obscure diary of a sixteenth-century explorer he had come across in the British Museum. No, all he hoped for at the museums was to see if there were a similar object which might give him a clue as to its origin and date, for the sixteenth-century explorer had been lamentably vague. Without that kind of precise information, his search, he said with a mournful sigh, was doomed to eternal failure. The curator and the keeper were sympathetic, for it was such a pleasure to talk with a foreigner who knew so intimately a subject so close to their own hearts, but unfortunately they could not help him, though each, attempting to diminish the disappointment of their charming visitor, came up with spontaneous speculations as to where he should look.

His real obsession was not a missing piece of jewelry, but society, and the obsession took a polarized form in his mind: he aligned himself with revolution in contemporary South America and at the same time sought, with an anthropologist's enthusiasm, a tribe that observed hierarchical principles and found its harmony in the tyranny of tradition.

Now in his mid-fifties, Mark Kessel had had a colorful career without ever having had a profession and had achieved absolutely nothing. Given to boyish adventures in his youth, he had remained an adolescent all through his twenties when he was prone to playing practical jokes of the kind a boy of fifteen would be embarrassed to be caught at. His father died when he had just turned thirty, leaving him an apartment building which brought a tidy fortune in rents each month. Kessel decided that the time had come for him to settle down and to find some serious occupation. But there was nothing that he really wanted to do. A university education in history had given him the habit of dreaming about the past in a rather sentimental manner; life in the modern world he found unbearably dull and unspeakably silly. A corporation which had hotels all over the world offered him an enormous sum of money for the apartment building, wanting to construct a hotel on its site. He accepted and went on a tour of Europe, ending by residing in London for two years. He found diversion in visiting museums and began to be interested in the objects of antiquity—Greek pottery, old maps, even the bones of prehistoric animals. He became acquainted with a number of exiles from South America, men and women of his own age who had escaped the horrors of military dictatorships and who now passionately talked of bringing democracy and social justice to their countries. He became interested in their cause, and when he returned to his own country he financed the publication of an underground paper that preached an extreme form of socialism. Kessel himself was not interested in the ideology; in fact, it did not even occur to him that should the cause which he was promoting succeed, he was the very sort of person who would be its first victim. He simply enjoyed courting danger. Because he was generous with his money and also willing to travel at his own expense to carry out their missions, the revolutionaries assumed that he was converted to their cause. For Kessel, however, the money he gave them was like paying dues to a club whose membership he enjoyed and he undertook the travel because he relished the sense of danger that he believed it entailed. At least he had a purposeful reason to be seeing countries other than his own in South America, and the several trips back to London for conferences with the exiles afforded him the opportunity to spend time at the museums again. Entering middle age, he

43

had acquired the manner which conformed to the common idea of a scholar—inattentive to immediate questions, occasionally quoting Thucydides, being extraordinarily struck by an old print—and he also presented an image of himself as a somewhat eccentric person capable of doing outrageous things.

But recently he had come to the somewhat painful realization that his own extravagant life and the appalling inflation had reduced his great fortune to practically nothing. And as if he did not care and wished to throw away what little was left, he bought a Lincoln Continental and derived considerable pleasure from being seen in it. He had a vague notion that he would marry into a rich family and settle down. He had never had to face a real problem in his life and so assumed that if a problem now existed, it would surely solve itself in a manner most satisfactory to himself. It was at this time that the revolutionaries had come up with a new mission for him. Having dimly begun to perceive what their ideas really meant, he was no longer interested in associating with them, but they offered something that he could not resist. He decided that he would have one last fling and enjoy himself enormously.

What they had to offer him was an old map, drawn in the hand of a missionary of the sixteenth century, which he had often talked about when trying to impress his friends with his eccentric interest in arcane knowledge. The map was supposed to depict an area east of the Andes where, his reading had hinted, a tribe that had peculiar habits was to be found. All his boyish enthusiasm for adventure returned. He would find the tribe and thus discover the principles on which a unique society was based. He almost believed that he was indeed a great scholar and explorer and that he was about to have a brilliantly glorious success. Thus the two pursuits that he had given everyone to believe were his chief obsessions—to help the revolutionaries to alter present society and to discover an ancient tribe—neatly came together in this one mission which he decided to undertake flamboyantly in his new Lincoln.

The backrests of the two front seats, both of ample width and depth, were filled with gold bars. His instructions were to drive to a certain street on the edge of the city at a given hour, walk half a kilometer away after parking the car; he would find himself at a perfect spot where he could enjoy a view of one of the most spectacular peaks of the Andes, and after doing so for ten minutes he should walk back to his car. The gold would have been taken out by the agents of the revolution who were planning a major campaign across several countries and who were due to receive arms from certain foreign countries who had to be paid in gold; and he would find, in the glove compartment, the old map he so passionately wanted.

Kessel had followed the instructions and found that the view of the peak was indeed magnificent. On returning breathlessly to the car, he had opened the glove compartment with trembling hands. The map was there! He unfolded the fragile paper eagerly; it had been eaten by time and was practically torn along the folds, but he saw through eyes that had become moist with emotion, the hand of the ancient priest making the firm lines leading to that village in the interior where once, and perhaps still, existed the strange tribe he had read about. Inscribed at the bottom of the map was this curious legend, or injunction, or riddle:

> Deliver this not, but in your bosom keep,
> As in the heart of a lake a golden sheep.

He put the map in his wallet and drove away, thinking how the gold would finance a new order in South America and how he would pursue the other quest.

But the police car bothered him now. Something must have gone wrong. Someone must have given away his identity. Of course, he had nothing in the car to incriminate him, but he did not want to take a chance with the country's police if he could help it. The police car must still be behind the truck, he thought, looking at the rearview mirror and seeing no one behind him. He was driving at a hundred and ninety-five kilometers an hour and had gone a good half a kilometer past the road that branched off to a farm by the time its presence registered on his mind and the idea occurred to him that he could go there. He braked, went off the road onto the dirt shoulder, swung around, and came back to turn into the road to the farm. The road went through some undulating land that was forested with eucalyptus, thus obscuring his car from the main highway. A thought came to him. He slowed down and finding an obscure spot under the trees, carefully drove off the road and parked the car where it could not be seen from the road. He went to the backseat and worked the hidden lever below the headrest of the front seat by raising the headrest and then inserting a finger in the opening to trigger the concealed lever. The rear panel fell back. The gold was still there! He could not understand it. The map had been delivered but the gold not taken. Whoever had been expected to take the gold must have known something, perhaps that the car was under observation. He had no way of knowing what really happened and it was no use trying to work it out now. His immediate need was to avoid the police. He quickly closed the panel and returned to the driver's seat, deciding to go to the farm.

The road became an avenue lined with eucalyptus trees. Kessel drove slowly, watching some peasants going about their work. He came to a large house and drove into its courtyard. He emerged from the car and was looking around before walking to the main door when it opened and a young man came out.

"Good morning," Kessel called out, walking toward the young man.

Rafael extended a hand to him and returned his greeting.

"The name is Mark Kessel," he said, shaking Rafael's hand.

"Rafael Rojas."

"Forgive me for having arrived suddenly from nowhere, but I didn't mean to intrude on this lovely paradise, this charming land."

He was going to offer an explanation but decided he did not need to when he heard Rafael say, "That's a terrific car!" And seeing that Rafael was walking toward it, Kessel, knowing that young men are more impressed by figures than by abstract remarks about design, said, "Cruises at two hundred kilometers an hour and is as silent as a whisper."

Rafael made a whistling sound to express his amazement at the fact.

"Go ahead, sit in it, see what it feels like, you won't find such velvet upholstery in a drawing room in Paris."

Rafael sat in the driver's seat, his hands at the steering wheel. He made little appreciative statements, and got out, closing the door with a careful, considerate gesture and finding a pleasure even in the precise way in which the door clicked itself closed.

"Is this your land?" Kessel asked.

"My father's," Rafael said.

"Well, that's the same thing," Kessel remarked, laughing, and Rafael noticed his blue, friendly eyes. "The reason for my most ungraciously unannounced visit is that I, too, am a farmer, and driving past on the highway a couple of times and noticing what appeared from a distance to be an efficiently run ranch I could not help being curious. I hope your father will forgive my presumption on wanting to inquire into his methods, but I do believe that farmers all over the world are brothers and have no secrets from one another."

What a charming man! Rafael thought to himself. He talked so politely and with such grace. "My father's away," he said, "but I can show you around."

"How kind of you!"

"May I offer you some breakfast first, or at least a cup of coffee?"

"I've had breakfast already, thank you. No, no, you are indeed very kind to take up your time with a curious old man."

"Please. It's my pleasure."

They walked to where the pickup truck was parked and climbed into its cab. Kessel had decided to spend two or three hours away from the highway in order to give himself the time to think what he should do, and he hoped that the police would be sufficiently frustrated to abandon their pursuit. For nearly two hours, Rafael drove to the various parts of the ranch, fording rivers, or cutting across the country on the narrow dirt road, and making many stops. They saw the cows being milked and in a nearby shed women making butter. They stopped at the timber mill with its mist of sawdust where the trunks of pine trees were being cut into planks and the wood-shavings being transformed into particle board. Rafael was pleased to see that Kessel was impressed by the up-to-date machinery. They saw the granary where corn, harvested from the fields near it, was being mixed with other products to make feed for the cattle. Finally, they came to the cold-storage warehouse.

"You must excuse the smell of disinfectant," Rafael said and explained the disaster that had taken place when the refrigeration plant failed.

"Oh, I'm used to the smells of farms," Kessel said and walked about the warehouse. "What impresses me most with everything on this ranch is the sense of order that prevails. Everything is carefully designed to be productive. There is no waste. You use the best machinery and get the most out of your land."

"Except here!" Rafael said, trying to make a joke of this one failure which, in the context of Kessel's praise, he felt to be a personal humiliation. "The best is sometimes not good enough."

Kessel went out of politeness to look at the refrigeration system. He was familiar with the make and said to Rafael, "You've got the best, and I see, like with all your machinery, you keep it spotless."

"There's a man who checks it over once a month. But it's no use having a brightly waxed Rolls-Royce whose engine is dead."

Kessel opened a cover and looked at the machinery. He checked the hoses, and Rafael, watching him probe some attachments in the engine whose function he himself was ignorant of, said, "You know how it works?"

"I know a little of everything, one has to nowadays since you can't depend on getting competent help, even from professional mechanics."

"An electrical engineer checked it over yesterday," Rafael said. "He said it needed a transformer and some other parts."

Kessel looked at him in disbelief and said, "My friend, you are being taken for a ride."

"What do you mean?"

"Simply that these machines don't have a transformer. They have a *compressor*. Your engineer either did not know what he was talking about or he's exploiting your ignorance to make himself rich."

Rafael wondered whether his memory of the engineer's words was precise; could he have said "compressor" and not "transformer"? No, he distinctly remembered hearing "transformer." Perhaps if his father had been here he would not have grown so desperate as to call in an engineer from the town but would have known a person he could trust; in his own inexperience, Rafael had called in an engineer recommended to him by no more reliable an authority than a large display ad in the Yellow Pages of the telephone directory of the nearest town. He had no proof of the man's competence.

Kessel was still probing the machinery while Rafael stood thinking. "Well, well, what do we have here?" he heard Kessel say.

Rafael saw Kessel pull out a long rag from the machine. Kessel looked around the place and, seeing where it was, walked to the fuse box. He opened the box and looked at the switches. He saw the one that had been tripped and flicked it back. The engine came on.

"That's incredible!" Rafael shouted.

"No, it's very simple, really," Kessel said. "The rag had blocked a vent, the engine became overloaded, and a fuse tripped."

Kessel helped Rafael to close the large gate by the loading bay and the two men came out of the warehouse, closing the front door behind them.

"Your coming has been an unbelievable piece of luck," Rafael said as they walked back to the pickup.

It was nearly time for lunch when they returned to the house. The table had been set for three. Rafael introduced

Kessel to Violeta and said to her, "You'll need to set an extra place at the table."

"I don't think so," she said. "I can't find Mother anywhere."

Rafael was too excited by his providential visitor making the refrigeration plant work again to be concerned by his mother's absence, though vaguely her words of the previous night came to him and he absently thought of going to see her later at Julio Reyes's widow's cottage, where she had said she would go, and to reason with her to come back. His disturbed night had given way to a perfectly harmonious day and he saw no reason to be tormented by his mother's nebulous anxieties; there was nothing like having machinery that worked efficiently to give one the sense that everything was fine in the world.

They ate an enjoyable lunch and even Violeta, taken by Kessel's charming manner of speech, talked animatedly. It was by far a pleasanter lunch than they ever had with their parents.

"You have been kind hosts," Kessel said at the end of the lunch. "I must be on my way now."

"Your coming has been like a miracle," Rafael said warmly. "You don't know how much trouble and money you've saved us."

"Think nothing of it," Kessel said, rising from the table, "it was just a stroke of luck. But tell me something," he added after a pause when he had walked to the window from where he could see his car in the courtyard. "You know that village north of here on the highway?"

He turned around to look at Rafael, who said, "You mean Palmira?"

"Yes, that's the one. Is there any way of avoiding it? It's a terribly dusty little village with pretensions to being a town."

"Yes, it's horrible, isn't it?" Violeta said, and Rafael wondered why she had said that since she rarely had occasion to go there.

"As it happens," Rafael said to Kessel, "the boundary of Palmira touches our land to the north. We have a large pine forest in that area, and there is a road to bring down the timber. The road comes out on the other side of Palmira."

"Splendid! I'll take that. It will be a fine diversion and I shall have the added pleasure of seeing more of your beautiful land. How can I find this road?"

Just then they heard a motorcycle, and Rafael knew that Emilio had come to the courtyard on some errand to the house.

"I know what we'll do," Rafael said. "There's our foreman, Emilio. I'll come with you in your car and get Emilio to drive the pickup after us so that I can return."

"No, no, I don't want to give you any more trouble," Kessel protested.

"Trouble? Listen, you've saved me a ton of trouble. And another thing. There's a tricky crossing in the forest where a dry riverbed looks like a junction. You come to it without knowing it and unless you have a guide you could get stuck or break the axle. But you want the real truth?" Rafael added with a broad smile. "I'd like nothing better than to take a ride in your beautiful car."

"Well, in that case . . . " Kessel smiled back at Rafael.

Rafael went out to the courtyard and Violeta went running up to her room. Rafael gave some orders concerning the refrigeration in the warehouse to Emilio and then told him to follow the car in the pickup when they drove away.

"But the pickup's needed to take the cornfeed to the corral," Emilio reminded him. "The feed has to be there within the hour."

"That can be done in thirty minutes, if you try," Rafael said, having a ready answer to any objection since he did not want to delay his guest, nor lose the opportunity of taking a drive in his car. "Take the pickup now, do the job, and come up the road. I'll be waiting at the junction of the dry river."

Soon they were ready to go. Kessel and Rafael got in the car, the latter finding it thrilling to be in the luxurious seat. Kessel switched on the ignition. The car started at once. Nothing like a perfect machine, Rafael said to himself. Just then Violeta, in jeans, T-shirt, and sneakers, came running out of the house, leaving the front door open behind her. She wanted to go, too.

51

7

When Emilio was transporting the cornfeed in the pickup the steering wheel began to shake violently in his hands and he realized that one of the tires had punctured. He stopped and climbed down from the cabin. The rear tire on the left was flat. It took him fifteen minutes to change the tire and then he discovered that the spare needed to be inflated; it was no use driving with that absurdly low pressure, for he would only have another flat which would make the pickup completely immobile. He needed to go back to the main house and find the air pump in the garage, a walk of nearly two kilometers from where he was, there and back. Fortunately, he ran into a peasant on a mule and borrowed the animal. The peasant sat down under a tree, quite happy to have nothing to do. Emilio was back in twenty minutes and by the time he had inflated the tire and was on his way to deliver the cornfeed, another fifteen minutes had passed. There was nothing he could do, he decided, the young master would simply have to wait by the dry river and accept the fact of the flat tire that had delayed him.

When they had driven through the dark and seemingly endless pine forest for some forty minutes, Rafael began to be apprehensive. He believed he knew the road well, though, when he thought of it, he had not actually come to this part of it for over two years. *Where* was that dry river? They should have come to it by now. Violeta, who had been excited by having the sumptuous backseat all to herself and had been thrilled by the air-conditioned luxury of the car which, though it went over an uneven dirt road, seemed to float over the land rather than follow its contours, had become bored after twenty minutes in the dark forest. Kessel, having his own problems to think of, kept silent and was aware of neither Violeta's boredom nor Rafael's apprehension.

Rafael threw a glance through the rear window and said, "I see no sign of the pickup."

"Perhaps I've been driving too fast," Kessel said, looking at the speedometer and noticing that he was scarcely doing fifty kilometers an hour.

"No, you can go faster," Violeta said, wanting the journey to end. "The road is quite smooth."

"We should have come to the dry river by now," Rafael said.

"Well, what is *this*?" Kessel asked, bringing the car to a stop.

They had come to a crossroads which Rafael had never seen before. Not wishing to appear a fool, however, he pretended that he was acquainted with the junction, and said, "Keep on straight here, we should be five or six kilometers from the river."

Kessel drove on. Rafael hoped that chance would prove him right. He did not want to tell Kessel that he had had enough, that he and Violeta could be dropped off right there to wait for Emilio, for he did not want to admit that he had lost his bearings on his own land. Also, he did not want to alarm the old man by confessing his worst fear, that he had no idea of where he was. He had no notion of the source of his error, which lay fifteen kilometers back where the road had bifurcated without their realizing it: the road they should have taken dipped down and was invisible as they followed the fork to the left which seemed the obvious continuation of the road they were on. They were, in fact, traveling parallel to the highway, just half a kilometer away from it. Rafael sat trying to look composed and searching his mind for something amusing to say, but he could think of nothing and was beginning to be vexed with himself.

Suddenly, Kessel pressed down on the accelerator and the car surged forward and in spite of the suspension which on a smooth paved surface, or at a slower speed, made it float like a steamer on a calm ocean it began to bounce and vibrate like a plane going through turbulence. At first Violeta shrieked with pleasure and then she began to scream in fear, for they had come out of the forest, the road had begun to curve and bend as it descended to a valley, and the speed at which Kessel was negotiating the turns and twists in the road made the car snake and drift and come terrifyingly close to the precipitous fall on their right. Rafael looked back to see what Kessel had observed in the mirror. Behind the cloud of dust raised by the rear tires, a bright-yellow Volkswagen could be seen coming right at them when Kessel braked at a bend and receding when he accelerated out of it.

"What's going on?" Rafael shouted above Violeta's screams. "Why are they chasing us?"

Kessel threw a glance at him and laughed. "No one's chasing us," he shouted back, turning the steering wheel quickly and taking the car round a bend with its outer tires less than a quarter of a meter from the edge of the road.

"That's the *cops*," Rafael shouted. "They must know your car."

"Everyone knows my car," Kessel shouted back. "There isn't another golden Lincoln in the entire country that I know of."

"But why are they chasing you?"

At that moment a sudden dip in the road made the car bounce, throwing Violeta up from her seat and she screamed a moment before her head hit the roof. She was thrown right back to her seat, and went silent.

"Violeta!" Rafael called, turning on his seat on his knees so that he could reach a hand to his sister from over the backrest. She seemed unconscious. Having seen something of Violeta's collapse in the mirror, Kessel turned his neck to take a quick look at her.

The next thing the car seemed to be flying through the air and then bouncing uncontrollably down some sloping land and finally coming to a halt with its front bumper smashed into a tree.

Thrown against the roof, then down to his seat, thrown

again but this time against the windshield, and finally hurled against the door, Rafael collapsed on his seat when the car came to a stop. The fact that he had turned with his knees on the seat just before the accident perhaps saved him from having his head smash through the windshield, for when he had been thrown against it, the padded dashboard had caught his buttocks and bounced him back. He opened the door and staggered out of the car. He looked up at the curving road from the depression in the land where he was and saw the yellow Volkswagen driving on as if the people in it were only out for an afternoon's drive in the country and not in pursuit of anyone. It must be, Rafael concluded when he had thought about it, that they had not come around the bend when the accident occurred and therefore did not see it and, concentrating on pursuing the car they imagined had gone around the next bend and was therefore invisible, they failed to see the golden beast that had fallen off the road.

Rafael noticed the torn bushes through which the Lincoln had crashed and saw the direction taken by the car in its uncontrolled descent. He observed that they had had the good fortune of leaving the road just where the drop was comparatively small and gentle: for beyond the tree that halted them, after about fifteen meters, there was a sheer drop of seven or eight hundred meters, and had their accident happened at any other point on the road they would surely have missed the tree and been dead by now. The thought of it brought sweat to his brow. He stretched his arms and bent his legs, testing his body. He did not even feel pain from the bruising he had received.

He went back to the car and opened the rear door and touched Violeta. Her heart was beating and she appeared to be breathing regularly. He turned her face from where it lay on its side. There was not a bruise on it. He went around to the door on the driver's side where, he could see through the window, Kessel was slumped against the steering wheel. He opened the door and touched him gently, drawing his head away from the wheel. Kessel seemed to lean back when he was touched, letting his head fall on the headrest. There was a tiny scratch on his forehead, a fine red line no more than three or four centimeters long. With his head thrown back and his mouth open, he was breathing noisily, almost snoring, like a man fallen asleep in a chair after a little too much wine with his lunch. Not knowing what to do, Rafael walked a little distance away from the car. He went up to the road with the intention of stopping a passing vehicle. There was no traffic there at all and after about fifteen or twenty minutes he came back to the car. Violeta and Kessel were as he had left them. If they were not injured, and they appeared not to be, then perhaps he should leave them alone in their sleeping state for a while, he thought. He went and sat near the edge of the precipice.

8

Although far to the southeast he could see the peak of the Andes that was visible from his father's house, the land around him seemed unfamiliar. Surely, the line of the pines in the distance must be on their own property? He could not be sure. He looked again up at the road and at the torn bushes as though the moment of the accident contained a revelatory secret that could be discovered by staring at the place where it had occurred; but he quickly looked away, for the replay of the crash in his mind filled him with horror.

It was a charming view from where he sat under a tree, if one could see it without the bewildering context of one's immediate situation. The sun must have shifted, for he saw the gleaming reflection of a river deep in the valley. And the light falling across the mountainside created an effect of cascading greenery, especially with the breeze moving through the leaves and making the light ripple in the fluttering foliage. Rafael leaned back on his elbows and looked dreamily at the landscape. The grass around him was soft and cushiony, the air like a soothing balm, and soon he fell asleep.

He did not know how long he had slept, for when he awoke it was completely dark. A gentle rain had begun to fall and had awakened him. It took him a few moments to realize what had happened to him and where he was. With the rain falling, the night was pitch-black. He remembered that the car was a dozen meters away from him, but he froze as soon as he had taken one step in order to go to the car. In which direction was the car? And how did he know which way he faced when he rose from the ground? The step he had taken might well be toward the precipice. He could see absolutely nothing, not even his own hand when he raised it before his eyes. A wild and terrifying fear possessed him as he stood frozen to the spot.

"Mark!" he found himself shouting. "Mark! Mark Kessel, Mr KESSEL! Violeta! VEE-O-LET-AAAH!"

His own voice terrified him as it rose and fell in the darkness, replaced by a deadly silence. He remembered that the windows of the air-conditioned car had been closed, but surely his voice would have penetrated the glass? But the air-conditioning must have gone off when the engine went dead. A new fear made his body turn cold. Could Violeta and Kessel have suffocated in the closed car? Why had he not thought of opening the windows? He shouted out their names more loudly, and waited, the rain falling on him.

He tried to sit down but found that the terror which filled his body had taken away from him any control over it. The body made not the slightest gesture to respond to the instructions of his mind. All he possessed were the menacing figures of his imagination. If only he had remained asleep and not woken to this overwhelming darkness: for there, in the immensity of the mountains, in the vast wilderness of space, he was the prisoner of the spot on which he stood.

He must have fallen unconscious at some stage in the night, for opening his eyes, he saw the great peak of the Andes lit up by the rising sun, the sky a deep blue behind it. He sat up and looked around him. Shadows in the valley, the brightly lit rim of the mountains. And *there*, behind him, was the car! He stood up and ran to it.

Violeta and Kessel had gone! The car was exactly where it had been halted by the tree, its bumper still stuck in the tree trunk, but there was nothing to indicate that some hours earlier two passengers had lain unconscious in it. Rafael went and sat in the driver's seat. He touched the steering wheel, flicked the directional levers up and down. He was surprised to see the key was still in the ignition. Pushing the automatic shift into N, he turned the key. The engine started at once. He pushed the shift to R and pressed the accelerator. After a slight straining of the front bumper, the car moved back so easily and with such power that Rafael, in a moment's panic, slammed the brake pedal. He switched off the engine, engaged the emergency brake, and pulled out the key.

He unlocked the glove compartment. It contained only the car's papers. Rafael went out and unlocked the trunk. Except for the spare tire, it was empty, its floor covered by golden-colored plush carpet. He inspected the area of the rear seat and found nothing. The car had no secret compartments that he could find. So it was not contraband, he thought. The police had been after Kessel himself. Who was he? Rafael wondered.

He went and looked at the road to see if there was any way he could drive the car back to it. After studying the terrain he decided that the most possible route was diagonally across the one along which they had fallen; the shoulder of the road offered the greatest obstacle, but if he aimed for it at an angle and came charging up with maximum power, he ought to be able to climb over it. He started the car and turned it around, aiming it in the direction of the path he needed to take. He held the steering wheel firmly in his hands, took a deep breath and threw his foot on the accelerator. The car bounded forward, bumped, the rear tires roared, there was a terrible screeching from the bottom of the car, the steering wheel turned back and forth although he tried to hold it firmly, the thick branches of a bush tore at the side of the car, the shoulder of the road rose before him like a sheer cliff, and for a moment it seemed as though the car would fall backwards and go somersaulting into the valley, but it leaped up and a moment later he was amazed to see that he was driving on the relatively smooth surface of the dirt road with the air-conditioning making his sweating body go cold.

His pleasure at being on the road so exhilarated him and his sense of release from the night's tyrannies was so intense that he did not realize until he had been driving for some ten minutes that he was going in the wrong direction. The road was too narrow for the car to be turned around safely, and he was obliged to continue. How, he wondered, had Violeta and Kessel gone away? Could the police have come back when it was dark? But they must have had flashlights and could easily have found him, and surely Violeta must have said to them that her brother was there, too, and should not be left behind. Or could it be that Violeta and Kessel, regaining consciousness in the dark and not finding him in the car, assumed that he had left them, perhaps to go and seek help, and seeing the light of a passing vehicle on the road, they had decided to walk in that direction and hope for another vehicle to pass by and pick them up? There were several other hypotheses, but the only certainty was that he had no way of knowing the truth.

He arrived at a village and stopped to ask a man who was standing outside a hut whether he could get a cup of coffee somewhere, for he needed some refreshment before turning around and driving back to his father's ranch. The man pointed up the road. There was a town there that could be reached in one hour on a mule, the man told him, and pointing to the car made a gesture which showed his open palms and indicated that with that car he could surely get there in no time. Rafael had never heard the name of the town and wondered whether the man knew what he was talking about. But by now three other men and several kids had gathered around the car, and one of the men mentioned the names of several cafés—there was one by the bus station, two on the main square—and he was enjoined to avoid the one named Estrella because it was dirty. Where do the buses go from there? he asked. Oh, everywhere, they said, naming several cities. At least the town was on the main highway, Rafael concluded, deciding to go there. He would be certain of not losing his way. Also the fuel gauge showed he would soon be low on gasoline.

It was a busy, bustling market town, the square thronged with Indians setting up their stalls in the early morning. As soon as he parked outside a café, a crowd of boys surrounded the car. He went and sat at a table just inside the door of the café from where he could observe the car. The café was no more than a small room with half a dozen tables. It was dark and dusty and smelled of dried meat that was being cooked in an adjoining room. There was no one there and he tapped on the table. A middle-aged man with graying hair and a slight stoop came out and looked at Rafael with expressionless eyes.

"Can I get some coffee?" Rafael asked.

"Yes."

"And some bread?"

The man shook his head.

"All right, just coffee then."

After ten minutes, the man brought him a muddy cup of coffee. Rafael swallowed half of it, threw a coin on the table and left. The crowd of boys parted, looking at him with awe as he went to the car.

"Which way to the bus station?" he asked the boys.

Several arms went up but the fingers pointed in different directions.

"Forget it," Rafael said, and drove away. He cruised up and down the dusty streets until he found the bus station.

There was only one bus there, an ancient vehicle crowded with peasants. Rafael went and talked to its driver, wanting to know where he could find the highway. The road out there would take him straight to the highway, the driver said pointing in the direction. Only two kilometers to the junction. Rafael thanked him and drove on.

The Shell station was the most reassuring thing he had seen since leaving home. A pleasant young man refueled the car, checked the oil, and cleaned the windshield.

"Takes a lot of gas," he said with his hand at the nozzle and his face turned to look at the pump. "With this much gas in a smaller car, you could get to Caracas."

"I didn't know you could get to Caracas from here."

The young man had not meant to be taken literally since he was making a point to do only with gasoline consumption, and he said ambiguously, "You can go anywhere from here."

"I only want to get home."

"Where's that?"

"The Rojas ranch. Just off that highway where the Equator crosses it."

The attendant tightened the cap on the gas tank and said,

"The Equator doesn't cross *that* highway."

"What are you talking about?" Rafael said. "There isn't another highway in this area."

"You're right there," the man said, wiping the windshield with a damp cloth.

"Then it *does* cross the Equator."

"No, sir, you're wrong there."

"Where does it go, then?"

"East," the young man said.

"And west in the other direction?"

"That's right."

Rafael looked at him intently and said, "Listen, if you think you're being funny . . . " But he stopped, seeing that the man stared at him perplexed. "All right, tell me then how I can find the highway that goes south."

"The one that goes to Panama?"

"That's north. What about the one that goes to Lima?"

"That's the same one, going the other way."

"You got it! That's the one."

"Take this one and go east. You'll come to the turnoff in about twenty kilometers. It's marked, you won't miss it."

Rafael brought out his wallet and was surprised to see how much money he had with him and then remembered that he himself had taken it out of the safe on the previous morning before breakfast in order to make some payment in the nearby town, but Kessel's arrival had made him forget that he was supposed to send Emilio to the town with the money. He paid the garage attendant who was saying, "I told you, that highway takes you anywhere."

It was a good paved highway and Rafael drove fast, wanting to tear away the skeins of confusion that had become woven around him. He desperately wanted to see a familiar landscape, or even a mark on the road that would give him a certain knowledge of where he was. He seemed to have been wandering in a puzzling maze ever since he left home. He tried to figure out the actual time he had spent in the car, driving first with Kessel, and then, this morning by himself, and tried to calculate the distance he had come from his house. He ought not to be more than fifty or seventy kilometers from the ranch—a hundred kilometers, say, making generous allowances for all sorts of errors. Yet he could not tell where he was; he had never heard of the town he had stopped at, and this highway that presumably went to Caracas—surely, he could not have lived his entire life a hundred, or less, kilometers from it without ever having heard of it. Something was wrong, somewhere, and he was beginning to get the terrible feeling that each determined attempt to find the way back home was taking him farther away from it. And now, surely more than twenty kilometers had passed, and there was no sign of the turnoff.

In his state of growing anxiety while he calculated distances and time and went over in his mind the many turnings and stops made since leaving the house, he did not see the sign—that had fallen down in a storm and had never been re-erected—which would have shown him the name of a familiar city. Also, he was looking with such alertness to see a sign that a picture of one was vividly present in his imagination, putting him in that peculiar state of mind in which one does not see the thing one is looking for because one is seeing it too clearly in one's fancy. When the Shell attendant had mentioned the turnoff, Rafael had imagined an intersection of highways, one of them arching up to leap over the other with ramps connecting the several lanes of the two highways. In fact, there was only a narrow dirt road which dropped off the highway just past the fallen sign and one had to travel on it for several kilometers before joining the highway going south. The Shell attendant had not tried to mislead Rafael with his description of the junction; he himself had never seen it and was merely repeating what he had heard from truck drivers.

Rafael looked at the speedometer. A hundred and eighty kilometers an hour. He had not made a note of the time when he had left the Shell station but thought that he must have driven for at least an hour since then. He slowed down, wondering whether he should not go back to the Shell station. Surely, there had been some mistake? But he feared that it was one of those situations in which, if he turned back, he would be turning back from within a few meters of the very place that he was seeking, and that if he continued, he would be making the mistake of not turning back in time. He stopped and got out of the car and stood leaning against its side. He realized that he was hungry, and then laughed, telling himself there was nothing he could do about it. He just stood there for some time, staring at the distance and trying to understand the landscape. It had become barren. The cool air indicated he was on some high plateau. No mountain peaks could be seen, however. He heard a sound. A truck was coming up the road. He began waving at it from a distance, standing in the middle of the highway. The truck stopped just behind the car. A man in his thirties, wearing a black leather jacket, climbed down, his hands in his pockets.

"Hello, friend," Rafael said to him. "I seem to be lost. I was looking for the highway to Lima."

The man stared at him, threw a glance at the car, and stared at him again.

"Where are you going?" Rafael asked him. "To Caracas? A guy told me this highway goes to Caracas. It's funny, but I never knew this highway existed and I don't live too far from here."

The man pulled out his right hand from the pocket. He was holding a handgun.

"Give me your wallet," he said.

"That's a nice way to help someone who's lost his way!"

"I don't want to know your problem; just hand me the money."

Rafael looked up and down the road. No traffic at all, nothing, just the strip of road in a barren, silent landscape.

"Don't try anything funny," the man said.

Rafael was struck by the steadiness of the hand that held the gun. He took out the wallet from the back pocket of his trousers and handed it to him. The man snatched it from his hand and looked at the money in it. Obviously pleased with what it contained, he put the wallet into the breast pocket of his jacket.

"Hey, wait a second," Rafael said. "What about giving me

my papers? My identity card's in that wallet. You don't need that."

"Forget it."

"But what if I'm stopped by the cops and need to show my papers?"

The man did not want to open the wallet and look for the papers, for the act of doing so might put him momentarily off guard and give the young man a chance to snatch away his gun. "I told you," he said, "I don't want to know your problem. Take off that watch and give it to me."

Rafael gave him his watch.

"And that ring."

"That's my family ring," Rafael protested. "See the letter R on it? That's for Rojas, the family name."

"Forget the history and just give me that ring."

Rafael gave him the ring. The man walked backward to his truck, keeping the gun aimed at Rafael, hurriedly climbed into the cabin, and drove away.

Rafael looked at the license plate of the receding truck. A rag, hanging out of the truck, covered the plate. He rushed into the car and started it, deciding to chase the truck; but he changed his mind and switched off the ignition. The man was armed and if he saw he was pursued, he would simply shoot at the car. It was not worth risking his life because he had been robbed. He just sat there, his hands on the steering wheel, staring at the lifeless road. He did not know what to do and sat in a stupor, hungry and helpless, and beginning to feel wretched.

He noticed in the mirror that a Volkswagen coming up the highway had slowed down. When it was some twenty meters from him, its driver appeared to stop behind the Lincoln, then accelerated and drove slowly past it. The driver's large, light-brown face was trained on the Lincoln and its occupant as he drove to its front and parked there. Rafael got out of the car, thinking to himself that if this were another holdup it would be better for him to be in the open. The man was tall and broad-shouldered, Rafael saw, as he came out of the dark-blue, dented and dirty Volkswagen, and had very bright black eyes.

"Any problem?" he asked, walking up to Rafael.

"Not really," Rafael answered cautiously, not wanting to say anything until he was certain the man was to be trusted.

The man came and stood near Rafael. "That's a fine car," he said, looking at it. "But you'd never get it fixed in this country if anything went wrong. Too bad about the scratches. It will be impossible to match the paint, you'll need to respray the entire car."

"I wasn't worried about that," Rafael said, wondering if the man's idea was to steal the car. He would gladly swap it for the dirty little Volkswagen, he thought, if in return the man could show him the way home.

The man looked at him and put up his hand. "The name's Tomás Oyarzún."

"Rafael Rojas." They shook hands.

"Where are you headed?"

"I was just debating whether or not I should go all the way to Caracas." Rafael's irony was directed at his own self, for his mood had become bitter.

"Caracas?"

"Well, it was an idea I had."

"There is no way you can get to Caracas from here," Oyarzún said. "What gave you that idea?"

"I was told this highway goes to Caracas."

"Must have been some joker," Oyarzún said. "We are in the northern cordillera but still south of the Orinoco. You couldn't get to Caracas unless your car could sail over the river and fly above a thousand kilometers of swampy jungle."

"Maybe this car could do just that!" Rafael said, laughing.

"It's a beautiful car," Oyarzún said, "but I don't think it will perform miracles."

Rafael noticed that while talking to him, Oyarzún kept looking up and down the car as if he desired to possess it.

"You can have the car if you can get me out of my predicament," Rafael said without thinking of what he was saying. "All it has done for me has been to cause me problems."

Oyarzún did not think Rafael meant his offer to be taken literally. "What problems?" he asked.

66

Without going into too many details, Rafael described how he found himself where he was, ending with an account of the robbery. "Taking my family ring and not giving me back my papers was too much," he concluded. "All I need is to find the highway to Lima."

"That's no problem," Oyarzún said. "I tell you what. I'm returning to my land. About two hundred kilometers from here, only two hours' drive. Why don't you come with me? We could be there in time for lunch. You could rest yourself. And we'll put you on the right road."

The mention of lunch took away from Rafael all ideas except those concerning food. He saw heaps of rice and beans and a large roast, bottles of iced beer, mangoes and bananas. "All right," he said, "I'll follow you."

"Follow me closely, otherwise you'll miss the turnoff."

"Don't worry. I'll follow you. I don't have a choice."

9

They had descended down a wide valley and were driving on a narrow dirt road just above the bank of a river which could scarcely be seen through the dense growth of the tropical jungle. The road looked like a tunnel under the branches of the great trees, which the early afternoon sun penetrated here and there to light up dark-red and purple flowers on vines and bushes. The road turned away from the river and they came to land that had been cleared of the jungle. A cluster of palm-thatched huts, each with magenta-blossoming bougainvillea climbing on its sides, stood on either side of the road. Small children playing in the doorways of the huts saw the two cars go by and jumped and shouted and grinned. The road entered the jungle again for a few more kilometers. They went past a large pond whose water under the canopy of the jungle looked black, making the half-dozen flamingos standing in it look startlingly conspicuous beside the water lilies. They came out under a brilliant blue sky. A flock of parrots went flying overhead toward the jungle. And suddenly, around a corner, there was the huge iron gate set in a high stone wall—both merely symbolic, however, Rafael noticed: the wall ended abruptly after about fifteen meters on either side of the gate and its line was continued by thick bushes, growing high, which made as secure and forbidding a barrier as the stone, while the gate was wide open.

Going through the gate, they entered a paved drive lined on each side by royal palms through which could be glimpsed wide areas of well-kept lawns, ponds with ducks on them, and little pavilions under tall trees which spread their branches in horizontal layers. A large house, made of great blocks of granite, stood like a castle at the end of the drive. Its central structure went up to four floors, with six windows spaced ten meters from one another on each floor. At the top left-hand corner was a tower, its high column crowned by a dome-shaped roof. On either side of the central structure, the house spread out laterally, the wing on the left forming a semicircle. There was a paved apron in front of the entire width of the house, some fifteen meters deep, on which no trees or bushes grew. Oyarzún drove onto the apron and stopped outside the front door, and Rafael parked the Continental just behind him.

Rafael did not know what he had expected, but he would certainly never have imagined this huge fortress in the middle of the jungle. By now, since leaving his own house, he had taken so many turns, driven at high altitudes and then in valleys, that he had lost all sense of direction and did not know where he was or how far he had come.

Two young male servants in white cotton shirts and trousers, with their black hair neatly combed, appeared at the door. Oyarzún instructed one to show the visitor to a guest room, wait on him till he was ready, and then bring him down to the dining room. Rafael followed the servant down a dimly lit corridor; the latter stopped and pressed a button on the wall. They entered the elevator which took them to the fourth floor. They came out into a large hall which was brightly lit with sunlight pouring through the high windows and falling on the beige carpet with its geometrical pattern of orange and green. The servant led the way to the room at the far end and opened the door for Rafael to enter, closing it when he had done so and remaining outside.

The room was large and appeared dark in spite of having windows on one wall which gathered in the outer brightness, an effect created by the tapestries hanging on the other three walls and covering them almost completely, except for the wall on the left which had an arch in it. Rafael recognized the scenes the tapestries depicted, all to do with the Spanish conquest of the Andean countries. There was a bed in one corner of the room and, next to the windows, a small bamboo sofa with cloth-covered cushions, in front of which was a low marble-topped table. Rafael walked across the room and looked out of a window. He saw vast lawns with royal palms and flowering acacias and flamboyant trees on them, a small lake with an island in the middle of it overgrown with lush vegetation through which part of a sloping roof of a building could be seen, and in the far distance, the immense jungle.

He came away from the window and walked through the arch which led to a bathroom. Its floors and walls were of white tiles, all spotlessly clean and polished. There was a rack filled with thick white towels, and beside the washbasin, on a gleaming marble surface, there was an array of men's toiletries, everything from a toothbrush in its clear plastic container to an after-shave lotion. Rafael examined himself in the mirror and realized he looked rather scruffy after his night in the open and his subsequent adventures. He stripped to his underwear, brushed his teeth and shaved, enjoying the beautifully soft English-made brush producing a rich lather on his cheeks. He then took a shower, dried himself, and sprinkled talcum powder on his body before putting on his clothes, regretting that the seat of his trousers and the back of his shirt were rather soiled. When he went out, the servant was standing patiently beside the door.

Oyarzún had just arrived in the dining room when Rafael was brought there. It was a high-ceilinged room with a large table in its middle. A white cloth covered the table and at its center was a vase of red and purple flowers. They sat opposite each other, across the narrow width of the table with the flowers between them. Oyarzún pushed the vase a little to the side, so that they could see each other, and said, "I hope you found everything you needed."

"A happier accident couldn't have happened to me," Rafael said, feeling nearly intoxicated when the aroma of the soup that the servant had just served him reached his nostrils. "You've no idea how hungry I am," he added, spreading butter on a piece of bread and beginning to eat.

When the soup plates had been taken away, Rafael said,

"While following you in the car, I thought we'd come to some town where you had a house. Or that we would come to a ranch. I didn't expect to find myself in a kingdom."

"It is a rather large piece of land," Oyarzún said and wiped his lower lip with his napkin.

"And *that* is rather an understatement, I should think! But what brought you to this land? You could not have been born here."

The servant brought in grilled steaks, boiled potatoes covered with melted butter and parsley, and cauliflower in a cream sauce. Rafael took a long swallow of the ice-cold beer that had been served and began to eat while Oyarzún said, "No, I looked for this land for several years."

"*Looked?* That would imply you had an idea of what you were looking for before you found it."

"Yes, but sometimes we keep looking in a negative sort of way. Rejecting the alternatives that come up one after the other. They are not satisfactory, somehow. If we are persistent, we do discover that which satisfies. You see, one's imagination is a tyrant."

"And you found this?" Rafael asked.

"In its primitive form, yes," Oyarzún said. "The house and its surrounding landscapes had to be created. You see, life is not simply a matter of being—even an ant or a poor wretch fallen exhausted with hunger in a street in Bogotá has that—it is a matter of creating an existence: the passions have to be attended to. The imagination's cravings are a greater nutrient than one's mother's milk. You see, we seek dimensions of reality which have no real presence in the visible world."

"This is all very interesting," Rafael said, "but I get the impression that you are carefully avoiding saying anything about yourself."

"What can I tell you?"

"Oh, the simple things. Where did the wealth come from to provide you with this existence? Where is the rest of your family? What do you *do* here to keep yourself from dying of boredom?"

"Where does anyone's inherited wealth come from?"

71

Oyarzún said, again not making a personal statement. "One's father or grandfather happens to hit upon silver or copper, or happens to be in a new country where a railway has to be built. And as for boredom, you could live in London with a season ticket to the Royal Opera House and still not escape it."

"You've said nothing about your family."

"My wife lives in Paris," Oyarzún said, showing no emotion, "where her wealth buys her a place in the society of the decadent aristocracy. No doubt she has an old duke for a lover. Before she left several years ago, she did me the honor of bearing two children. The son, who was about your age, was too ambitious for his wings when he joined the air force and was killed training to be a pilot. The daughter, Oliva, is in Miami at the present, on a shopping trip. Like so many South American women, she is infected with a passion for super-fluous things, and goes to Miami three or four times a year with the devoted zeal of a pilgrim going to a holy shrine."

"Forgive me if I say so, but you speak as if you did not care for your family."

"I loved my son, but he's dead. I loved my wife, for why else should I have married her, but she cannot accept this existence. I have wept in one case and remonstrated in the other. However, I cannot bring back the dead nor change someone's will. As for my daughter, I love her, but she's nineteen and of an independent mind—the very kind of mind I educated her to have, and therefore I cannot complain when she exercises her independence."

A feeling of intense contentment filled Rafael as he finished the meal. "How very interesting," he said out of politeness. "One day I'd love to hear your whole history. But I've had such weird experiences since leaving home that my mind is dizzy. To tell you the truth, I can scarcely stay awake."

"You ought to go and rest for a while," Oyarzún said.

"I will, if you will excuse me."

Rafael went to his room, removed his clothes, and fell into the bed. The breeze coming through the window was warm and finely scented. It touched his heavy eyelids and slightly open mouth, putting him to sleep just when unspecified desires were evoking a sensuous languor in his semiconscious mind.

There was a dim light outside the window when he awoke after a profound, dreamless sleep. He rose out of bed and stood at the window. The sun was red on the horizon. He remained standing for several minutes to see the darkness come over the land. Instead, it got lighter and the birds which had been making sleepy sounds soon began to sing loudly. He realized that the sun was not setting but that it had just risen, and that he must have slept for some fifteen hours.

He took a leisurely bath, put on his clothes, and went downstairs.

It was only seven o'clock, he noticed when he went to the living room. It was a large, beautifully decorated room with Oriental rugs completely covering the floor and paintings of landscapes and allegorical scenes hanging from the walls. The windows looked out on a fine prospect of royal palms and to the left of them a pond with ducks on it. Rafael walked down the hall and entered another room. From the wall where the door was, the room spread out in a wide circle, and Rafael realized that this must be the vast circular wing on the left of the house that he had seen on his arrival. The huge circular wall was lined with books from floor to ceiling. A narrow ladder of polished wood was suspended from a rail in the ceiling. There were leather sofas and small tables beside them, and a large table covered with magazines. It was the largest library Rafael had ever seen, and he felt as if he was in the presence of all the knowledge that mankind had accumulated.

Hearing sounds from the hall, he walked toward the dining room where a servant was laying the table for breakfast. Soon, Oyarzún came down and the two exchanged joking remarks about Rafael's siesta which had turned into a long sleep.

At breakfast Oyarzún said to him, "I must get one of the men to fill up your car's tank with gasoline."

"Where could he do that?"

"We have a pump. A tanker comes once a month to keep us amply supplied. In fact, we have a workshop with two mechanics. You see, there are so many vehicles on the land that it makes sense to have a complete service and repair facility here."

"It certainly does," Rafael said, swallowing some coffee. "I'd like to look at your land," he added. "I might learn something from your organization."

"You're welcome, but it'll take you days to see everything."

The coffee was rich in Rafael's mouth as had been the homemade butter on freshly baked rolls and he found himself saying, "I'd love to spend a few days here, if I may."

Oyarzún gave him a surprised look and Rafael said, "Please forgive the vulgarity of my inviting myself. But I love this place."

"As I say, you're welcome. You can stay for as long as you like."

Rafael thanked his host as they rose from the table.

A few minutes later, they drove away in Oyarzún's car. Rafael, not wishing to be an incumbrance, had insisted that he not be shown anything in the sense of being taken on a tour; instead, his host was to go about his normal business: Rafael would accompany him and see the land for himself without the necessity of a conducted tour.

At the service station, which was as large and as well equipped as any in the city, a tractor was being repaired. Oyarzún had a few words with a mechanic, left his car there and took a Jeep. The small lake that Rafael had seen from his room appeared on their left as they took an unpaved road that dipped down into the jungle; and after a few kilometers they came out to a vast prairie where several hundred head of cattle were grazing. Three men on horseback were riding across the land and Oyarzún drove toward them. When he stopped beside them, the three riders sat erect on their stationary mounts on Rafael's side of the Jeep, the land shimmering behind them with increasing heat and, on the horizon, the jungle dark and still. Oyarzún spoke to the men, but only one of them answered his questions and made a mental note of his orders. The other two, their dark, tanned faces sweating, stared with a dumb awe at their master.

During the next three hours, covering some twenty to thirty

kilometers going back and forth but apparently in a logical progression, for after visiting the stables they were back on the road next to the lake, they visited the vegetable gardens, which, with water drawn from a well, had their own automatic sprinkler system; a plantation of corn where Indian women, their eyes alive with movement, worked in a slow, monotonous rhythm; they visited the slaughterhouse and a dairy plant, going from the pungent smell of blood to the fetid smell of butter and cheese. In a large shed, a group of Indians was making pottery and wooden objects. It was, Rafael saw, a busy, prosperous land where a fine harmony prevailed between machines and human beings: mankind's traditional impulses had not vanished, only the burden of heavy labor had.

Coming out of the stables, Oyarzún said, "It's almost time for lunch. You see how time-consuming it is only to inspect what the workers are up to. And you haven't seen half of it yet!"

"When I said yesterday that you had a kingdom here, I was only using a figure of speech," Rafael remarked. "I realize now that I was being literally precise."

The road had come to the edge of the lake which, when Rafael had seen it from the bedroom window, had seemed small. He saw now that it was a kilometer wide and perhaps three kilometers long. Oyarzún stopped by a pier where two motorboats were moored and said, "Come, let me show you something."

He started one of the boats and they rode out in it to the island in the middle of the lake. The island was fringed with royal palms, some four or five deep, and other tall trees behind them, and from the water one could not see the large barnlike building in the middle of the island, it was so densely surrounded by vegetation. The building had a large gate which Oyarzún opened with a key from the ring of keys that he carried, saying, "This is my madness, if you like. You can never tell, can you, what another person's secret obsession is?"

The first thing Rafael saw was a gleaming 1928 Dusenberg. Next to it was a Rolls-Royce which was older still, and beside the Rolls a 1912 Renault. There were twenty cars in all, each one perfectly restored to its original specifications, down to the stitching on the leather upholstery. Oyarzún's face was flushed, his eyes shone brightly as he showed each of the cars to Rafael, talking animatedly about the history of each one, how he came upon one in a country house outside Buenos Aires and bought another from an aristocrat in England. Rafael was affected by Oyarzún's boyish enthusiasm and shared his pleasure in touching the shining brasswork on the headlamps of a 1932 Bentley or looking at the engine of a Lagonda.

"This one is not so old and not as breathtaking as the Dusenberg or the Bentley," Oyarzún said, showing Rafael a more modern car. "But it is the rarest of them all, being the only one made."

"What is it?" Rafael asked, staring at the car.

"An Armstrong-Siddeley. Its history is vague, except that it was designed by a Swiss engineer named Graber, possibly for a British officer a few years after the end of the Second World War. It was first registered in Bristol and last in London. I came across it at an auction of repossessed cars. Its last owner had been a schoolteacher who could not meet the monthly payments and had to give up the car. It seemed a sad end, almost as if your favorite sheep were about to be slaughtered. I bought it for practically nothing without realizing it was to be my rarest possession. Sometimes, a little sentimentality pays off. The bodywork, by the way, is all aluminum and it has a curious electrical gear system, just like the London buses. What I like are the clean, functional lines. It is really very handsome as an open tourer. But you must understand that while I appreciate style and mechanical details, what thrills me most of all is that there is only one of it in the world and that it is mine."

At the back of the museum was a paved courtyard and as they went to it, Oyarzún said, "Now you understand why I drive a dented old Volkswagen. You see, I have a contempt for modern cars just as I have a contempt for the modern world. The earlier cars came from the human imagination, they glowed with an intense passion; now they are shaped by a computer and made on an assembly line by workers whose minds are on a football match or the next weekend's fishing. The same with modern life. The old passions are gone. Vulgarity reigns supreme."

The courtyard was a wide rectangle enclosed by flowering hibiscus bushes.

"What's this!" Rafael exclaimed, looking at a strange object.

"This is the other side of me," Oyarzún said. "Call it a folly, if you like."

They were looking at a large head, some three meters high, made of crushed and contorted metal. Oyarzún described how a 1958 Buick was transformed into that ugly oval shape first by being mechanically crushed and then hammered into its present form by a sculptor who used the headlights for eyes and part of the radiator grille for an ugly mouth. At the opposite end of the courtyard stood another piece of sculpture: a large globe of crushed metal mounted on four bumpers which were fixed vertically to the ground.

"It took two Toyotas to make that," Oyarzún explained.

"Tell me something," Rafael asked. "How did you transport all these things across the lake?"

"It's an artificial lake. The cars were brought here before there was any water. The crushed cars we managed to bring across on boats."

Rafael looked again at the crushed Buick and said, "That really is very funny."

"You know," Oyarzún said, "when I met you on the road yesterday, it was your car that caught my attention. I probably wouldn't have stopped if you'd been in a less conspicuous car."

"You were just saying that you have a contempt for modern cars. If I remember right, I think you said the Lincoln was beautiful."

"Yes, your memory is correct. I had an idea when I saw that car. An inspiration, if you like. It is a beautiful car to be crushed into a cube or some other object and sprayed with

77

gold paint. A monument to human vanity and vulgarity—the two usually coincide in modern life. I would love to have such a monument here. In fact, if the car were yours, I'd offer to buy it from you."

"We can do better than that," Rafael said. "Since the car is not mine, I will be happy to give it to you."

10

When Kessel had come to consciousness in the car, he had at first been confused. It was dark outside, a soft rain was falling. He switched on the dashboard light and saw that it was just nine o'clock. He switched the light off and remembered the earlier events of the day that had ended in his crashing the Lincoln against the providential tree. In all his years of running errands for the revolutionaries, he had never had a brush with the police or any accident which might have tested his character. It had all been an amusing lark. Now for the first time a sudden scare had thrown him into a panic and revealed to him what he himself was really made of: not much courage and hardly any sense. His first thought on coming to and realizing what had happened was to make himself scarce as quickly as possible.

What he had considered to be bravado and superior intelligence in himself—the idea of coming to a foreign country on a risky mission in a glitteringly conspicuous car—he now considered an act of sheer stupidity. He had been carried away by a boyish sense of romance. He had been absolutely silly. His lust for an ancient map, his infatuation for the chimera of El Dorado, and his craving for solving the mysteries of antiquity— all of which were supposedly aspects of his "scholarship"— had nearly been his death. What scholarship? he mocked himself—only the grandiose self-delusion of an imbecile! In this mood of self-abuse, he chided himself also for his association with the populist revolutionaries. A bunch of idiots, all! He swore aloud at them and at himself. He ought to grow up. At fifty-five, it was time to stop pretending to be a boy. He should have gone into business with his brother-in-law, made a pile of money for himself, and bought himself a huge estate. El Dorado was not where you might find it but where you created it for yourself. Idiot, idiot! he swore at himself.

Suddenly, he remembered the young man and the girl who had been with him in the car. "Oh, my God," he called aloud, "I hope I haven't messed up their lives too!" He switched on the interior light. The seat next to him was empty. But he heard the girl. She had been awakened by his voice and was saying something. He got out of the car, opened the rear door and stooped in, saying, "Are you all right?"

"Where are we?" she asked.

"Wish I knew. Are you all right?"

"Why, yes, I'm fine."

Just then he heard the sound of a vehicle. He stood up straight and turned to look in the direction of the sound. The headlights had already come around the curve of the road and gone, and he stood staring at the receding tail-lights.

"Where is Rafael?" the girl asked him, emerging from the car.

"I don't know," Kessel answered. "But there can be only one reason why he's not here. He must have come to some time ago and gone to get help. That would be the logical thing to do."

"What can we do now? It's horribly dark, and it's raining too!"

"It's only just gone nine," he said. "We could wait here till Rafael returns, which could mean sitting here all night."

"Oh, no!"

"Or we could go and wait by the road. It's still early in the night and there could be some traffic."

They decided to go up to the road. Kessel switched off the light in the car. It did not occur to him to try starting the car, for he assumed that the engine must have been damaged by the impact; and in his haste to get to the road in case a car was already approaching he forgot to remove the key from the ignition. He had a vague notion of coming back the next morning with a tow truck and having the car towed to the nearest town where he would leave it in a garage until it was repaired. It was much later that he realized he had been stupid in not having a well thought-out plan when he left the car that, in his haste, he appeared to be abandoning as if it were a worthless toy; he had not given a thought to the police who might still be hunting for him; he had not quite forgotten the gold bars, but his responsibility to the owners of the gold was not at that moment uppermost in his mind. As he realized later, in thoughtlessly running away from the car he was simply demonstrating how inexperienced he was in coping with a crisis: facing the first real problem in his life, he ran away from it expecting everything to work itself out without his presence being necessary—somehow the gold would reach the people it was meant for, the car would come back to him in perfect running order, and the girl would find her way back home by herself. In his haste and confused state of mind, in which he was forcefully rejecting the love of romance and adventure that had brought him to this predicament, no objections occurred to him.

In the darkness they slowly made their way up the hill, and by one of those strokes of chance where that quickly happens which we had wanted to happen, thus creating in us the conviction that the course we had chosen for ourselves was the correct one, no sooner had they reached the road when a small car came around the curve and, seeing them, stopped. A light-skinned man opened the door. He looked to be in his thirties and spoke in a soft voice, inviting them in. Violeta flipped forward the backrest of the front seat and sat in the rear, and Kessel sat beside the driver, saying, "Thank you, thank you! We've had a long and terrible wait."

"What happened?" the man asked.

"We had an accident," Violeta said. "It was quite frightening."

She has a beautiful voice, the man thought, while Kessel went on to describe what had happened. Violeta was amazed at what she heard. "We were out for a drive and had just stopped to look at the view. I parked there on the edge of the road, just where you picked us up, and walked out to take in the view. Next thing, we saw the car rolling down the slope and crashing down into the valley.''

She must be quite a whore, the man thought, to be going out on a drive with an old bull like him. He was glad he was carrying a gun. Always carry a gun in the country, he recited to himself as if it were a proverb. She must have a tight little cunt, he thought, unless this old bull has opened it out wide.

"What's the name of that town?" he heard her beautiful voice say. There were lights in the distance, about five kilometers away.

"That? Let me see now," the man said. He stopped the car and switched on the interior light. "There's a map somewhere here."

"It's not that important," she said.

He glanced back at her. Pretty, too, he thought. "It's no problem," he said, and reached across Kessel's lap. He opened the glove compartment, probed inside it and quickly pulled out his hand, holding a gun.

"You, old man, go take a walk," he said, aiming the gun at Kessel's head.

"What's this?" Kessel demanded. "I was just blessing you in my mind, what's this, eh?"

"I said, go take a walk, unless you want to lie out there with your skull ripped open."

Kessel moved to open the door, performing the action slowly and deliberately to gain time. Behind him, Violeta had begun to sob, her face in her hands.

"Don't try any tricks," the man said, nudging Kessel's shoulder with the gun. "Just get out and leave your whore behind."

Violeta gave a little scream at those words and Kessel, who had opened the door but not as yet pushed it out to facilitate his exit, said, "Now, look here, young man, you're making a mistake. That is not a kind word for an innocent young girl."

"I'll give you five seconds in which to get out in your own skin. Otherwise you're going to go out as a stream of blood."

Kessel pushed the door out and shifted in his seat. The man put the car into first gear and revved the engine. Violeta was crying loudly. Kessel made to leave the car. The gun that had last been at the level of his shoulder was near the top of the backrest of the seat. Suddenly, Kessel threw himself out and in the same movement tipped the backrest forward. The top of the backrest hit the man's hand. The gun went off, the bullet going clean out of the window, Kessel fell out onto the ground, the car sped forward, the door banged shut, and the backrest tipped back with the sudden momentum, all simultaneously.

"Now you can cry, my sweet whore," the man said, driving fast. "Just cry your pretty little heart out."

"You are a pig!" she said, continuing to cry.

He laughed. "Say that again, my lovely."

"You are an inhuman criminal, a barbarian, a *pig*!"

"Just keep calling me names, anything," he said. "Just keep using that beautiful voice of yours."

They were going through the town, and she saw that he was driving quickly through some back streets, avoiding the main square where the only people and traffic were likely to be at that hour. One drunk staggered across the street and at a corner a group of boys was playing. They saw no one else and nothing held up the car. Within a few minutes they had driven out of the town. The man stopped the car. It was dark outside with a light rain still falling.

"Come and sit next to me," the man said, tipping forward the backrest of the seat beside him.

Violeta stared wildly at him. The only light was from the instruments on the dashboard and all she could see were his eyes and the outline of his head against the windshield. She opened the door.

"No use trying to run away," he said. "There's nowhere you can get to. It's a wilderness out there."

But she had to step out in order to sit at the front. For a moment, she stood outside, feeling the rain fresh on her face. Why was this happening to her? she thought. Why had she ever left home? She made a move to reenter the car, but froze, being filled with the horror of what she must submit to if she entered.

"Quit the drama, girl, get into that seat," the man said.

She stared at him, still standing outside the car. He was leaning toward the open door and she saw his teeth flash in the darkness as he smiled. The image came to her of a beast licking its lips in anticipation of biting into her flesh. She collapsed on the ground. She heard him swear and mutter something. She heard the click of the door as he opened it and heard his footsteps coming around the front of the car. She could not rise. The feet were in front of her, below her face. He was wearing boots, she saw.

"Look, girl, you're going to have a great time. We're five kilometers from my little farm. There's a nice warm bed made for two in a cozy little room. See, I want to be gentle and romantic and not do it in the dirt here."

She flung her arms at his legs, holding them just below the knees. *"Please,"* she cried, "please let me go."

He bent down and raised her by the shoulders. She stood before him, his hands still at her shoulders. Her body had gone tense, almost frozen again, and she struggled against the helplessness of the body not being able to follow the commands of the mind. She fought the fear and the feeling of being frozen. His hands were pressing her shoulders and he was smiling at her. She realized he did not have his gun with him. That gave her the strength to fight her fear, to discover motion in her limbs.

"I want to be gentle, see?" he said, coming closer to her, bringing his face to hers.

She held her face back and he had to lean a little forward in his attempt to kiss her. His lips were close to hers when she flung up her arms, tore her nails through his face, heard him yell, and began to run into the darkness toward the town. She heard him running after her and slowed her pace so that he would not get the impression that it was futile to chase her and thus be persuaded to pursue her in the car. She knew she had enraged him, drawing the blood on his cheeks, and momentarily taken away his capacity for reason. She knew he was now the maddened beast who is driven to pursue the creature who has wounded him. He was running with long, heavy strides, and she realized that his boots must weigh him down. He was panting and cursing as he ran, wild with himself that he had not forced the girl soon after getting rid of the old man instead of giving himself to the romantic scheme of taking a pretty young girl to his bed. She saw that they had come some thirty or forty meters from the car and slowed down, so that he was within a couple of meters of her, giving him the impression that he had gained on her and was within a moment of grabbing her. She looked over her shoulder and seeing that he was now within a meter of catching her, she shot away in a burst of speed. Another twenty meters away from him, it was too dark for him to see her while she, turning around, could see him because the lights of the car behind him still showed him in outline. She quietly walked off the road and went under some trees. Slowly, a step at a time, and holding her breath, she began to walk back in the direction of the car. He had stopped in the middle of the road and was shouting incoherently. She caught the odd obscene word, and thought that it was good that he shouted in his rage, he was not likely to hear if her foot accidentally snapped a fallen twig. Now she was directly in line with him, just beyond the edge of the road. She did not want to risk going on slowly in case by some chance he saw her and with the extraordinary energy that enraged animals discover when they are threatened, be able to catch her; and so she took the other, perhaps more daring, risk. Not that she thought of what she was doing, for she had become a creature entirely of instinct. She bounded out of the darkness onto the road and seeing only the car, ran to it for all her life was worth. It took the man a moment to realize what had happened, and he made a wild rush at her. For some distance he found the extraordinary strength to pursue her with a sense of certainty that he was going to get her but she, who stood to lose more in this contest, found a greater strength. He was far away from the car when he saw her jump into it.

The engine was still running and since the driver's door was open, the interior light was on. She jumped into the seat, put the car into first gear, pressed the accelerator flat down, and shot off, the two open doors banging shut. She could not see behind her in the darkness where he had fallen panting and helpless on the road.

In the exhaustion that overwhelmed her mind after her ordeal, she could not think of what she was doing, only that she must press on farther and farther away from the man on the road. Clutching the steering wheel tightly and staring out with glazed eyes, she had no sense of her existence, only that she must continue to flee from the terror in the darkness behind her. Where the road entered a curve or a bend, her hands automatically steered the car, and where it was straight her foot kept the accelerator pedal pressed flat to the floor. What land she was going through and in which direction were questions that did not come to her mind. She had no sense of time or space, seeing only the tunnel of light created by the headlights through which she was flying at a speed which was both dangerously fast and at the same time seemed like an unbearable stillness. Occasionally, the tormenting images returned to her and she felt sweat trickling down her inner thighs as if the passage there had indeed been forced and what poured out was her blood. She gave a start, a small scream escaping her lips, and pressed harder on the accelerator although the pedal was already flat against the floor.

The darkness of the night turned to gray and then to a diffused light and then quickly to a blue-skied brightness. She was driving down a series of bends into a wide valley where she could see a river and houses. She had begun to have a sense of herself and to understand what she was doing. The horror of the night remained vividly with her, but now she had a grip over herself and, seeing the brightly lit landscape, she felt a moment's pleasure that she was still alive, still whole, that her body had found the strength and courage to escape from her tormentor. The car was nearly out of gasoline: the needle on the gauge was on E. She was thankful that it had had enough gasoline to bring her thus far, but wondered what she would do next since she had no money.

She stopped outside the iron gate of the first house she came to in the town. It stood behind a high stone wall cemented to the top of which were broken bottles and bits of glass. The gate was open and she walked in to find herself in a large rose garden with the white stucco of the house beyond it. She took a few steps on the gravel path and stopped. Just outside an open French window three people sat at a round white table, having morning coffee; a middle-aged couple and a young girl of thirteen or fourteen. They had become immobile, watching her with curious expressions. She saw the man rise. She took a few steps toward the group, walking on the lawn past the rosebushes. She suddenly felt faint, and stopped. The girl had risen, too, and the man had begun to walk toward her. She collapsed on the grass and passed out.

After he had been rudely forced out of the car, Kessel had collected himself together and, cursing his own stupidity at having become involved in the foolishness of revolutionary politics and swearing obscenely at himself for having harbored an insane lust for an old map for so many years, he had walked the five kilometers to the town. He had only one idea in his mind: to find the fastest way out of the country and to join his brother-in-law on the northeast corner of South America. He felt remorse, and even despair, when Violeta's cries came to his mind, and in those moments he cursed the inhumanity of man, and he wondered at the accidents of life that plunged people into situations of barbarism and terror. It was terrible what the poor girl must be suffering, he thought, seeing images of the brute entering her flesh. And he cursed aloud again, it was all his fault. His grand attempt to further a cause which was intended to make people happier was responsible for the rape of an innocent girl. It was too horrible to contemplate. He spat on the ground, cursing himself afresh, and cursing all of mankind that thought it could create a perfectly harmonious world and did not see the basic fact that man was a brute concerned only with petty gratifications. Forget it all, he said to himself, just get to Pernambuco as fast as you can.

But he had to see about the car, for he could not abandon it. The idiot revolutionaries would hold him responsible for the gold, he supposed, though it wasn't his fault that the person or persons deputed to take it at the appointed hour had not done so. In fact, he would not have known the gold was still in the car had he not become suspicious after he found himself being chased by the police car. But he knew that his reasoning, though fair, would not be accepted. It was nearly eleven o'clock by the time he arrived at the town. One dirty bar on the square was open but everything else had closed down. Kessel was obliged to pay the price of a room in a luxury hotel in order to find a bed for the night. He thought of Violeta as he lay in bed. His attempt to knock the gun out of the man's hand by flipping the backrest of the seat as he got out of the car was the one small action he could be proud of. It was the only heroic deed of his entire life which, he now chided himself, had been wasted on all sorts of foolishness. But what could he do about the poor girl? He ought to give a description of the man and his car to the police, but how could he risk going to the police? As it was, he would have to exercise all his caution; it was not going to be easy towing the wretched Lincoln without the whole world seeing it. In fact, *what* was he going to do? he wondered.

The next morning he went to a garage in a street off the main square. The man there told him that there was no such thing as a towing truck in the whole town. The best he could do was to offer to use his old Jeep which, with ropes and chains, could probably do the job. Kessel gave a roar of astonishment when the man mentioned the price. The man turned away coldly to resume working on the engine of an old Ford. Kessel was obliged to accept the exorbitant price, but the man kept him waiting to show him who was boss. Had they left immediately after Kessel had agreed to pay what he demanded, they would have, on coming to the main square, seen the Lincoln parked outside a café. But by the time the man, who had become sulky and incommunicative because he harbored a contempt for the stranger whom he was obliging to part with a lot of money, had brought out his creaking old Jeep, Rafael had already gone from the town.

It was a slow, tortuous journey back to where Kessel had had the accident. He hated the man who drove the Jeep at thirty kilometers an hour. Finally, they arrived at the bend in

88

the road where the accident had occurred. But the car had gone! There were the torn bushes; there, too, the tire marks: he could not be deceived about the place. Could Rafael have come back with help, or could the police have taken the car? The man from the garage sat calmly in his Jeep, watching Kessel rage and fume as he stamped about the ground, and suspecting him to be slightly insane. Kessel mumbled to himself as they drove back to the town. The man paid him no attention.

Late that afternoon, Kessel took a bus to the nearest city with an airport. He realized that there was nothing he could do but flee the country. Once he was safe, he could write to the people in Bogotá who had sent him on this mission. They would have to accept his explanation. He had done what they had asked him to do; indeed, it was they who owed him an explanation as to why the gold had not been taken; and it was he who needed to be compensated for he had lost his car and very nearly his life. The conviction grew within him that he himself was blameless; the thought drove away his anxieties and by the time he had caught the first flight his own sense of himself as a gentleman of quality and impeccable honor had been restored to his mind.

He had to change planes in Lima and São Paulo, where he had long waits, and two days later he arrived in the northeast where his brother-in-law, Benedito Carvalho, ruled over a large tobacco plantation and a cigar factory whose products rivaled the best cigars from Cuba. His nephew, Jason, met him at the door and Kessel was both surprised and pleased to see him.

"Hey, Jason, I hardly recognized you! Boy, have you grown!"

"It's great to see you, Uncle Mark."

"One can't go away from you for a year, and you grow another ten meters," Kessel joked, going into the house. "How old are you now?"

"Fifteen."

"Why, look at you," Kessel said, holding Jason's arm and squeezing it, "you're already as big as a bull."

"Father's in the library," Jason said, his face clouding over.

"Good, good, I'll go see him there. Let me go and surprise him."

Kessel went to the library and quietly opened the door. Carvalho was sitting in an armchair, reading a book. "Hey there, Benedito!" Kessel called and raising his arms and laughing uproariously, walked toward his brother-in-law who rose from the chair to greet him with extended arms.

After the two men had met in a warm embrace, they sat down and before Kessel could begin to tell what had brought him there, Carvalho said, "You come at a sad time, Mark, but perhaps your coming is providential and is meant to save me."

"Why, what are you talking about?"

"Your sister, Mark." Carvalho began to cry, and added through his sobs, "She's dead, Mark. Dead."

Tears filled Kessel's eyes, too, and he asked, "How? When?"

"Two months ago," Carvalho said, wiping his eyes with a handkerchief. "I phoned you at the last number you gave us. There was no answer. It was leukemia, there was nothing we could do."

"Horrible, horrible," Kessel said, tears flowing down his cheeks.

"You find me a broken man, Mark. You find in me a man with a tormented soul."

"Oh, Benedito!"

"No, I was already a broken man before Julia died. That tragedy just made it worse."

"Why, what's happened?" Kessel asked, wondering if Carvalho's business had collapsed.

"God forgive me, Mark, for having the thoughts I do."

"Benedito, what are you trying to say?"

"I have prayed, I have fasted. I have submitted myself to a long retreat. I deprived my body of its legitimate pleasures. But I have not been able to find an answer to my torment. That this life . . . not only is it empty and without meaning. It is an abomination. Why, I asked in my prayers, do *I* come up with such a belief? I who love my family. God's answer was to take my wife away. That was His will. I still believe in Him. Still pray and ask again. Why I, given His bounty and enjoying the wealth and the peace that I do, cannot escape staring at a horrible blackness. There is nothing, Mark, nothing. I do not want this life. I want my mind to melt into that nothingness. My very breath torments me. But I will not *take* my own life. No, I will not. I still believe in God. And that is a terrible contradiction. To stare at nothing and to believe in Him. It worsens the torment."

Kessel thought he could help his brother-in-law by letting him talk, by asking him questions and trying to draw out the source of his appalling torment. For two weeks, Kessel accompanied Carvalho to his office in the city, saw him go through the motions of business, and accompanied him back home. The two sat together in the library after dinner, talking late into the night. Instead of restoring Carvalho's mental health, the conversations only led Carvalho to perceive more clearly what he must do, and finally he came up with what he had determined.

"This life is not for me," Carvalho said gloomily. "I want to go away, perhaps to some remote corner of the world where I am far from the burdens, the responsibilities of the physical world that surround me."

"Come, come," Kessel tried to joke, "you're not ready for the Himalayas yet, the Buddhists won't have an answer for you!"

"No, Mark. I see no meaning in this wealth, this repetition of quarterly profits. I have decided what I must do. You will not question me. You will not try to find out where I go."

Kessel stared at him in bewilderment. The man was being perfectly serious and could not be restrained on the grounds that he had gone mad, which he had not.

"I want you to promise me one thing," Carvalho said. "Look after Jason. Treat him as if he's your own son. See that he gets a good education. Will you do that for me, Mark? It's the only worldly happiness which I still have a need for."

Kessel tried to persuade him not to be so precipitate and that he should at least wait himself for Jason to finish his education, it was only a matter of a few years. As for the business, Kessel protested that he would not know how to run it, not having the experience; but Carvalho answered that it was in the hands of able executives, he would only need to be a figurehead and watch things. He had a sound answer to every objection and was unmovable from his resolve: the more Kessel tried to argue with him to stay, the more he hastened his departure from his familiar world.

A month later, Carvalho went away without announcing the time of his departure. Kessel explained the situation to Jason as best he could. Jason was in despair. To him it seemed that his father had abandoned him, leaving him virtually an orphan. But his uncle spoke kindly to him and reassured him that his father was bound to return, for he would soon discover the error of his ways. In the meanwhile, they must get on with their lives. The boy calmed down and was prepared to listen to his uncle's reasoning.

The two talked about Jason's education. Kessel was of the opinion that he should have the very best education that money could buy. After talks with the British Consul and a phone call to the headmaster of a famous school, Jason flew off to England where the school would prepare him for entrance to the London School of Economics.

The only possession with which Kessel had arrived at his brother-in-law's house from his absurd adventure in the Andes had been the contents of his wallet and the old map. Now, to all intents and purposes, he was the head of one of the largest businesses in the country. One day, he took the old map to his office and put it in the safe there. It was the only evidence he had of his earlier existence which he had begun to despise. He had neglected to write to the men in Bogotá and now he decided it would be best not to; if they looked for him, it would be in the big cities or in the European capitals. No one was likely to guess he was stuck in a corner of Pernambuco. He was finished with that foolish existence, involving himself in the game of idiots; and he was finished with exploration. There was nothing more to look for. He possessed his own El Dorado now. Fate had been remarkably expeditious in granting him

92

his wish. His only remaining desire was to find himself a young wife. He had finally outgrown his boyishness, and wanted boys of his own.

When Violeta awoke, she found herself in a bed at the foot of which a woman was standing. The woman smiled at her and said, "I just came to see how you were."

Violeta looked about her. She saw that she was in a brightly lit room with photographs of smiling and laughing people on its yellow walls.

"You fainted when you arrived," the woman said. "Carlos and I brought you here and I washed your face."

"Carlos?" Violeta's voice was weak.

"Yes, Carlos. He's my husband. My name is Sylvia. The family name is Antúnez."

Just then the young girl whom Violeta had also seen in the rose garden came into the room, and Sylvia added, "This is my daughter Madeleine. She was born on a trip to Europe and we gave her a French name."

Madeleine came and stood beside the bed. She had vivid green eyes and black hair. She put a hand on Violeta's arm and said, "Are you all right? You gave us such a fright."

Violeta smiled faintly at her and at Sylvia and said, "I've had a terrible—" but she stopped, breaking down in a fit of crying.

Madeleine sat on the edge of the bed and clutched Violeta's right hand in both of hers. "Can I bring you some water?" she asked.

Violeta tried to control herself and looked at Madeleine through her tears. Madeleine's eyes were bright with solicitous regard for her. Violeta wiped her own eyes with the back of her hand and Madeleine pulled out a handkerchief for her. "I'm very hungry," Violeta managed to say.

"I will bring you some soup," Sylvia said and went out of the room.

"What's your name?" Madeleine asked.

"Violeta. And you're Madeleine. That's a pretty name. How old are you?"

"Fourteen. I think Violeta is a prettier name."

Violeta was happy that the young girl was holding her hand, it was so comforting. What an innocent age, fourteen! she thought. One could be so lively and curious and smile at everything. Only five years older, she felt so aged after last night.

Sylvia returned with soup and some bread and butter on a tray. Madeleine helped to prop Violeta up with pillows, and her mother placed the tray in front of Violeta, saying, "You don't need to talk. Eat and feel better first, and you can tell us everything afterward."

Later in the day, with Madeleine sitting on the edge of the bed and holding her hand and Sylvia sitting on a chair nearby, she told them her story. How she had left home wearing only jeans and a T-shirt. She was only going for a drive to the edge of her father's land with her brother and the charming visitor. Madeleine gasped when Violeta described the accident, how they had all nearly died, and Sylvia said, "God saved you."

But when she came to the story of the man who had picked them up early in the night she paused and looked at Madeleine. The young girl's breasts behind her white cotton dress were small and the skin on her face was soft and unblemished. Madeleine understood Violeta's look and said, "You can say what you have to say. I know about sex."

Slowly and pausing frequently to wipe away her tears, Violeta told them of her ordeal with her night's tormentor. Sylvia moved her chair closer so that she could pass her sympathizing hand over Violeta's brow and stroke her hair gently. Madeleine wept with her, holding her hand to her cheek. And when, through her tears, with Violeta's hand in both of hers beside her cheek, her head bent a little with the black hair falling over her shoulder, Madeleine looked at Violeta, her vivid green eyes seemed to be overwhelmed with affection. And Violeta noticed that when she told of her worst moments, Madeleine's eyes flashed with ferocity as she threw a look at the window—as if all the hateful men of the world were crowded there.

"You will stay with us for some days," Sylvia said when

94

Violeta had ended her story. "You have had a terrible shock," she added, stroking her hair. "You are in no state to go anywhere."

"I'm sorry to be so much trouble to you," Violeta said.

"Don't say that!" Madeleine protested, and Sylvia said, "Why, don't be so silly! It's no trouble at all."

"The three of you looked so pretty in the rose garden when I arrived," Violeta remarked. "When I fainted, I thought I was dying and that God had willed that I should see beautiful, happy people before I died. To make up for the evil He had shown me in the night."

Mother and daughter were profoundly touched by this declaration. Madeleine pressed her cheek to Violeta's and Sylvia bent forward, rising from the chair, and kissed her forehead.

"Could you do one thing for me?" Violeta asked a few minutes later. Sylvia's expression indicated that she would do anything she was asked, and Violeta said, "That car I left outside your house. I don't ever want to see it again."

"Carlos will look after it," Sylvia said. "He'll probably let the police take it so that they can trace the man. You'll have to go and give a statement when you're well."

Soon Violeta fell asleep again and Sylvia went to attend to her household duties. Madeleine sat in the chair to watch over Violeta. What sorrows women had to endure, she thought to herself. She had only recently, during the last year, awakened to sexuality and had been filled both with confusion and a vague longing. She was attracted to some boys she knew but was also terrified of the physical power they possessed. She imagined a perfect romance for herself, one in which her existence was immersed in a rosy light and in which the experience of love was a fluid mingling of essences and did not involve the harsh solidity of the male body. She had enjoyed going to the parties where the youngest girls were of her own age and the eldest sixteen, and the boys all fifteen to eighteen. It had been natural to dance, but one boy, Rudi, had held her close and she had been startled by his pressure at her thigh and the leery look in his eyes. She had pushed him back and he had laughed. Was *that* how men and women came together, she had wondered, with the woman always obliged to retreat, or were there other passions that she did not as yet comprehend which made woman the aggressor? She longed to grow up, to understand. She had a vast reservoir of kindness within her, of love even; but the fear that there was an element of brutality natural to men, graphically confirmed now by Violeta's story, made her apprehensive and brought to her the understanding that she must be on her guard and not be taken in by the first sweet words spoken in her ear. And when she had heard the worst part of Violeta's story, she, too, had wanted to tear her nails into the faces of men. She herself had no reason to; but she understood that nature had balanced man's brutality by giving women a boundless capacity for revenge.

Violeta remained in bed for four days. Added to her terrors, the damp rainy night had given her a slight cold. On the fifth day, she was well enough to leave her room and sit out in the garden or take short walks among the rosebushes. She was enchanted by the house. It was so airy and bright and had such a beautiful orchard of oranges and lemons at the back, she loved going from room to room or walking in the fragrant air. She and Madeleine were always together. The young girl was so mature, she thought. She herself had never had such thoughts of boys when she was fourteen. And her mother was so gentle, such a kind person, Violeta almost wished she were her own mother.

She saw the father only at mealtimes. Carlos Antúnez was always polite and attentive, never raised his voice even at a servant. Madeleine told her that he was a timber merchant and spent his mornings in a forest nearby, which he owned, and afternoons at his office in the town. He also owned a share of a manganese mine, in Amazonas, which was run by his partners in a multinational corporation, and two or three times a year he flew out there in a small plane. She had gone once with him; it was quite breathtaking to see the jungle from the small plane.

One evening, when Violeta felt strong enough, she went to

see the town with Madeleine. They walked there hand in hand. There was an excited eagerness in Madeleine's gait. The main square was only a kilometer away and on the way they passed other large houses. Madeleine told her who lived in them. In this house there were two daughters the same ages as they themselves were, nineteen and fourteen, both quite pretty but not beautiful, Madeleine remarked with a gleeful giggle. Ah, and in this one lived Luis Rejano. *Was* he handsome! He had gone to a boys' school in Argentina and was nineteen. He really was sophisticated.

"I think, Madeleine, you've fallen in love with him," Violeta said, laughing and squeezing her companion's hand.

"Why, what an idea!" Madeleine, too, laughed.

They arrived at the square where a crowd of young people walked on the paths around the flower beds and the taller flowering bushes. It was an animated crowd. Laughter and the murmur of voices filled the air. Madeleine greeted several of the boys and girls but did not stop to introduce her new friend to them since she was afraid it would tire Violeta. She was convinced that Violeta's health was still too fragile for the strain of conversation with new people. Across the road on each side of the square the houses had been painted different colors—white, pink, blue and green—and at two corners were cafés where people sat drinking. The musicians in the cafés were playing the boisterous rhythms of northern South America. Violeta was delighted by it all and said to Madeleine when they were walking back to the house that she lived in a little corner of paradise.

"Oh my God!" Madeleine exclaimed when they had reached the house and saw a young man just coming out of the gate. "That's Luis Rejano!"

Madeleine was obliged to introduce Violeta to him. He was, indeed, handsome, Violeta thought, with his wavy hair, clean-shaven face that emphasized the fine proportion between the cheekbones and the jaw, and an upper lip curved like a bow.

"I just came to invite you to a party," Luis said to Madeleine.

"I'm sorry, I can't come. I have to be with Violeta and take care of her."

"No, Madeleine," Violeta protested. "I absolutely will not let you stay with me and miss the party."

"It's no ordinary party," Luis said, "and it's not till next week."

"Why, what do you mean?" Madeleine asked.

"It's at Oyarzún's. Oliva's back from Miami. I got the invitation today. It's a weekend party. I am to take a girl and I thought I'd ask you."

"Oyarzún's?" Madeleine said thoughtfully. "But my mother will never allow me to go if I have to spend the night away."

"I just asked her." Luis was smiling. "She knows old man Oyarzún and knows you will be treated like a princess. In fact, she was delighted that you have a chance to go there."

"But I'm too *young!*"

"Oh, nonsense," Violeta said, for she saw that Luis was sincere. "If your mother agrees, you should go. Luis will look after you."

"Yes, of course," the young man said eagerly.

Madeleine looked at Violeta and said, "If you promise that you will still be here when I return, then I'll go."

"All right, I promise."

"I'll pick you up on Saturday morning, next week," Luis said, going away.

"Who is this Oyarzún?" Violeta asked when they went into the house.

"One of the richest men in South America. He has an estate which is huge, but *huge!* It's about two hours' drive from here. I went there with my parents when I was a little girl and while I've forgotten much that happened to me then, that one experience was so unique that it has stayed with me. Oyarzún was still receiving people in those days. His wife was with him at that time, but she left him and then I heard his son had been killed training to be a pilot. He doesn't see people anymore. But he has a wild daughter who gives parties. He disappears to the city and the daughter just takes over. The house is like a fort. There are gardens, rivers, a lake—it's an incredible place.

You know, Violeta, I wish you were going instead of me. You would enjoy it."

"Why should you not enjoy it?"

"Because you won't be with me."

"Oh, Madeleine, how can you say such a thing! It's only a weekend and I've already promised that I will be here when you return."

"I don't ever want you to leave," Madeleine said.

11

Three days had passed since Rafael had come to Oyarzún's house and he was sitting after lunch on a leather sofa in the library, with the intention of reading a novel set in eighteenth-century Brazil, which he had begun the previous day, but he sat there, the book in his lap, thinking and daydreaming. Kessel's Lincoln Continental had been taken away. He had said to Oyarzún that he could have it and was delighted to see how much pleasure he had given his host with that one short sentence. It did not occur to Rafael that he had a responsibility to the owner of the car; the fact that Kessel appeared to Rafael to be involved in some criminal business was enough, Rafael thought, to absolve him of any necessity to make at least a token attempt to restore the car to its owner: after the accident, Kessel seemed to him to have lost his normal rights.

Oyarzún had sent it to the sculptor of the two pieces with the Buick and the Toyotas that were in the courtyard on the island, and had commissioned him to have the Lincoln crushed by a compacting machine and to shape the resulting compressed metal into an object of his own imagination.

"I accept your gift," Oyarzún had said to Rafael, "on the condition that I can reciprocate by giving you something of equal value."

"But the car has no value to me! It means nothing for me to give it away since it is not mine. Besides, I can't think of anything I want other than the happiness I already possess simply by being your guest."

"But I am in your debt," Oyarzún protested.

"Please! That is a terrible distortion," Rafael insisted.

"I wish you would ask me for something. It makes me uneasy to take something for nothing."

"All right," Rafael said. "Give me a promise."

"A promise?"

"A promise that if the time comes for me to ask you for something, you will not deny it to me. You see, there's nothing I can think of right now that I really want."

"Very well, you have my promise."

Rafael was pleased to have given away the car. It gave him an excuse to stay on at Oyarzún's, for he could tell his host that he was interested in seeing what the car looked like when it came back from the sculptor.

He picked up the book from his lap, read a paragraph which had something to do with life on a plantation in the state of Pernambuco, could not concentrate, and began to think of his father's land. What had his father been up to, why had he disappeared? Business probably. Unless there were a woman. He recalled his last conversation with his mother. She had wanted him to go away and to take Violeta with him. She was a superstitious woman. But he realized with a start that that was exactly what he had done the very next day. It was an accident that Kessel had turned up from nowhere and, of course, his own intention had only been to see Kessel to the end of the land. Emilio was going to pick him up at the junction of the dry river. And Violeta only came at the last minute, running to the car in her sneakers and blue jeans. It was a sudden caprice on her part, nothing more. But the fact was, he realized now, that they had both left the land. He expected that Violeta had returned home; but when he thought of the sequence of events, all a consequence of one chance leading to another, he wondered whether Violeta had not also been involved in a similar unfolding of unexpected events. If chance had willed that he should carry out his mother's intentions, then perhaps in a way unknown to him, as his was unknown to Violeta, she too was in some strange place and perhaps as perfectly content to be there as he was at Oyarzún's.

He crossed his legs and enjoyed the feel of the linen slacks he was wearing. A wardrobe full of Oyarzún's late son's clothes had been made available to him, each item could have been made to measure especially for Rafael. He could not tell why he was so content and why he had no desire to return to his father's land. He suspected that what his mother had said was based on more than intuition; that his father had a mistress and that he planned to bring her to the land in defiance of all the laws of matrimony, plain decency, and consideration for the children. He imagined the house with the strange woman, whom he saw only vaguely, a tall pretty creature in silks, a fluid beautiful presence, who ordered the servants to remove those objects which had been the special delight of his mother. He expected that it would be a house of silences and hysteria by now, of sinister tensions, of a painful awareness that the father's whispered words to his mistress contained the vocabulary of a secret passion. No, he had no desire to return to that atmosphere of a father's regression to adolescence. He would rather that a few months passed and the father realized his error. Better not to be there to give the father the excuse that his son was to blame for his own failures; better to give him the time in which he could come to understand that the failures stemmed entirely from his own vanity.

He heard a car door slam, and went to a window to look. A maroon-colored Porsche 924 stood in front of the house, and walking away from it was a young woman wearing a bright-orange blouse and matching trousers, broken at the waist by a pink belt, a wide-brimmed straw hat on her head with a pink ribbon around it floating away in a tail below the shoulder-length blond hair. She stopped for a second and looked back at the car; he saw the high cheekbones, the square jaw, the lips painted pink and slightly open, and the eyes which were brilliantly blue. She turned back and walked to the house, taking long, decisive steps in her pink patent-leather shoes with high heels.

Oliva's voice rang loud and clear and changed the atmosphere of the house. Hearing it through the open door of the library, Rafael realized that a house is empty without a woman's voice floating down corridors. Now it came in a warm rush, now it was high-pitched with excitement; it came as a low murmur, and now it was raised in a tone expressive of disbelief. How thrilling was the laughter of a woman, how lovely even the little vocal gesture, "Huh-huh!"

Rafael wondered whether he should go and meet her, but decided he should not intrude on a family reunion. He tried to read the novel but there was more meaning in the rise and fall of her voice than in the words before his eyes. He must, however, have become interested in something on the page, for he did not realize that her voice had stopped and then suddenly returned, closer to him, with the single word, "Hello."

She was standing in the doorway, smiling at him. Taken by surprise, he stood up hurriedly, the blood rushing to his face.

"I'm Rafael," he said, offering her his hand and being struck by her deep-blue eyes. She was larger than most native girls and looked as if her parents could have been English or German.

She touched his extended hand softly, quickly, saying, "I know, Father just told me. I'm Oliva, his crazy daughter."

"Crazy?"

"Father thinks it's mad that I fly off to Miami every time I need a new tube of toothpaste."

"That *is* rather extravagant."

"Not at all," she said, walking about the room, her bright-orange silk trousers falling in diagonal pleats across her thighs. "It takes three hours to drive to the city and one has to spend the night there to get any shopping done. It is too boring. The flight to Miami takes four hours, one can sleep on the plane and thus actually save time." She sat down on the same sofa on which he had been sitting, leaned back, stretched her arms, so that he saw the fullness of her bosom which the loose blouse had obscured, and added, "There, isn't that absolutely logical?" She brought her arms down, put a hand across her mouth, and suppressed a yawn.

"It makes a funny sort of sense," he said, wondering how she had such gloriously blond hair. Perhaps it came from her mother as must those terrific blue eyes. "But," he added, "you still have to go to the city first to get to the airport."

"What of that? It's fun to go abroad. What's this you're reading?" She picked up the book Rafael had left on a table next to the sofa, looked at its cover, pouted her lips and made a dismissive sound, and said, "This is a waste of time. You should read Latin poetry. Catullus and Ovid. There's nothing like it."

"I never studied Latin," he said.

"So, you're going to stay with us?" she asked.

"Only for a few days."

She looked at him, her dark-blue eyes flashing, as if she disbelieved him. "Why, that's my brother's shirt!" She had seen the monogrammed initials.

"And his trousers," Rafael said.

"Well, you should stay at least till my party. A million people will descend on us." She stood up and began walking out of the room, saying, "Am I tired!"

He could hear her saying some words to her father and a little later, when the elevator door had closed, silence again fell on the house. Rafael sat down on the sofa, pressing into the cushion where she had sat a moment ago, and closed his eyes, throwing his head back. He lost himself to a pleasant fantasy, finding it easy to convince himself that all the freak chances that had brought him to this place were the elaborate design of a destiny that had in store for him a great happiness.

From what Oyarzún had told him, Oliva was nineteen and attached to the land. The father sometimes worried about her; he would have preferred her to spend more time in the city and be with people her own age. Her answer always was, "They can come to me." And she had never told him that the main reason why she would not leave the land was because she did not want her father to be left alone; that she herself had no attachment to the land at all.

In his reverie, and with his partial knowledge, Rafael already saw how perfectly matched they were, both with a love of the land and not caring for the city. He was prepared to admit that he preferred her land to his own, from which he now felt alienated because of his father's behavior. He was overjoyed to think that they were the right age for each other and he assumed that like him she could not have had the opportunity as yet to fall in love. The sweet, precious angel must be a virgin! he said to himself, sinking deeper into enchanting visions and blessing the fate which had brought him to this land.

12

Having done her duty to her father and his guest, Oliva had gone to her room, fallen in bed with her clothes on, kicked off her shoes, turned her head to the pillow, and begun to cry. It was her first real opportunity, for while she had not been able to restrain her tears in Miami, a hotel room seemed an inappropriate place in which to have a good cry. She needed her own pillow.

When she was checking through the immigration control on landing in Miami, the man thumbing through the large black book looked up at her, looked at her name in the passport and looked again at the page before him in the black book. She could tell that something was wrong. She was taken to be interviewed by some officer in a small glass cubicle at the back of a larger office.

The questions appeared silly at first. Why had she come to Miami? To shop. She had been coming quite frequently in the last three years. Obviously, she replied, I need to keep up with changing fashions. Where did she stay? At the Miramar the last three times, but different hotels before then, she could try and remember, but she'd grown quite fond of the Miramar and didn't propose to stay anywhere else. Had she ever gone anywhere else in the United States? Only once, on her first visit, which had been with a group of schoolgirls when she herself was one, to Disneyworld. She had stayed at the Miramar the last three times, did she remember where she had stayed the time before that? It could have been the Sheraton, she could not be sure, but she preferred to be in big hotels, in a room on the twentieth floor with a balcony where she could sit and watch the ocean. Alone? Alone, or with company, what did he think, she was not a nobody, she had friends.

But there was one time when she did not spend her entire visit at a hotel, was there not?

She crimsoned. "I don't know what you're talking about," she said. "I come to Miami to shop. I spend money in your country. Thousands of dollars in a few days. Why are you asking me these questions? What have I done?"

"But that one time," the officer said softly. "Where else did you check in apart from a hotel?"

"You obviously know everything. Why are you asking me all this?"

"To hear the truth from you."

"Well, yes, I can't deny I spent two days at a clinic."

"What for?"

"What do people do in clinics, watch elephants dance? To get a checkup, of course, what else!"

"Try that again, miss. What for?"

"You're beginning to be embarrassing," she said, and stared at him. "I had a woman's problem and had to see a gynecologist. *All right?*"

"No."

"What do you mean, *no?*"

"You can be more precise than that," he said.

"Oh, all right! To have an abortion, that's why! I wasn't breaking any law."

"No, you were not."

"So, what's this all about?"

"Apart from that one visit to the clinic, you come to Miami to shop. Only to shop. That's what you say, correct? You are positive there's no other reason?"

She looked away from him but kept him in the corner of her eye, wondering what he knew and why it was important. "Well, I have some friends here whom I visit. You can't help getting to know people when you come to a city so often. There are so many South Americans who keep apartments here."

"Is there any friend in particular you like seeing? I mean a beautiful young girl like you must—"

"*Stop that!*" she cried imperiously. "I will answer your questions if I must but I will not suffer vulgar remarks."

"I'm sorry, miss," he said, and was surprised at himself that he had been forced into an apology by the authority of her voice. They're quite something, he thought, these upper-class Latin dames. "But, please. I do have to ask you the names of the people you visit here."

She was tempted to rattle off a list of a dozen girls whose names she remembered from her school days, but realized that that would be impetuous folly. It was obvious the man knew everything and was merely drawing it out of her. She might as well tell him the truth and get it over with; then at least she would know what the reason was behind the questioning. She looked boldly at him, making her resolve, and said, "I have a lover in Miami. His name is Claudio Matta."

"A Cuban."

"Yes. There are thousands, hundreds of thousands of Cubans in south Florida, what's wrong with that?"

"Nothing, so long as they live by the laws of the United States."

"Claudio loves the United States," she said. "He has told me many times how he hated the revolution and how lucky he has been to flee from Communism and to be able to live in the greatest democracy in the world." She was not inventing noble sentiments in order to make an impression on the American official; those were Matta's very words.

The officer looked at her coldly and said, "I have to tell you that Claudio Matta was arrested last month."

She was horrified and felt suddenly dizzy, but tried hard to keep a hold over herself. "What for?" she asked in a weak voice.

"He was an agent of Communist Cuba."

She felt faint and even her strong will could not give her the strength to say anything. Weakly, and as if from a great distance, she heard the man say, "I'm afraid we will have to detain you for questioning. It is likely that you are innocent and were only one of Matta's mistresses. Oh, yes, we've had to interrogate several," he added with a smile that was almost malicious. "But if you're innocent, you have nothing to fear. On the other hand, we can't take any chances. We know very well that the people in South America who are the most keenly committed to revolution are the children of the upper classes."

Four days of it. Questions, questions. She fought back the anguish, suffered the indignity of detention, and gave the answers until they were satisfied that she was not plotting to overthrow the legitimate right-wing military dictatorship that ruled her own country—the irony of which conclusion was completely lost on her fair-minded democratic interrogators. But she could not restrain her anger when she was finally free and spent two nights at a hotel to recover from her ordeal. *One of Matta's mistresses*. The officer's words returned to her again and again. *One* of his goddamn mistresses, how do you like that! She had given Matta her virginity at the age of sixteen, kept herself chaste for months, and then returned to Miami so that he could possess her twenty times in five days. She had loved him so much she had become careless in her passion and conceived his child. Even the pain and the trauma of an abortion she had borne cheerfully in the innocence of her love. *One* of his fucking mistresses! She was in a rage. How terrible it was to be lied to, to be robbed, to be utterly deceived! He had never loved her. He had only loved the idea of himself as a successful seducer of beautiful young girls. The villain, the criminal! What she had foolishly believed was hers only, that which she had held and kissed and drawn into her womb, was the plaything of countless whores. Oh, the unendurable horror of it, the last torment of having been deceived in one's love, the pain of knowing that your virginity has no more value than what can be bought at a brothel! Oliva cried until she could have wrung tears from her pillow.

13

Now a time of anxiety began for Rafael. He could not understand Oliva. If he ran into her in the house (and he frequently contrived opportunities to do so), she talked to him cheerfully, her brilliant blue eyes shining on him with their natural brightness: a brightness which he interpreted as sympathy or even an incipient love. When she laughed, the points of sparkling light from her teeth so overwhelmed him that he was filled with desire. And in the dining room, at the meals with her father, her conversation was animated and Rafael thought that she looked more often at him than at her father. But when he chanced upon her in the grounds of the house loitering aimlessly between the flower beds, she scarcely recognized him and looked sadly away from him, or, seeing him from a distance, simply avoided him by turning around and walking in the opposite direction. He did not have the experience with which to try and understand these signs. Perhaps she was confused, he thought, and did not herself understand what was happening to her; and perhaps this was a sign that she was falling in love with him. Rafael longed to believe this idea but he was convinced that he was only interpreting her behavior in a way favorable to himself. Or perhaps, he thought again in his anxiety, it was her feminine instinct that made her present confusing facets of herself—nature's way of so bewildering the male that he is drawn to the woman, insuring a union by making the male become obsessed by the object of his desire. Because she confused him, she was always present in his reflections. To himself, Rafael became a theoretician of love wandering in a maze of speculations, and the more he pondered the more he realized that he understood nothing. There was no one he could talk to except her father, and he was the last person Rafael could have consulted on so intimate a matter.

Elusive in person, she was ever present in his mind, always looking so fresh and pure. He saw her in so many different guises—in shorts and a T-shirt in the house, in blue jeans and a light sweater on some evenings, in a bikini by the lake, diving into the water from the pier, in a silk dress at dinner. He loved to see the glow that her body transmitted as she walked back from the lake, trailing a towel behind her: a sensuous vitality seemed to pour out of her flesh as the light touched her bosom and thighs. He loved to see her wrist encircled by the cuff of the silken sleeve as she raised a glass of wine to her lips. The light that flowed from her concentrated itself in a beam and struck his loins, intensifying his desire to an unbearable pain; and when her lips opened to receive the wine he felt that it was he who had become distilled and was entering her body. It was both a pain of knowing that he existed and an intoxication of not knowing whether he had not already become the substance which flowed in her arteries.

When he was most lucid, he was, he felt, most mad, for he saw her when she was not there and could not see himself when she was. On days when she was more distant than ever and it appeared that he could never obtain her, he was given to the extremest fantasies in which he made exquisite and unending love to her, touching every part of her with his lips and kissing her virginity before possessing it. His despair then was great as he lay sweating and exhausted in bed, although the night air was cool.

He thought that he should embolden himself and confess his love to her when he next saw her alone. But several opportunities came and went. The uncertainty was preferable to a curt dismissal; a vague and distant hope was better than an immediate and irrevocable rejection. He could live with despair as long as he could live near her. On some days, he thought he had gone truly mad; or that she had cast such a spell on his senses that when the air touched him it was her

110

fingers caressing his cheeks. When he saw a butterfly hover over a flower, he felt the stem of his body stiffen, for the two dots on the butterfly's wings were her eyes and he saw her come closer, closer where the petals were opening in eager anticipation. Then the sky filled with butterflies and he was the cloudless blue. Or he was a forest of flowers where migrations ended. In a delirium of desire, his body was saturated with sensations. He could not drink water without experiencing ecstasy, for the water contained her in its icy bubbles. Mangoes were shaped like her breasts, plums like her buttocks, and he devoured them. Even the tips of his teeth had terrible longings. There was no darkness at night, for her body hung over him as a rosy light, her form both vividly naked and obscurely abstract, an illumination that could be alarmingly both a representation of her as well as a diffusion of her, so that as he reached out for her in his madness he found himself possessing emptiness.

One day he was in the library, standing in front of a book-shelf with his back to the door. Oliva came in and without thinking she said, "What are you looking for, Alberto?"

Alberto? he wondered, turning around and seeing her closing the door behind her.

"Oh, excuse me!" she said, her face coloring slightly. "You looked just like my brother with your hand up reaching for the book."

"I'm sorry," he said, walking toward her and seeing the line of her white shorts halfway across her thighs, "if I've given you a shock."

"*Alberto* suits you, though," she said casually and went and stood by the table where the magazines were. He watched the outline of her breasts in the dark-green T-shirt as she walked. "Al-ber-to. It sounds nice, don't you think?"

He would have agreed if she had said that an obscene word sounded beautiful, and he said, "You can call me that, if you prefer it to my own name."

She looked at him with a little astonishment, and he quickly added, "If it gives you pleasure, and the idea is not offensive. I don't mind what you call me."

111

He wanted to go on with: "Provided you speak to me, look at me, hold me, love me." But he did not dare.

"Alberto, come here," she said with a serious look on her face.

Rafael walked over to her, and she laughed. "You walk as if you were trying on new shoes!"

"What can Alberto do for you?" he asked.

"Alberto, please go and fetch me the volume of Catullus."

He walked to the wall lined with books. "On second thought, please forget about it. I don't think I want to read."

He stopped and stood by the sofa.

"Yes," she said. "*Alberto* suits you. You will be *Alberto* for me. When my friends come to the party, I will tell them, 'Meet my friend Alberto.' "

After a pause, Rafael said, "Oliva . . . ?"

"Yes, Alberto?"

They both laughed.

"Well?" she said.

He was hoping that she would help him by understanding that which he did not know how to express. But she simply stood there waiting for him to continue. He was in agony. Not knowing what to say and yet feeling that here was an opportunity he could not miss, he blurted out, "What does Catullus write about?"

"Love." She spoke the word in a neutral tone, as if she had said, "Cement."

But her use of that one word thrilled him. A lucky chance offered him an opportunity to talk about love, for he had had no idea that that was what Catullus wrote about. But before he could think of a suitably generalized statement about love, Oyarzún came in and said, "Oh, there you are, Rafael! Listen, could you do a small piece of work for me? There's a package of cattle vaccines in my car that needs to be taken to the corral. I was there just now and stupidly forgot to take it out of the car."

When he had gone, Oliva asked her father when he thought their guest would leave. "He seems completely unaware of time," she added.

112

"You know, I've got used to having him here," Oyarzún said. "He relieves me of many burdens."

"So, you don't want him to go?" she asked.

"I told him when he came here that he was free to stay for as long as he liked. So far, he has not talked of going."

"You really like him being here, don't you?"

"To tell you the truth, I've not thought about it," Oyarzún said. "I've just got used to him. Somehow, it seems natural that he should be here, although that's a strange thing for me to say."

"Admit it, Papa," she said with a smile, "you see Alberto in him. He wears Alberto's clothes and sometimes from the back he looks just like him."

"The resemblance had occurred to me," Oyarzún said. "But I wasn't aware that I was trying to keep him here because he fits the figure of my dead son. Isn't that your implication?"

"Well, yes," she said. "You do appear to be fond of him."

"I hadn't thought of that. But it hasn't escaped me that he is fond of you."

"Yes, I have noticed," she said calmly. "The poor boy is madly in love with me."

"And you? What do you think of him?"

"Oh, I don't know," she said offhandedly.

Oyarzún did not want to tell his daughter that he worried about her future. The withdrawal from the world which he had created for himself had never been intended as an attempt to establish a petty empire to be inherited by his descendants. If the expression of such gross vanity had been his interest, he would have desired more children. His interest was entirely selfish: to dispense with the world by creating one of his own. Having contempt for man, he had made himself a superior man; being disenchanted with God, he had made himself a god. But he recognized now, seeing a certain sadness in his daughter's face, the force of instinct: as if there were emotions within her breast that he was eager to share.

"Have you ever thought of going to Paris?" he asked her.

"I don't know how to speak French," she said, and he

wondered why she had phrased her answer as an evasion.

"Your mother could help you," he said.

Oliva laughed and said, "You know her better than that! She wouldn't want competition from her daughter."

"She might have changed," Oyarzún argued, the idea occurring to him that his wife too might experience an instinct that she had not known before.

"She has not been too eager to tell us about it," Oliva said, and Oyarzún was struck by the fact that the daughter hated the mother more than he the wife for her desertion of the family. "Besides," Oliva added, "a person has to be stupid to leave this beautiful world."

He did not know whether to approve of his daughter's sentiment because it coincided with his own view or to condemn her harsh dismissal of her mother. "But this is *my* world, Oliva. You are not obliged to suffer it."

"I know of none other," she said.

"Will you be going to Miami again soon?" he asked after a moment.

"I don't plan to," she answered.

"Listen, Oliva. I don't know how to say this. It is difficult for a father. I mean . . ."

"You don't have to say anything," she said when he paused. "I know what you're trying to say. It's all right. You don't have to worry about me."

"You fill me with a sense of failure. Inadequacy. You are so young and there is so much I have not done for you."

She walked over and kissed him softly on the cheek, saying, "You don't have to worry."

He touched her arm as she withdrew. "But it's worse than a nunnery here. For you."

"Far from it," she said, smiling brightly. "I could play my stereo so loudly you could hear it the other side of the Andes. I can go for a drive in my Porsche. Oh, there's a million things I can do! I'm completely free, and this is your precious gift to me. As for meeting people, there's a million who'd gladly come here if I sent them an invitation."

14

The cars began to arrive before midday. Oliva had spent several days preparing for her party. She drafted the menus for the three main meals that her guests would be served; inspected, with one of her father's workers, the rowboats in the boathouse and ordered them to be lined up beside the pier on the first morning of her party; she rearranged the furniture in the long gallery so that she could receive her guests there for the buffet luncheon with which the weekend party would begin. There were not enough bedrooms in the house to accommodate the forty guests, and she ordered a number of cottages on the estate to be prepared, and had drawn up a plan, assigning each guest his living quarters, the men and the women being strictly segregated since her party was not to be an occasion for debauchery. She had taken a very fast trip to the city in her Porsche, leaving early in the morning before sunrise and returning in time for dinner; she had bought wines and liquors, boxes of chocolates and other delicacies which were not produced on the land, as well as ten records of new music.

While driving there and back, with the music from the cassette player loud in the car, she asked herself why she had busied herself with this party when she had so little desire for the company of people. Perhaps it was an elaborate disguise with which to hide her own depression, for her father must not know of what she had gone through and the sadness within her must not be seen in her eyes. Perhaps it was something deeper—an attempt to repress the image of Claudio Matta by surrounding herself with younger men, for it could be that her mind refused to accept the degradation of her body by Matta and wished to wipe away the memory by engaging with young men and women of her generation, all carefully chosen from established families, in the traditional rituals of her society. Young people must get together, dance and flirt, and participate in the overtures of mating in the game of choosing a lifelong partner. Or perhaps there was something else going on inside her which had been bred by the bitterness of her recent experience, enlarged by resentment and made so huge a monster by her anger that she could not see it, something that, demanding she play the game of love, was empassioned by a contrary emotion; something that, unknown to her, was whispering that she should bewitch men with longings for her and, drawing them into the sweetness of her embrace, transmit poison into their flesh with her kisses. She knew how overwhelming was the sense of rage within her; and that her independent spirit gave her the reputation of being wild: but the thought that inside the eye of the storm of her rage was the still, cold center of cynicism and vengeance which was silently moving with a destructive fury made a shiver run down her spine as she drove over the Andes at a furious speed.

And now the cars were arriving one after the other almost in a procession. A servant received the young people as they emerged from their cars, taking each to his or her assigned room, from where, after they had changed, they were to go to the gallery on the second floor. Seeing each other, nervous young men joked loudly to cover up their nervousness. Young women looked timidly away from others' eyes.

They began to assemble in the gallery, walking up the four white marble steps which curved in a wide bow at the entrance just past the hall outside the elevator. High heels clicked on the marble of the floor and then stepped onto deep rugs where heavy colonial furniture had been arranged to make it possible for people to sit in groups of six or eight. The earlier arrivals loitered about the gallery looking at the paintings of pastoral scenes and kept away from the large table in the middle of the room which was covered with food, for the sight of all the meat and salads and desserts made the mouth water and reminded one how hungry one was. The nude nymphs on the river-banks in the pictures or just the cattle looking stupefied under the summer sun in a European landscape were at least passingly distracting and offered a subject for low-voiced hesitant conversation. Two servants mingled among the guests, offering them a glass of wine or lemonade.

Madeleine took a lemonade and sipped from it nervously. She looked rather frail in her simple white dress with its dark-green satin belt; her straight black hair, parted in the middle, and her brilliant green eyes had the effect of making her appear intense and serious as she glanced from the paintings to the other girls in the room. They were all older, she observed, with fully developed figures, the hair elaborately done, the dresses especially purchased for the occasion. They had an assured air about them as if they were all members of an exclusive club and this gathering a regular event or cere-mony whose prescriptions were known instinctively to each. They seemed to know at once what they had to talk about, what gestures to make as they threw quick glances at the young men. Madeleine's companion, Luis Rejano, took a glass of wine and said to her, "You're going to enjoy this." She smiled at him, and he added, "Although you've come with me, feel free to mingle."

She took this as a hint that she might expect to be deserted by him and looked away, slightly hurt that she was too young for him to feel other than a brotherly attachment for her. Seeing the people around her and knowing the names of the families that Luis mentioned as they saw more and more couples come into the room, Madeleine understood why he had asked her to come with him: there was no one else in their town from a distinguished enough family whom he could have asked. She almost regretted having come, for she felt she was being used; she would have been happier, she thought, with Violeta, and for a few minutes she did not see what was going on around her but imagined instead that she was walking with Violeta among the orange trees at the back of their house. The thought filled her with pleasure, and it gave her a start when Luis squeezed her arm and said, "There's Oliva!"

She was wearing a dark-blue gown and was walking up the steps with her hand on the arm of a young man. Her lips, glossy red with makeup, were held open in a brilliant smile and her eyes shone brightly. Her mannered walk and her terrific smile, which flashed at everyone but was directed at no one in particular, made her appear to be imitating the bearing and gestures of a beauty queen walking on a stage. She certainly looked dazzling and Rafael, feeling her hand on his arm and breathing in her perfume, was in heaven. After she had asked him the evening before to escort her to the reception, he had spent sleepless hours having fantasies: he was her partner!

Someone cried, "Oliva!" and rushed up to meet her, and she and Rafael were surrounded by six or seven people. Soon she disentangled herself from that group and went about meeting the others, taking Rafael's hand each time she moved from one group to another. Luis and Madeleine were standing with a couple called Rufino and Celia when she came to them.

"Luis!" she said, greeting him. "I hope you're not going to abandon us again for Argentina."

"I've finished school," Luis said, thrilled that she should remember. "Oliva, I'd like you to meet Madeleine Antúnez."

She was enchanted. She knew of the Antúnez family, of course. How very nice of her to come. Then she said, "I would like you all to meet our house guest, Alberto."

Madeleine was struck by his eyes which somehow reminded her of Violeta. Just a funny coincidence, she thought as they shook hands. Although he was smiling and looking at her when he did so, Madeleine noticed that he quickly turned away to look at Oliva. He was the first to laugh when she made a witty remark, agreeing with her when she said something controversial, and could not take his eyes off her for more than a second. Perhaps they love each other, Madeleine thought, but then Oliva suddenly left the group, saying, "There's Andrés! What a *gorgeous* surprise!" She walked off quickly by herself to where Andrés, a tall young man with reddish hair, was walking up the steps. Madeleine noticed that whereas Oliva had met her other guests with a handshake or with a light kissing of cheeks, she met Andrés with a tight hug.

118

Madeleine looked at Alberto just then and felt a distinct pleasure at seeing the smile go from his face and his eyes be unable to conceal a moment's jealousy.

Rafael wanted to go and hear what Oliva and Andrés were talking about and did not wish to lose the illusion he had been enjoying of her being exclusively his. But their gestures and laughter and the fact that they easily moved together to a group of people suggested to Rafael that he would probably be snubbed if he attempted to assert his possessiveness. He decided to wait. He did not want to give any of the other young men, who had earlier looked at him with envy, the satisfaction of a public humiliation.

Luis had moved away on seeing a girl standing by herself, Rufino and Celia had gone to the table where several people had begun to make up plates of food for themselves. Rafael looked at Madeleine and saw that she was staring at him.

He was struck by her brilliant green eyes, noticing them for the first time, and observed, too, how young she was.

"Whose sister are you?" he asked, assuming no young man could have brought her as a partner.

She was offended, for she quickly grasped the implication, but she said quietly. "I am an only child."

There was an austere dignity to her voice and he sensed a reprimand. "Oh, excuse me," he said. "I did not mean to be rude. It's funny, isn't it, that women over thirty don't want to be reminded how old they are and girls under eighteen hate to be told they're too young."

He had a frank manner and she was prepared to forgive him. "I don't mind being alone," she said, "if you want to go and join Oliva."

He looked in Oliva's direction. She was whispering something into Andrés's ear, and from where Rafael was it seemed as though she was kissing his cheek.

"No, that really would be rude of me," Rafael said to Madeleine. "Why don't we have something to eat?"

They served themselves and took their plates to a table where a couple was sitting, eating silently. They introduced one another and began talking about how excellent the food was, how wonderful the place was, and what a marvelous person Oliva was, and then exchanged stories of their favorite resorts in the mountains and on the ocean.

Voices and laughter and the sound of silver on china plates filled the room. By now everyone was seated at the tables. Madeleine began to feel more at ease and secretly sympathized with Rafael, whom she saw stealing occasional glances at Oliva, and liked him for giving her more attention. She imagined that he did so out of a sense of duty since both of them had suddenly been abandoned by their friends, but thought that a man who was so considerate deserved to be liked. Besides, he was good-looking and had a distinctive air about him which made him superior to Luis.

Oliva rose from her table and ringing upon a china plate with a spoon, had everyone's attention. "After siesta," she said, "we will meet at the lake. At four o'clock. Please remember the rule about the lake. No one is to go onto the island. I repeat, the island is out of bounds. Anyone trying to get on it will be in for a shock."

The guests began to disperse. Rafael politely took leave of Madeleine and went toward Oliva who was just leaving her table. Before he could reach her, a dozen other people crowded around her to compliment her on the excellent fare she had provided and to exchange pleasantries with her. Presently, she disengaged herself from the crowd and began to walk away. Andrés walked with her as if he were her acknowledged partner.

"Oliva," Rafael called from behind her.

She stopped and turned around. "Oh, there you are, Alberto!" she said. "Thought you had disappeared."

"I was at a table across the room from you," Rafael said, and felt foolish that he had to offer such an explanation.

"Have you met Andrés?" she asked. "Andrés, this is Alberto."

Andrés offered a hand and a generous smile. As the two men were shaking hands, Oliva said, "See you all later," and walked away.

Now what? Rafael wondered. He heard Andrés say, "Well,

I'll be off to my room." And he saw Andrés walk quickly away as if he hoped to catch up with Oliva. Rafael's impulse was to follow him and see if he did not rejoin her, but his pride restrained him. What if he followed and saw the two of them go away together? It would be unbearable. But a few minutes later, he regretted not having followed Andrés, for now the uncertainty of knowledge made his condition worse: not having seen them go off together, he began imagining that they had done so and saw them vividly in his mind, making rapturous love. He was miserable. The last couples were leaving. And that shy little girl, Madeleine, had gone. After the triumph of his entrance with Oliva two hours earlier, he was left alone with an empty glass of wine. The servants, who had done their work discreetly and unobtrusively, were now making a great din clearing the tables and one had even plugged in a vacuum cleaner to sweep the rugs.

Madeleine returned to the cottage in which one of the two rooms had been assigned to her. It was in a charming wooded setting with a stream behind it which produced a pleasant sound of water falling over rocks. Her bedroom had a small window just above the bed through which she could hear the water and the recurring songs of birds and see rosebushes in the area between the cottage and the stream. She lay down, glad to be by herself again. Her initiation into the society of these smart, cultivated people had not been so terrifying, she thought. The parties she attended in her home town were modest affairs by comparison; besides, *there* she did not need to seek attention, for her family position guaranteed that everyone was anxious to be seen with her. She realized now why her mother had so easily given her permission to let her spend the weekend away with a young crowd: her mother's ambition was seizing an opportunity from which could come an attachment and lead in the future, in three or four years when Madeleine was old enough, to a brilliant marriage. The mother's ambition was premature and was born of an anxiety that the society of the town in which they lived, although it contained some respectable families, did not have the kind of quality that she wished for her daughter; she had been prepared, therefore, to take the risk of sending off the un-chaperoned daughter to spend a weekend with forty strangers without observing the irony that the young man who was to accompany her was a neighbor and was considered distinguished enough to be invited.

At fourteen, Madeleine had an intuitive understanding of the eternal game of chess that went on between the sexes and had a perception of her mother's motives. But while her mind was precocious, her emotions were not; she had a sense that she had reached an age when her vague longings would begin to acquire a particular focus, when the idea of falling in love would begin to attach itself to some young man. She was disappointed in Luis Rejano, having realized in the first twenty minutes of the reception that his motive was to make a superior conquest. She thought of the young man named Alberto who had entered with Oliva and then spent so much time with her. Perhaps he had done so only because he could not escape his situation, for clearly he was strongly drawn to Oliva and, equally clearly, she was not drawn to him, for she had abandoned him as soon as Andrés had arrived. She thought of Violeta and wished she were with her, sitting beside her, so that she could talk with her about these things which she was beginning to understand, and be puzzled by.

Rafael awoke from his siesta to find that it was nearly five o'clock. He changed hastily and went to the lake where the party was to have resumed at four. On his way out of the house, he ran into Rufino whom he remembered meeting at the reception.

"I overslept, too," Rufino said with a grin. "Had too much wine. By the way," he added, "what is this prohibition about the island? Why is it out of bounds?"

"I have no idea," Rafael said, deciding not to tell Rufino what was on the island, for he assumed that the prohibition came from Oyarzún. "Maybe it's some kind of an enchanted island where men fall in love with monsters."

Rufino laughed and said, "It certainly makes me curious and want to go on it. But, boy, does Oliva have authority in this place! If she says no, it means no."

"That's right," Rafael said.

"Did you see that girl Diana?" Rufino went on chatting. "Wow, what a beauty! Her father owns the biggest coffee plantation in the country."

As they came up the road, they could see from a distance that some couples were in the boats, the men rowing in a lazy motion, the girls trailing their hands in the water. Several people stood by the pier, many of them in their swimsuits. Some were diving from the pier, a number were already in the water. A lot of splashing and foolery was going on, with the loud laughter of men and the shrieking of girls. Rafael searched for Oliva but could not see her until he came up to the pier and observed behind the crowd that she was just going out in a boat. She was wearing a blue bikini and leaning back, the line of her bosom pushed high and her breasts bulging out of the narrow band of the bikini top. Andrés was working the oars and talking and she was laughing. In a few minutes they had rowed some distance away. Standing in the boisterous crowd, Rafael saw Oliva throw her head back as she laughed and he wondered who this Andrés was who had the gift of making a girl laugh so much. More couples were rowing out and soon there were a dozen boats scattered on the lake. In two or three the men had stopped rowing and the boats drifted slowly on the water while the couples sat looking into each other's eyes and talking. Rafael saw that one of the girls who was diving from the pier was Madeleine. She was wearing a one-piece white swimsuit which showed her tanned shoulders and legs to advantage and covered her small breasts in two neat swelling circles.

When Madeleine had come to the lake she had found herself standing on the edge of the crowd without being able to start a conversation with anyone and, seeing that some people were swimming, she had gone back to her cottage and changed to her swimsuit. She had decided that one could dive and swim and thus not be seen to be alone. Rafael watched her climb up the pier, walk to its end and dive from it. She swam out in a wide arc and climbed up the ladder to the pier again. Rafael walked toward her, enjoying seeing the flawless skin of her glistening shoulders and back. He watched her stand on the edge of the pier three meters away from him, put her arms up, and spring into the air. He saw her arms and head disappear as she arched out and the line of her buttocks appear against the sky and then her legs, and then she disappeared entirely out of his view. He heard the splash and soon saw her swimming out again. When she came up again, he bent over the side of the pier and held out his hand to help her up. She was surprised, and smiled.

"Why, hello, Alberto," she said. "Aren't you going to swim?"

"You'll tire yourself out," he said. "I've seen you do three dives in five minutes."

"That's nothing," she said, smiling.

Her eyes really were extraordinary, he thought, being struck again by their brilliant green. The moisture on her skin, the wet black hair hanging straight down, and the general quality of a young girl whose beauty is still unfolding made her look very appealing.

"Would you like to go rowing?" he asked.

"I know a girl who has eyes just like yours," she said as Rafael slowly pulled at the oars.

"Oh, yes? What's her name?"

Madeleine was about to mention his sister's name but something in her censored it and she said, "Pilar." Violeta, she thought, was her very special friend and she would only share her with another very special person.

Rafael shrugged his shoulders. "A coincidence."

"Why can't one go on the island?" she asked.

"I don't know. I suppose there's some secret treasure there."

He said that with a laugh and she smiled, saying, "Do you realize you're rowing straight toward it?"

"I'm not responsible for the direction," he said. "You are the one with the tiller."

"Nothing stops us from going to the island. Only landing there isn't allowed."

"I tell you what," Rafael said. "Let's go around the island."

"You sure you can row that much?"

"Young lady, you're looking at a descendant of the great navigators of the sixteenth century," he joked.

She was enjoying his company and steered the boat about twenty meters from the edge of the island. They passed a boat which was drifting on the water; the man in it was playing a guitar and singing softly. Another boat went by in an opposite direction and the girl in it called to them: "Don't put your hands in the water, there are electric eels!"

"Is that true?" Madeleine asked Rafael.

"I doubt it," he said.

They had come halfway around the island and Rafael looked over his shoulder. There was an area on the shore where instead of the royal palms that grew on the edge of the rest of the island there were half a dozen or so large trees with thick dark foliage; creepers and roots hung down into the water from the outer branches, so that between them and the tree trunks there appeared to be an archlike entrance. The higher branches hung far over the water and thus made a green leafy cave. Just then Rafael saw a boat come out of the opening. The back of the man rowing was all he could see of its occupants. He turned around to look at Madeleine and said, "Steer that way, where that boat's coming from."

Madeleine looked in that direction and hesitated for a moment. It seemed too secluded. But just then she saw that the girl in the boat coming out of the dark opening was Oliva, and she knew at once that in this game of chess Oliva was the queen who had somehow to be vanquished; her instinct drove her to match Oliva's daring. Rafael had not looked back again and Madeleine was not sure if he had seen Oliva. They had begun to row away in a direction which would keep them out of Rafael's sight.

"I wonder where I've seen that man before," Madeleine said, surprised herself at her own cunning.

"Who?" he asked.

She jerked her head in the direction of the boat behind and to the left of Rafael. He looked back and saw Oliva with

Andrés and was again pierced by jealousy. The emotion was so strong that Madeleine could see it on his face and she was thrilled by the triumph of her own cunning.

"I don't know," he said weakly, and Madeleine realized what her instinct had led her to do: remind him of Oliva's rejection of him.

As they entered the green cave, Rafael was filled with misery. It was a perfect spot for lovers and he had no doubt that Oliva had steered the boat to this place in order to find an opportunity to make love with Andrés. Impossible, he tried to convince himself, looking at the boat in which he himself was. At best a couple could sit together side by side. It would be difficult even to embrace. But it was not impossible to turn one's head and kiss, the jealous part of him whispered to him. It was not impossible to lower one's head to where her breasts rose out of the bikini top. It was not impossible to take the bikini top off! The thought of it was unbearable as he imagined all that a man and woman could do by way of touching and stroking and kissing in an uncomfortable position in a narrow boat.

"Look at that!" Madeleine pointed to an area behind Rafael. By the time he turned to look the boat had moved up to near the spot where there was a muddy bank which sloped down to the water. Two sets of footprints were clearly marked on the damp mud. Rafael saw that by tying the boat to a hanging root it was possible to secure the boat in that spot to enable one to leap onto the bank. So the constricted space of the boat was not enough for their illicit lovemaking! the voice of torments inside Rafael said to him. And sure, that is why Oliva had decreed the prohibition. Rafael was startled to hear Madeleine voice the same idea, for she said, "Now I know why Oliva didn't want anyone to alight on the island."

There was a bemused smile on her face and he smiled back at her, wanting to suppress his own feelings. What he thought of as Oliva's treachery was clear to him, but there was still a tiny rational part left in him which doubted if she could have been doing what the jealous part of him was convinced she had been doing. He needed proof. There must be, he thought, an area of crushed grass somewhere not far from the bank. He rose and began tying the piece of rope that hung from the boat to the root.

"What are you doing?" Madeleine asked.

"I just want to see where those footsteps lead," he said.

"Alberto, you're crazy! What if someone should come?"

He looked out of the opening and said, "There's no one near here, and I'll only be a minute."

He leaped off the boat and followed the footprints. They vanished after a few paces. There was a grassy path just above the bank. He walked along the path, looking for a clearing on the side which might appear as an appropriate setting for lovers. There were only thick bushes on either side. The path turned to the left behind a tree trunk and came to a clearing. There, instead of seeing an idyllic spot for lovers, he saw a concrete slab some ten meters square and on it what looked to him to be the kind of installation used for the transmission of electricity. Perhaps they had simply done their embracing standing up under a tree, he thought, staring in puzzlement at the installation.

"Alberto, where are you?" He heard Madeleine's voice through the woods.

He walked back around the tree and saw Madeleine walking up the path, looking to her left and to her right.

"Come and see this," he said to her.

"What is it?"

He took her around the corner.

"It looks like a little power station," she said. "Do you think Oliva came to check it for some reason?"

"I don't believe so," he said, taking her arm and guiding her back to the path.

"It's scary here," she said, holding his arm. "I didn't want to come but I could see a boat which seemed to be coming toward the opening. I was scared someone would find out you had broken Oliva's law."

They walked quickly back to the bank from where he could see that no one had come into the leafy cave. He held Madeleine's hand to help her leap back to the boat but the moment she was about to do that, he brought his other hand around to her shoulder and turned her body to face him. Her green eyes shone brightly even in that darkness of green foliage.

"Have you ever been kissed by a boy?" he asked.

She looked at him intently and found herself lying. "Yes," she said.

He brought his closed lips to hers and pressed them there briefly, and said, "Like this?"

Again the lie and the gesture came to her without thinking. "No," she said, "like *this*." And she brought her open mouth to his.

As her tongue entered his mouth, he thought of Oliva and drew his face back. Madeleine was left with her eyes closed and the tip of her tongue between her lips kissing the air.

"Let's go," he said, "before anyone comes."

She did as he told her, for she was overwhelmed by what she had done. What had come over her? she wondered and felt relieved that the lovemaking had not gone any further; she would not have known what to do and not been able to reject the lover had he become possessed by a stronger passion; but at the same time she was vaguely annoyed that her cloying kiss should have made him withdraw so abruptly, and obscurely she understood that her female vanity demanded that she should have been the one to have decided the point beyond which they should not go, not the man, whose role was always to insist upon the unobtainable.

Rafael rowed away from the island and out of the opening of the cave, feeling once again the intensity of his misery. If this little girl could kiss him suddenly with such ardor, then what was Oliva not capable of doing with Andrés? If Madeleine's kiss could be so sweet, would not Oliva's be a taste of heaven? If he looked morose as he rowed back, Madeleine did not notice it because she was puzzled by her own thoughts. Occasionally, their eyes met and they smiled at each other. Rafael felt annoyed with himself for having tried to give Madeleine the embrace that he longed to give to Oliva; and Madeleine was annoyed with herself for having been so forward. But when he smiled at her it was an expression of his gratitude at her unprotesting simplicity and at her marvelous spontaneity; and when she smiled at him it was to convey a kind of affection, for she was thankful that he had spent so much time with her without taking advantage of her.

Back on the land, people were dispersing to go and change for dinner, and Rafael and Madeleine went their separate ways.

They assembled again in the evening on the wide lawn at the back of the house where several rectangular tables, each covered with a white cloth, had been joined together to form one long table. Gold-rimmed white china, silver cutlery, and crystal glasses gleamed from the table, along the center of which arrangements of flowers—cascading nasturtiums, erect zinnias, and drooping pomegranate blossoms—alternated with silver candlesticks. Andean flute music played from speakers in a nearby room. A dozen of the guests were standing in scattered groups on the tiled patio between the house and the lawn when Madeleine arrived. She suffered a moment's nervousness but seeing Rufino in one group, and recognizing him from the reception, she went and stood near him and was surprised at the ease with which she joined the conversation, which was about a seaside resort on the Pacific coast. She had not met the other two men in the group and of the three girls she remembered Celia as having been with Rufino. Yet, she felt perfectly at ease with herself, and found herself talking as with old friends. No one was introduced and yet in the course of the conversation they used one another's names and Madeleine found herself using such expressions as, "You should know, Gerardo . . . " or "Believe me, Leticia . . . " And they listened to her as if she knew the entire coast and could tell them of beaches no one had ever seen. Some twenty minutes passed in this animated discussion. The patio was now crowded with all the guests assembled there. Madeleine was surprised when she noticed, for she realized how quickly time passed when she commanded everyone's attention. She was pleased that she had spontaneously

129

acquired the facility to be natural with people. It filled her with a sense of power. She was beginning to enjoy herself.

Dinner was about to be served and they were called to the table. There were place-cards beside each plate and Madeleine found herself sitting halfway down the table with people on either side of her whom she had not previously met. But she quickly fell into conversation with them, Horacio on her left and Mercedes on her right. It was a wonderful place, was it not? The time on the lake had been so enjoyable, and wasn't this setting for dinner just spectacular? After the small talk, while soup was being served, she herself asked Horacio what he thought of the inability of the Colombian government to control the drug traffic, and they entered into a heated discussion. While she talked, she glanced up and down the long table and noted that Oliva sat at the head with Andrés to her right and another young man, whom Madeleine did not know, to her left. Alberto, her lover of two minutes under the dark foliage on the bank of the island, was down to her own left, placed between two girls and all three of them seemed to be doing nothing but eating. She felt sorry for him, for he obviously had nothing to say to the girls, nor they to him. And her sympathy for him made her feel all the more enchanted with herself, for here she was manipulating a clever dialogue with someone she had never met before. The many courses of the dinner passed for her in complete happiness.

Not, however, for Rafael, who was again miserable at not being able to be with Oliva. He was certain that she was deliberately scorning him, even insulting him. Perhaps, it occurred to him, she resented his presence on her father's land and her present disdain of him was a hint that he should go away. No, he could not believe that; he was, after all, her *Alberto*, and whatever nonsense that signified to her he was certain that it did not signify rejection. The two girls on either side of him had made two or three opening remarks but he responded so woodenly that neither attempted to continue the conversation and had turned to talk to other people, obliging him to sit out the meal in silence. Which was worse for him, of course, since he could not help looking up the table in the direction of Oliva and seeing her having a hilarious time with Andrés. It was a relief for him when the dinner was over, and he realized when he rose from the table that he had consumed an entire bottle of wine by himself since the girls next to him drank only water.

Now the sound from the speakers in the nearby room was the popular music of Spanish America and it was natural that several couples should spontaneously begin to dance on the tiled patio, especially as Oliva herself had given the lead by beginning to dance with Andrés. Rafael went back and sat at the table with another glass of wine and watched the dancers with a resentful look on his face, noticing that even Madeleine was having a great time. There was a sensuality to Oliva's movements. She would take a number of steps then stop as if all rhythm in the world were taking a pause, and the effect was quite thrilling, being almost erotic, before she burst into movement again, attracting one's eye with the renewed vigor with which she flung her limbs and allowed her breasts and hips to move. But whereas she caused a sensation in the eyes of men, Madeleine was, Rafael noticed, more alluring and graceful, more feminine in an old-fashioned sense and, therefore, in the end, more exciting to observe. He drained his glass and remarked bitterly to himself that he had been reduced to the role of a spectator when he ought to have been the leading male at the party. He turned around at the table and noticed that all the bottles of wine had been taken away. There was only a jug of cold water before him. He sat for a few moments in a slumped position, his hand on the jug of water as if he did not have the will to drag it toward him and fill his glass.

"Can I have some water?" he heard a familiar voice behind him.

It was Madeleine, her face wet with perspiration, her eyes shining brilliantly. "The dancing makes me awfully thirsty," she added.

She took his glass and held it for him to fill it with water. She drank it all down and said, "Don't you want to dance?"

"I don't know," he said weakly.

131

"Come on," she said, "the music's terrific." And she dragged him away to the patio.

He felt clumsy-footed at first, but Madeleine had such grace that he found himself responding to her movements and soon began to enjoy himself. Once, the two of them, whirling around the patio, came close to Oliva and Andrés, and noticing that Oliva seemed completely oblivious to everyone else but her companion, Rafael seized the whirling moment to press Madeleine close to him for several steps before the rhythm dictated they separate.

In a pause in the music, Madeleine wanted to drink more water and he walked away from the patio with her. After she had drunk from the same glass at the table, they walked away from the light to sit on the grass under a tree. Neither had suggested that they do that, but several other couples were walking toward the darkness and it seemed natural that they should do so too. They sat side by side for some time, not saying anything. Then she threw herself back, letting her head fall to the grass, and he turned to look at her.

"It's enchanting here, isn't it?" she said.

He did not respond to her banal words and she found herself saying, "But not so enchanting as it was on the island."

He leaned his head on his elbow, his face close to hers, and since her words could have only one meaning for him and she saw that she had conveyed it, she wondered at her own capacity for sexual provocation.

"There we were on forbidden ground," he said.

She laughed, flinging her arm and letting her hand fall on his shoulder.

"And what is this, then?" she asked. "Sacred ground?"

"Why should it be sacred?"

"How else can you describe where we are?"

There was pressure from her hand at his neck, and he responded to it by drawing his face closer to hers. He looked up toward the light. Several couples were still dancing. They were in shadow, under the tree.

"I would describe it as a place where a man loses his mind," he said and put his lips to hers.

132

She scarcely heard his words as she drew him closer, and in a moment he was pressing against her along the entire length of her body. She had never believed, when she had imagined it, that such an embrace could be without pain for the woman, for she had assumed that a man's weight must crush the woman. She was astonished to find how delicious it was to have a man pressing her into the earth. But she pushed him away a few moments later, for his thighs were beating against hers and she felt afraid. He fell on his side, but their faces were still together, and remained thus for several minutes. She felt his hand reach for her bosom. She held it with the intention of pushing it away because she did not want to permit him more than her lips. She pushed his hand down to her stomach and held it there a moment, and then found that it was her own hand which jerked his hand quickly back to her left breast and held it there, hoping that he would not find it too small. But she stopped him when he began to attempt touching the buttons on her blouse, and sat up.

"This is madness, Alberto," she said, smoothing her hair.

"I'm sorry," he said. "I don't know what overcame me."

They rose and walked slowly back toward the patio. The dancing had stopped. Someone had opened a bottle of Scotch and Rafael got himself a glass.

"Where's everyone gone?" Rafael asked the man who had the bottle in front of him.

"Some to the woods," the man said drunkenly, "and some to the loneliness of their beds."

Madeleine decided that it was an appropriate moment for her to leave, for she imagined that the few men left together would probably proceed to get drunk. Saying that she needed a glass of water, she left them and quietly walked back to her cottage.

Going to bed, she lay for a long time in the dark, listening to the sound of the stream outside her open window. It had been the most incredible day of her life. Had she fallen in love? she wondered. And what was it in her that made her say the things that she did? And from where had she discovered the knack to draw a man to herself? And who had taught her to kiss with her tongue in the man's mouth? It had all happened suddenly, without her attempting to do anything deliberately. And it was all very wonderful. Poor Alberto! she thought. He had seemed so attached to Oliva, his longing for her seemed to have been written on his face, and a few hours later, he was hers. *She* had drawn out a passion from him, *she* had begun to make him mad with the sudden currents of sensuality that she transmitted into his body, *she* was affecting the emotions of a man! She could not believe the strength she possessed and was amazed at herself. But again the question came to her: had she fallen in love? The question afforded her the opportunity for a long debate with herself, which was pleasant whichever point of view she took: she was in love and had got her man; or, she was not in love and enjoyed the power of arousing love for herself in a man; or neither of them was in love and yet she could manipulate the man to love her. Life was better than she had expected it to be: it offered a variety of ways in which to find happiness. She was smiling to herself when she fell asleep.

Rafael sat till three in the morning with two other men drinking Scotch. The two had been disappointed in their attempts to make an impression on certain girls, and Rafael, whose despair at Oliva's treatment of him had been mixed with a few moments of exhilaration he had experienced with Madeleine, decided that he suffered from the despair more than he experienced the happiness that he had found with the younger girl and carried on a dialogue of disenchantment with women with his two drinking companions. It was a crazy world, they all agreed, in which women could get away with teasing men or with deceiving them. Rafael asked if either of them had seen Oliva leave.

"Oliva," said one of the men, "now there you have a woman who doesn't tease. She sticks with her man. Never mind if that Andrés is a tall prick, at least he doesn't get the runaround."

This was worse, Rafael felt, than listening to his own thoughts, and he decided to go to bed. Better the unconfirmed torments of his own mind than the words of others that carried a greater force and were therefore too painful to hear. He spent a night of great misery, being able to sleep only sporadically, and when he finally rose from his bed it was with a severe headache. He took two aspirins and fell back into bed. It was past eleven by the time he got out of bed and nearly noon before he had taken a shower and was ready to go down.

Most of the party had breakfasted by nine and had been driven to the stables in a pickup which made three trips to transport those who wanted to go riding. Madeleine, who had run into the man called Horacio who had sat next to her at dinner, decided to go and Horacio went with her. The horses were splendidly groomed with beautiful saddles on them. Madeleine and Horacio followed the other riders out of the stables. Oliva, dressed like a member of the English nobility at a hunt and mounted on a marvelous black horse, indicated the alternatives before them: there were the fields and pastures for those who wanted a brisk canter; a narrow path into the jungle for those who wanted adventure; or if they just wanted to amble, they could stay on the roads on the land. She herself galloped away toward the pastures and was followed by a good third of the party, including Madeleine and Horacio. Madeleine, in blue jeans and white T-shirt, spurred her horse and overtook the rest of the group and came abreast of Oliva, some twenty lengths ahead of the others.

The two rode side by side, their faces flushed. They looked at each other and wide smiles came on both their faces, their eyes shining brilliantly. Oliva tried to go faster; Madeleine kept pace with her. Having come across a field and put more distance between themselves and the others, they entered a wood through which Oliva led the way.

"You ride well," Oliva said over her shoulder.

"You're pretty good yourself," Madeleine said.

"But I have the better horse."

"Where is Andrés?" Madeleine asked.

"He left early this morning."

They came out of the wood to another field, and again galloped away.

"Isn't this terrific?" Oliva shouted, trying to go faster than Madeleine.

"It's great," Madeleine shouted back, determined to gain on Oliva.

But they remained precisely next to each other to the end of the field. They returned at a slower pace.

"I've not really had much chance to talk to you," Oliva said. "Who did you come with?"

"Luis Rejano."

"Oh, Luis! I heard that he's mad about Diana and she's been giving him a difficult time!" Oliva looked at Madeleine when she said that to see if she had provoked jealousy.

"I've hardly seen him since we came," Madeleine said without revealing any emotion. "I've been having a great time with all the other people."

"That's good. It's foolish to have attachments when one is so young."

When they came out of the wood they saw that the rest of the group was riding around in a wide circle in the first field, and they joined them. Horacio rode up to Madeleine and asked, "Where did you disappear to?"

He was blaming her because he himself was too poor a horseman to keep up with her. "There's another field there, past that wood," Madeleine answered casually. "We had a race."

"Who won?"

"No one," she said, galloping away from him.

Returning from the stables, each went to his or her room to change, and at noon they all began to assemble in the gallery for the luncheon with which the party was to conclude. When Madeleine arrived there, a group of six was standing in a corner and she went up to it and immediately began to take part in the conversation. Gerardo was describing how he had gone into the jungle and seen a jaguar.

"But that's impossible," another man said. "There are no jaguars in this part of the country."

"I tell you I saw it with my own eyes," Gerardo insisted.

"What you saw was an onça pintada," Madeleine said with the conviction of one who knows the facts, and put an end to the argument.

They proceeded to discuss the species of wildlife in the country. More people were arriving and when Madeleine looked away from the group she was in, she noticed that Rafael was standing alone by a window. She went up to him and said, "Hello, Alberto, how do you feel this morning?"

He smiled at her and said, "I woke up with a monstrous hangover."

"Oh, poor thing."

"And you?"

"I've been up since eight," she said. "We went riding across the fields. It was great. I wish you had been with me."

Her eyes were glowing brightly, and she added, "There was a wood there where we could have got lost."

The words produced a sudden thrill within him. She had such a natural way of expressing a desire for intimacy. A group of people had gathered near them. "Let's go to the balcony," he said. "There's a beautiful view of the lake from there."

They stood alone on the balcony, the murmur of the party coming from the open door.

"Look, there's the island." She pointed, suddenly holding his arm.

He held her by the shoulder. She looked at him with a smile. He touched her hair and she leaned her face against his shoulder.

"Down there," he said, pointing. "See the lawn where the table was last night?"

"Yes?"

"And across there, see those trees? Which one was our tree?"

"*Our* tree?" she asked coyly.

"You know what I mean."

"Show me what you mean," she said, raising her face.

He kissed her softly; then with some passion. She was beautiful, he thought, really quite wonderful. Then why did he feel the hesitation toward her, why did he torment himself with thoughts of Oliva?

Yes, Madeleine thought to herself, this *is* love, it has to be. She withdrew her face from his and looked at him in wonder, this object of her love. Her smile was dazzling and he again kissed her, with increased ardor.

"Perhaps we should be going in," he said.

"I'm not hungry. Are you?"

They stood there a while longer, leaning against each other, each with an arm around the other's waist, looking at the lake. She was wondering what would happen when the party ended. Would he make her a promise to come and see her at her parents' house? Just then they heard a sound behind them, someone clearing his throat. It was a servant.

"What is it?" Rafael said.

"Could you please come with me?"

Rafael looked at Madeleine, excusing himself with his eyes, and followed the servant out to the hall.

"Miss Oliva is in the living room and would like to see you," the servant said. He had had the discretion not to relate the message in front of the young girl he had seen Rafael embracing.

Rafael's eyes brightened and he ran down the steps and arrived breathlessly in the living room. Oliva stood by a window looking ravishingly beautiful in a dress of light blue.

"Alberto, please do me the honour of escorting me to the gallery."

He walked up to her and held out his arm for her to take. They proceeded out of the living room. The servant was holding the elevator door open for them. In the elevator he asked, "Where is Andrés?"

"He went away," she said without feeling.

Madeleine was just coming back to the room from the balcony when she saw them enter the gallery. Her dear Alberto's face was that of a saint who has just seen a beatific vision. Anger surged within her, her face went crimson, but she suppressed her emotion. Perhaps it was only a task he had to perform for the tyrannical mistress of the house, perhaps his face was only a mask he had put on. She would pretend that nothing had happened. She would join the others, for surely he would soon come back to her.

The luncheon proceeded with more gaiety than the day

before. There was a great deal of talk and laughter. Madeleine stayed with a group which included Rufino and Celia, and Luis, who seemed to be the only person in the party who found it impossible to disguise his dejection. Madeleine looked in the direction of her Alberto from time to time and received no evidence from him that he was aware of anyone else's existence than Oliva's.

The party ended. There were embraces and the kissing of cheeks. Oliva stood by the door and said goodbye to each of her guests and received effusive declarations of their thanks. Rafael had gone out before the dispersal began, for it had crossed his mind that he might have a confrontation with Madeleine. It had been a mistake. He would rather not have to explain anything to her. He joined Oliva at the door when he had seen Madeleine leave.

Soon the cars began to glide away from the drive in front of the house. As Luis drove away, Madeleine saw from her window that Oliva and the man she thought she had fallen in love with were standing at the door waving goodbye to the departing guests. Luis was profoundly depressed at having been rebuffed by Diana; Madeleine was seething with anger; neither said a word as they drove back to their town.

"One thing I always do when a party is over," Oliva said, "is to drink a bottle of champagne and go to sleep."

"That's a wonderful idea," Rafael said.

"You may join me if you wish."

They sat in rattan chairs in the back patio, a small table between them with a bottle of champagne in an ice-bucket.

"Did you enjoy yourself?" she asked.

"Not so much as I could have if I had seen more of you."

"Oh, nonsense!"

"Believe me, Oliva, I was depressed half the time. You spent *all* your time with Andrés."

"That's funny," she said, laughing. "You know who Andrés is? My first cousin. My father's sister's son. I hadn't seen him for three years. He was in the United States studying to be a computer engineer. It was a coincidence that he arrived during

139

the party. We had so much to talk about. He has to go back to the States for another year, and God knows when we'll be together again."

What she did not tell Rafael was that she had been delighted that Andrés had turned up, for it relieved her from having to appear gracious to her guests. She had behaved as though Andrés was a close boyfriend because no one, seeing her in a superficial closeness with a supposed lover, would make any demands on her. She could not have wished for a better arrangement; she had given the party to create an impression for her father that nothing had changed in her life, and she had feared that it would be something of a trial to be with so many people pretending to be perfectly happy. With Andrés present, she had not needed to be with all the guests for much of the time. He gave her the perfect alibi to go away from the guests when she felt like it and to appear before them as a wildly unpredictable and passionate person, confirming their idea that she was wonderful and yet mysterious.

"It was quite obvious to everyone," Rafael said, "that there was more between you than a family relationship."

"Believe what you like, but it's not true."

"I saw you on the lake," Rafael said. "You rowed around to the back of the island. There is a secluded spot there."

"What a first-rate spy you are!" she mocked.

"You said that no one should go on the island, and yet you yourself, with your first cousin, as you call him, went on it."

"Were you watching us through binoculars?"

"No, you left your footprints on the mud-bank."

"Why, you are a superdetective! Very well, then, let me explain. There's a power station on the island. The electricity on the land comes from there. I wanted Andrés to check something. He knows all about electricity. He's a genius with anything to do with the mechanics of things."

"I don't know what to think."

"Listen, I do not care what you think," Oliva said.

"I wish you did."

"And what about you?" she cried at him. "It happens that I saw you right there, under that tree, after dinner last night.

You were lying there with a girl."

"Do you care about that?" he asked.

"Yes. This is my father's land. *My* land. I despise debauchery. Especially when it's so shamefully public."

She rose and went away, leaving him the champagne bottle, which was still a quarter full.

When she went to her room, she wondered why she had cried aloud at him about lying under the tree. Could she really be jealous of the girl? The phrase about her despising debauchery had been an attempt to cover up what had slipped out: one could always feel righteous when one did not wish to show a hurt. Why should she have felt anything when she saw him under the tree with that little green-eyed girl? And why had she felt so miserably lonely when she lay alone in her bed last night? She had thought of Matta, wept again for a precious part of her youth that he had stolen away from her, and when the tears had dried and she still had not fallen asleep, she realized a need within her. But she refused to face it, having decided after the wretched affair with Matta that henceforth she could only hate men. Then this morning that green-eyed girl had come riding with her and would not let herself be outpaced. A slip of a girl who seemed to receive love so easily. Seeing her ride her horse so effortlessly, Oliva had been furious at the power the girl possessed, and had been reminded of Rafael. Last night she had finally fallen asleep with the resolution to suppress the need within her, but now, finding that she had come close to spontaneously confessing that she was jealous of the little girl, a new thought came to her: if she wished to hate men, the way to do so was not necessarily by keeping away from them. A liberal and promiscuous attachment to them was a more amusing way. She would devise ways of making them suffer the torment of needing her body.

The day after the party the normal routine of the land resumed itself. Oyarzún, who had gone away to the city for the week-end, returned in time for lunch. Rafael informed him that he had supervised the shipment of pottery that morning: the

141

pickup had been carefully packed and sent off to the dealer in the city. After lunch, at which Rafael found Oliva remarkably attentive, the two men went off to inspect some work being done to add an extension to the corral.

During the rest of the week, Oyarzún often asked Rafael to go along with him on the many tasks that had to be performed on the land. On some days, the two were away from an early breakfast till lunch and then out again till sunset. Oyarzún began to assign tasks for Rafael to do on his own, and he became familiar with the operations of the land and began to be treated by the peasants and the workers on the same terms as their master. Sometimes, out in the fields, he would run into Oliva, who would happen to be riding by on her black horse. At mealtimes she was always radiant and agreeable, and one day when he was in the library after dinner, she came there and picked up the volume of Catullus. He was sitting on a sofa reading a novel, and she walked and stood in front of him. He looked up and saw her gazing at him with her deep blue eyes.

"Listen to this," she said.

She proceeded to recite a poem. Her voice rendered the Latin as a rich, musical sound. It was entrancing, moving, and beautiful.

"What is that about?" he asked when she had finished.

"About the inconstancy of women." She put the book down on a table, and added, "But don't you believe the poets, they can only utter a partial truth."

"What do you mean by that?"

"Women can be terribly faithful, and *that* is an extreme form of inconstancy men can never understand."

He was confused. She began to walk to the door.

"I wish you'd read some more Latin," he said.

"Some other time," she said, going away.

The next day a van drew up to the front of the house just when the three of them were having lunch. Rafael went to see and came back a few minutes later.

"It's the sculpture," he said, taking his seat again. "I've got the men to unload it."

They went out after they had finished lunch. The men had

142

just brought down a huge crate from the van, which had a hydraulic lift above its rear bumper. Oyarzún ordered the men to open the crate. It took them ten minutes to do so. Long sheets of brown paper which had been wrapped around the sculpture were removed, and there it stood! Oliva gave a gasp and said, "That's fantastic!"

"It really is something," Oyarzún said, filled with pleasure.

Rafael was quite awed by the beauty and the size of it.

The Lincoln had been crushed till it was less than three meters long and a little under two meters in height. The sculptor had then beaten it with his tools until he had turned it into the form of a sheep and then sprayed it with gold-colored paint.

The van went away, and three of the men from the land who had come to help with the unloading returned to their work. Oyarzún, Oliva, and Rafael remained there, admiring the work, walking around it, or standing at a distance. It was unbelievable, and amazing, what the hand of an artist could do.

Oyarzún and Rafael were standing next to each other, and Oyarzún said, "When you gave me the Lincoln, I offered you a choice of a gift in return."

"But this golden sheep is priceless," said Oliva.

"I believe I can match even the priceless," Oyarzún said almost with severity as if he resented the suggestion that anything was beyond his means. He turned to Rafael and added, "Well? Do you have a wish?"

Rafael looked at Oliva, who was staring with amusement at her father.

"Yes," Rafael said. "Your daughter's hand."

Oyarzún looked at him coldly, and then at Oliva. She seemed to have turned into a statue, her eyes wide open, staring at her father.

"If my daughter will permit me to do so," Oyarzún said.

She turned her eyes from her father to Rafael. The stare turned to a piercing gaze. A smile, as if of triumph, came to her face and her eyes shone brilliantly as she said, "What else can be so priceless?"

15

After his "honeymoon" with Margarita and a few more days in the city, which were necessary for Margarita to tidy up her affairs, Rojas returned to his land with his young mistress. She was slightly apprehensive as they drove up to the house, but resolved that she would meet his wife and children with the coldest severity.

All her life she had been mild-natured and kind; timid in the company of people, she listened rather than talked; and although she had her own views on subjects she was acquainted with, she did not reject a contrary opinion but considered it with agreeable politeness. But now, going through the door, her very soul seemed to change; for she was beginning a new life and though Rojas had conjured up a beautiful vision of it, she perceived now that it was not to be a life without its own terrors: the transformation that came over her as she took the first step into the house had its source in some instinct buried deep within her which informed her that the only way in which she could inhabit this house was through the exercise of tyrannical power. She must abuse Rojas's children, scorn his wife, whom she was bound to find pitiful, and be merciless in her demands of Rojas himself; otherwise the established traditions of the house would crush her.

There was no one in the living room when they entered.

"What is *this*?" she cried as if greatly alarmed.

Rojas looked at her, surprised at her tone, and said, "What do you mean?"

"Where on earth did you pick up all this rubbish?"

"What are you talking about?"

"You call this *furniture*?" she said, waving a hand which indicated she meant everything in the room. "Why, I thought you had better taste than this. This is most disappointing. It's the kind of rubbish poor country people have."

"Margarita, I inherited all this. It's old furniture, I know. Some of these pieces must be quite valuable as antiques by now."

"I don't care about antiques. I want to bury the past. I couldn't possibly live with this."

"What do you expect me to do?" he asked, exasperated.

"I'd rather return to the city than live surrounded by this rubbish," she said coldly.

"Margarita, what are you saying!"

"Get rid of it, Jorge, and the sooner the better. I want to be surrounded by new and beautiful things."

Rojas left the argument at that. It must be the shock of coming to the house, he thought. He would reason with her later. Perhaps she would begin to get used to her new environment in a few days. But where was everybody? He went to the hall and shouted, "Rafael! Violeta!"

He went to the kitchen, Margarita going with him. There was no one there. The sink was clean, the pots were hanging from their hooks, the stove was spotless.

"I happen to enjoy cooking," Margarita said, "and can make some terrific French dishes."

"That will be wonderful," he said.

"But we'll have to redesign the kitchen. It's *primitive*. Just look at those burned aluminum pots!"

Rojas led the way upstairs. "These pictures are *awful*!" she said, climbing the stairs and referring to the simplistic watercolors of Andean peaks that hung on the wall.

All the rooms were empty. Rojas was shocked to see that Violeta's room was littered with rose petals, which had blackened. When they went into his own bedroom, Margarita said, "Please don't expect me to sleep in *that* bed. The heavy headboard will give me nightmares."

On the rooftop terrace he found there was not a single flower on the rosebushes. "Where has everyone gone?" he said in exasperation, and irritated that Margarita followed him everywhere and made sarcastic or abusive comments on the objects she saw, added, "Will you *please* stop tormenting me with your remarks?"

They returned to the ground floor and he went out of the house. He found a worker and asked him to fetch Emilio. He returned to the house and going into the drawing room saw Margarita standing on a chair removing the curtains.

"Margarita, *what* are you doing?"

"Jorge, have you ever seen brown flowers in your life? *Brown*! And on a dirty beige background, too!" She flung the curtain she had just removed to the floor.

Emilio arrived.

"Emilio, where is Rafael? And where are the others?"

All Emilio could say was that some days ago Rafael and Violeta had driven away in a gold-colored car with a man with white hair. They had taken the road that goes through the pine forest to the north. Rafael had asked him to follow in the truck and pick up him and Violeta at the dry river. He'd had a flat and been delayed, but he'd gone to the dry river. There was no one there. He'd searched the forest for two hours, walking on the paths or driving on the narrow tracks. He'd seen no sign of them. They'd just disappeared. He'd come back and sent four men on mules to search the entire forest. They'd returned at sunset with no luck.

"What about the Señora? Where is she?"

"I don't know, sir."

What did all this mean? Rojas wondered.

Meanwhile, Margarita had flung down all the curtains and, abandoning them in a heap on the floor, had stomped out and was taking down the pictures on the wall by the staircase.

"What happened with the cold-storage warehouse?" Rojas asked.

"That was fixed," Emilio answered.

"That's good."

"But we had to burn all the beef that was in it. A hundred

146

and twenty carcasses. And we're losing more. It's a bad time for the cattle."

"What do you mean?"

"I found seven dead cows three days ago. It was mysterious. Then I was in the corral and noticed. Vampire bats have been getting at them. There are hundreds who've been attacked."

Rojas was walking about the room pensively. Emilio was silent and after a minute Rojas asked, "Any other bad news?"

"There has been no rain all these days, and this is the time of the year when the land needs it. We need water for the new corn."

They heard a crashing sound from above.

"All right, you can go," Rojas said to Emilio. "Find the cook and tell her to make lunch. I'll see you in the corral later."

Rojas went upstairs. The watercolors of the Andes had been taken down, leaving rectangular marks on the wall, and thrown in the hall at the top of the stairs. He went into the bedroom.

"*What* on earth are you doing now?" he shouted.

Margarita had pushed the bed away from the wall. By kicking and pulling, she had managed to separate the headboard from the bed, sending it crashing to the floor. Stepping back from it when it was about to fall, she knocked over a side table, sending an alarm clock crashing to the floor, where its plastic shell cracked and glass face broke in fragments.

"I didn't think you could get a new bed by tonight," she said, "and decided I might as well make this one bearable until a new one can arrive."

"Margarita, what's come over you?" he asked sadly.

Her eyes seemed to be touched by violence. "Nothing," she said.

"Then why are you going around tearing down things?"

"I'm doing what any woman must do," she said coldly.

"But you don't have to start breaking things the moment you arrive at the house."

"It's *my* house," she said. "Instead of standing there like a fool you might at least have the sense to go and send me a servant to clean up this mess."

147

Rojas left her and went up to the terrace. But the sight of the Andean peak did not soothe his eyes. From another corner, he saw his cattle grazing in the distance. How many of them would be alive next week? The sun was scorching his land. His children had disappeared. His wife had vanished. The woman he had brought to his house had entered it like a fury.

He had been convinced that it had been in his power to rearrange his life in order to bring himself a perfect happiness. He had expected nothing but adoration and tender expressions of love from Margarita. He had seen nothing but the beauty of her body, which he saw himself entering each night. He had imagined nothing but ecstasy and harmony. But as he looked at the parched land and the dying cattle, he understood that he was not exempt from the long history of torments suffered by mankind for thousands of years. He saw the error he had committed and wondered if the years that remained to him would be sufficient for expiation.

Margarita came up and he saw her do a happy little dance among the flowerless rosebushes. She looked out on the land from near where he stood.

"It's beautiful," she said. "It's like paradise here."

And she rushed up to him and hugged him for the joy she felt.

"When I kiss you," she said, kissing him, "I kiss your land also."

He felt her loving words to be cruel; her kiss cold.

PART 2

The Dead Labyrinth

¡Haber nacido para vivir de nuestra muerte!

César Vallejo

1

Mark Kessel sat on the front veranda of the house looking out past the front lawn with its flowering oleanders on the Atlantic Ocean, drinking his morning coffee. He smoked one of the smaller cigars manufactured by the company that his brother-in-law Benedito Carvalho had left in his trust four years earlier to be given over to his son Jason when he had finished his education. During these years, Kessel had taken effective control of the company, found himself a young woman from a distinguished family in Minas for a wife, and was now the proud father of two boys, aged two and one. His wife, Heloise, though still only twenty-four, was devoted to him and although he was now fifty-nine, he had every hope of continuing to father more children for several years to come.

Benedito Carvalho, who had left in a state of spiritual ill health, leaving the care of his son Jason to Kessel, had ended his days in Spain. Kessel had received a letter from the monastery about three months before with the news that Carvalho had died in a fit of hysteria in which he had screamed out against existence but, in the last moments, had gazed at a crucifix with a wild and amazed stare—which was to be interpreted as his final reconciliation with God.

Kessel had burned the letter and lit a cigar with the same match. He had not communicated the news to Jason, who had finished his schooling in England and had just begun his third term at a provincial university, not having been able to win a place at the London School of Economics. It suited Kessel to keep the fiction alive that his brother-in-law had gone in search of a place where he could cease suffering from spiritual

151

torments and to broadcast a picture of Carvalho as a man who was so troubled in his mind that his spirit demanded a profound and irrevocable withdrawal from the world for many years. Kessel's usual answer on the rare occasions when anyone inquired after Carvalho was to say, "For all I know, he's in the Himalayas right now, conversing with the Buddhists. What do you expect from a spiritual maniac?" It was extraordinary how a joke satisfied everyone as being the true answer.

He let the ash drop from his cigar and sipped his coffee. Heloise came up to him with a jug of fresh coffee to replenish his cup. She stood beside his wicker chair, and while she poured coffee into his cup, which he had placed on the small table in front of him, he passed his hand over her stomach across the cotton morning gown which she was wearing. She smiled at him with her dark eyes.

"It's going to be a girl this time," she said. "I can feel it."

"That will be wonderful, Heloise, just wonderful," he said, putting his hand up to her neck as she was bending down just then and drawing her face toward him to kiss her lips. "There's no one more beautiful when your breasts are full of milk," he added, squeezing her right breast.

"You've only one idea on your mind," she teased, stepping back. "You're quite shameless, Mark. What if a servant is watching?"

Ah, it was a wonderful life, he thought, watching her walk away with a slow, swaying motion of her hips. He had been such a fool in his earlier years, wasted all that time in the pursuit of utopian chimeras that he was not really interested in. He had squandered a good part of his inherited fortune backing a press which printed underground revolutionary propaganda in which he had never believed. What a waste of time all that was! It had taken him the best part of his life to understand that the true political goal was not to seek equality for all but to seek that inequality which placed one in a superior position to the scum of mediocrities who populated the earth. But he felt fortunate to have recovered from idealistic illusions—or, in his case, the silly games with which to fill

152

one's idle hours, for he had never really *thought* seriously about anything—in time to still have a few years in which to enjoy the freedom that came from being the master of a company in which a thousand people were nearly his slaves. Life was glorious not because the workers were free but because he was the master who kept them in chains.

He was about to rise and drive to his office when a man rode up to the house on a motorcycle and delivered a telegram. It was from Jason in London and announced that he was arriving the next week for the long vacation. Since having been sent to England four years ago, Jason had returned only once, when he finished school and before he began at the university. Kessel had enjoyed his nephew's visit—Jason was very boyish and naïve—and Kessel had experienced a pleasure in reacquainting him with the customs of his native country. But now he was not so sure if he liked to have Jason visit. Carvalho was dead and he did not like the idea of having the son, who was its legitimate owner, in the house. Besides, he rationalized, it would be inappropriate to inform Jason at this time that he had inherited his father's estate, for the boy had only just finished his first year at college and it would be best for him if he were to continue his studies without suffering emotional stress. That was it! Kessel thought. An excellent reason for not telling Jason the truth; after all, he was only doing it for the good of the boy: he would be grateful for his uncle's silence in due time.

But what would happen *after* the two years? The question occurred to Kessel while he was driving to his office. No, there was no reason to worry about it, he thought, dismissing the question. But the question echoed in his mind from time to time until the day that Jason returned. He did not come alone. He had with him a young man his own age, an Englishman named Bob Bradford, and after the first conversation with the two, Kessel had the answer to the question that had been bothering him.

Jason had grown up to be a handsome and cultivated young man. He was tall and slim but strong in his muscles; he had his father's brown hair and Kessel's sister's light-blue eyes; but

Kessel also noticed that he possessed the same boyishness and love of adventure which he himself had in his earlier years. He was more interested in roaming the streets with Bob Bradford, going surfing with him when the beach was declared to be too dangerous for swimming, or riding on horseback across the tobacco plantation, than he was in going into society or visiting the office. With the concern of a surrogate father, Kessel asked him about his studies at the university. "I trust," Kessel added, adopting a deliberately ponderous tone, "you have your father's business paramount in your heart and that your studies are preparing you for taking over as the company's chief executive in due course."

"Well, Uncle Mark, it's rather fun to be studying all sorts of things."

"That's hardly a satisfactory answer," Kessel said, looking severe. "Whatever can 'all sorts of things' mean? One can study all sorts of things in a brothel!"

Jason was shocked and his pale skin reddened a little. "Well, you see, Uncle Mark, we are not taught how to run a business, but we study widely in the field of economics as well as in politics, philosophy, and anthropology. It prepares one for life." Jason grinned at the end of his statement.

Kessel was glad that the education was too general to give the young man a particular ambition for business, but he said, feigning annoyance, "What kind of a degree program in economics is that!"

"A rather good one, actually," Jason said with enthusiasm. "You see, Uncle Mark, it has really nothing to do with business but is indeed a very good course for people who go into all sorts of things. I mean," he added quickly after his last phrase, which he saw made his uncle's eyes widen, "former graduates of the university have filled very high positions in the Home Office in England and similar positions in foreign countries. Indeed, one of them is a cabinet minister in Nigeria."

"I see," Kessel said in the tone of one who did not approve of what he had heard.

"I'm also rather good at languages," Jason said in order to

convey a favorable impression of himself. "I had to take a foreign language at school to fulfill the entrance requirements. I could easily have breezed through with Portuguese but I didn't think it was a sporting thing to do, to use one's native tongue to get into a university and so I took Spanish. It was extraordinary how quickly I mastered that. Since then, it's a kind of hobby with me to be learning a new language. I've been doing Latin to give myself a solid foundation. It's great fun!"

Kessel pretended to have no interest in such a time-wasting pursuit and pointedly changed the subject by asking, "Who is this Bob Bradford you've brought along with you?"

"He's my closest friend. We were at school together and won our rugby colors at the same time. He's awfully good, and a rather fine cricketer too, bowls a jolly difficult inswinger."

"But what's his background? What does his father do to be able to afford to send his son to such an expensive school and now to a university?"

"Actually, he was at school on a scholarship," Jason said. "The family's rather poor. His father used to work for British Leyland but the poor man's been laid off for three years and lives with his wife in a council flat in Birmingham. It was rather a crushing blow when BL stopped making the MG. They're awfully lucky to have such a brilliant son as Bob."

"Am I right in thinking that you paid Bob's air fare to come here?"

"Well, I helped him out a bit," Jason said, and quickly changed the subject. "Bob's a brilliant speaker and ought to be elected president of the debating society next term. He caused a sensation with a speech on imperialism the first term we went up. Everyone predicts he's going to be Labor leader."

Kessel was reminded of his own idealistic days and understood precisely the kind of foolish young man Bob was—championing the latest cause, arguing passionately for reform, a complete ass in fact.

"And do you take part in debates, too?" he asked his nephew, using a tone of voice which managed to suggest that debating was a completely reprehensible activity.

"Actually, I've spoken a couple of times," Jason answered guardedly. "But I must confess I didn't enjoy standing there with everybody hanging on to my every word and waiting to hear a witty remark. I find it awfully difficult to be witty. I prefer to work with people. We had a field trip to a mining town for a sociology class. I enjoyed that enormously."

"Does Bob enjoy that kind of work, too?"

"Oh yes, indeed! Our favorite subject is anthropology. We love to observe people. As a matter of fact, we thought we might camp out on the plantation for a week and study the habits of the workers."

"We'll see about that," Kessel said as though he wished to decline permission for such a venture, but inwardly forming a different resolution.

Jason was glad the interview was over. "It was rather grueling," he told Bob later. "I'm jolly glad you didn't have to witness it. My old uncle is a stickler for getting me the right education for the business. I suppose he means it for the best, being so strict with me. He's been awfully decent all these years, I must say, sending me a generous allowance, reminding me of my duty to my father's business—yes, he's been awfully decent."

"I suppose when one's born to inherit a kingdom one has to be prepared for it properly," Bob said, being vaguely sarcastic, for, coming from a family which offered him no expectations, he had long been of the opinion that all property should be inherited by the state—and yet was unaware of the contradiction that inherited money had paid for his ticket to South America.

Bob was a tall, lanky youth, narrow-shouldered with thin long arms. His face, too, was narrow, and looked best when it was seen in profile: the slightly curved nose and a strong chin together with full lips which were rarely closed together because his upper teeth were long and somewhat protuberant, all these features combined to give the face an appearance of authority in profile, especially as the mass of unruly brown curls looked like a mane when seen from the side; but the effect was lost from the front; the weak gray eyes on the narrow face with its pale sallow cheeks made him look inconspicuous and frail. He stood with a slight stoop as though he were about to collapse. His strongest feature was his voice, which was deep and rich.

"I don't suppose you had the chance to ask him if we could spend a week on the plantation," he said.

"Actually, I did bring it up," Jason replied. "He said he'd see about it."

It was morning and the two took a bus to the market. Bob always carried a notebook with him in which to jot down his impressions of local customs and Jason carried a camera with a telephoto lens to photograph scenes which illustrated those customs; the two planned to do a book together and to astonish all the undergraduates of England with their brilliance. For Jason, the market, and indeed all else in the country, provided a curious experience. He was a native and yet after his four years in England he was seeing his countrymen as members of a remote tribe. He remembered coming to this same market as a child, accompanying his mother when she would come here early in the morning to buy fish which had just been brought in by the night fishermen. Seeing the mulatto fishmonger now putting a fish on the weighing scales, calling out a price, taking down the fish, and deftly cleaning its insides, he saw precisely the same gestures he had seen as a child and yet how exotic it all appeared! The heaps of garlic beside which sat a fat Negress, her white skirt spread out around her over the ground, was surely an image from his childhood but he saw it for the first time as possessing an alien charm.

They wandered about the stalls, looking at everything, observing people trade.

"It's bloody strange, isn't it," Bob remarked, "how colors are so vivid here? I mean, look at those aubergines and tomatoes. I bet you they're no different from the ones you see in the market in Soho and yet they look so awfully bright here."

"What do you think of the dried meat?" Jason asked.

"Gosh, what a stink! It must be like eating the soles of one's shoes that have been boiled with a lot of dirty socks."

Jason laughed and said, "I remember being presented with boiled cabbage for the first time in England. Talk of a stink! It's all acculturation, you know that, Bob."

"I suppose you're right. Jason, me old mate, I just had an idea. Why don't we go into the interior and observe the people there? Aren't there any Indian tribes in this area?"

"I'm afraid not," Jason said, taking a picture of an old woman selling beads. "Civilization's encroached all the way to the Amazon, and penetrated there, too. But it would be jolly fine if we could do some real fieldwork and take back an article for the anthro mag. That would impress the old prof!"

"Jason, do you observe that the beads in front of that poor woman are the same sort of rubbish the first encroachers took to the Indians?"

"Perhaps we should buy some and take off for Amazonas!"

"That's a great idea, but I don't suppose your uncle would care for it."

In the evening they walked on the sidewalk on the waterfront above the beach that led from the residential area to the city. Fishermen were beginning to go out already. The sea bathers and surfers had gone home, the beach was empty except for a few couples strolling by the water's edge. They came to the end of the beach where in a brightly lit area were stalls of street vendors selling snacks and soft drinks. Across the road, on the sidewalk in front of some closed shops, was a line of girls, each one a couple of meters from the other, stretched out for blocks.

"Who are *they*?" Bob asked with astonishment seeing the girls were all dressed in brightly colored dresses and were heavily made up.

"You surprise me, Bob," Jason said. "Who do you think they are but whores?"

"My God, what a dis*gust*ing sight!"

"Don't be an awful prude, Bob," Jason said. "When I was fourteen, some of the boys from school and I would go and tease them. There was one boy, Jaír, I remember his name, boasted that he'd fucked ten of them. I believe he had too."

"How awful! And what about you?"

"I never did."

"Let's go across and walk past them," Bob said, seeing a car drive away with a girl.

They crossed the road and began to walk past the girls.

"I must remember to make a note when we get back home," Bob said. "Their jewelry is particularly interesting. It's all fake."

"What do you expect? They're from poor families."

"Pity you can't photograph them, we could have some sexy pictures in our book for perfectly sound sociological reasons."

"That can be done," Jason said. "There's an area in town where you see them in the daytime."

"*Day*time?"

"Understand, Bob, that without prostitution some fifty thousand people, or some seven to ten thousand families, would have no income at all."

"An interesting observation, if I may say so," Bob said, "coming from the heir apparent to the local kingdom."

But Bob's sarcasm was lost in the flow of invitations that had begun to be directed mainly at him by the girls. "Hey, Mr Thin, wanta buy some sin?" "Hello, skinny, want some flesh on your body?" "How 'bout some meat, Mr Bones?" "Nah, he's a vegetarian!" "How 'bout a coupla juicy mangoes to go with your banana and yogurt?"

"Shit, this is intolerable," Bob said. "Let's get back to the other side, it's too fucking filthy here."

They ran across the road with the whores jeering at them, and began walking back to the house. Bob felt a little insulted that all the remarks made by the whores had been inspired by his lanky body. He had come out in a sweat. "It must be easier doing fieldwork in an Indian tribe than trying to walk past fifty whores," he said in an attempt to restore his dignity.

At home, Kessel wanted to see them in the library. He was sitting in an armchair with a snifter of brandy beside him, smoking a cigar, and reading a book.

"Did you have an adventurous day?" he asked them in an amiable tone.

"It's been rather charming observing the customs of the people," Bob said sententiously.

"But we can hardly call it adventurous," Jason said.

"Listen, boys," Kessel said with a sparkle in his eye as if he had something very exciting to tell them. "You, Bob, are an Englishman. Have you ever heard of Colonel Fawcett?"

"Yes, of course. He disappeared in the Mato Grosso on an expedition early in this century. I think it was 1920 or thereabouts."

"Very good," Kessel said. "I like a man who knows his facts. But do you know anything about the nature of his expedition?"

"He was looking for a lost civilization," Jason said.

'You, too, know your facts, Jason." Kessel beamed a congratulatory glance at his nephew. "Very good, very good." He paused and looked at the boys thoughtfully. "You know, Jason," he went on, "when we were talking the other day about your studies and you mentioned that you were both interested in anthropology, well, I was taken right back to my earlier years. You cannot know that I was something of an explorer once. Oh yes, I've had many adventures in Amazonia and have been near death in the high wilderness of the Andes. Ah, yes! In the frantic world of business one forgets there is a world out there still waiting to be discovered. Being reminded of my earlier life, I got a bit nostalgic and took out one of my old notebooks this evening. Come, let me show you."

He rose from the chair and walked to the desk. The two boys followed him. There was a thick notebook on the desk; some traveler's inscrutable notes, he had chanced upon the volume in a dusty corner of a bookshop, finding it perfect for his present purpose. He flicked the pages, pausing here and there. They were covered with a minute handwriting. Occasionally, there was a sketch of the layout of a village. The young men were greatly impressed. Kessel closed the notebook and walked back to his chair, remarking that even his handwriting had changed over the years.

"Well," he continued, sitting down and taking a puff at his cigar, "listen to this."

160

He picked up the book he had been reading earlier and said, "This is a diary written in the eighteenth century. It was one of the things which impressed Fawcett."

He read a long passage.

"That's the legend about El Dorado," Bob said, almost disappointed that all the suspense had been about a banal old story.

"Yes, but wait a minute," Kessel said, sipping brandy. "This account is an *eighteenth*-century one. You see, by Fawcett's time, the truth had already become diluted. The failure of people to discover the place gradually made it appear larger and richer and more fantastic as succeeding generations transformed the basic simple truth with the florid embroideries of their imagination. Now, Bob, I don't know whether you have ever spent any time in your wonderful British Museum, but I have sat there for months. Literally for *months*. It was there, of all places, that I came across a *sixteenth*-century diary. I have notes from it which I shall show you later and I will prove to you that the El Dorado of legend and Fawcett's quite crazy idea of an Atlantis in the Mato Grosso are nothing but a tribe of people living in the most perfect harmony—if, that is, the tribe is not already extinct. And I will show you a document in my office tomorrow which will take your breath away."

"What is it, Uncle Mark?" Jason asked excitedly.

"Be patient, Jason. Wait till you see it. For I have something else to say. Just over four years ago, when your poor father entrusted me with the grave responsibility of looking after his business until you were ready to take charge of it, I came across an important clue to solving the mystery of the missing land. If my family responsibility had not weighed me down here, I would have undertaken the exploration at the time. But out of consideration for your father, and for *you*, Jason, I thought I'd postpone the idea."

He paused to sip some brandy and to puff at his cigar, and continued, "Little did I know your father would not return for so many years, for I assumed that after he had spent a few months in a monastery he would be bored to death and come

161

right back in the best of spiritual health which, believe me, cannot be enjoyed without having material goals in life. However, this is another matter, and I shall faithfully carry out the promise I made to your father. But I am nearly sixty years old now and have been leading a sedentary life for four years."

He paused again to take another sip and continued, "I have had to face the fact today that I shall never have the stamina or the health with which to go on an exploration. Four years ago it would have been child's play for me, today I cannot leave your business, and in another two years when you finish your studies I shall be lucky if I possess the health to walk without the assistance of a cane from here to my bedroom. Now you two are young and eager to explore the world. You are keen young anthropologists. You have three free months in which to do anything you want. So, what do you say? Would you like to go and discover the lost land?"

The boys were ecstatic. Would they like to go! Wow, what a coup! They couldn't wait to see the old prof's face when he read the article they would publish. They'd have to appear on television talk shows. What incredible luck!

Kessel sipped his brandy and watched the healthy enthusiasm of the two boys with eyes which gave every appearance of being benign. Incredible luck, indeed, he thought. The jungle would devour them in two days. "Well, come with me to the office tomorrow morning, I'll give you the document I mentioned and we'll work out the details of your exploration."

He finished his cigar and went to the nursery. His two little boys were fast asleep in their beds. He leaned over and kissed them softly. In the bedroom Heloise had propped herself up in bed and was sewing a baby garment. Kessel undressed and lay beside her. He pulled up the skirt of her nightdress and stroked her belly. He raised himself and kissed her navel and said, "How I love life!"

The next morning at his office, making a little ceremony full of drama and suspense of the simple act of opening the safe, he

162

brought out the old map with trembling hands. Jason and Bob were overawed.

"What is that inscription, Uncle Mark?" Jason asked, pointing to the lines at the bottom of the map which he read aloud:

> Deliver this not, but in your bosom keep,
> As in the heart of a lake a golden sheep.

"What on earth can that mean?" Bob asked.

"Can you not guess?" Kessel said.

"I don't believe I can," said Bob.

"It's an injunction and a coded message," Kessel informed them. "The first line is telling you to keep the knowledge of this map to yourself. And the second, which appears at first only to be a figure of speech, is really a cunning device. It is giving you a truth so openly that you do not see it."

"But what is it *saying*?" Jason was impatient to know.

"That there is a lake on the land, and in the middle of the lake there is a treasure to be found."

"All right," Kessel said, "you will need money and provisions. I would suggest to you that you spend today and tomorrow preparing yourselves. Work out what equipment you need, how you will travel, et cetera. Show me your plan this evening, we'll discuss it to make sure you haven't left anything out. You can buy everything tomorrow and set out the day after. Don't forget you'll run into Indian tribes for whom you'll need gifts, you'll have to be ready with medicines against diseases common to the region, et cetera, et cetera. But above all, I want you to be absolutely certain that you're men enough for such an exploration, that you know the dangers involved and are certain you have the strength to overcome them. God forbid, if anything should happen to you, it will be the despair of my old age."

Of course, the concluding remarks only intensified the boys' desire to set out on the journey.

2

They had a large-scale map of Amazonas, Mato Grosso and the eastern slopes of the Andes across their laps and pored over it as they flew to Manaus where their journey into the interior would really begin. They circled with a green felt-tipped pen the names of the villages and the abandoned missionary outposts that appeared in minute letters on the map and pinpointed the last-named place along the great river up to where they could find reliable transportation. It would be comparatively easy until they reached it; and at least on the map it was reassuring to see that from there to the area where they hoped to discover the lost land was really no more than three hundred kilometers, perhaps five hundred, allowing for the fact that they could not hope for a direct route in that terrain. It seemed to them almost an accomplished fact that within three or four weeks their names would be as well known as those of Fawcett, Rondon, Humboldt, Orellana, and Aguirre.

When they were waiting to collect their luggage in the crowded room at the airport, a boy of about twelve or thirteen came up to Bob and said, "Mister, you want hotel? I take you. Real cheap."

"Oh, go away, stop being a pest!" Bob said to him.

"You wanta go river trip?" the boy persisted.

"I said, *no!*"

The boy turned to Jason and as if to suggest that the Englishman was being unreasonable, said, "Good cheap hotel. I take you."

Planes from Europe and the United States had landed just before theirs and the wait for their luggage continued for twenty minutes.

"Many tourists come in jumbo," the boy said, coming back to Bob and Jason. "All big hotels booked. Amazonas, Ipanema Palace, Lider, all booked. Many tourists. I do you favor. Take you to good hotel. Real cheap."

"We'll see," Jason said to him.

When they had collected their luggage and found a taxi, the driver confirmed what the boy had said. The major hotels were all booked. The boy had followed them out and was standing near the taxi.

"We might as well take his offer," Jason said to Bob. "It's only for a couple of nights."

"It probably stinks," Bob said, with an expression of disgust.

They ended up by going to it. The taxi was an old Chevrolet, which creaked, bounced, and swayed although it did not go faster than twenty-five kilometers an hour.

"It's like being on a bloody mule," Bob remarked.

"We're in the interior now, Bob," Jason said. "And we're not tourists, we have our work cut out for us."

The hotel was near the market, two blocks away from the river. A pretty, young dark-brown woman with her hair in curlers showed them to their room. It was small with two low, narrow beds.

"No bathroom!" Bob said.

There was a communal toilet down the hall and next to it a small cubicle with a shower, and between these two facilities a small rusted washbasin stuck to the wall in the corridor.

"Stinko is the word," Bob remarked when he had inspected the conveniences. "A bloody hole in the floor and dirty newspaper with which to wipe your arse. In Portuguese, too!"

"Cheer up, old boy," Jason said. "Luxury hotels are the same the world over, here at least you're getting local color."

"My dear Jason, squalor and filth are the same the world over, too."

"I should have thought that you for one would prefer to be

with the working classes rather than with capitalist tourists."

Jason's remark was perceptive, for while Bob was virulent in his attack on the upper classes, it never occurred to him that all he was doing was expressing a contempt for his own background. Sharply ironical about others, he did not see the irony of his own companionship with, and now complete financial dependence upon, a rich young man.

"We should go and see about chartering a boat," Jason said.

Another pretty young woman was sweeping the narrow hall downstairs when they left. They walked through the market and became briefly absorbed in it. It was larger and more colorful than any other that Bob had seen.

"You know, one could do an interesting study here," Bob said.

"I suppose one could, but there's been an awful lot written about Manaus and I doubt if there's anything left here to discover."

They walked past the customhouse, and Bob remarked, "Just like my bloody countrymen, to export to the steaming tropics a building fit for the Merseyside."

"I think we're going the wrong way," Jason said. "The dock's there, but that's for the ocean-going vessels."

"Why don't we go and look at the town while we're here?" Bob said. "Let's go see the bleeding opera house."

"Bob, you amaze me. You're behaving like a bloody tourist."

They walked back through the market to the river. Bob resented being called a tourist and was sulking, and Jason talked with the boatmen. No one had a boat available. It was the European and North American tourist season, and it was more profitable to take the tourists on day trips than to charter out a boat for three months. Besides, no one wanted to leave his family behind for that long.

"It's obvious they're hoping we'll get desperate and offer a lot more money," Bob spoke at last when Jason had inquired for the seventh time.

"I don't know," Jason said. "We'll have to keep trying."

"The humidity's killing me," Bob said. "I'm dying for a drink."

They walked back toward the market and went to a bar.

"Something's bound to turn up," Jason said. "No use being depressed."

"I'm *not* depressed, I just don't like being called a bloody tourist, that's all."

"Oh, is that what's been eating you? Come out of it, old boy."

"You know, for a foreigner, you're more English than the English. Old boy, indeed!"

"You know, I was thinking of the old explorers," Jason said. "How slowly they were obliged to proceed. Waiting for days for a vital supply or to make an important contact. For months sometimes. And here we are, having flown in on a jet, anxious because in three hours we haven't found a boat."

The cold beer restored Bob's spirit. "I suppose you're right, something's bound to turn up," he said. "This beer's fucking good."

They had another bottle between them and without having a particular aim, walked out of the bar in the direction of the customhouse. They strolled through the small park between the customhouse and the church and proceeded to wander about the town. They saw several old mansions, some dilapidated past hope of restoration, and accidentally came to the square where the opera house stood. The imposing building made a strong impression on them and even Jason forgot his resolution not to behave like a tourist.

The sun had set by the time they finished seeing the opera house and they decided to go to a restaurant for an early dinner. They talked about the inevitable topic—what life must have been like in Manaus in the days of the rubber boom. While in his imagination he saw himself as a wealthy merchant drinking champagne at the opera house, Bob harangued against the treatment of the native rubber tappers whose misery he was certain he could see in the faces of their descendants.

They walked back to their hotel through the dimly lit streets. Many people were strolling about in the area of the docks. A continuous sound of voices and the noisy clatter of traffic on the narrow cobblestoned streets filled the air. There was a greater crowd of people in the market area, where

167

many of the shops were still open. They ran into the boy who had pestered them at the airport.

"You find hotel okay?" he asked with a grin.

"Just like the Hilton," Bob said to him.

"I told you. Good hotel, real cheap."

"With running water and air-conditioning," Bob said.

"Water no problem," the boy said. "Plenty water, straight from river."

"Ugh."

"You need girls?" the boy asked. "Pretty girls, real cheap. Give you good sex."

"No, thank you," Bob said and began to move away with Jason.

The boy followed them. "Pretty girls, real cheap. Give you real good time any way you like."

"Will you stop pestering us?" Jason said to him sternly.

"You need nothing?" The boy looked amazed. "I get you anything. Imported whiskey, real cheap."

"No, we don't need *any*thing," Jason said.

"You want boat tomorrow? Go on river trip. Big boat, small boat. I get you anything. No problem."

Jason stopped and looked at him. He was about to tell him in very strong language to make himself scarce, but said instead, "We need a boat to go upriver."

"Upriver?" The boy looked puzzled.

"Yes, we need to charter a boat for three months," Jason said.

"Hey, that's real business," the boy said, grinning broadly. "You need good strong boat. Sure, I get it for you. Big boat. Just like a ship. Real cheap."

"First thing tomorrow morning?"

"Sure. No problem. I get you anything."

"All right, we'll see if you can live up to your promise," Jason said. "See us in the morning."

They began to walk away from him, and Bob said to Jason, "I don't think I trust that boy. I expect the boat he can get will be of the same luxury class as the hotel."

"Well, we'll see," Jason said. "At least we've got rid of the pest for now."

The pretty young woman in curlers who had shown them to their room earlier in the day was standing outside the hotel when they arrived there. She was wearing a pink dress that had a plunging neckline; her black hair hung to below her shoulders in luxuriant waves; she had a lot of makeup on. Her mouth was held open in a smile and she looked brightly at each passer-by. She caught Jason and Bob with her gaze, her eyes darting from one to the other, her head jerking back slightly in a gesture of invitation. Bob went red in the face and Jason simply said, "Good night," to her as he walked past. Going up the stairs, they saw the other young woman, whom they had earlier observed sweeping the hall, coming down the steps. She, too, was gaudily dressed. A wave of strong perfume hit them when she went past. A few steps behind her followed a middle-aged man who had a contented look on his face. He winked at Bob as he went down.

"God almighty," Bob exclaimed when they were in their room, "this is a fucking brothel!"

Jason, who did not suffer from Bob's sense of revulsion, laughed and said, "Nothing like living in the den of sin."

A few minutes later, Bob was returning from the toilet. He saw the girl in the pink dress walk down the hall with a short, slightly stooping gray-haired old man, and go into the room next to the one he and Jason occupied.

On returning to the room, he told Jason what he had seen and added, "The man must be at least seventy years old!"

Jason put a finger to his lips. They could hear the girl's voice clearly through the thin wall. "You know I'm worth it," she was saying. Jason with amusement, and Bob with disgust, listened to the sounds from the other room—mainly an intermittent moaning cry from the old man. The couple left ten minutes later. Bob and Jason heard the door close and the footsteps fade away. They switched off the light and lay in their beds, talking in the darkness. A few minutes later, they heard the door of the next room open. The man's voice suggested a young, robust person, and the sounds that began to come from the room indicated a more vigorous activity than on the previous occasion. "A little with the mouth first," they heard the man say. "Shit!" Bob muttered under his breath, turning in bed and squeezing a pillow against his ear.

Their sleep was disturbed several times in the earlier hours of the night by the activity in the next room. When they went down the next morning, they saw the girl in the pink dress, now wearing a soiled cotton smock and looking sleepy-eyed, going about cleaning as if that was the only work she did at the hotel.

The boy appeared at the restaurant in the market where they were having breakfast. They had forgotten him and had been talking about the women at the hotel, for Bob had expressed his disgust and Jason was saying, "No use being a puritan, Bob. That's the lot of mankind. To sell oneself one way or another."

"It's plain and simple exploitation," Bob said. "It's evil."

"It's reality."

"A horrible life!"

"What would you not do to survive?" Jason asked.

"What would you?"

"I suppose I would kill if necessary," Jason said.

Just then the boy appeared and said, "Hey there, friends! I got boat for you. Good clean boat. Real cheap."

They went to see it, expecting to find a broken-down little dinghy, and were surprised. Some fifteen meters long, it looked like a miniature ship. It was a dazzlingly white launch in a new coat of paint, and when Jason and Bob went on board they found everything on it spotless and gleaming. A tall man of light-brown skin, wearing white drill trousers and a white short-sleeved shirt and a white peaked cap on his head introduced himself as Afonso Furtado. He had a neatly trimmed black beard and he gazed steadily at the two young men, who asked him several questions. Yes, of course, he knew the river, he told them. Have you ever woken up in the middle of the night and without needing to switch on a light have been able to walk to the bathroom? That's how well he knew the river. There were two cabins on board. They would have the one with the two bunks. Food? He would supply the food. There was Esteban whose job it was to cook and clean, there he was polishing the brasswork, he slept in a hammock on deck. No, no problem, he had the charts, they did not need to buy any. How much? Five thousand U.S. dollars, to be paid in advance. They wanted the launch for three months, did they not? He could earn more taking tourists on day excursions, but he loved the river. The great Amazon. He knew its every bend all the way to Iquitos, and would rather be sailing on it than listening to the squawking of tourists. That was his only interest in obliging them. It was cheap at five thousand dollars. They'd be lucky to find a vessel of this quality for under seven thousand.

Jason and Bob went aside to have a consultation.

"I think we'll take it," Jason concluded. "That's half our money gone, but we have a splendid little ship to ourselves and Afonso seems awfully knowledgeable. It's great luck finding him, we could easily have got stuck with some ignorant fool with a dirty little boat."

3

And afterward Jason remembered the feeling, which at the time he had thought to be a distillation of exhilaration and anticipation when they set out from Manaus, that there had been a different sort of intensity to it, providing him with a clarity of vision which was inexplicably bright and sharp. For a sense of wonder had filled him with vibrant excitement as they sailed out of Manaus, gliding quietly over the glassy black surface of the Rio Negro with the diesel engine not yet much higher than idling speed, flowing down with the stream till they reached the great expanse of water where the muddy brown of the Amazon met and transformed the black current of the Rio Negro to a dark brown. There they made a wide loop and began the voyage west up the river. And afterward Jason remembered how he had stood for a very long time on the deck, his glance fixed on the wide expanse of the interior, and even where the jungle presented itself as a dark impenetrable barrier along the bank he saw the passages in it, labyrinthine tunnels with no more light in them than is afforded by a glowworm, and how he had witnessed the courageous progress of the early explorers in that world of mystery and unpredictable torments. And he had a clear sense of his self as a perception of the mind of the body's desire for dissolution in the larger and overwhelming body of all creation.

Afonso Furtado, whom they began to call Captain Afonso, stood on the deck, his steady eyes calmly gazing at the river. Bob, whose English seafaring instinct had perhaps surfaced, stood at the helm, turning the wheel gingerly, imagining to himself that he was taking a nineteenth-century clipper around Cape Horn.

172

"Watch out for that tree floating downstream," Captain Afonso called.

Sometimes they saw whole islands, torn from the bank by erosion, come floating toward them. One of them even had a cleared patch of ground on it with a little shed and half a dozen banana trees, and on the shed several crates in which live chickens could be seen. "There goes someone's plot of land," Captain Afonso said, taking the wheel himself to avoid the danger. And even as the island was floating past, part of it broke and slowly began to sink.

They stopped at several small villages which were little more than clearings a kilometer square so that Bob and Jason could spend half an hour observing how the people lived in such a wilderness. It was only an excuse to break the monotony of the slow journey and to stretch their legs, for all that they observed was twenty to thirty people standing outside their thatched huts in scarcely any clothing and staring right back at them, professing, no doubt, the same degree of anthropological interest in the visitors as they in them. At larger villages, like Caori and Tefé, where Captain Afonso took on supplies, there were shops and a church and a few stucco houses together with several huts. Here, the people having a daily commerce with the traffic on the river went about their business, expressing no curiosity in the visitors, and Jason and Bob were able to roam about drawing each other's attention to some exotic fact or other. At one place they walked to the end of the little town and found that it ended abruptly at a wall of trees. The jungle formed a vast horseshoe around the town. They wanted to enter the jungle for a short distance to discover some rare moth or even just to see some monkeys but found themselves frozen to the ground and unable to step past the first tree.

And afterward Jason remembered how numbing had been that terror and how the warm perspiration on his body had turned into a cold sweat. The body desired to enter the darkness but the riot of fears in the mind would not permit such folly.

That he looked at it for hours from the launch and stood

scared on its edge in a town was a measure of the jungle's fascination—almost as if there were more in that darkness than trees, beasts, and reptiles which only a daring penetration of the darkness would reveal. And afterward Jason understood that it was not merely the accidents of travel that took him into the jungle. He was satisfying a need which had been born in him much earlier.

Whenever they stopped at the larger villages to take on supplies, Captain Afonso would finish his business quickly and return to the launch and wait there for Jason and Bob to come back from their explorations. He always rose and gave them a hand when they jumped aboard from the rickety pier and offered them cold beer as soon as they had begun to sail away. He was very observant and attentive. At one village he had picked up a small wooden object and he gave it to Jason. The painted piece of wood had tiny beads and feathers stuck to it and was no larger than the palm of his hand, and Jason asked, "What is it?"

"A miniature *kuarup* log. Must have been made by a small boy. It's quite rare to come across a *kuarup* fashioned as a toy. I thought you might like to have it since you're interested in the Indians."

"Why, thank you," Jason said. "But what's it supposed to be?"

"*Kuarup* logs are usually the size of people. The painted part which has attached to it two armlets of macaw feathers is really a representation of a human being. The idea is that you're symbolically bringing a dead person back to life."

"How interesting," Jason said. "You do know an awful lot about the Indians, don't you?"

"One picks up stories. It's a strange world behind that silent shoreline. Teeming with sacred objects. Even the leaves whisper superstitions when they rustle. The moon stays in the sky because the jaguar will not let it come down. The sun calls the trees to come to it, for he wants their fruit to quench his thirst. There is no mystery in that world except the mystery of the imagination's capacity to invent fantastic stories. From

174

where does it come, this intuition of truth from fantasy?"

"It's quite remarkable, isn't it?" Jason said.

"The idea of heaven for some Indians in the interior is a beach on a river. Interesting, isn't it, that their fantasies lead them straight back to reality? Different from us, our Christian fantasies lead us to wild and implausible fictions."

Jason found this, and several other conversations, highly enlightening, as did Bob, who took part in some of the others. Once, Captain Afonso concluded a discussion by saying, "You should know this about any human being, however primitive. He inherits a code of symbols whether he's born in the jungle out there or in London. For we are all creatures of unaccountable compulsions. The mind does not respond so readily to the history of the tribe as it does to the symbols of the race. Your uniformed soldier is no different from a painted warrior. Your primitive may eat his enemy's flesh and your civilized man will do the same thing, though only metaphorically, but neither will sleep with his sister."

Later Bob said to Jason, "Our captain's a terrific chap, isn't he? I've learned more from him than from the old prof."

"Every time we've talked," Jason said, "I've wished we had a tape recorder. His observations about the Indians would make a fine article. He's a natural anthropologist, don't you think?"

"Just shows you, doesn't it," Bob said, "that study isn't everything, experience in the field teaches you as much."

In their naïve enthusiasm for the ordinary wisdom contained in Captain Afonso's ideas, they toyed with the notion of devoting their lives to a simple existence in the interior and emerging from it several decades later to astonish the world with their account of the real basis of society. But they could not do so quite yet, since it was their immediate destiny, as they reminded each other, to discover the lost land. After the tumult over that discovery had died down, they could then return to Amazonas for a lifelong study of its people. Two days passed in the discussion of such plans for their future.

The slow voyage up the river continued for twelve days. On the twelfth day, they were docked in the early afternoon beside a small clearing where there was only one hut encircled by a plantation of bananas. Captain Afonso had stopped there because he thought they should have some fresh fruit for their lunch. But after lunch, instead of proceeding to Benjamin Constant, the last Brazilian town on the river where they were to stop before they entered Peru and made for Iquitos, Captain Afonso decided that he needed to do some work on the engine. It was a small matter, he told them, just a gasket that needed replacing, but it was in a part of the engine not easily accessible and would regrettably take two or three hours.

Jason and Bob took the opportunity to go and talk with the man who cultivated bananas, for he seemed to them a singular object for study. He was a gray-haired man whose tiny body stooped when he walked. He lived in the small clearing with his wife and seven children, three of them grown-up sons. He had been living there for thirty years, ever since he was married. The young anthropologists were busy with their observations as they walked about the clearing with the man: they saw the division of labor, for two of the sons were carrying bunches of bananas to a boat tied to a tree on the edge of the river, and the wife with two small children near her was sitting outside the hut plucking the feathers off a chicken. The man seemed wise and some of his statements could have come out of the mouth of a distinguished statesman.

"It's extraordinary, isn't it," Bob said to Jason, "what a man can know even when he lives in a savage condition?"

They walked toward the hut and when they arrived there they heard a foreign voice. They were confused only for a moment, for they realized soon enough that the old lady had a transistor radio on inside the hut and what they were hearing was the voice of an American female pop singer whose latest song had been climbing up the charts even before they left England and was now a universal hit. This incident, however, did not at all impress the young anthropologists as possessing an ironical significance, for they soon walked away from the hut and continued to make their probing investigations into the life of the savage.

Captain Afonso welcomed them back to the launch by offering them bottles of cold beer and apologizing for the unscheduled delay. He really was very kind, they thought, and told him that far from having had their time wasted, they had had an opportunity to advance their study of man.

The sun had just set when they arrived in Benjamin Constant. Having subsisted on a diet of fish and turtle stew for twelve days, Jason and Bob asked if the town was large enough to have a restaurant where they could find a good steak or even chicken. Yes, indeed, there was the Churrascaría Real, Captain Afonso informed them, anyone would show them where it was. He himself could not join them immediately because he still had some doubt about the engine and wanted to check with a dealer in spare parts before he closed for the night. Perhaps he would join them later—with luck while they were still eating—but his concern for the engine had to take priority.

Jason and Bob walked off into the darkening streets. The day's heat had not yet begun to be relieved by a cool breeze, but they did not mind that their faces were shining and that their clothes had become damp with sweat. Within twenty minutes of wandering about the town they arrived at the Churrascaría Real without needing to be directed to it. It was brightly lit and was obviously a popular place for the local population, for it was crowded and they had to wait a quarter of an hour before getting a table. Apart from a plate of rice and beans, the food consisted entirely of a succession of meat dishes. The waiter would come by every five or six minutes with a large tray heaped with freshly carved roast beef, barbecued chicken, and pork sausages, and serve the diners generous portions of whatever they wanted. There were three fans on the high ceiling, which circulated some air, but the entire crowd of some fifty or sixty people seemed unconcerned by the hot, stifling atmosphere generated by the open wood-burning ovens in the far end of the room. The waiters' faces glistened, and all the people devouring large quantities of meat with a sort of desperate rapidity had glowing, shining faces.

"I must say this is the best beef I've ever had," Bob declared, and Jason said, "The sausage is jolly hot."

They drank two bottles of cold beer each, and by the time they had finished the meal nearly two hours had passed since they had disembarked from the launch. They staggered out, heavy with food, and slowly began to walk back toward the river. The spicy food and the still, humid night renewed their thirst and they stopped at a bar for a bottle of beer.

It was a dimly lit, cavelike room with small wooden tables and stools. Two men sat together talking over their drinks and two other men were drinking alone. Jason and Bob sat at a table near the entrance. The barman, who was also the owner of the establishment, was large and had a broad face and big black eyes. His thick white hair seemed to be a source of illumination, it appeared so bright in that dim room.

"Welcome to Raúl's," he said, coming up to the two new customers. "That's me, Raúl Osorio."

"Could we get some really cold beer?" Jason asked.

"Certainly," he said, making a slight bow and going behind a counter where the refrigerator was. For all his weight, he seemed to walk gracefully.

He brought them the beer. "We'll have a storm tonight," he said. "There's not a whisper of a breeze."

"It's the hottest we've known so far," Jason said.

"You're traveling on the river?" he asked, pouring out the beer into the glasses.

"Yes," Bob said. "Up to Iquitos."

"This area is opening up," Osorio remarked, standing near the table as they drank. "More and more tourists are coming."

"We're not quite tourists," Bob said.

"We're students of anthropology," Jason put in before Bob could absentmindedly reveal that they were explorers. "We're studying the Indians."

"Do you mind?" Osorio said, indicating with a gesture of the hand that he would like to sit down. The boys shook their heads and he took a chair. "I know these parts. I could give you a lot of information."

"We have a fair idea of where we want to go," Bob said,

anticipating that Osorio was about to persuade them to buy some entirely phony information from him.

Jason, too, had the same idea and said, "We have come prepared."

"Yes, of course, of course," Osorio said. "Modern scientists were not born yesterday, they know what they're doing. Even when they put a satellite into the sky to take pictures of Jupiter, they're not taking random shots. Everything's got to be thought out beforehand. But please don't think I have anything to sell you. That's what you thought, didn't you?"

The two looked at him and the thought passed through both their minds that he seemed an intelligent and sincere man. Before either could say anything, he went on, "The only thing I sell here is beer and liquor. The information I was talking about is my experience. Knowledge. You see, I've spent all my sixty years in this area."

"How do we get to the Equator from Iquitos?" Jason asked.

"You could take a plane to Quito from there, but if you're going by boat you don't need to go as far as Iquitos. You go up the Rio Napo, but that's a tough river. The rapids would smash your boat to bits. There are other ways. You see, there are so many rivers here not all of them are even shown on the standard maps."

Another customer came in, and Osorio said to the boys, "Are you going to be here for a day or two?"

"Well, we're spending the night on the launch," Jason said, "and were planning to sail tomorrow morning."

"If you can spare an hour, come to me," Osorio said, rising from his chair. "I've some old maps to show you, and if we have the time I'll tell you how I once went in search of gold."

When they left the bar, Bob said, "He's really a charming man, isn't he?"

"I thought he was quite genuine," Jason said. "At first I thought he was going to take us for a ride, but then I saw something of my Uncle Mark in him. He seems delighted to be able to share his knowledge with young people."

"I hope we'll be like that in our old age," Bob said with a laugh.

Talking and joking, the two walked down to the river. Reaching the pier where they had docked, they found that the launch was not there.

They looked at each other in consternation and Jason said, "What does this mean?"

"Perhaps he might have needed to take the launch to another dock to get the engine repaired," Bob speculated.

There were other boats on the riverside, and they inquired of some of the local sailors whether there was a place where boats were taken for engine repairs.

"Everything happens here," one said.

They asked if anyone had seen a white launch, but realized immediately that the question was a foolish one, for several other white launches were docked nearby. None, however, was as immaculately painted as Captain Afonso's. They asked if anyone knew Captain Afonso. People shrugged their shoulders.

"It has to be that he had to take the boat elsewhere for repairs," Bob said.

They decided to go to the restaurant to see if Captain Afonso were not there. Neither dared mention yet the first thought which had come to him: that Captain Afonso was right then sailing at full speed down the river; it was too terrible a thought to express. But even though the image of Captain Afonso was one of a kind and wise man, it was the one idea which was uppermost in their minds.

"Do you have the rest of the money with you?" Bob asked, thus indirectly expressing the thought.

"Yes. And the map, too. Those I always keep on me."

The restaurant was still crowded with people chewing large mouthfuls of meat. The smell of roasting meat filled the stifling room and where it had been a tantalizing aroma when they were hungry it was now an abominable smell. Jason and Bob looked at the glowing faces. The missing captain was not there. They asked the cashier if he knew Afonso Furtado.

"Never heard of him," he answered.

They described the man. Tall, black beard, steady brown

eyes, dressed in white like a sailor. The cashier pointed to two men in the restaurant who fitted that description but who were not Furtado. They left the restaurant, dejected.

"Don't you think we should go to the police?" Bob asked.

Jason gave him a despairing look, and Bob said, "Let's face it, he's plainly absconded with your money. It was absurd, giving him all that money in advance."

"But he was such a super guy," Jason said. "He was so kind."

"That is one of the masks of the con artist," Bob said. "Come to think of it, that business about replacing a gasket that took him three hours, he knew what we didn't, that we were only a couple of hours from Benjamin Constant. It's obvious now he was killing time. He wanted to get here when it was dark."

"You could be right. He was so wise, it pains me to think of him as a robber."

"But don't you think we should go to the police?" Bob repeated.

"Supposing we went and it turned out that he had in fact only gone somewhere to get the engine repaired? We'd look pretty stupid."

"Do you want to lose five thousand dollars, your camera, my notes, our clothes, our equipment, all just for the remote possibility of not needing to lose face? That's more stupid!"

They found themselves outside Raúl's bar. "Let's go in and have a beer," Jason said. "It's so bloody hot, I can hardly think."

Osorio was surprised to see them return so soon. "Welcome again," he said, bringing them the beer. "You make Raúl's the most popular bar in town."

He saw the look of dejection on their faces and asked, "Anything wrong?"

"We don't know," Bob answered. "The launch we came in seems to have disappeared."

"That's no problem," Osorio said cheerfully. "You can get another one easily."

"We'd already paid for a three-month charter," Bob said. "In dollars."

181

"Oh, I see," Osorio said sympathetically. "Four or five hundred dollars is a lot of money to lose."

"What do you mean four or five hundred dollars?" Bob said. "We paid five thousand."

"Five thousand!" Osorio expressed disbelief.

Jason had not been able to speak, for the horror of his situation was beginning to be clear to him. At last he whispered, "Yes, five thousand."

"It was a beautiful little ship," Bob said. "It seemed worth it to be traveling in luxury."

Osorio sat down and asked, "Where did you pick up this luxury liner?"

"Manaus," Jason said.

"Do you realize that you could have come from Manaus to Benjamin Constant for thirty dollars on a freighter? There's dozens of them which take passengers."

Jason and Bob were too depressed by this information to be able to respond. After a pause, Jason said, "It was such a wonderful little ship and Captain Afonso seemed so reasonable and intelligent."

"Captain *who*?"

"We called him Captain Afonso," Bob said. "His name was Afonso Furtado."

"My friends, you have been had," Osorio said. "I know this Afonso Furtado. He hasn't used that name in years. He's a pirate and a scoundrel. You've only to ask about him in any bar on the river between Belém and Iquitos, and everyone will tell you you're dealing with the most slippery fish the Amazon has known."

Jason and Bob looked aghast at Osorio as he went on. "He lurks around in the tributaries for months until one of his many connections procures a likely victim for him. He's a smooth operator. Very civilized and very urbane. The boom in tourism provides him with many a gullible victim whom he impresses with his style. He keeps his launch beautifully painted and polished, for that gives his customers great confidence and a great sense of security. Con men are very particular about exterior details, for a good impression is everything. I am sorry, my friends, but you've had the misfortune to run into the biggest fraud on the river."

"I suppose we had better go to the police," Jason said, finishing his beer.

"That will do you no good," Osorio told him. "Your Captain Afonso gives a cut to the police, and you will not find a single cop on the river who will not tell you that he's sorry for you, that he'll do everything to catch the criminal but who will then do absolutely nothing."

"Supposing we offered a bribe?" Bob asked.

"Go ahead and try it if you want to lose more money," Osorio said. "The cop will put the money in his pocket and tell you to come back tomorrow. On the next day, he'll show you a copy of a telegram he has supposedly sent to Manaus. A week later, he will even appear to make a phone call to Manaus. Two weeks later, if you're still patient, he'll produce a whole file for you to see. But his tactic will simply be that of wearing you out until you either go away in despair or die of malaria."

"What can we do then?" Jason asked.

"Reconcile yourselves to your fate," Osorio said. "You can get drunk if you want, and you can do that on the house. Be my guests. Otherwise all I can suggest is that you take the next boat back to Manaus and go back to your civilization."

"We can't just let a man walk away with five thousand dollars and do nothing," Bob remarked.

"If he operates from Manaus," Jason said, "surely, he'll turn up there looking for a new victim? Supposing we returned there and waited?"

"To do what?" Osorio asked.

"To get my money back or have him put in jail," Jason said.

"Did you get a receipt from him?"

Jason did not answer Osorio's question. The latter went to the bar and returned with two glasses and a bottle of Scotch. "Here," he said, "you might as well drown your sorrow."

There was a clap of thunder outside and heavy rain began to fall.

Jason was filled with rage and his hand shook as he raised the glass of Scotch to his lips. Bob was more philosophical; for him, the loss was not so personal. They drank quietly and refilled their glasses. After twenty minutes, Osorio returned to them and said, "There's a small hotel down the street where you can spend the night. It's not too clean but it's not too filthy either. When you sober up tomorrow you can work out your problem. As I told you, my best advice to you would be to return to civilization. But think of it tomorrow. Come and see me if you need me, otherwise good-bye."

The hotel was in fact superior to what they had suffered in Manaus. The alcohol they had consumed put them soundly to sleep. After two cups of coffee in the morning, they were sufficiently clearheaded to discuss their situation. Jason thought they should go to the police in spite of what Osorio had said: they should not believe what the first man they had talked to had told them—that had been precisely what they had done in Manaus and look where that had got them. But when they went to the police station they found the officer on duty behaving exactly as Osorio had predicted and although they left a statement of their experience with him, they realized the futility of the action. They had merely wasted the entire morning.

Both felt dispirited but neither would admit to the other the extent of his frustration or that he secretly wished to be back in England. The mystique of heroism, as they understood it, demanded that one maintain the pretence of resolution and fortitude. If each one had known that he was not the only one who preferred to abandon the scheme and go back to England, they would have burst out laughing, shaken hands, and made their preparations for the return. Instead, the conviction that an expression of a desire to retreat would be seen to be scandalous by the other kept both of them grimly resolved to pursue their adventure. Bob thought of Darwin's voyage on the *Beagle* to bolster his own resolution; Jason thought of his uncle and imagined the scene in which his premature return would provoke the uncle's sarcasm and abuse, and thus strengthened his determination to continue in spite of the setback. They decided to go and talk to Osorio.

It was after lunch and Osorio was just closing the bar to go and have his siesta. He let them in and took them to a small room at the back and brought out some hand-drawn maps. He spread them out on a small table and sat down on a wooden chair behind it, inviting Jason and Bob to sit across the table from him. "First of all," he said, "you have to be honest and tell me what you really have in mind. I hope you're grown men and not just boys with some foolish adolescent dream of discovering a treasure."

"No, not at all, we're serious students," Bob said.

"You said you were planning to go to the Equator," Osorio reminded them.

"Well, in that region," Jason said.

Osorio spread his hands across the maps, leaned forward and said, "My friend, you have to be more precise than that. I repeat, you have to be honest, otherwise we're wasting each other's time. You said yesterday that you're anthropologists and are curious about some Indian tribe. Now, that, too, is only vaguely true, is it not? And that which is true only vaguely is also half a lie, right?"

Jason and Bob looked at each other.

"Well?" Osorio asked.

"We're students of anthropology," Jason said, "at a university in England. We were hoping to discover something. But we are also explorers. There is a lost land that we are hoping to find."

"Ah, what is that lost land supposed to contain? Rooms full of gold conveniently left undiscovered for centuries?"

"Perhaps nothing at all," Jason said sincerely.

"We're not after treasure," Bob said, "but, of course, for a scientist to come across a fossil can be a great treasure."

"And how do you propose to discover this lost land?"

Osorio could not help sounding sarcastic; so far the boys appeared to him to be complete fools.

Jason, understanding his thought, hesitated for a moment and then brought out the map from his wallet and unfolding it placed it on the table. Osorio glanced at it and then, appearing to be startled, took a closer look.

"Extraordinary!" he whispered to himself. He raised his head and stared at the boys with a look of disbelief.

"I do believe you are serious," he said. "Here, look at this," he added, shuffling his own maps and placing one on the top.

Jason and Bob rose from their chairs and leaned over the table to look at the map.

"Why, it's a copy of the same map!" Bob exclaimed.

"Except for the legend," Jason said, reading aloud the lines at the bottom of the map:

> Go into the jungle, enter it deep,
> Come to a lake and find the golden sheep.

Osorio read the lines on the map Jason had produced:

> Deliver this not, but in your bosom keep,
> As in the heart of a lake a golden sheep.

"My map appears to be more recent," Osorio said, "and perhaps it's a copy."

"How do you account for the variation in the legend?" Bob asked.

"Who knows?" Osorio said. "Perhaps the earlier abstract injunction has become a particular command with the passage of time. Perhaps it was added later and the variation is due to the failure of memory to remember precisely. But otherwise the maps are identical."

"What do you know about the place indicated on the map?" Jason asked.

"Only that it's impossible to find," Osorio said. "It is as if you had a large-scale map of a city but the streets were not named and all you were told about it was that it was somewhere in Europe. Its immediate environment which could give you a point of reference is not known. The area outlined by this map can be no more than thirty or forty kilometers wide, probably less, and it could as easily be in the Congo as in Amazonas. Who knows?"

"*We* know," Jason said excitedly. "You see, we do have a point of reference. The Equator."

"Which cuts across the Congo with the same impartiality

186

as it does across Amazonas."

"No, we have more. There are two rivers which make the point of reference more precise."

They discussed the idea at considerable length, going into the bar, that Osorio needed to open. He was convinced that the young explorers had a reasonable chance of discovering the lost land—provided the kind of stupidity which had made them fall for that scoundrel Furtado did not lead them into other errors. There were no customers in the bar at that early hour in the afternoon and they carried on their discussion. Osorio showed them the route they needed to take. He had brought out one of his maps and pointed on it how far up the Rio Napo they should go.

"Let me mark it for you," he said. "Here. Note this point." And he pointed with the pen before making the mark. "You can take one of the small launches which carry fruit up and down the river up to here. But *here*, you will have to get yourself a canoe and after seventy kilometers northwest up the river, to this point here, you should take this tributary. If you continue on the Napo you meet the rapids head on and that will be the end of your worldly days. There are friendly Indians on the Napo who will show you this river in case you can't find it yourself. It's called the Rio das Mortes."

He gave them more detailed advice and concluded with, "And when you announce your great discovery to the world, don't forget that it was old man Raúl Osorio who showed you the way."

He laughed uproariously, and Jason and Bob laughed with him, being infected by his warm and generous spirit.

"I suppose," Bob said when they were walking back to their hotel, "that after our experience with Captain Afonso we ought to know better than to trust anyone, but I must say old Osorio is a terrific man."

"He's awfully kind, isn't he?" Jason said. "Of course we can trust him. He has nothing to gain except the satisfaction of passing his knowledge to a younger generation."

Bob stopped suddenly, put his hands to his stomach and groaned.

"What's the matter?" Jason asked.

Bent at the waist and still holding his stomach, Bob gave a short cry and said, "A stabbing pain." He straightened up and let his hands fall to his sides. "It's gone now, but I'd better run to the hotel, my stomach's about to explode."

They were not far from the hotel and Bob managed to reach the lavatory and sit over the hole in the floor just in time. His bowels let forth a hot, burning stream which poured out of him in such quantity and with such force that his whole body came out in a sweat. He sat there open-mouthed, gasping for air. The flow ceased. He felt utterly exhausted and it was only with a great effort that he was able to clean himself, rise, and stagger to the room.

Jason had just arrived there and was opening the door. "Good God, what's happened?" he asked.

Bob staggered past him and went and collapsed on his bed. The only sound he could make at first was to groan. Jason sat on the edge of the bed and saw that sweat was pouring down Bob's face and neck and that his clothes had become wet. His mouth was open and his tongue hung below his lower lip as he panted. Jason brought him a glass of water. At last Bob managed to say, "A touch of dysentery, I think."

Mention of the word renewed the pangs in his intestines and he had to rise and rush to the lavatory again. Jason followed him and stood outside the lavatory and helped him to return to the room when he had finished.

"Shit! Oh my God!" Bob groaned.

Jason brought a basin of cold water and a towel to the bedside and mopped Bob's face. He unbuttoned his shirt and passed the wet towel over his chest. Bob shivered and drew his shirt together. The supply of medicines that they had brought for precisely this kind of emergency had been lost with the disappearance of the launch, and Jason decided to send for a doctor.

It took nearly an hour for the doctor to come. He was a short bald man with heavy eyelids which made him look as if the world saddened him. He listened paiently to Jason's account of what had happened and turned his glance to Bob with a weary air. He took Bob's temperature and spoke aloud the alarmingly high reading on the thermometer as if it were one more dull fact that had to be noted. He prodded Bob's chest with the stethoscope, moving his small, damp hand lethargically. Finally, he wrote out a prescription and announcing that he would need to examine the patient again the next day, started to leave.

"But what's the diagnosis?" Jason asked.

"Dysentery."

"Will he be all right?"

"In a week or so."

But when a week had passed, Bob's condition had grown worse. Jason spent his time sitting beside him, leaving him only when he was fast asleep. Osorio came to sit with Jason several times and expressed his concern at Bob's suffering. He sympathized with Jason for the pain his friend's illness must cause him and was sorry that their journey to the interior had to be cut short.

"But we have time yet," Jason said. "Bob will recover in a week and once he's regained his natural vigor, say in another week, we can be off."

"Let us pray so," said Osorio.

But on the tenth day they noticed that Bob was spending more and more time in a state of unconsciousness as if he were sinking into a coma. He had lost so much weight that when he moved his arm one was struck by the conspicuousness of the bones. The doctor, too, began to be anxious and called in a colleague for advice. The second doctor, quicker of movement than the first, examined Bob and said, "It could be amebic dysentery, but I'm not certain. I'm afraid it could be something more serious. Some rare tropical disease that a European is susceptible to and of which we know nothing. We don't have the facilities to do the tests in this town. If you want to save him, my advice to you is to fly him out to Lima, or even back to London."

Jason accompanied Bob as far as Iquitos. From there he talked to the British consul-general in Lima on the phone and sought his advice. Since Jason had the necessary money to cover the expenses, it was decided that Bob be flown to Lima, where he would be met by an official from the British embassy who would put him on the next British Airways flight to London.

It was a sad moment for Jason when he saw his friend being carried to the plane on a stretcher. During a period of consciousness Bob had been told that he was being flown to England. The mention of his native land brought a momentary brightness to his eyes, leading Jason to believe that Bob had the peculiar tough quality of the English to win a fight when the prize was his own country. He was confident that he would make it and thought how in two months' time they would be together at the university again and talking about their experiences in Amazonas as if it had been a lark. But it saddened him to think that their adventure had ended in a failure and that their dream of glory was now over.

A day later, Jason was sailing down the Amazon in a riverboat to Manaus. As they were approaching Benjamin Constant, he was standing on deck watching the shore. He remembered afterward how this ordinary moment when he had stood bored with the sight of the jungle, and bored too with the overwhelming despair he felt at his condition, had suddenly become transformed into a moment of revelatory brilliance. The jungle seemed to open to his vision and to draw his imagination into its heart. He saw a profusion of gaudy leaves and flowers and had the peculiar sensation of his own body leaving the frame in which he stood and entering that riotous vegetation and becoming submerged in it with a sharp, ecstatic thrill. *This is my world*, he heard himself say as if it were not he who spoke but his soul. And afterward he remembered how a great happiness seemed to fill him as the conviction came to him that he must leave the boat at Benjamin Constant and go into the jungle in search of the lost land, and the belief entered his soul that he must, if necessary, lose himself in the pursuit of the vision which had revealed itself so briefly and yet with such compelling force.

4

Osorio was delighted to see Jason again. On one occasion during Bob's illness Osorio had wondered if Jason was not unconsciously glad that his friend's condition obliged him to abandon the search for the lost land; but seeing him return with such conviction, and hearing him express his desire to pursue the quest alone, filled Osorio with an admiration for the young man. While waiting eleven days for the next little freighter to take him up the Rio Napo, Jason spent most of his time with Osorio. The older man brought out his maps again and the two pored over them while Osorio described a village or a river or an area of jungle to be crossed, giving exhaustive information about each.

"These are the rapids," Osorio said, pointing to a mark on a river, "that a British team tried to go over in a Hovercraft some twenty years ago. And *this* is where they came unstuck. The technology hasn't been invented for such navigation. You've simply got to haul your canoe out and drag it for two kilometers through the jungle."

Jason expressed no fear at the prospect of having single-handedly to transport his canoe and equipment, and Osorio smiled at him and said, "My friend, I was just testing to see if you had the nerve for this kind of expedition. Actually, the really ferocious rapids are farther up the river and you won't encounter them if you go off on the Rio das Mortes. Obviously, nothing is going to stop you. Be happy to learn, then, that you'll have no problem on this river. Those rapids won't bother you if you keep to the eastern bank."

Much of their time together was spent in Osorio teaching

Jason the important words and expressions of the Indian language common to the area. There were several Indians who lived on the fringes of the town and Osorio got one of them to come and talk to Jason in his language, so that Jason, obliged for long hours to try to understand the man, began to pick up his tongue; and having an innate facility with languages, as he had found with English and Spanish, Jason very quickly acquired a working knowledge of the Indian language. Osorio also taught him facial gestures and hand signs that would serve Jason to communicate in case he came across a tribe which did not understand his words. When the time came for Jason to leave, Osorio presented him with a rifle, saying, "I hope you will never need to use this except to hunt for food."

And so, better prepared than he could have hoped to be, Jason set out on his expedition. The launch, loaded with bananas, slowly labored up the Rio Napo and after five un-eventful days, which he spent lying in a hammock on the deck and watching the jungle on the shore, took him to the small town from where he had to proceed alone. He spent two days there, picking up information from people who had traveled up the river, and looking for a suitable boat. At first he had inquired about buying a canoe, but a man at the bar in the main square told him, "How far do you think you'll get in a canoe without killing yourself? You are going against the current, you've never been in a canoe before, you'll be ex-hausted after half a kilometer."

Jason was persuaded to buy a small boat with an engine and also bought fifty liters of gasoline in five cans. By the time he had paid for these, and for the other necessary provisions, he had not more than six hundred dollars left of the ten thousand his uncle had given him. But he embarked upon his lonely voyage feeling serene and happy, confident that he was enter-ing a world that was somehow more real than that served by jet liners.

Sitting in the middle of the boat by the wheel, with the engine clanking away behind him, he set out early in the morning. He had computed that it was a matter only of traveling some three to four hundred kilometers before he would be in the region outlined by the map given to him by his uncle; no doubt there could be some problems and even a confrontation or two with hostile Indians, but he imagined that after ten days or so, spent mainly in a quiet meditation, he would arrive in the region that included the lost land. And so, for the first two hours of his journey, he proceeded cheerfully, wondering from time to time about Bob's condition. He began to regret not having his friend with him, for after three hours of solitary navigation he felt the need for comradeship. There was so much that he observed, from the toucans in the trees to the alligators in the river, that it was a shame not to have someone with him to point these things out to, for experience, he realized, even when it was commonplace, was worthless unless it could be shared. A thing could be beautiful and unique but a knowledge of it was of no value unless it could be communicated to another being.

Late in the afternoon, he came across three Indians in separate canoes. He steered toward them, hailing them and making friendly gestures when he had their attention. They had seen him long before he was aware of their presence on the river. They were not greatly interested in the stranger but had seen people of his tribe before and felt unthreatened by him. He asked them if they knew about the Rio das Mortes. He knew well enough that the river was at least two days' journey up the Rio Napo, but it was the only thing that occurred to him to ask of the Indians. He realized that his anxiety was really only a need to talk to another human being. The Indians merely pointed upriver and made a gesture of going to sleep several times, and paddled away from him quickly. He called out after them the word in their language that signified gifts, but the three appeared determined not to turn back to look at him as if he represented some omen that they needed to avoid.

He sailed on and came to the bend in the river where their village was located. The sound of his engine had attracted a crowd to the shore, mainly of little children, and as he sailed by close to the bank, they screamed and laughed, throwing up their arms to point at him as though he was the funniest thing they had seen in their lives. He waved back at them, provoking louder yells and jeers. Some of the girls clapped their hands to their mouths while the boys threw up their heads in uproarious laughter. Jason cut off the engine and came to the bank. The children ran away, their voices raised in one piercing scream. A few youths and adults watched him tie a rope from his boat to a root of a tree. He spoke the friendly expressions of greeting that Osorio had taught him, and one of them answered back in like manner. He asked if he could alight and enter their village to take a gift to their chief.

They conducted him past the thick vegetation along the bank to the clearing, where ten or twelve huts had been constructed in a wide circle. The children, who had begun a game in the open space, were amazed to see the stranger enter the village, and ran off to the huts. Women, pounding manioc outside some of the huts, made shrill remarks to the children.

The chief received Jason courteously on being presented a dozen macaw feathers. Jason wanted to question him about his tribe but found that his small vocabulary was inadequate and that while the key words came to him he could not put them into meaningful sentences; it was one thing to repeat phrases after Osorio and the Indian at Benjamin Constant when the mere fact of correct pronunciation gave one the illusion of knowing the language, but something altogether different and exceedingly complex when it came to expressing ideas. He was obliged to utter single words and accompany them with gestures. The chief, having no idea of what the visitor was saying but feeling the necessity of responding, answered with rhetorical discourses. When Jason asked him if his tribe lived exclusively on hunting or whether it also cultivated manioc and corn, the chief catching the word for *corn*, or perhaps some other but hearing it as the word in his tongue for *jaguar*, made a neat little statement about how he as a young man had had the power and the swiftness of a jaguar and, by way of illustration, narrated a feat he had accomplished concluding which he laughed for a full minute. In the end, neither understood a thing the other had said but each was satisfied that he had said the correct thing and felt a considerable respect for the other.

There was some commotion outside. Two young men who had been out in the jungle for three days had just returned, having captured a wild pig. There was jubilation in the tribe, for it had been without meat for several weeks. The visitor had brought the tribe good luck, and he was invited to share the meal. When the pig was butchered and divided, the chief himself handing out parts of it, Jason observed that the tribe consisted of twelve families, a total population of some sixty. Though the pig was fat, the portion that each family received was therefore small. The sun had set by the time the meat was cooked. The children had been making boisterous noises in expectation of the feast, but otherwise there was no ceremony. Everyone simply ate and put up their hammocks and went to sleep.

Early the next morning when Jason was leaving the village, the three men he had seen in canoes the day before returned with a large catch of catfish. There were shouts of joy from the children who ran after Jason and yelled at him from the bank as he sailed away, for they too had understood that he had brought them good luck; and Jason understood why the three men had been so reluctant to talk to him the day before: they were out on the serious business of finding food for their tribe and to have allowed themselves the distraction of talking to a stranger would have been an act of such frivolity as to have dissipated the magic spell of the religious chants with which they had set out.

Again he entered the silence of the jungle on both banks of the river with the engine of his boat clanking away. He thought of the friendly tribe that had shared its meat with him, and was filled with naïve sentiments about the instinctive goodness of human beings in a savage state.

The engine made sputtering sounds and went dead. Jason came out of a reverie in which he had been giving a talk about the habits of a friendly Indian tribe to a learned society in England and was filled with fear. What now? The boat had begun to drift downstream. He took out the oars and placed

195

them in the rowlocks on the two sides of the boat and began to row. He could hardly make any progress against the strong current. "Shit, what am I thinking of?" he suddenly said aloud. For he realized that the engine had not broken down but that it had merely run out of gasoline.

It was with a great sense of relief that he heard the engine start again. The current had become stronger and occasionally the water rose in a swell, rocking the boat. He came to a series of rapids and remembering what Osorio had told him, made for the eastern bank. These could not be the rapids he had been warned to avoid, he thought, for he was still a long distance away from the Rio das Mortes. He found the water calmer by the eastern bank but had to watch out for sunken rocks. He was gliding through a tunnel made by the over-hanging vegetation near the bank and could see the rocks jutting out of the river where the water became collected and was then forced out by the pressure of its accumulated volume. It made a wonderful sound as it splashed and tumbled over the rocks, and near the western bank there was a wide stream which fell some ten meters, making the roaring sound of a waterfall.

After an hour of slow navigation, he was past the rapids. Though the current continued to be strong, the river was again serene. The roar of the water could still be heard over the sound of the engine, and Jason decided to cut the engine off and to stop by the bank just before a wide bend in the river. He found a spot where he could tie the boat and climb up the bank. He ate some salted beef and bread and an orange before leaving his boat. The forest was sparse and he was able to stretch his legs for a short distance without losing sight of the river. Suddenly, he heard a shout in the distance. He quickly crouched down behind the wide trunk of a tree and raising himself gingerly peered in the direction of the noise. A number of Indians, some thirty or more, their bodies red with *urucu* paint, spears and clubs in their hands, were running down to the river in a direction away from Jason on the other side of the wide bend in the river.

Even from a distance their broadly grinning faces and the

tone of their shouts seemed expressive of jubilation, as if they were returning after a successful hunt. But they carried no trophies, only the spears and clubs that they were waving in the air. Jason wondered at the miraculous chance that had led him to turn off the engine and moor his boat at the place where he did and the chance, too, of the loud rapids which drowned all other sounds on the river; otherwise, he would almost certainly have run into the armed band, and he shuddered to think what they might have done to him in their boisterous mood. He waited behind the tree for ten minutes until the last of them had gone out of his view; he walked quietly, stopping behind trees and bushes every few steps, to see where they had gone down to the bank. He reached a point from where he could see the river while remaining concealed in the forest. The first of the men had already rowed across the river in their canoes and the last of them had reached the middle of the stream. Presently, a great cry of jubilation came from the opposite bank, so loud that it rose above the noise of the tumultuous river, sounding as if many more members of the tribe had been waiting there and now received some wonderful news that made them give a spontaneous shout of joy.

Jason waited where he was. He expected that the tribe had a village not too far from the river and he was afraid of returning to his boat and starting the engine. He decided that he would need to wait for dark. He heard some shuffling behind him, and turned around and crouched. A tapir was scurrying through the underbrush. Jason stood up and seeing where the tapir had gone, noticed the well-worn path down which the men had come running. He walked along it for some fifty meters, looking back every few steps to make sure he did not lose his bearings, for he had heard frightening tales of the jungle closing in on people who ventured into it. But the jungle had obviously been cleared here and the beaten path indicated more than a casual traffic. It was then that he saw the vultures.

He had come out to a large circular clearing with huts on it, and the first thing he saw was a vulture flapping up and descending on a human body and flapping again in an attempt to pull out its intestines. There were a dozen other vultures on other bodies lying in pools of blood and many more of the birds were swooping down from the sky. The wide open space was covered with the bodies of men, women and children who had been speared and clubbed to death. Jason saw a vulture jab its beak into the eye of a girl. Three young women, lying on their backs with crushed skulls, had their legs kept open by wooden struts placed between their knees, and he saw their vaginas were covered with green flies and trails of ants were making journeys up their faces and into their mouths. He found a hammock below a tree which contained the mutilated remains of six babies, and seeing the blood on the tree trunk, he concluded that some maniac must have put them together in the hammock and then, drawing the two ends together, swung it repeatedly against the tree until the babies had been battered to death. Some carnivorous animals the like of which he had never seen even in a zoo, the size of bobcats, had entered the clearing and were competing with the vultures at tearing up the bloodied human flesh.

It was not until he had turned away and begun to retreat that Jason felt the full impact of the sight of the massacred tribe, and he doubled over with nausea and began to vomit. His mouth went sour, his throat hurt, and his stomach muscles suffered from cramps, he vomited so much. He slowly began to walk back to the river, not taking the path on which he had entered the doomed village but going straight for the point on the bank where his boat was, for he could see the river through the sparse jungle.

He had read accounts of how modern man had destroyed Indian tribes, and how with the construction of the Transamazônica highway a new frontier had opened up where the white man was systematically destroying the Indian and taking his land.

But the Indians were doing the same thing themselves!

The thought startled him. The difference between one Indian tribe wiping out another with spears and clubs and the European invader doing so with rifles or clothing contaminated with smallpox was one only of degree. It was sentimental rubbish to think that the Indian, living in a supposedly natural state, was therefore justified in expressing an aggressive instinct through which he made more room for himself and restored the ecological balance threatened by overpopulation: Western man was doing precisely the same thing but he was supposed to be cruel, avaricious, and barbaric!

Sobered by this thought, Jason felt relieved of the nausea and clearer in his head. Just then he heard a sound and he froze. It was a sobbing, wailing sound and was coming from behind a bush quite near him. He approached it stealthily, going out in a circle rather than making straight for the bush. He saw a naked boy, twelve or thirteen years old, curled up there, his legs drawn up, his fists close together by his chest. Not wishing to alarm him, he approached him softly and bending down, touched him gently on the shoulder. The boy gave a start and a short scream and looked up with terrified eyes. Jason remembered some words of kindness and spoke them in a sympathetic voice. The boy sat up and began to cry loudly. Jason tried to indicate to him that he meant no harm. After about fifteen minutes, the boy calmed down and began to understand that the stranger whose kind he had never seen before didn't mean to hurt him.

He began to talk in a confused sort of way. But Jason did not need to understand his words to know his story. The poor boy had somehow escaped the massacre but had been a witness to the horror. Jason managed to persuade him to walk to the bank with him. There, he fetched an orange from the boat and gave it to the boy. The boy ate it greedily.

It was late afternoon and since Jason had resolved not to resume his journey until nightfall, he tried to converse with the boy. After half an hour's misunderstanding and confusion, he managed to establish that the boy was named Cocoró. Each time Cocoró spoke in a rush of words, Jason raised his hand and gestured that he repeat the words slowly, one at a time. Cocoró did so and in the process Jason not only understood what the boy was saying but began to be able to formulate phrases himself. Each time he put together a phrase of four or five words which precisely communicated an idea to the boy, Jason had the sensation of being marvelously fluent in the Indian's language. He asked Cocoró to accompany him up the river.

The boy gave him a bright smile. Did he know the Rio das Mortes? Cocoró nodded vigorously and pointed up the river. They should go quietly when the sun set. The boy understood why Jason wanted to leave in the dark, and he looked angrily across the river. Was there a village there where the bad men lived? He nodded resignedly. Well, they wouldn't harm him, he would take him away. Cocoró smiled.

Using words and signs, Cocoró told Jason to stay where he was and went away for a few minutes and returned carrying a live hen by its legs. He twisted its neck and killed it and then deftly, with remarkable speed, plucked its feathers. They collected dead wood and lit a fire and roasted the bird. The sun had set by the time they finished eating it.

They sat side by side in the boat and taking an oar each, slowly moved away from the bank. Jason found Cocoró a deft oarsman and as they proceeded upstream in the darkness, Jason heard the young Indian talk and partially understood him to say that he had a good memory of the river since he had sailed up it several times on fishing and hunting expeditions. When the boat suddenly hit something and made a terrible grinding sound, Jason was afraid that they had hit a submerged rock and immediately had a vision of the boat springing a leak and sinking. Cocoró laughed at the thought. It was nothing but some dead branches of a tree floating downstream.

After rowing for two hours, Jason was too tired to continue and proposed to start the engine. Cocoró advised him not to; although they had come a long way on the water, the river had been making wide loops and they had not come far from the village of the hostile Indians, who would be bound to hear the engine. Cocoró took over Jason's oar and continued to row. Jason slumped over in his seat and fell asleep. After a night of dreams and discomfort and waking to the sound of wild beasts,

Jason awoke in the early morning light to see that Cocoró had fallen asleep on the bottom of the boat. He had had the sense to tie the boat to a tree which grew from the crevice of a rock in the middle of the river.

All that day they proceeded slowly up the river with the engine running, stopping for two hours in the late afternoon at a spot where Cocoró knew game could be found. It was the wrong time of the day, however, for their brief expedition into the jungle was a failure. Jason still had a good quantity of salted beef but before he could bring it out, Cocoró had dived into the river and come up with a large fish, having caught it with his hands.

When setting out from the place where he had bought the boat, Jason had thought, and in fact had been led to believe by his informers, that the Rio das Mortes could be reached in two days. But he made very slow progress against the strong current and the river wound around so much that it took them several hours to make a real advance of half a kilometer. It was not till the eighth day that they reached the Rio das Mortes. During these days, Jason got to know his young Indian companion well, enjoyed going hunting with him and learning some of the instinctive ways in which a savage coped with his environment. By the eighth day, Jason realized that the greatest advantage of having Cocoró as a companion was that he had become remarkably fluent in the Indian language.

The sun was setting when they came to the mouth of the Rio das Mortes. Jason remembered what Osorio had said about it: "Don't be scared by its name, there are several rivers in this region which have that name. And there's only one that I know of, and this is to the south, where the name once carried a literal truth. A hostile tribe commanded its entrance and killed anyone who ventured into it. But that, too, is old history now, for you cannot exercise such power without arousing another tribe's envy and making it determined to overthrow such tyrannical control. Sometimes I think the politics of the Indian tribes are no different from those of the Greeks of Homer's day. It's curious how without knowing the idea of freedom men will always strive for it."

The Rio das Mortes was a narrow tributary made dark by the vegetation of the two banks forming an arch over it. Jason thought it best to stop for the night, and wanted to climb up the bank and hang a hammock from two trees. Cocoró pointed to the alligator concealed in the dark, muddy bank, and mentioned the prevalence of snakes in the region. It would be safer to cut off the engine and row quietly to where they could moor the boat and sleep in it.

The bottom of the boat was curved and narrow and the two just managed to lie there next to each other. It was uncomfortable but the advantage of relative security made it acceptable. Jason found it curious to be lying next to a naked boy. In the gray light of the morning, Jason awoke suddenly in an attempt to stop a bad dream from continuing. In the two or three moments it took him to remember where he was he became conscious of Cocoró's penis, which was erect and pressed against his thigh. He looked at Cocoró's face. The boy was fast asleep, breathing regularly through his open mouth. Jason looked down his body, moving himself a fraction away from the Indian. The erect penis was thick and remarkably large for the boy. Jason touched it with a finger and then held it between his fingertips and thumb. Cocoró moved in his sleep, sighed, and turned over. Jason's hand slipped to the side of his thigh and he fell back to sleep.

The sun had risen above the canopy of trees when he awoke again. The trees were moving away and he had the sensation that the boat was slowly traveling upstream. But the engine was quiet. There was a sound of oars splashing in the water, but it was not Cocoró who was rowing. In fact, he realized after a moment, Cocoró was right next to him, still fast asleep.

Jason sat up, facing the rear of the boat. They were definitely moving! He could even see the narrow wake made by the steady forward motion of the boat. He stood up and turned to look to the front. In his confused state of consciousness and in the darkness of the river, he saw that a larger boat was ahead of them, towing his boat. He discerned six figures plying the oars and it took him a few minutes to see clearly that the six figures belonged to young women. They appeared to be wearing nothing but necklaces of palm-nut beads. He slipped down in his boat again and awoke Cocoró. By making gestures and pointing to the other boat he managed to convey the situation to the young boy. Cocoró stood up, stared at the rowing women, scratched his head, and yawned, and turning to the side of the boat, urinated into the river.

Jason looked up to see if the women were watching this piece of instinctive male arrogance. As far as he could see in the dim light, they were grimly concentrating on the task of rowing.

Cocoró sat down and putting his elbows on his knees rested his face between his palms. Jason asked him if he knew who they were. Cocoró shrugged his shoulders and pouted his lips. He seemed quite unperturbed and gave the appearance that as far as he was concerned it was a relief to let the girls do the work; he had no reason to complain at such a satisfactory arrangement. Jason brought out two oranges and gave one to Cocoró. They continued up the river slowly with no sign or word from the girls who, however, observed them closely as they rowed.

They proceeded thus for some two or three hours. The boys had nothing to do but stare at the river and its banks. It had occurred to Jason that their position might well be a perilous one, for they were obviously prisoners and were being taken for a particular purpose. Several gruesome ideas came to him, including the appalling one that the girls might belong to a tribe of cannibals. When they were going through a particularly dark stretch of the river, he wondered whether they should not slip out of their boat and swim to the shore and take their chances with the interior. But he could see alligators on both banks and there were piranha in the river. Then he had the idea of cutting the rope with which their boat was being towed, starting the engine, and making a retreat downriver. But he could clearly see the bows and arrows beside the girls, and their grim expressions indicated that they were experts with their weapons. He had Osorio's rifle with him, but though the situation was potentially perilous, for the present it seemed so peaceful and even idyllic that the thought of using the rifle to commit cold-blooded murder seemed repugnant to him. And in any case, he had no experience of using a gun and did not trust himself to hit his mark at the first try, and the attempt to do so would probably be so clumsy that it would give the girls all the time they needed to get him with their arrows. They seemed awfully well disciplined, he thought, rowing with such precision and power for such a long time.

They came out of the canopy of trees and the river widened and became two diverging streams as if they were the tributaries that formed the Rio das Mortes. In fact they were two limbs of the same river, as soon began to be apparent to Jason, embracing between their two long arms a large island. The girls rowed into a small cove where some canoes were moored. The boys were ordered to alight and come up the bank. Three girls in front and three behind them, they were conducted through a narrow tunnel in the vegetation until they came out to an open space. There was a village there. The island, though some two kilometers long, was too narrow for the huts to be built in a circle, so they had been erected facing each other with a narrow alley of cleared ground between them. A few women were pounding manioc outside the huts, and they gave a nervous sort of shriek when they saw that of the two captives one was of a kind they had never seen before. Their cry brought other women out of their huts who, seeing Jason and not knowing whether he was some strange animal or a human being in some perverse guise, began to jeer loudly at him.

The girls conducting them stopped outside a hut and one of them went in. By now Jason had realized that there were no men in the village and he had observed that there were very few children and they were all female. The girl came out of the hut with an old woman with shriveled breasts and a thin, wrinkled body. She looked up and down at Cocoró and seemed pleased with what she saw. She muttered a word to the girl who took Cocoró into the hut, thrusting him rudely through the doorway. The old woman then appraised Jason. She rapidly intoned some words which Jason could not catch.

Two girls immediately turned to him and began to tear at his clothes. He was horrified when he heard the material of his shirt ripping off his back, and feeling a girl's hand at his waist, quickly had the presence of mind to prevent his trousers being torn by rapidly assisting in removing them and letting them fall to his feet. The old woman came up to him and spitting on her fingers rubbed them on his chest. She appeared disturbed when his color did not come off and she mused to herself for a moment, looking at his eyes and then down at his penis.

Jason noticed that the other girls were similarly gazing at him and that one with small pointed breasts and a beautiful face with her black hair cut across her forehead and dreamy brown eyes seemed particularly struck by what she saw of the male sex. Secretly, he gave her the name *Anna*, a fact which would have been irrelevant but for the events that took place later.

The old woman frowned and took her eyes away from his penis. She appeared not to like what she saw. Perhaps, thought Jason, she had never seen a circumcised one before and was confused. She gave a command to Anna and the other girls. Three of them marched away in the direction of a hut. Anna and another girl began to conduct him away. At least he had got his trousers back on, he thought, as he again marched past the jeering women.

There was a natural hollow in the land, some four meters deep, which formed a small subterranean roofless room with a circular floor four meters at most in diameter. A thick piece of bamboo with holes cut into it at intervals was placed in it, and the girl who was not Anna indicated to Jason that he should go down into the hollow. It took him a moment to understand that the holes in the bamboo were meant to be footholds. The girl held the bamboo, which projected a meter above the ground, while he shakily made his way down. As soon as he was on the floor of the hollow, the girl raised the bamboo up and pulled it out. Jason understood that he was a prisoner. He had the sky and the free air above him but there was no way he could scale the wall of his room to escape. The girls looked down at him. He could not quite see their faces, for they appeared in silhouette against the light, but he heard them giggle and thought he saw a bright gleam in Anna's dreamy eyes as she turned her head to share a glance with her companion. Soon, they went away.

The ground was covered with a short, prickly vegetation, and Jason began to tear it up and to heap it at the side in order to make a space bearable enough to lie on. The work kept him busy for a good hour, but it also made him hungry and thirsty. He looked at the wall which surrounded him. It, too, was covered with the same vegetation, but any attempt to hang on to it and pull himself up only resulted in his falling back onto the floor, clutching a handful of weeds.

He sat down and then lay back, tormented more by thirst than by any fear of what the old woman might be planning for him. He must have fallen unconscious for a long time; when a voice awoke him the sky had lost its brilliance. Something was being lowered down to him. A kind of cradle had been woven at the end of a rope and placed in it were a pot and a basket. They contained a small amount of food and water. As soon as he took them out, the rope was pulled up and the girl disappeared. He drank a few sips of the water. The food was coarse and he chewed it morosely. It was some comfort for him to reflect that at least the women had not left him to die of hunger and thirst. And given the meagre quantity of food, they did not appear to be fattening him for a cannibalistic feast either.

At sunset, a more pressing problem concerned him than his ultimate fate. His stomach was rumbling. He had eased himself with a series of farts but the pressure in his bowels was now such that there was only one natural way in which it could be eased. He was obliged to sit against the wall. After the unusual foods he had eaten in recent days, or perhaps because of the tension generated by his present situation, the bowel movement was painful, the stools were slimy and smelled horribly. When he had finished, the relief within his body was replaced by a new torment in his senses: he would need to live with his own terrible smell. And worse, the slimy excretion had smeared his buttocks. He stood with his trousers and underpants fallen to his knees, not knowing whether he should let his clothes be soiled by the gooey mess. He sat down on a part of the ground which he had earlier cleared and with a clumsy movement dragged his buttocks across the earth. All he succeeded in doing was to attach a layer of dirt to his buttocks.

Such fastidiousness and concern for cleanliness bothered him only for the first few days of his confinement in the hollow. As the days, and then the weeks, passed, filth became his natural condition. What his body did and what his senses suffered were trivialities compared to what his mind was beginning to suffer. The girl who came once a day with the little food and water, performed her task quickly and went away without answering his questions. What were they trying to do to him? What was happening to his friend Cocoró?

He upbraided himself for the foolishness of having undertaken such an expedition. What had he thought it was like to cross Amazonas, a day's hike across the Pennines? He had been so stupid! He could not believe that his uncle and even the kind old Osorio could have counseled him with such enthusiasm to enter a world where savagery prevailed. Bob was lucky to have fallen ill and returned to England. How many weeks had passed since he saw him off? Could the new term already have begun at the university?

Reduced almost to the life of a worm in the hole in the ground, he had lost count of the days he had spent there. At first, he had not expected to remain imprisoned for more than a few days, for he had expected that whatever the women were up to they could not want to keep a stranger incarcerated indefinitely. Why he should have thought so, he could not say since he had no idea at all of the life on the island.

One day it began to rain. He crouched against the wall as the slanting sheets of rain came down in a heavy thunderstorm that lasted several hours. He was cold and spent the night shivering. The rain, however, had performed the valuable service of cleaning out his pit, and the new freshness in the air in the confined area briefly made him cheerful. Very early the next morning when the sky had scarcely turned from black to gray, a girl appeared and lowered a basket of food to him. He was astonished, for this event usually occurred later in the day. Since the light behind her head was not as strong as the one beginning to come from the eastern horizon, he saw her face clearly and recognized her as the girl he had named Anna.

He opened the basket and found that instead of the usual coarse food, it contained a roasted fish. She spoke slowly so that he could understand, and told him that she herself had caught the fish. To him it was a rare delicacy and he thanked her. He asked what had become of Cocoró. She did not answer, but indicated instead that she would return the next morning.

There were thunderstorms every afternoon now but the sun shone brightly the rest of the day, drying up the pools of water. Anna began to come every morning, always bringing him something to eat. She would stay up on the rim of the hole for ten minutes and talk to him, and began to stay for as long as half an hour after a few days. From her, he learned the story of the island and its women.

The old woman, who was the island's chief, and fifteen other women of her age, belonged to a tribe two days' distance away. Their husbands had gone to take revenge against another tribe. They had killed all the men of the enemy but instead of killing their women also, they had fallen under a spell and seduced the women and brought many of them back to their own tribe. Thereupon, their own wives, outraged by their lewdness, plotted and killed them and left the land that had brought the curse of shame to the tribe. They took with them only their daughters, having decided that men brought nothing but evil in the world, and finally came to this island.

After meeting Jason in the early morning for several days, she let slip the information about Cocoró. The boy had been captured to help the women make babies.

"But he's only twelve or thirteen! How can he know anything about it?"

She did not grasp Jason's statement, and said that that was what they did—captured a youth from time to time and kept him there until at least ten of the women were pregnant. When

208

the babies came, they kept only the females. The males were given to another tribe up the river who liked eating small children. This way they kept at peace with the neighboring tribe, and were not molested by its men. They made babies only with strangers whom they captured. The idea of a family was hateful to them. They only wanted to remain women.

Jason was horrified but realized that an attempt to express his sentiments would mean nothing to the girl, even if he could find the difficult words with which to state his idea. And he understood in that moment that a complex morality depended on the prior development of a complex language. Even if he commanded the girl's language fluently he would not have been able to formulate the idea in his mind. Could it be that an idea did not exist outside a sophisticated language, he wondered, finding the thought difficult and perplexing; and if it did not, then was the tribe which did not comprehend that idea absolved of all the associations attending it, including that of guilt? Obviously, these were questions he could not raise with the girl, and so he asked her instead what would become of Cocoró when he was considered to have fulfilled his duties.

Oh, he will be sent away to the neighboring tribe, too, she answered without any feeling for the boy. The tribe would appreciate that and would send back gifts. When Jason had thought of the baby boys being given away to the cannibals, his horror had been generalized and abstract, for they existed only as an idea; but Cocoró! Before this girl had begun to come to him, he was the last human being who had been his friend. The poor boy had scarcely escaped the massacre of his tribe when he was being readied to be sacrificed in the most appalling manner known to man.

On one morning the girl told him in a roundabout way why she came to him so regularly with the presents of food. She was angry with the older women. They already had had children but they were the ones who were making the most use of Cocoró. At first their excuse had been that the boy needed to be taught what to do; after that, they had allowed some of the younger women to go and lie with him. But on the pretext that Cocoró could not do it with more than three a day, the older women were restricting his use to themselves and to a few of their younger favorites. It was clear that her own chance would not come; she was considered too young. She was angry because she knew she was not that young, for she felt inside her that she could make a baby.

Jason pondered her remarks after she had gone. She could be preparing the way to coming down to him. The very fact that she had been taking the risk of coming to him with food early in the morning indicated an independent spirit, a person of natural individuality who resented the life imposed upon her. So that when she came the next morning, Jason proposed that he could offer her his services if she could find a way of coming down or, he added jokingly, help him to climb up.

The bamboo on which he had descended was lying near where she leaned over the edge to talk to him. She quickly put it down the hole and came scampering down in a minute. Jason held her shoulders and face. He had no way of telling her that, like her, he was a virgin. But she, driven entirely by instinct, knew precisely what to do.

From the following day, she came at an earlier hour, when it was still quite dark, so that she could spend a longer time with him, making him enter her twice. She let him kiss her and fondle her breasts but remained passive when he did so, for her interest was entirely in the animalistic one of coupling with him. After a week of this, he asked her if she was not afraid that he would knock her out and make his escape on the ladder on which she had come down.

She was not afraid, she said, because she knew there was nowhere he could go. One of the girls was in on her secret and kept guard a short distance away. She would shoot him with an arrow if he appeared aboveground.

Is that how she cared for him? he asked. To keep him her prisoner or have him killed if he tried to escape? But these questions, ill-phrased in her tongue, were beyond her comprehension.

By now, Jason had no idea how many weeks or months had

passed. His life was made bearable by the girl's morning visits and miserable the rest of the time by a consciousness of despair at his situation. He wondered if she realized that if she did have a baby that it would be a half-caste; he doubted if the elder women would accept such a progeny and presumed that the girl would find herself in serious trouble as a consequence. She was a willful creature, the kind who almost deliberately gets into trouble as a demonstration of independence.

The afternoon thunderstorms continued regularly, and he was surprised he had not caught his death from the elements. Apart from the weakness that came from a lack of exercise, he seemed healthy enough, and the extra food brought in the morning by the girl ensured that he did not suffer too much from malnutrition.

One morning she told him that she thought that she had a baby inside her. But she wanted him to come to her again because she was sure that that would make the baby bigger. He was surprised at the pleasure he felt at the idea of fatherhood and idly pondered to himself the happiness that could be theirs if they could go away and live together somewhere. But he soon realized the empty sentimentality of his thought when she told him casually that Cocoró had been sent away to the neighboring tribe. A dozen women were happily pregnant. He could not find strength to penetrate her a second time that morning since his thoughts were on the wretched fate of his friend. She asked him if anything was wrong and he excused himself by telling her that she needed to be careful if she already had a baby.

The rains intensified and instead of an afternoon thunderstorm, there was now a continuous downpour which went on for two days. The girl did not come in the morning and no one else came to bring him his food and water at the usual hour in the afternoon. The memory of the girl coming to him so regularly to make love with him now seemed bizarre, as though the entire episode had been an invention of his imagination. He tried to think what the experience had been of embracing her and realized that he would never have a clear idea of that experience unless he possessed her again. That, he supposed,

211

was what gave repetition its interest; if we understood a thing after doing it once and could re-experience it without needing to do it again, life would be awfully boring. Repetition guaranteed renewal—nature used the cunning device of novelty, making one believe that the next repetition would be a rarer experience than before.

Odd to be having such thoughts while the rain poured down on him and he had had nothing to eat for over a day! But there was nothing else for him to do but think in order to distract himself from his misery; and he found some satisfaction with the idea that he had a hold over his life as long as he continued to think.

A strong wind began to blow in the middle of the night. He heard crashing sounds in the distance. The rain beat down harder than before. He longed to be in his father's house. How he used to love the rain from the comfortable shelter of the veranda, hearing it beat down upon the tiles on the roof and seeing it pound upon the ocean! Now he hated the rain that was hitting his skull even though he was pressed against the wall in his terrible little hole in the ground. Was this to be his life forever? And how he had never minded the rain when playing rugby in England with Bob at his side! That mud, those blows on the field when you flung yourself through the air to tackle a man and fell flat on your face in the mud, how delicious all that was compared with this meaningless downpour on his tormented body.

The wind was thrashing at the trees, whistling and roaring through the branches. Suddenly, there was a great crashing sound above him. The wall opposite to which he was clinging seemed to collapse; the upper part of it turned to mud and slid down to the floor, making the mouth at the top wider and at the same time producing a slope where there had been a sheer wall. Jason could scarcely see it in the dark, and he was terrified to think that the wall to which he clung would collapse next. But the crashing sound had not been made by the wall collapsing; a huge tree some ten meters away from the hole had fallen and some of its branches now hung down the hole. Its uprooting must have caused the earth to break, he

212

thought, and produced the mudslide. During the moment in which Jason became aware of the branches falling into the hole, he thought his end had come, for he expected some huge limb to come smashing down on him. But the tree seemed to have come to a neat rest across the top of the hole, and soon the storm abated though it continued to rain steadily.

He touched the limb of the tree that hung before him, pulled at it, and strained upon it. It held his weight! Within a minute he had climbed out of the hole, and he threw his face up at the rain feeling the thrill of liberation. But where was he? Which way was the river where they had docked? He decided that instead of running any risk, his best bet was to wait patiently until it was light. He walked some distance away from the hole and sat down under a tree. The rain diminished, then ceased. He struggled against fatigue and sleep, for he needed to get to a boat the first moment he could see for more than ten meters.

He rose in the gray light, listened carefully to sounds, and gingerly made his way toward the river. By the time he reached it, the light had brightened though the sun had still not come up. He looked intently up and down the bank and saw where the boats were. To his surprise, he found his own boat exactly where he had been obliged to leave it. Obviously Indians did not see things that did not involve them in immediate action.

He rowed slowly, watching the shore as he went. The island's length of two kilometers seemed to him the coastline of a continent, but finally he had left it behind and could begin to breathe more easily. He rowed for two more hours before the exertion, on top of a sleepless night and not having eaten for two days, totally exhausted him. He pulled up under some overhanging branches, to one of which he tied the rope.

The provisions he had begun the journey with were still on the boat. But the salted beef had gone putrid, the basket of oranges rotten. He had nothing to eat. He scooped up some water from the river and drank it. Aware of his dirty, stinking body, he wished he had the strength to take a swim in the river and change his clothes. But he feared that his weariness would not alert him to any dangers that might lurk in the water. It looked clear and innocent enough, but piranha and electric eels were always a threat in these waters. Better, he thought, to be dirty and alive than clean and in the mouths of a thousand piranha.

He checked to see how much gas he had left. Just one full can. He poured it into the tank and started the engine. He should have gone back! he suddenly thought. After all his suffering, he ought to have turned back from the island and gone back down the Rio Napo. He would have been safe, at least he would have known where he was going. Why had he not thought about it? What made him choose the unknown without his consciously thinking about it? It was too late now; he dared not try to go past the island of the vengeful women. Half-asleep and hungry, he proceeded slowly up the river like a prisoner who has been flogged in the yard and then walks staggeringly down a long corridor in a dungeon, hearing successive iron doors close behind him.

For five days, traveling very slowly—for he had run out of gas—and stopping frequently to climb up the bank to look for fruit or merely to rest from the overwhelming fatigue, he had made his way up the river. His hunger was now great and sometimes when he crawled up the bank he found that he did not have the strength to rise up on his feet and continued into the jungle on all fours. He had not changed into a clean pair of clothes since leaving the island and wore only the pair of trousers he had on when the women stripped him; they were torn at the knees as he crawled in them. Only the sight of fruit on a tree gave him the strength to rise up on his feet and on two occasions even to climb up a tree; so powerful was the force of hunger that in the absence of anything edible he could scarcely move, but in the presence of something that he could bite his teeth into he was driven to comparatively heroic action. He craved for some meat and longed to catch an animal. There were plenty of beasts in the area but once when he had decided to take his gun with him, he found that while he could drag the rifle along he did not have the strength to raise it to his shoulder without its shaking so violently in his hands that he could have no hope of hitting his mark.

In his hunger he saw the world about him as a blur. His mind had no thoughts in it, only a confusion of memories which were meaningless. If anyone had come to him and asked him who he was, his answer would have been a grunt or a howl. His eyes searched only for food.

On one afternoon he sat slouched in the boat, not finding the will with which to make his body go up the bank. He heard oars splashing in the water, and looked up wearily. He saw three men in a canoe. Their bodies were painted blue-black; wooden disks in their lower lips held their mouths open. Jason watched them with sleepy eyes as they paddled downstream and vaguely wondered why they did not see him and put an end to his suffering. He opened his mouth to call to them but his cry remained choked in his throat.

Later, he rose out of the boat in order to try and go on shore. His attempt to leave the boat resulted in his falling in the water. The river was shallow there and its muddy bed was firm. Dimly in his consciousness he wondered if this were not the end, for surely the piranhas and alligators would come and tear him up in a minute. But nothing happened. He began to be conscious of a vague enjoyment, for the water refreshed him. He had not felt so well for a long time. He submerged his head in the water several times, finding the action to possess a certain exhilaration and also alleviate his fatigue. When he crawled up the bank, he found that he had the strength to stand up and walk, albeit shakily. Coming out of the water, he had unthinkingly put his hand to the rear pocket of his trousers to see if his wallet was still there. That little action and his ability to walk surprised him, for it indicated that his mind was eager, however obscurely, to work for his survival, that some instinct within him was concerned only with his preservation.

He walked a little distance away from the bank but found no fruitbearing trees, and ventured a little farther. He saw a bright-yellow bird on a tree and picking up a stone threw it at it. The stone fell a few meters in front of him with a plop. The bird flew up and landed on the next tree. He walked forward, his eyes trained on the bird with a lustful stare and seeing himself bite into the raw, bloody flesh of the bird. He picked up another stone and with a greater effort threw it in the direction of the bird. This time the stone went higher and the bird flew away a greater distance. Stumbling, he ran after it and when he found it again it was sitting on a higher branch than before. He took slow aim with a stone and flung it up. The stone rose, as if in slow-motion, in an arc a meter above his raised hand and then fell to the ground. The bird looked down sideways and then raised its head and pointing its beak to the sky began to sing.

Jason collapsed to the ground and let out a howl. He cried, stretched out on the ground, sobbing convulsively. He prayed for a boa to come and swallow him, for a jaguar to tear up his miserable body. But though the jungle was infested with the bushmaster snake, and preying animals large and small roamed the interior, they somehow failed to discover this creature who would have welcomed their venom or claws in his body.

He heard a rustling sound in the trees and looked up. Soon, there was a great commotion, the branches of the trees seemed to be swinging as if in a storm. But the air was still. Then he heard laughter, loud echoing laughter. He must be going mad, he thought vaguely. But then he saw that the trees were crowded with monkeys whose jabbering cry sounded like laughter and whose faces were opened and gave the appearance of a wide grin. They were the laughing monkeys he had read about. It was a maddening, vicious sound. A whole theater full of monkeys laughing at some crazy comedy.

He saw them look down at him and almost believed that they were pointing at him in derision as they laughed aloud. He rose up and shouted at them. His voice came out as a howl. Their laughter seemed to grow louder. He yelled, raised his fists, and beat the air. They seemed wildly amused. Some had come down to the lower branches and were staring with round, merry eyes at him from a few meters away while continuing to laugh. He dashed at them or tried to throw stones at them. They swung out of reach. Some of them, while swinging on hanging roots, seemed to make a deliberate point

216

of brushing over his hair or jabbing his shoulder. They gave the impression that they had never had such fun before. Jason tried to run, to get away from them, away from their horrible laughter. They seemed to be screaming with joy at his stumbling attempt to escape. He fell, and heard a renewed roar of concerted laughter as if it were the funniest thing they had ever seen.

They disappeared as suddenly as they had come, their jabbering laughter echoing briefly from a distance and then vanishing. Jason lay in his exhaustion for some time as if the laughter had been violent blows inflicted on his body.

When he came to and rose, he realized that he did not know which way the river was. He had come too far into the jungle in his vain attempt to catch the bird. He remembered that he had been out of gas for several days and that now he no longer had the strength to row for two meters let alone to some safe and civilized harbor. But still, the boat was his home, offering him a measure of security. He looked around him, trying to see if he could identify the tree on which the bird had begun to sing. He remembered that he had fallen below it; surely, there would be marks on the ground, he thought, stumbling about erratically. A feeling that he would be lost forever if he did not make the effort to find a way out of the jungle gavé him the strength to stumble on. He was not conscious of the passing time or how far he went, for his only obsession was to take one more, and then one more, step forward.

He stood, looking wildly at what he saw. He had come out on the edge of a clearing and was looking at an Indian village, larger than any he had seen before. There was a hut in the middle of the circle of huts, and the sound of men's laughter was coming from it.

Children playing in the open space spotted him and raised a cry. Some men came running out of the hut in the middle of the circle and, seeing his strange figure, approached him slowly. They could not believe their eyes. He was a man but a different sort of man. They touched his arms, and exchanged glances as if to say, "Not much flesh." On being touched and pinched,

Jason fainted. They carried him to the hut from which they had come. Other men squatted there, sipping a fermented drink. There were expressions of amazement and delight when they saw the body of a man carried in and placed on the floor. There was a lot of animated talk, several of the men talking simultaneously. Someone thought of pouring some of the fermented drink down the stranger's throat.

Jason sat up, choking. He used the word for water, which he had learned from Osorio. The men were astonished that he knew their words. Someone brought him water in a gourd. He sipped it slowly, staring at the circle of men surrounding him. Someone remarked how thin he was. All bones. Not much good for anything. Another shouted something to a boy peering in at the door. The boy ran away, and the men debated some question which Jason could not follow. They talked too fast and perhaps they spoke a different dialect than the one which he had practiced with Cocoró and the girl he had called Anna. Those two figures passed vaguely through his mind as the blurred memories of a dream. His physical and mental states were so near total exhaustion that he was in no condition to follow an intellectual discourse, however elementary. The small boy returned, bringing a basket with him. It contained a meal made out of corn. Jason put a little in his mouth. It was cold and tasteless, but his teeth snapped eagerly at the soft mess. He ate all the rest and licked his fingers, and managed to smile weakly at the men around him.

The men laughed. Another command was given to the boy, who had again stationed himself at the door. He went off with the basket and returned a little later. Jason was overjoyed when he saw what he was being offered. Meat! The little pieces were soft and cold, but he ate them all greedily. There were a few bones which he sucked with great relish. Taking one out of his mouth, he stopped and stared at it, becoming suddenly frightened. It looked like a human bone. Yes, it was a knuckle. And this other one which he tried to chew. A thumb. He turned his face away from the basket but though he thought he should be overcome with a great revulsion he felt only the satisfaction of having fed his body.

They kept him in the hut for several days, bringing him more food than he could eat and insisting that he swallow it. He understood that they were fattening him in order to eat him. He thought of his confinement on the island as a beautiful time and of the days of crawling up the river with nothing to eat as an idyllic experience. Now the men would pinch him from time to time to see how much meat he had put on and make jokes to each other, and the horror of his situation intensified each moment. By now he understood clearly what they said to each other; the word for *feast* was often on their lips when they talked about him.

One day, three men he had not seen at the village before entered the hut. They had returned from some expedition. He heard them say something which made him prick up his ears. The women had liked the cloth and pots they had sent in exchange for the gift of the boy. They would get the boy's male children next year. A cry of delight went up when the men heard that. Jason realized that though he had traveled up the river for five days after leaving the island, he had not come very far. He had stopped so often in his vain search for food and rowed so slowly that it had taken him five days to travel a distance these men covered in less than a day without the benefit of an engine. He tried not to think that the meat he had eaten on the day of his arrival had been the leftovers of Cocoró.

On some days the torment of boredom was greater than the horror of knowing he was soon to be killed. Sometimes, watching the men lounge around doing nothing all day and the women outside their huts passing the time picking lice from the hair of children, Jason was struck by the essential mildness of the tribe; the people around him certainly did not live up to the expectation of cannibals as savages who went about armed and on finding a human being instantly roasted him on a spit or cooked him in a huge cauldron. Instead, these were a lazy people. Perhaps the fact that they received a regular tribute of male flesh from the island women had contributed to their laziness. Their hunters did not venture too far in search of fish and game. Jason remarked to himself that, contrary to popular belief, the cannibals, these cannibals at any rate, ate human

219

flesh in much the same manner as Western societies ate venison: it was not something that they did every day of their lives, for fish and game were much enjoyed by them, and there were days when there was no meat at all.

Jason would not have thought a few days earlier when he was desperately trying to find something to eat that he would come to loathe the sight of food. For his hosts brought him fish and game and large quantities of cornmeal almost by the hour and obliged him to eat. Sometimes he would vomit, and that would arouse the disgust of his hosts. The thought that each bite that he swallowed brought closer the hour when they would deem him ready to be slaughtered took away all his appetite. But they forced him to eat, and it was horrible for him to reflect that the people who had saved him from dying had done so only to prepare him for a more ceremonious death.

He was surprised to see one afternoon, when someone had just shaken him out of his stupor to make him eat again, that two girls had arrived from the island of women. There was some dialogue going on just outside the hut, which the girls could not enter since it was the exclusive abode of men. The discussion became heated, and all the men stood in a circle around the girls to listen to what their chief and the girls were saying. Jason was glad to have the opportunity to turn away from the food before him and he, too, listened. The women had discovered—Jason did not understand how—that the man who had escaped from their island was with this tribe and they demanded his return. The chief argued that the man had come by himself and belonged to them. They had been feeding him for several days and were going to eat him during the celebrations following the Javarí festival. The girls reminded him of the obligations of the two tribes to each other. They added that their chief was planning to send them four baby boys for the Javarí festival; the boys had been born two festivals ago and were nice and fat.

The chief pondered the idea and exchanged remarks with three or four of the men standing near him. The girls, who seemed very well briefed by their chief, added at this point that twelve women were going to have babies. The implication was obvious: if the tribe wanted to continue receiving these gifts, then it ought to cooperate. The chief went away with three men to hold a council. They returned ten minutes later. Apparently, they had weighed the future advantages against losing the young man, and the chief had also been persuaded by one of his advisers that the man, being of a different-colored skin, might contain poison in his body—an idea which became a neat face-saving formula in the diplomatic defeat. The girls were allowed to take Jason away.

His happiness was great as he walked with the girls to the river and sat in the middle of their canoe, one girl in front and the other behind him. They began to paddle away in the late afternoon with the sun some two hours from setting. He made remarks to the girls, suggesting how he regretted having left their island. They paid him no attention and paddled away with remarkable power. He wondered what would happen to him now. These were crazy people who followed an inscrutable code. It was conceivable that they might end up by returning him to the cannibals as a gift, for they were given to being absurdly ironical without realizing it. He wished one of these girls had been the one he had called Anna, he might have been able to reason with her; but perhaps not, he thought, she probably resented his going away and would be revengeful and in all probability would denounce him for having seduced her when he returned to the island.

But he began to talk about her, describing her, so that his two captors could identify her, and asking them if they knew she was going to have a baby. The one in front of him turned her head around and looked at him in amazement. Sure, he went on, sensing a possibility, she came to him in the mornings in the hole where he was kept. She was smart. She knew how to get what she wanted, although she was very young. She must be younger than they were and was already going to have a baby. What about them, had they had the chance to mate yet? He thought not. The old women were too greedy. They were too jealous of the young girls who were more beautiful than they and made excuses to keep the young girls from being mated. Wasn't that true? That is why they had not mated yet. That little girl was clever. She got what she wanted. She did not wait around for old women to tell her when she could be happy. It was a shame they had to wait. It was great to make a baby. Their bodies were ready to do so. Their bodies wanted nothing more.

Jason talked on in little phrases trying to convey the idea that they had been cheated of their natural right to enjoy the pleasures of mating. The girl in front of him had ceased paddling and had turned to stare at him. The girl behind him soon stopped paddling too. They were drifting downstream, and now a strange coincidence took place. Jason saw his own boat moored to the bank under some overhanging trees. He realized that he had the girls' attention, and he realized, too, what his imagination had been leading up to as he talked in a primitive way of the pleasures of sexuality. And so he talked on. They might not have the chance when they got to the island. Here, they were alone. They could stop by the bank. They could lie under those trees there. First one and then the other. It was a chance not to be missed. What had they to lose? No one would know.

The girls were persuaded to stop on the bank opposite to the one where his boat was. When they had climbed up the bank, Jason asked them which one would like to be the first. The two pointed at each other simultaneously, and giggled. Well, you come first, Jason said to one, taking her hand and drawing her away. He told the other to stay by the bank, her turn would come very soon. The mating had to be done without anyone looking, it was a secret thing between a man and a girl. The girl, both excited and apprehensive, obeyed him and stayed by the bank while he took the other some distance away in the jungle, telling her that they must find a good soft area on the ground.

When he was certain that he had come far enough away, he stopped and embraced the girl. She did not understand the gesture and he told her to remove the belt on her waist and the strip of bark that went between her thighs. He removed his own trousers. He lay with her on the ground. She giggled when he kissed her breasts. His mouth on her lips was even more ticklish. He stroked her clitoris, and that was the only action which made her close her eyes in the experience of pleasure. Her vaginal entrance was tight, but spreading her legs out wide, he succeeded in forcing it. She gave a sharp little scream. Quiet now, he said, pressing on her, your baby is going to come soon. His hands just above her shoulders, he raised himself. She had closed her eyes and her hips were pushing up in a natural rhythm. God forgive me, he said to himself, and pressing her hard down at the thighs, he threw his hands at her throat and put all the weight of his body behind the fierce grip. She convulsed, tried to beat her legs and to shake her head. But he held her down; his own body tensed and became one immense force, his eyes looking wildly at her.

She was dead. Now for the other, he thought grimly as he put on his trousers and walked away. When he reached the bank, he told the girl that her companion wanted to rest where she had found such pleasure. He led the girl to below a tree near the bank. His face was a mask of kind consideration and tender affection and he guided the girl down to the ground. Not having ejaculated during the previous intercourse, he was ready for his second victim.

Her interior was more accommodating and he saw the look of astonishment come over her that such a thing was possible. He bent over her and rubbed her nose with his in a gesture that conveyed his concern to please her. Hers was a softer, less rigid body, and he thought, in a passing moment as he experienced an intense pleasure in the act of making love to her, how in another situation in another place he could easily be content to live with so wonderful a girl, but the thought passed from his mind quickly, for his raging blood was attuned not to the sexual act but to murder. And he saw himself as some other, a wild and perverse maniac, a man with clenched teeth and bulging eyes, his strong hands tightening their ferocious grip around her neck. She struggled, fought back. His penis slipped out of her and for a moment he thought he was going to lose hold of her. A terrible scream came from her in that moment before he tightened his grip again, pulling himself up to sit on her stomach. Her hands and legs were flailing and beating, but he held on, shouting to her, "Die, damn you, die!" Incredibly, and to his great horror, he ejaculated and spilled his semen over her stomach in the final violent moment in which his hands destroyed her life. He fell on her, exhausted, panting loudly.

He walked back to the bank and sat down on the edge of the river to wash his hands. He found himself crying. It was a terrible existence which obliged one to commit murder in order to continue to have breath oneself. And what for? Only to keep oneself alive, even when that life had an expectation only of suffering the torments of the body and the greater torments of the mind. After such knowledge, what could he do?

He looked at the river. Downstream, the women would be on the lookout for his return. Up the river, the cannibals lounged in their huts. And where he was two girls lay dead, two beautiful girls whom he could easily have loved had the circumstances been different.

He went into the canoe and paddled across the river to where his own boat was. He found that the canoe was a more natural vehicle for the river than his own boat, which was comparatively cumbersome to row now that its engine was useless since he had run out of gasoline. He transferred his clothes, the rifle and the few other items he had to the canoe. He removed his trousers and bathed in the river. Putting on clean clothes, he was ready to continue his journey. The sun was near to setting and he calculated that it would be dark by the time he paddled past the village of the cannibals. He remembered that by sunset anyone who had gone out hunting was usually back, the women were busy cooking and the men lounged about drinking in the men's hut. If he ran into anyone, it would just be bad luck. After what he had already experienced and especially after what he had done he was possessed by a confidence which was a kind of abandon.

Now he entered a vast labyrinth of rivers in an uninhabited wilderness where the jungle offered little light, and it seemed that he was condemned to spend the rest of his life crawling through this darkness in his canoe. Neither map nor compass could help him choose a direction. One river led to another. Sometimes there were two or three tributaries with only a few meters separating their banks, and it was pure whim that made him choose the one he did. He discovered the knack of using his rifle to kill game. He found a way of catching fish. But when would he come out into the light, he wondered, how long must he spend in this darkness?

Several times he had the impression that he had already traveled the river he was on, and he was struck by the panic that he would never escape from this world of circular streams in the dark jungle. He resolved to turn to the right and to the left at each succeeding tributary and to avoid turning altogether the third time to insure that he did not go in a circle. Having no course to follow, a random one was as good as any other. If craziness of direction was the only way in which to make any progress, then he was willing to be crazy.

Then came the rainstorms that battered his head. And then came the swarms of insects that pinched his skin till he was screaming. But he survived these, too, though for days his body shivered in a fever and itched.

One day when the rains had stopped, though the forest still dripped wet, he caught a fish and ate it raw, spitting out the scales. He paddled away a little later with a burst of energy, and came to a jolting halt that threw him out of the canoe. It had hit a jagged submerged rock. He held on to the canoe but saw that water was pouring into it and that its rear end was already sinking. His attempt to climb into it only helped it to sink more quickly and without having the opportunity to save anything, he was obliged to jump out and reach for the nearest bank. He was left with nothing but the clothes in which he stood.

Now he left the rivers for the land, the dripping jungle thick around him. He had made himself a club from a fallen branch and walked carrying it on his shoulder. By now he was past having thoughts. A memory of his earlier life simply did not concern him. Nothing made any difference. It was all ridiculously irrelevant. What use was it for a termite crawling on the floor of the jungle to know it had been the emperor of China in an earlier life? Its destiny was only to crawl on. Nor did he question what it was in him that insisted that he go on, what kept him alert against dangers, what made him bear the terrors of the dark jungle. Why this anxiety not to die when the life he held on to was merely a haphazard circuit of an uninhabited wilderness?

And so he endured, not knowing why he must. There were days when he lay in a shelter he had made, unable to move, like an animal which must patiently sit out the duration of an illness. Then he would crawl out and continue to proceed on his hands and knees, fighting the loss of strength and the loss of spirit. To go hungry for long periods of time became his natural condition. But he taught himself to be patient, to sit for two or three days near the traps that he made in which to catch animals and birds. Snakes were the easiest to kill when he came to them, and he found that rattlesnakes provided him with a good meal. Whatever he ate, he chewed it raw, sucking at the blood that was still warm. It was as if by doing so he absorbed the very juices which gave life to the jungle itself.

He came out into the open one day and thought he was having hallucinations. The brightness hurt his eyes and he put a hand across his forehead and peered at the distance. If he had not gone completely mad and was not having delusions, then what he saw were tractors on a landscape that had been stripped of its vegetation. He walked toward them, staggering in the manner of a drunkard. He quickened his pace, his gait becoming more clumsy, and began to make sounds from his throat that came out as howls. The men driving the tractors had seen him and had stopped. Open-mouthed and howling,

226

his arms in the air, he made a rush toward them, fell to the ground, and passed out.

Afterward, when he was flown in a four-seater Cessna to a town in the eastern foothills of the Andes, he remembered that he had regained consciousness in a tent and found a middle-aged man sitting beside him. The man had talked to him kindly, giving him water and some food. His name was Carlos Antúnez, he had said. They were camped out beside a manganese mine of which he was part owner. Jason smiled weakly at him and opened his mouth to thank him; but he found that only a muffled grunt escaped his lips.

"No, don't try to speak," Antúnez said. "We'll fly you to a hospital this afternoon."

From the airfield in the town where they landed, he was taken in a car to a hospital. A doctor came with Antúnez to see him when he had been placed in a bed. The doctor examined him for some fifteen minutes and after giving some instructions to a nurse, went away with Antúnez.

Antúnez was assured by the doctor that the young man would be all right. All he needed was rest and nourishment. Antúnez went home and was greeted by his daughter, Madeleine, who expressed surprise that he had returned earlier from the mine than had been expected.

"I have an extraordinary story to tell you," he said, "and will tell it over dinner when your mother and Violeta can also hear it."

"What is it?" she asked eagerly.

"We found a young man who seems to have crossed all of Amazonas all by himself. It's incredible."

5

When three months had passed and Jason and Bob had not returned from the expedition which he had encouraged them to undertake, Kessel began to feel hopeful that his scheme to have his nephew perish in the wild interior had been successful. His wife, Heloise, was a month away from giving birth to their third child and it gave him great pleasure to stroke her belly and to contemplate at the same time how easily and without any wrongdoing the Carvalho plantation and cigar factory had become his empire. He wished he could receive some proof that Jason had indeed perished in the interior, and he went to the police. He could, showing the proper concern of a loving uncle who suffers from a keen anxiety for the missing nephew, implore the police to send out a description of Jason to the police stations in the interior to see if information on his whereabouts could not be found. When two weeks had passed and no information had been received, Kessel, looking downcast as he sat in the office of the chief of police, stated that he would offer a substantial reward to anyone who could help him find his nephew. "You see," he added, "my sister's memory is very dear to me and I love her only child as my own."

Just as in his younger days he had plunged into adventures without ever pausing to reflect on the morality of his actions, without considering, too, that some of the activists he served were only political thugs, but had done so because the adventures provided him with excitement, so now concerned only with selfish gain, he had no qualms at all about the evil intent of his real desire. And just as he had never stopped to think of the cost in human life that was caused by his association with the activists, so all that the living body of Jason represented in his mind was an obstacle in the way of his complete triumph. Only that existed in the world which gratified him or brought him wealth; he had no idea that anyone else could suffer pain. It had not occurred to him that in sending Jason away with the hope that he would perish he had also sent his young companion to the same fate; he had never reflected upon the evil that must exist in his mind, which thought nothing of committing a perfectly innocent person to a course that very probably led to his death.

Kessel had little doubt that the two young men must have got themselves into some absurd situation and been killed, and the passing of the weeks without their returning seemed a confirmation of their deaths. But then one day he was surprised to see a letter arrive from England addressed to Jason. He opened it and was even more surprised to see that it was from Bob. The Englishman thanked Jason for saving him from certain death and then proceeded for two pages to describe how he had remained near death for a full month in a London hospital; but he had made a very good recovery and though he was not going to play any rugger this season he was indeed fit enough to return to the university for the Christmas term. But, he added, why had Jason not returned to England and why had he not been in touch?

Kessel was puzzled and tried to imagine what might have happened. If Bob had fallen so seriously ill that he had had to be flown back to England, then what had become of Jason? He surely could not have wanted to go among the savage Indian tribes alone. But since he had not returned, the evidence pointed to his perishing in the interior. Kessel began to be convinced that Jason had died. He wrote Bob a letter in which he expressed his alarm that Jason's whereabouts could not be traced.

Instead of being glad that Bob had not unnecessarily perished to further his, Kessel's, schemes, he was at first distressed that there was a survivor to tell the story; but then he had the cheering thought that, in the event of Jason's death

229

being a certainty, Bob could always attest that there was no foul play, that the uncle had been sincere in his attachment to Jason, whom he had duly warned, in front of Bob, about the dangers before him. Bob would be a perfect witness to confirm that the sorrow to be seen on his face was genuine.

Heloise gave birth to a daughter, and Kessel was happy that she had had her wish. He was thrilled himself and already saw her grown into a great beauty whose long fingers played a Chopin sonata with graceful ease and whose eyes maddened a European prince. Her existence and the conviction in his mind that Jason was dead seemed to make his happiness complete.

But a new, more troubling event began to darken his days. For over four years, the South American revolutionaries whose gold he had carried in his Lincoln had not been able to find where he had disappeared to and they were eager to find him, for the gold had been worth two million dollars at the time of the Lincoln's vanishing. And after four years, they had finally tracked him down, having realized after all that time that instead of living obscurely under a new identity in some remote part of Paraguay, where and in other favored retreats of fugitives they had searched, he was living quite openly where they would have found him in a week had they not assumed that he was a cunning, clever person who would not be such a fool as not to go underground. He received a letter from one of the leaders who ran the group's financial operations from Bogotá who told him in blunt terms that the gold he had stolen was now worth six million dollars. He could return the gold or pay the money, or his life would not be worth living. Not knowing what to do, Kessel let several days pass. Leaving his office one day, he found the tires of his car had been slashed and a piece of paper had been stuck to the windshield. "The people cannot wait," the note said.

Kessel decided to alert the police. He said nothing about his past association with the revolutionaries but spoke instead of examples of international terrorism: how rich industrialists in Italy were kidnapped, how wealthy businessmen who brought prosperity to their countries were the victims of blackmail, and so on. It was clear that he was being made just such a victim, he argued; it was the duty of the police to protect him. His safety was important to the city, indeed to the country; at the very least if the Carvalho plantation and cigar factory collapsed because of the actions of terrorists, the economy of the state of Pernambuco would go down with it. The chief of police was sympathetic and assigned two men to guard his house and one to serve as Kessel's personal bodyguard.

For a time, Kessel lived content that he and his family were secure, and happily watched his baby daughter grow. She had his blue eyes and it was a great joy for him to see her smile. But the shadow of the underground movement would fall across his mind at night and he wondered if any amount of security could ever free his mind from the torment of fear. He began to get headaches in the middle of the day and to find it difficult to sleep at night. Nothing had happened for three weeks since the tires of his car had been slashed; the two policemen on duty outside his house were a reassuring presence; but he realized that even if he lived in a castle he would not be free of fear. He began to watch the servants suspiciously and one day peremptorily dismissed the cook when he had a stomach ache after a meal, for he could not take a chance with a cook who might be bribed to poison him. Heloise was grieved by the cook's dismissal since she had known the poor woman for many years before her marriage, for the cook had worked for her own family in Minas. But Kessel, who had told his wife nothing about the fear in which he lived, was adamant that she would have to go; instead of seeing the poor woman thrown in the streets, Heloise quietly gave her a sum of money and told her to return to the family in Minas. Heloise was a mild, unquestioning person who, through her upbringing and her own temperament, believed that her life consisted of doing her duty to her husband. Kessel was more than thirty years older than her, making her relationship with him more that of a dependent than a wife. Their conversations concerned themselves entirely with children; he told her nothing about his business, and it was assumed that when he sat in the library after dinner with his cigar and cognac, he was to be disturbed by no one, not even his wife. The cook's dismissal saddened her but she did not question her husband's decision.

Leaving his office with a headache early one afternoon, Kessel was about to open the door of his car but stopped. What if a bomb had been planted in it? It was one of the commonest traps, he suddenly realized standing frozen beside his car, to wire a detonating device so that the car exploded the moment the ignition was switched on—he had read of one such incident only the other day; it was in England, he remembered, a member of the government killed in his Jaguar, the work of the Irish. He went back to his office; the policeman who guarded him followed him thinking that he must have forgotten some papers. Kessel asked one of his employees to drive him home, he himself felt too ill to face the traffic. Kessel gave him the keys to his car and told him to go and start the engine, he would come down in a minute. He followed the employee like a detective tailing a suspect and stood concealed behind a column in the underground garage and watched the man enter the car and switch on the ignition. The car started quietly and Kessel, relieved that the drama had only been in his mind, that life continued to be uneventful, quickly walked to the car and entered the rear seat. The next three days, while he looked for a reliable chauffeur, he went to the office in a taxi.

But no amount of precautions would relieve him of his fear; instead, each attempt to improve the security around him only intensified the fear, for it made him think that there must be something else which he had overlooked which offered an open door to his tormentors. After a month, the chief of police took away the three men assigned to Kessel, arguing that the men were needed for other duties and suggesting that Kessel hire his own security guards. Kessel remonstrated at first but then realized that he could place a greater trust in men he had himself chosen, and hired six guards to watch his house around the clock and six more to watch his office.

Heloise went to the beach one morning with the two boys and the baby. It was something she did every weekday, believing it healthy for the children. As usual, the beach was crowded with hundreds of other mothers with their children. Scores of vendors, carrying soft drinks and ice cream, were busy walking about the crowd, making their daily living. Heloise took her children through the mass of people under parasols or in the sun and found a spot near the water where it was cooler and the sand was firm.

The older boy, who was three years old, set about shoveling wet sand with a toy spade with a view to erecting vast architectural masterpieces and his younger brother commenced with equal determination to undermine what the older one erected. It took the older some time to understand his continual failure, for his brother, with a gleeful smile on his face, was subtle in that he gave the impression that he was admiring the older brother's work while casually digging in a toe at the foot of the structure so that it gradually collapsed. The inevitable fight ensued. Heloise had to rise from where she lay under a parasol with the baby and separate the quarreling brothers. It only took a minute since the boys were no more than three meters away; she scarcely needed to take a step. It was sufficient to rise, make for the boys with an aggressive gesture, use a loud scolding voice, and the fraternal quarrel was at an end. But in that moment the baby disappeared.

She stared at the vacant spot under the parasol with horror and gave a scream. People sitting near her looked. She began to shout that someone had taken her baby, staring wildly all around her. All she could see was the crowd of people sitting or lying on the sand; the vendors walking around with the cylindrical aluminum containers of soft drinks hanging on straps from their necks, calling out the name of what they had to sell; games of soccer and volleyball in the distance. There was nothing unusual about the scene.

Some people had come up to Heloise, for she was screaming quite hysterically by now. The baby, the baby! Everyone was shouting that a baby had been stolen. People began to run around the beach and in a few minutes the whole length of the beach seemed to be echoing with *the baby, the baby!*

No one saw the very common sight of a large black woman dressed in great folds of white with a white turban on her head

233

and on the turban a basket walk away from the beach, in a slow, labored rhythm. There were others like her on the beach, walking in precisely the same manner, bringing down the basket from their heads whenever someone offered to buy one of their homemade pastries. The woman slowly climbed up the road from the beach, crossed it, and laboriously walked to a side street. There, she lowered the basket in front of the open window of a car inside which two men sat, and held out her hand for the money she had been promised.

Kessel rushed back to the house on receiving a phone call from a servant and heard the loud wails of his wife as he opened the door. Her normally pretty oval face looked terribly haggard. She had been tearing at her hair and her body with her nails in a feverish frenzy of hysteria. Seeing him enter, she screamed all the more wildly and in the torrent of words that followed the scream he distinguished words of abuse she was hurling at herself, for she was berating herself for having lost the child. He tried to calm her down but she cried all the more loudly. Finally, he called the doctor to come and give her a sedative, for she was in danger of doing serious injury to herself. His despair was great. He needed to think what to do in order to try and get his child back, but his ears were burning with the cries and screams of his wife. She would go insane if the baby were not returned quickly. But how? The kidnappers might not make a demand for days, or weeks; and though he knew what that demand would be, he could do nothing until it came except to make a report to the police.

After the doctor had given Heloise an injection and she had fallen asleep, Kessel went to the police station. He was furious with the chief of police for having taken away the officers who had guarded his house, and intended to give him a piece of his mind. But by the time he reached the chief's office, he realized that he had merely been wanting to find someone to abuse, for the kidnapping was hardly the consequence of the policemen no longer being outside his house. His own privately hired guards were and they had not been able to prevent the horror. It had really been Heloise's fault. But then he could not blame her either, for he could not expect her to remain a prisoner in the house with the children, especially now that the two boys were bursting with energy all day long. Also, apart from telling Heloise vaguely that she should be careful, he had not told her the danger with which they lived and had not even properly explained the presence of the guards outside the house. He could blame only himself, but this notion did not occur to him as yet; to himself, he had never committed a wrong in his life. All he could do at the police station was to make a report of the kidnapping and return home.

He closed the windows as if they had been responsible for letting happiness escape from his house. The elder boy was making a row and Kessel slapped him so hard that there was a trickle of blood at the boy's lips, and he looked at his father with eyes of such profound hatred before he yelled out in a great cry that Kessel, filled with a horror of what he had done, shut himself in the library with a bottle of cognac.

Heloise's cries roused him from his stupor. He found her writhing on the floor of the bedroom. He raised her up and was terrified to see the wild look in her eyes, and was even more terrified when he realized that the roar that filled the room was coming from his own open mouth which he found he could not immediately shut. Heloise froze for a moment, seeing him roar, and then opened her mouth and let out a piercing scream. The two held each other and fell on the bed and cried convulsively until their bodies could only heave with exhaustion and all that came out from their mouths were slow moans.

After some days, Kessel persuaded his wife to take the children and go to Minas, where she could stay with her family. He was finding it unbearable to live in a house in which his wife cried and the two little boys screamed all day long. When at the office, he wondered constantly if some new disaster had not taken place at home; and when at home, he suffered from looking at his wife's strained face, her swollen eyes and the mouth that could not stop quivering. She was helpless and emotionally weak, and it was no use trying to console her with a hopeful optimism. And watching her suffer so profoundly, his own pain intensified; hearing the sound of grief echo continually in his house, he could hardly think what he could do. The noise from the boys was a source of great vexation; if they were not running around the house unchecked, screaming and yelling, one of them would be crying at the top of his voice for some injustice inflicted upon him by the other.

The silence was blissfully sweet when he returned to the house after seeing them safely off on a plane. He sat down with a glass of cognac in the leather chair in the library and lit a cigar. For a few minutes it seemed as if all problems had been lifted from his mind and that he had at last found a wonderful tranquillity. The distant sound of the ocean and the slight wind knocking softly on the closed shutters were peaceful noises which encouraged the illusion that life was bearably pleasant and that it was only the occasional bad dream which made it seem otherwise. A second, and a third, glass of cognac made the illusion seem a reality.

A servant knocked timidly on the door and gave him a package which had arrived while he was at the airport. Kessel came out of his reverie of happiness. His hands trembled as he opened the package, feeling certain that it came from his tormentors. It contained a cassette. At last, he thought, the message had come. The kidnappers were stating their terms.

He rushed to the drawing room and snapped the cassette into the tape deck. The tape ran silently for several seconds and then the room filled with the noise of the loud and terrible crying of his baby daughter. A great roar of pain came from his mouth as he flicked a switch to cut the tape off. Then he ran the tape forward, stopping at several places to hear if the baby's crying did not cease and give way to a message from her captors. But at each point she was crying.

He thought that perhaps the message was on one of those parts of the tape which he had skipped. He was obliged to listen to the tape from beginning to end. He sat there, his head in his hands and tears flowing from his eyes, listening to his child crying for forty minutes; and when the tape ended, he found that the silence which he had obtained by sending his family away did not return. The child's crying continued in his ears.

He did not leave the house for the next ten days and lay slumped in a chair in the library for most of the time. He hardly ate anything but drank a bottle of cognac a day and smoked one cigar after another. Then another package arrived. He kept it on the table and stared at it wildly while swallowing a glassful of brandy. He opened the package and found that it contained a small box. He gave a loud howl and collapsed in his chair with the box in his hands. On a cushion of cotton in the box was one of his daughter's fingers.

When he could think again, he wondered why his tormentors did not make their demand instead of torturing him and mutilating his precious little girl. He had to stop drinking and do something. But he found himself pouring himself another glass of cognac. What did they want? he wondered. The gold or six million dollars. He did not have the gold. Was his business worth six million? Perhaps. But whom could he negotiate with? He suddenly had the idea that he should go to Bogotá. Several of the activists lived there and it was from there he had been sent on his mission in the Andes, and the only way he could contact them was by going there.

Having made the reservations on the phone, he drove alone to the airport on the next day. The large car park at the airport was quite full and he had to drive to an outer extremity of it to find a space; he intended to leave his car there for the few days that he was going to be away. A plane was coming down to land just when he left his car, and was flying low right above him, its engines making a frightful noise. He looked up, thinking vaguely that it was the plane he had to catch, and did not see, nor hear, the car that had come down fast through the narrow lane between parked cars. Two men ran out of it. They had followed him and when they saw that he was going to the airport, had concluded that he was attempting to escape and was probably about to disappear to Europe. Kessel was still looking up at the plane, the noise from whose engines had a louder, piercing pitch than half a moment before, when the two men came up to him. He scarcely saw them before both of them fired into his chest from a meter away.

6

Jason's condition improved rapidly at the hospital and after ten days he was discharged. He needed, the doctor told Carlos Antúnez, a long rest, a lot of wholesome food, and the tranquil atmosphere of a family where domestic happiness prevailed; for his sense of civilization, which had been rudely damaged by his experiences in the interior, could best be restored in the environment of a happy family life. And so, cleanly shaven and wearing a new set of clothes, Jason came to live with the Antúnez family and was given the very bedroom in which Violeta had convalesced from her ordeal nearly five years ago.

Violeta was in the living room with Madeleine and the two saw Jason come through the gate to the front garden and walk up to the front door, Madeleine's father with him. Having heard some of the young man's history, as narrated by Antúnez, the two girls already felt a great sympathy for him, but seeing the slim, tall figure they exchanged glances and were prepared to believe that even from a distance his light-blue eyes expressed a profound sadness. They met him with shy smiles when he was brought to the room by Antúnez.

Jason's presence had an overwhelming effect upon them, for one could not look at him without remembering that it was this being—whose slim and handsome body was made for that leisurely existence in large houses where one perhaps played croquet on the lawn or sat in wicker chairs among roses, drinking tea, and thought of poetical little phrases to speak to the girl who adored him with a great secret passion—that it was this person who had crossed the great wilderness all by himself.

"It is so good to be with real people again," he said. And looking at the citrus orchard through the french windows, he added, "You have quite a little paradise here."

Madeleine took that to imply that he had come through hell and said brightly, "In that case you must stay to enjoy its fruits."

"You won't find it easy to leave," Violeta said quickly, for she saw that Madeleine had realized even as she spoke that she herself was one of the fruits of this particular paradise and had turned her blushing face away. "For look at me, I came here five years ago and have not been able to leave."

She tried to make a joke of it in order to amuse Jason and to draw Madeleine back into the conversation. It was, indeed, true that she had been with the Antúnez family for five years but not because this little paradise, as Jason called it, had cast a spell on her; it was a charming place, of course, and she had never known such perfect happiness, but it was also true that she had tried to leave the place.

After she had been there for some three months, she decided to return to her parents' land; but Madeleine, being an only child, had become terribly attached to her and was reluctant to let her go so soon, having discovered in her the most wonderful companion she could wish for, and Madeleine had persuaded her that she should write a letter to her mother to tell her where she was and that she expected to return home shortly.

"I know, I'll phone her!" Violeta had said at first.

But Madeleine had argued, "No, don't phone! You won't be able to refuse if your mother tells you to return home immediately."

So she had written. When a month or so had passed without her receiving a reply, she thought she should return at once, for it was unlike her mother not to reply to a letter, but Madeleine would say, "Wait till tomorrow, perhaps there'll be a letter." After several more weeks when Violeta again expressed the necessity of her going, Madeleine came up with a new idea to keep her friend with her a little longer. Why didn't she write to her father? For Violeta had said that she thought, though she had witnessed nothing, that her father had become estranged from his wife, that she had suspected a simmering despair in him and had been saddened to see him look at his wife with a cold hatred. It could be that something awful had happened since she left and that her mother was no longer at the house. She took up Madeleine's suggestion and wrote to her father, and let another month pass while she waited for a reply. She realized then that the reason why she was so easily persuaded by Madeleine, each time she came up with a new excuse for her to stay on, was that she herself did not want to leave.

But one day she said to Madeleine, "I can't go on like this! Of course, I want to stay with you, but I've *got* to find out what's happened to my parents."

Madeleine watched her walk to the phone and noticed that her hand˙ shook when she picked up the receiver. "Poor Violeta!" she said, going up to her and touching her cheek. "Nothing can be wrong."

Violeta looked at her before dialing, her eyes moist. "There can be no trouble," Madeleine said.

The operator said there would be a half hour's wait before she could connect the number, she would ring back as soon as a line became available. Violeta put the receiver down with a sense of relief, but soon became tense with having to wait and wished there had been an immediate connection so that she could have got over her ordeal by now. Madeleine, noticing her agitation, talked of a young man who, she was certain, she said teasingly, had fallen in love with Violeta.

"Oh, but that's impossible," Violeta said, convinced that Madeleine was only trying to distract her.

"I have a gift for knowing these things," Madeleine asserted.

"You should have been a fortune-teller!"

"But seriously . . ." Madeleine began to offer an elaborate proof. Violeta was greatly amused by her friend, she had such a charming way of engaging one's heart!

Suddenly the phone rang. The two girls stared at each other. Even Madeleine suffered a moment of apprehension. Violeta picked up the receiver and whispered a soft "Hello."

240

She hardly understood what the operator said and was soon hearing the phone ring at the other end. She saw the living room at her parents' house, where the phone was on a table, just by the entrance. When it was picked up, a crazy sound invaded her ears; it took her a moment to realize she was listening to disco music. She heard a woman's voice shout, "Hello, who is it?" Violeta could not speak and stood frozen. The disco music seemed to be pounding fists at her ear. "Hello, hello," the voice shrieked. Madeleine, believing that her friend had become petrified with fear, took the receiver from her and immediately said into it, "Hello, Violeta is calling you." It was only after she had spoken that she heard the loud music, and she looked at Violeta, raising her eyebrows. Just then the phone at the other end went dead.

"Well, what on earth was that?" Madeleine said going to Violeta, who had collapsed in a chair.

"Some woman answered," Violeta said. "I don't understand it. I don't know what has happened. Oh God, what could have happened!"

Madeleine, seeing that the experience had been too much for Violeta and that she was on the verge of tears, said brightly, "A wrong number, that's what has happened."

She walked back to the phone and called the operator, asking her to check if the number had been dialed correctly. "I can try again if you like," the operator said.

"Do."

This time the operator got an immediate connection. Madeleine stared calmly at Violeta when the phone at the other end was picked up and she again heard the disco music and the woman's voice cry, "Hello!"

"Can I speak to Jorge Rojas, please?" Madeleine said sternly.

Violeta gave a start.

"Who are you, what do you want?" the woman seemed to be screaming over the din of the disco.

"I said, can I speak to Jorge Rojas?" Madeleine's voice was raised, commanding.

"Rojas?" the woman burst out laughing. "Who are you,"

241

she yelled in an ugly voice, "some old mistress of his? Find yourself a new lover, lady!"

And the phone was abruptly disconnected. Madeleine understood. During the moment in which she replaced the receiver she comprehended the larger sorrow that saturated her dear friend's family. Slowly, with kind eyes turned to Violeta, she walked toward her to console her, instinctively having the sense that she herself possessed the power to save Violeta from despair. It would take time, she knew, but that, to Madeleine, was a reason for joy, not concern, for she would be certain of having her friend to herself.

As the weeks passed, she managed to create a conviction in Violeta's mind that she was happier in her ignorance of whatever the reality was at her parents' house. It had all turned out well, for, really, was she not perfectly happy where she was? Madeleine was sure that a great happiness was in store for Violeta, because, she argued, life did not cause these accidents for nothing. Eager for sympathy, Violeta was easily persuaded, and when a letter finally came from her father she was less alarmed by it than she would have been had it arrived earlier; for, by the time it came, she was completely enveloped in Madeleine's magical kindness. The letter was brief, vague, and rather cold. Everyone was fine, he wrote. He was glad she was living in a town and hoped it offered her a varied society. She should get married, he added, much to her astonishment; he would, of course, make a handsome settlement on her, she need not worry about her future.

Violeta had been greatly perplexed and not a little hurt. It almost seemed that her father was rejecting her and telling her in so many words that she need not return. Why had he not said anything specific about her mother and about Rafael? And what made him think she expected to get married? She interpreted his offer of a handsome settlement as meaning that he would prefer to give her money rather than have her back at the house. It must be, she concluded, that he had a mistress living with him; that explained why her letter to her mother had never been answered. He must have torn it up. And that also explained why he made no mention of Rafael; he had probably settled him somewhere, too. Madeleine concurred with her conjectures and sympathized with her for the hurt she felt. But remarkably, after a few days of bitter thoughts about her father, she felt a marvelous sense of relief — as if she had been relieved from the burden of her own family and were now free to do as she pleased. Madeleine sensed this and was enormously happy: there was no danger that her friend would leave her now.

They loved each other deeply, but as sisters. There was no experience, no idea, however trivial, that they did not share. Madeleine had told Violeta all about the party she had gone to at Oyarzún's land, especially about the disgraceful behavior of a young man named Alberto who seemed madly in love with Oliva but whom she had succeeded, if only briefly, in attracting to herself. She described how they had embraced, lying under a tree, and she had thought she was going to fall in love; except that he had gone running back to Oliva at the first opportunity. He was horrid, she hated him! But when he had been with her, he had been so gentle, and if it weren't for that bitch Oliva, she was certain he would have fallen madly in love with her. She was never going to forget him.

She must really love Alberto, then, Violeta mocked, if she was never going to forget him! Madeleine was amused by the thought but said firmly that she hated men who were fickle. If he really loved Oliva, why had he not remained constant and accepted *her* inconstancy with fortitude, why should he have turned to Madeleine for consolation in his misery? It was disgraceful behavior, taking advantage of a young girl's emotions. She was not going to accept the role of the weak woman who passively suffers the silliest little insult from a man, she was going to show the silly fool what a woman could do.

She was so passionate in her resolve! Violeta remarked to her. And why not? she had cried with a seriousness Violeta found so charming. Men were such scoundrels. She described how Luis, whose particular partner she was supposed to have been, had abandoned her completely at the party and then felt sorry for himself that a conceited little girl called Diana, with *curly hair*, had given him the cold shoulder. What a silly fool he was, too!

Violeta loved to hear her friend talk with such passion. She was so shrewd and perceptive and so remarkably precocious, almost as if she and not Violeta were the one who was five years older. Her reasoning was always precise and her resolution to wreak vengeance on any man who slighted her, even absentmindedly, which might be thought by others to be a streak of feminine cruelty was in fact, Violeta thought, a perfect sense of justice. No one ought to be allowed to trifle with a girl's emotions, and Madeleine was quite right in her expressions of outrage. Besides, she looked so beautiful when she was incensed!

There was a circle of young people in the town who cultivated their friendship but who were treated by Madeleine much as a person from the city with a high opinion of his cosmopolitan culture treats provincials, with sublime condescension and, occasionally, crushing irony. By the time she was sixteen, she had acquired a contempt for young men who gawked at her and Violeta and for girls who gave the impression that now that they knew how to make up their faces and to keep their painted lips open in what they thought was an alluring smile they had nothing more to do in life but wait for the man who would marry them. She and Violeta were above such nonsense, for surely, she argued, life was more than the triviality of sexual attraction, and she astonished Violeta by exclaiming what a bore all ideas concerning sex were, including chastity! It was worthless to waste one's youth with longings which one was supposed to suppress until one achieved the holy state of matrimony, and she scandalized Violeta by adding, if all the young men of their acquaintance were not such buffoons she would long have done away with her own virginity, the importance of which, of course, had been invented by men, who were certainly the most possessive and selfish and conceited idiots nature had made the mistake of creating.

Violeta would laugh at such impassioned denunciations of men, but she enjoyed Madeleine's unconventional ideas and even found herself agreeing with them. It was not long before Jason arrived that Madeleine had come up with the most scandalous idea yet. They must break down the tyranny of accepted ideas concerning sex—oh, but promiscuity was not the answer! she added. That was only another kind of failure of the intelligence, one was no better than a dog if one went around sleeping with everyone. One ought to be more deliberate. Violeta should promise her that when she, Madeleine, ever found a man worthy of her bed that she, Violeta, would agree to sleep with him first. Violeta had let out a sharp exclamation at this proposal, but Madeleine had gone on to say that it would be a reciprocal agreement, for if it was Violeta who first found an acceptable partner then she, Madeleine, would be obliged to sleep with him first. "This way," Madeleine added, "we will guarantee that we will never be jealous of each other, for neither of us will need to desire the man the other loves, for we will be certain to have him before the other."

It was an oddly logical scheme, Violeta thought, but of course it was not the sort of thing that was ever likely to happen, for they were only two girls talking about the kinds of things, Violeta imagined, that girls usually talked about, making scandalous proposals at the expense of the opposite sex—and of course they had not considered at all what the young men who were supposed to submit to such a scheme would have to say. Madeleine, however, insisted that they make a solemn promise to each other and Violeta, seeing no objection to committing herself to something that was not likely to happen and since they were both laughing at the thought, said of course she promised, she would do anything for Madeleine.

Violeta remembered this promise some days after Jason had come to live in the house. His pale-blue eyes never seemed to lose their sadness, but he was beginning to gain color and enjoyed taking short strolls in the citrus orchard with the two girls. It was flattering to have such beautiful companions who were so solicitous for his health that they would not have walked half the length of the orchard when one or the other of them would say, "I think this is far enough, don't you think? You don't want to overexert yourself."

Madeleine, recently turned nineteen, possessed a peculiarly Latin beauty of which the stereotype in Jason's mind was to be summed up by the words "dark" and "mysterious." In fact, she had grown to be taller than was the average among women in the Andean countries and her vivid green eyes, which would have been remarkable even on a Scandinavian blond, were conspicuously foreign on her light-brown face. Her broad forehead and high cheekbones would have made her face appear square did the cheeks not curve in a clean line along the jaw to a perfectly rounded chin. Her black hair, parted at the middle, hung down below her shoulders to the small of her back, some of it falling at the front over her breasts, which had remained small, giving her an appearance which was both mature and girlish.

Violeta was slightly lighter in complexion and though a full-grown woman of twenty-four she seemed as youthful as her constant companion. Jason loved to see the dimples appear on her soft, fleshy cheeks when she smiled and was much taken by the fullness of her breasts and never failed to glance at her when she raised herself in her chair and leaned back, heaving her chest.

The two would sit for hours listening to Jason's accounts of his experiences, and in this they were two Desdemonas listening to Othello. Madeleine was fascinated to hear about the island on which only women lived and Jason, knowing by now that some of Madeleine's views were strongly feminist, teased her by saying, "Do you know what women do when they acquire power? They become slaves to the ideal they serve. They exile men from their society and yet go hunting for them, and when they find one they become contentious and conniving and enter into tortuous intrigues. Why? In order to possess the man! It is a perfect example of a society which, professing to be unique and based upon exclusive principles, is behaving precisely as any other society does. Is it not extraordinary that whatever their condition people always remain selfish and nasty?"

Madeleine was not perturbed by his remarks, for he maintained such a charming smile on his face when he talked with, she guessed, a deliberate attempt to provoke her—which, of course, was a well-known symptom: a man teased the girl he was attracted to by expressing ideas contrary to the ones she held. In any case, she was not going to challenge the point he had made about the women on the island, which had to do with baser instincts and not with the more abstract concept which concerned her, having to do with freedom of the self; not only *of* but also *from*, she would have insisted had there been a real dispute on the subject.

But Jason had begun to tell the story of his poor friend Cocoró who, escaping the massacre of his tribe, had had a princely time with the women. Jason did not know, of course, precisely how happily Cocoró had performed his not too unpleasant duties since he himself had been thrown into a pit, and he carefully refrained from mentioning the Indian girl whom he willingly obliged with the same service. He dwelt instead on the horror of his experience—but not because he calculated that an account of his terrible suffering would win him the admiration of his two ardent listeners but because *that* was, indeed, the experience which had made the strongest impression on him. Since leaving the jungle, he had never had a dream of making love to the Indian girl, but his nights were a torment of dreams of the horrors he had endured; and he needed to tell the worst that had happened to him—as if once his suffering existed in the imagination of another as a vivid reality then its pain somehow diminished in his own mind.

That the girls admired him for what he had endured was an incidental advantage of his telling them his story, but not an unwelcome one. He had never been so taken by female companionship; it seemed altogether superior to the rough and boisterous company of men. Simply to be able to glance at the sympathetic eyes of a girl looking at one with so much interest was extraordinarily thrilling. And at night, waking suddenly from a nightmare, it was a great comfort to see in his imagination Madeleine's wonderful eyes fixed on him or to

247

hear Violeta's sweet voice express a phrase of pity when he paused in an account of some harsh experience. He was convinced that the sympathy of the girls was instrumental in the sense of reality being restored to him; they made the world bearable, their eagerness to hear his story had possibly saved him from going insane, and it was a pleasure to wake up in the morning knowing that the three of them would soon be strolling together in the orchard. Only one thought cast a shadow across his mind: he could not love them both, though after four weeks at the house he began to believe he was equally in love with each.

Having lost all sense of time in the jungle, it had come as a shock to him that it was ten months since he had left home. He intended to write his uncle to tell him that he was well and to ask him to send him more money so that he could return, and he had also thought of writing to Bob's parents in England. But the days passed with his charming companions. Lunch was always a long affair, with Sylvia, Madeleine's mother, fussily attentive and Antúnez asking him questions about his journey. Unless he deliberately denied himself the pleasure of these people's company, there really never was a moment in which to sit down and write a letter.

"This is the only thing I've held on to at all times," he said to the girls one day, bringing out his wallet.

"What use was money with the Indians?" Violeta asked.

"No, not money," he said, bringing out the map that his uncle had given him. It had been folded a dozen times to fit the small wallet, and when he opened it out and placed it on a table he saw how it had torn at the creases; the plastic pocket in the wallet had preserved it, for it had withstood many drenchings both in rivers and during the many torrential downpours. "This is the map," he went on, "of the lost land that I set out in search of. It seems to be falling apart and going the way of the dream I had of discovering the land."

Madeleine, who had been staring at the map with some amazement, said, "Poor Jason, you or your uncle have been taken for a ride. Everyone knows where that land is!" And she

248

sat down with a look of disappointment on her face: the dénouement had been anticlimactic.

Both Jason and Violeta looked at her in astonishment, and she said casually, "That's Oyarzún's land. It's two hours' drive from here."

"Who on earth is Oyarzún?" Jason asked. "Sounds as though he were an Inca chief."

"Only insofar as he's at one with the Incas," Madeleine said, "being like them, dead. But in life he was of the tribe that destroyed the Incas, being a descendant of a sixteenth-century Spanish general. Ask Father, he knows the history of all the great families in this region."

"What is his land like?" Jason asked.

"Rather large, rather beautiful. But then this entire region is beautiful, don't you think? Oh, Oyarzún made it into a grand place, as close to anyone's crazy idea of a sensuous paradise a person can create on earth. It's quite an extraordinary place, actually."

"Tell me something," Jason said. "Does it have a lake?"

"Yes, of course, it has a lake. Any large estate will have at least a pond. And Oyarzún, doing everything on a grand scale, had a lake."

"I should like to see this land," Jason said.

"We could all go for a day," Madeleine said. "But the dear old man is dead and I'm not sure you'd like what you'll see there."

"What do you mean?"

She meant, but did not say it, that the young man, Alberto, who had slighted her five years ago, had married Oyarzún's spoiled daughter, the conceited Oliva. She understood herself well enough to know that any remark she might make about Oliva would be necessarily bitchy and did not as yet wish to talk in such a tone in front of Jason; and if he ever heard her talk about Alberto he would wonder whether she did not hate all men, and that was a risk she was not prepared to take. Therefore, she answered Jason's question with the vague words, "You will see that paradise is not necessarily a desirable habitat."

But she was curious to return to it herself, for she longed for an opportunity to be nasty to Alberto. The image of his face in those tender moments when she had embraced him would surface on her mind occasionally, but she would force it to sink right back. Now, seeing Jason's map, she had seen Alberto's face imprinted across it, and wondered if an opportunity had not presented itself for her to go and torment the man who had slighted her. She had not returned to the land since the party, and had only heard of the wedding when it was gossiped about in town. She imagined that after nearly five years, Alberto must be heartily sick of Oliva; she was perceptive enough to see at a glance what sort of woman Oliva was—self-centered, greedy for male admiration of her person, and bored with life in the country. And Madeleine was well aware of her own singular beauty and knew how to improve on nature to make herself into a vision which must surely madden Alberto and torment him with the thought that had he not been such a fool five years earlier *she* was the one he should infinitely have preferred.

7

Oliva had not wanted to go on a honeymoon; nor had she wanted a ceremonious wedding in a cathedral in the city with hundreds of guests. Rafael was surprised that she, who appeared so much to enjoy attention, insisted that all that was necessary for their marriage was for a priest to come to the house and get the business over with as quickly as possible. In the end, Rafael did not mind giving in to her, for he himself, after all, was interested only in her and not in making an impression on society. He tolerated, too, the fact that when the priest came on the appointed day, Oliva, who often wore a stunning gown for dinner with only Rafael and her father present, appeared in blue jeans and a T-shirt. He was slightly hurt, having dressed himself meticulously in a dark blue suit, a white shirt and a silk tie, but had said nothing after the hint of disapproval in his glance had made her say, "What's the use of a gown when you're going to make me take it off anyway?" And he had suppressed his anger—for she seemed determined to make even this briefest of ceremonies look ridiculous—when she insisted that the cook and a housemaid be the witnesses. She had stifled his attempt at remonstrance with, "They're most appropriate, don't you think, since your main interest is to have me served up as a dish."

When her father opened a bottle of champagne after the ceremony, she declined the glass Rafael brought to her, saying, "It's too early in the day for champagne, it'll only give me a headache." She drank a cup of coffee and suddenly got up and left, taking the Jeep to the stables, where she mounted her favorite horse and spent three hours riding across the fields and into the forest. She was so tired when she returned, she went straight to the suite of rooms on the third floor that had been prepared as their apartment and fell asleep.

In the meantime, Rafael felt more and more foolish in his dark blue suit as he sat drinking champagne with his father-in-law.

"I'm sorry," Oyarzún tried to console him. "Oliva has her moods sometimes. She tends to be contrary."

"This is the first I've noticed of it," Rafael said morosely. "Why should she have agreed to get married if she had such a contempt for the idea?"

Oyarzún sighed and blamed himself for having left Oliva to be too independent in recent years. Her behavior toward Rafael had been so blatantly insulting it had been embarrassing, even the priest had raised his eyebrows seeing her dressed the way she was. But Oyarzún said, "Women are unpredictable, I'm afraid." He wondered to himself if Oliva did not resent having been given away in exchange for an object.

He had some work to attend to—for he had expected that after the ceremony the couple would want to be together alone and so had not arranged to keep himself free for longer than normal courtesy deemed appropriate—and he left Rafael alone with the first of the three bottles of champagne still a quarter full. Feeling a mixture of rage and self-pity, Rafael sat looking as if he saw a ghost and drank all the champagne himself. There was nothing else for him to do. His head was beginning to spin and he rose and walking unsteadily with great difficulty on legs in which the bones seemed to have become rubber, he reached the elevator. In it he had the curious sensation that the elevator was going down when it was in fact going up. He staggered out of it and fell on his knees. He crawled across the carpet for a few meters and then, taking a deep breath, raised himself and somehow succeeded in entering the room. He took off the wretched suit and flung it to the floor and threw himself on the bed and passed out.

He was awakened some hours later by Oliva who demanded, "How can you insult me like this on my wedding day?"

He was so astonished by what he considered her arrogance that he found himself speechless.

"To drink yourself silly," she went on, "and then to crawl back to your former room as if you did not have a wife! It is scandalous!"

He raised himself and realized that it was not only her voice which was pounding on his brain but also that he suffered from a severe headache. "It never occurred to you," she was saying, "that I might be waiting for you in what is supposed to be the bridal chamber. Bridal chamber! That's some joke."

Rafael lifted himself out of the bed and suffered hearing her cruel ironical laughter. He staggered toward the bathroom and grinned sarcastically at himself in the mirror. He looked a sight with his hair standing up in two points, his eyes red and his face swollen. He still wore the tie on the white shirt but looked ridiculous since his legs were bare. Fumbling at the collar, he removed the tie and had a long struggle with the buttons of his shirt. Finally, he stood under the cold shower, finding the water refreshed his body. The water, hitting his head with its needle-points, had the advantage of drowning the voice that was continuing to taunt him, but he was suddenly surprised to hear it clearly and saw that she had stuck her head inside the curtain. "When you've finished sobering up," she was saying, "you might remember your duty to your family. Dinner's in forty-five minutes and it will be very distressing to your father-in-law if he does not see you escort your wife to the dining room."

When he came out of the shower, he took two aspirin and lay down. The idea that he should be left alone on his wedding day both amused and angered him. It was a relief not to be hearing Oliva's taunting voice, but at the same time it enraged him to think that instead of fulfilling his dreams of possessing her perfect body with those caresses and softly spoken words that he had rehearsed so often he was instead obliged to suffer her entirely perverse behavior. He had still to kiss her lips!

During the weeks of their engagement, she had studiously avoided being with him for any length of time, limiting their being together to a short walk in the evening or an hour in the library when, on several occasions, she contrived for her father also to be present. When he had attempted to direct her steps to a darker area of the garden, she, anticipating his move, would appear to have a sudden interest in pursuing a butterfly which happened to be fluttering in the opposite direction. In the library, she would take an armchair, making it impossible for him to sit next to her. When he had talked about his desire to have children, she had said, "All in good time." The answer was evasive if not meaningless; but in those days, Rafael—always having the vision before him of his approaching wedding and the pleasures that that would guarantee—had thought of Oliva's contrary behavior and inscrutable words as perfectly charming and natural. The poor girl was obviously in a state of agitation, he had thought, and if she gave him no opportunity for any sort of intimacy, surely it was because she had expectations of her own and was perhaps, at that moment, when she seemed absorbed in Catullus, actually having an elaborate fantasy of the first time they went to bed together! Seeing everything during those weeks from the point of view of the marital bliss to come, Rafael found it easy to interpret her refusals to talk about their future or to allow him a simple kiss as signs of her innocence. Her aloofness was, in his mind, proof of the intense intimacy to come; her most sullen mood was to him an expression of pure female instinct which was charged with a silent passion; and thus, the more she appeared to be cold the more he thought she possessed a desire for him which she was temporarily sup-pressing, and the more she frowned and turned her face away from him the more beautiful he thought she was. She would go away to the city for two or three days at a time, and he did not mind these absences for which she gave him no reason at all, thinking that they were an indication of her strong passion for him; she did not want to be always close to the man whom she desired, because that only increased the anguish of desire, and since she had apparently decided to save her virginity for the wedding night her absence from the sight of her lover was therefore perfectly understandable.

He rose from his bed half an hour later and dressed, putting on a T-shirt and a pair of cotton trousers. When he went down to the apartment to take his wife to dinner, he saw Oliva sitting on a stool in front of a dressing-table, brushing her blond hair. She wore only a bra and panty hose and high-heeled shoes. She put the brush down and walked toward the bed on which she had placed an orange-colored silk dress. This was the nearest he had come to seeing her without her clothes on, and being quite thrilled by what he saw, he said, "Hello, wife."

He walked toward where she stood beside the bed, about to pick up her dress but just then looking at him. He had never seen her appear so beautiful and the desire that welled in him made him want to forget what had happened, to forgive her her contrariness, and to enfold her immediately in his arms. When he put his hands on her bare shoulders, she took a step back, saying, "Your hands are sweating." And then looking at him critically, she added, "Please go and change into something proper. You're *not* going to go to dinner looking like a tramp."

Anger surged in him again, and he said, "I suppose it was all right for you to get married in blue jeans."

"Please," she said, her face expressing great patience, "I did not get married to spend my life having arguments and hearing criticism. We have to be down for dinner in a minute, and you can at least take off that ridiculous T-shirt. Wear a dark-colored one, it will at least distract attention from those shabby trousers."

Rafael sat gloomily at the table, finding it difficult to raise his head, for his gorgeous wife sat opposite him.

Oyarzún said: "I was looking at a newspaper I picked up in the city two days ago and came across a curious little item. You know that Lincoln you were so kind enough to make a present of to me?"

Rafael glanced sideways at Oyarzún and nodded his head.

"Well, what I read in the paper was," Oyarzún said, pausing to take a sip of wine, "that a gold-colored Lincoln Continental had disappeared. Could it be the same one, I wonder?"

255

"It is conceivable, but then it could be a coincidence," Rafael remarked.

"But the story is more complicated," Oyarzún said. "Apparently, the car belonged to some revolutionary who was taking two million dollars' worth of gold concealed in secret compartments in the car. It seems the gold was meant to finance several revolts all over South America."

"In that case," Rafael said, "it must be another car which looked the same. I can assure you that your Lincoln belonged to a man called Mark Kessel. He had white hair and was quite old, closer to sixty than fifty, I think, and you can be sure he was no revolutionary. He was a farmer with a wonderful knowledge of agricultural machinery."

"You *stole* his car?" Oliva accused him.

"He nearly got me killed," Rafael answered. "He abandoned me with his car. If I had not managed to bring the car up to the road again, it would have remained and rotted there."

"It would have been funny if it had been the car with the gold," Oyarzún said. "In that case I'd have thought the sculptor was some kind of a seer, making a golden sheep of a car which had a heart of real gold."

The conversation about the gold and the car took up much of the dinner and had the advantage of being a subject which was remote from one's personal preoccupations. Rafael was grateful to Oyarzún for his tact; obviously, he could not have been blind to his daughter's behavior and yet he pretended to have noticed nothing. He was a remarkably even-tempered man who had succeeded in creating a quietly efficient world around himself; nothing seemed to perturb him, he never needed to raise his voice, he did everything with discretion. He appeared particularly indifferent to any turbulent expressions of emotion, and whenever he sensed that his daughter was on the point of one such outburst he always remembered that he had to go somewhere else to attend to some urgent work. Once in a conversation alone with Rafael, he had said that he was a man who tolerated existence rather than one who enjoyed living. Rafael had asked how he who had created a paradise for himself could say such a thing. "That," he had said, "is only a vain attempt to create the conditions in which existence can be made bearable. Life really is not worth living and to be a human being has to be the worst possible condition to endure." Rafael had attributed Oyarzún's pessimism to the fact that his wife had deserted him and his son had died. But now he began to appreciate Oyarzún's refusal to take human concerns too seriously. One's emotions, one's desires—in short, all that had its source in human vanity—were merely aspects of a sense of self-importance and served as distractions, allowing one, while one longed for a particular pleasure or cried aloud how much one suffered, to forget the simple fact that existence was indeed unbearable.

And Rafael began to identify with Oyarzún's point of view the more he was tormented by Oliva's behavior. On the night of their wedding she wore silk pajamas and when Rafael, wearing only his underpants, came to bed, she accused him of being thoughtless. "I bought these pajamas especially for this night," she said, "and you haven't even noticed them!"

Trying to be patient and tolerant, he said, "They're beautiful, really beautiful. But Oliva, my dear wife, if I may say so, don't you think it would be more appropriate to dispense with clothes considering this is our wedding night?"

"You think of only one thing!"

"Oliva," he tried to remain patient and to keep the tone of irony out of his voice, "it is normal for married couples to make love to each other, especially on their wedding night."

"Well, go and fetch your condoms and the box of paper tissues."

"I don't have any condoms!" he said in a voice of complete despair.

"Well, then excuse me," she said, turning on her side, away from him. "There's no point in starting to make love when one is going to be left hanging in the end."

"We can have children, Oliva. I *want* children. Don't you?"

"Oh, how can you be so vulgar! I never want to have a child, I'm not a peasant!"

"You cannot mean that," he said calmly, though he was

257

beginning to be overwhelmed by despair.

"It's all right," she said ironically. "*I* will go to the city tomorrow and *I* will buy the pills that *I* will have to take. Please have the decency to switch off the light, I shall have to get up early in the morning in order to go to the city and return in one day."

The next night she again wore the silk pajamas but appeared to be more conciliatory when they were in bed. Rafael touched her cheek with his hand and said, "You have no idea how I missed you all day."

That was his attempt to keep the peace. Her hair, parted at the side and coming across her forehead in luxuriant blond waves, looked particularly lovely—she had spent an hour at her hairdresser's in the city—and he said, "Nor can you have an idea of how much I love you."

"Why do you have to make such old-fashioned speeches?" she asked, though not tauntingly for there was a pleasant smile on her face and she was passing a fingertip across his ribs.

"It's not a speech," he said gently, "only the truth."

"Oh, come on, no one talks such soppy rubbish nowadays!"

"What does one do nowadays?" he asked.

"One experiments with sex," she said, suddenly clasping his head and kissing him.

There was a look of amazement on his face when she took her lips away from his and pushed his head back a little. "Oh, Oliva!" he cried, putting his arms around her and reaching again for her lips.

"You are unbearably impatient," she said, pushing him back. "At least have the decency to undress me first and spare the silk from reeking of your sweat."

He swallowed the little insult and attempted to unbutton her pajama top.

"How can you be so *clumsy*!" she cried, pushing his hands away. "You don't undress a woman as though she were a child—you do it subtly, with caresses; imperceptibly, without the woman knowing it."

He tried to follow these instructions by passing a hand across her breast. She pushed him back, sat up and began to unbutton the garment herself, saying, "I said *caresses* and not that you should commence to play the violin!"

She took the pajama top off and threw it to the floor and then pulled off the trousers and throwing them away, too, lay back and heaved a great sigh. "Come, my silly little husband, you've a lot to learn."

He was about to lean toward her when she said, "And you can take those dirty underpants of yours off, they're stained yellow. Don't you know how to shake yourself clean?"

Rafael fell back to his side of the bed. He had lost all desire for her.

"It's just as well we don't try anything," she said. "The pills I got are new, I couldn't find the ones I used to take, and I have to wait after my period to be really safe."

Rafael had decided a moment before to shut out her voice from his ears. But what was she saying? The pills she *used to take*? He sat up and looked at her. The beautiful curving body with the beautiful breasts and the beautiful legs was as perfect as he had imagined it would be, but what new cruelty was she uttering now?

"What was that you said?" he asked. "About the pills."

"Only that the ones I bought today are new."

"You said something else, too."

"And that they're not the ones I used to take."

"I see," he said, looking at her legs and imagining them part to allow an erect penis to enter there. How many times, with how many men? He was about to groan but something distracted him. Her pubic hair was dark brown, nearly black, and he looked at her head.

"Your hair is not naturally blond," he remarked in a weak voice.

She pulled up the sheet, turned on her side, and fell asleep.

Rafael lay awake for a long time. Only his pride kept him from shedding the tears which had come to his eyes.

On his next visit to the city, Oyarzún stopped at the studio of the sculptor, Fernando Losada, who had crushed and hammered the Lincoln to create the beautiful golden sheep, in

259

order to pay him. The studio was on the outskirts of the city. Losada had bought a small farm and converted a derelict old barn into a studio and renovated a rambling old house to make a charming residence for himself and his Indian wife. Large sculptures in materials that ranged from rosy marble to rusting iron were scattered about the grounds: gigantic human forms in stone, a puzzling geometry in steel, and here and there an old refrigerator or an iron stove smashed into a startling shape. Losada was a popular figure in the country, almost a national monument himself, for, now in his late fifties, his work had won him an international reputation.,

Oyarzún parked his car outside the studio and was first struck by an unusual silence. He had never come there and not at once heard the sound of hammering. The studio was closed and Oyarzún drove to the house. A servant there informed Oyarzún that Losada had been taken to the hospital some ten days before. There had been some terrible accident. The servant seemed not to know the details. Losada's wife was obviously with him at the hospital? No, the servant answered, she had been there at the start but then she had gone away to her parents; he was quite certain she had gone to stay with her parents.

Oyarzún drove to the hospital and found Losada propped up in bed, a bandage over his forehead, and his right arm in plaster. Before going to Losada's room, Oyarzún had been able to have a word with the doctor. It had not been an accident, as the servant had said. Losada had been beaten up by a couple of men. They had broken his right arm ("But thank God," the doctor said, "his hand was not even scratched") and then knocked him unconscious with a piece of steel that was on the studio floor. He was going to be all right, but Oyarzún should not spend more than five minutes with him.

Losada smiled on seeing him, and Oyarzún said, "The doctor told me what happened. I'm sorry."

"It was that car you sent," Losada said, "that Lincoln. I had great fun working on that, but it brought me bad luck."

"What do you mean?"

"I think there was a big misunderstanding," Losada said. "The men wanted to know where the Lincoln was. I told them I had no idea, I was a sculptor and not a used-car dealer. How on earth they traced the car to me, I don't know, but I wasn't going to help them trace it back to you. They said it had been stolen. I told them they looked like a couple of thieves themselves. That's when they went to work on me."

He grimaced and Oyarzún said, "I'm sorry to hear all this. There must be a mistake. The Lincoln I gave you to work on belonged to a farmer. It's a long story but I'm certain it's not the car these men are looking for."

"Well, you must be careful," Losada said. He himself was going to hire a guard, he wasn't going to take any chances with such thugs around. He had sent his wife to be with her parents while he was recovering in the hospital. No use having the worry, on top of everything else, of having her alone in the house. Oyarzún insisted on paying his hospital bills and doubling his original fee by way of compensation.

"No, you don't need to do that," Losada said. "We're old friends. Besides, I have hospital insurance."

The two men who had attacked Losada had deliberately beaten him only to the extent that would make it necessary for him to spend some time in the hospital; for, they had calculated, if Losada would not give the information they needed, then among the people who visited him in the hospital there would likely be one who could. Consequently, with the help of two nurses and an orderly, they kept track of whoever entered Losada's room. And thus Oyarzún became one of the people who began to be followed discreetly until his identity and place of residence had been established.

Oliva often spent three or four days in the city, having begun to do so a month or so after her marriage. She had taken an apartment and kept a maid there. She would give impromptu parties, calling up all the friends she had, and herself began rumors that brought chaos to the marriages of three men who, as everyone was whispering, were Oliva's lovers. In fact, the lovers she had were all bachelors, and of these there were four

261

in two months. The price of going to bed with her, as these four young men discovered, was to be banished from her presence thereafter: she was reversing male hegemony in sexual roles— it was she who was making the conquests, and the men who were embraced with passionate ardor for one night were then obliged to remain figures of contempt. Nor did they have the opportunity to boast of their brief success, for she broadcast news of their impotence or inadequacy even before they realized they had been permanently dismissed from her presence. Seeing Rafael on returning from a visit to the city, she congratulated herself on having as a husband the most pitiable of men, one so enslaved to her that he swallowed any insult she hurled at him; it pleased her to have in him a completely despicable figure, one who represented in a singularly transparent manner all the qualities in men which she held in contempt.

Rafael began to comprehend the nature of her absences. He had no proof, of course, but when he had succeeded in sleeping with her only twice after being married to her for three months (both of them were drunk on the two occasions; he because he was intensely miserable, she because she had discovered that a man she was scheming to entice had been caught selling cocaine), Rafael began to sense what she must be up to. He could not, however, understand why she behaved thus. And his own two successes with her, far from making him elated, filled him with profound melancholy; he had derived no plea- sure but had merely emptied himself and ended up over- whelmed by self-disgust.

He felt trapped in evil and wondered if it were not a punishment for having abandoned, even unwittingly, his father's land. He could, of course, follow Oliva to the city to see exactly what she did there; also, he could return to his father's land and suffer whatever indignity and humiliation he had to suffer for having made an unfortunate marriage. But he saw no good coming from either course. He could not abandon the fate he had embraced. This was hardly a sound reason, he knew; for in truth it was only an excuse. The real fact was that he had lost his will. And he understood now what Oyarzún had meant when he had said that existence was unbearable and that life was not worth living.

Unlike his daughter, Oyarzún usually returned from the city on the same day that he went, the only exceptions being when Oliva had a weekend party, and she had given none since her marriage. On one occasion, three days passed and Oyarzún had not returned from a visit to the city. Oliva was at home, doing her best to be disagreeable, and Rafael busied himself in strenuous activity on the land in order to keep at a distance from her. Then a car arrived.

Two men in crumpled suits came out and solemnly walked to the house. They were police officers in plainclothes, they said. It was their unfortunate duty . . . one of them muttered. These are violent times . . . the other attempted a laborious preface. But the information they had to convey was simple. Oyarzún, coming out of the bank the previous day after drawing a considerable sum of money, had been shot and killed. They were terribly sorry, they said to Oliva who, Rafael observed, received the news with perfect composure. The assassins—there were two of them—were obviously urban guerrillas, the officers were saying. They had found a piece of paper in Oyarzún's pocket with an address scribbled on it. It was one of the places where the revolutionaries were to be found—the police knew perfectly well of all their movements but could never get the evidence on which to act. It was likely that he had either gone there earlier in the day or on the day before or that he had intended to go there after drawing the money. Something must have transpired or was about to transpire. Unless they caught the two assassins or found some witnesses who knew anything, it would be impossible to tell the motive for the murder. They were terribly sorry, there was not much they had to go on. The body was in the city morgue. They had assumed that she would wish to bury him in the city.

Some months later, Oliva, driving to the city, had the notion to stop at Losada's studio. He was surprised and pleased to see her, remembering her from the time he had twice visited her father's land—though, of course, she had to tell him who she was before the memory came to him. He was sorry about her father's tragic . . . He had been such a wonderful . . . Poor Losada was full of incomplete sentiments. And then he told her what he knew, beginning with the attack on his own person. The good Oyarzún had come to see him in the hospital, he had warned him . . . But you could tell the honest truth to these terrorists and they shot you for it because that was not what they wanted to hear. He knew from three other people who had visited him in the hospital that they had been trailed by the terrorists. Oyarzún must have been, too, there could be no doubt about it. There must have been some argument. Her father was a man of independent views, really a great noble human being. He must have answered the terrorists with contempt. Losada shrugged his shoulders to indicate that was how the world was, full of scoundrels who had no respect for traditional values and did as they pleased.

Oliva began to go to the city every week, taking more of her things each time. She had no desire to live on the land anymore, having remained there all these years for the sake of her father. It was all hers but she hated it; it had been responsible for depriving her of her mother for the last seven years, and now she was certain, without having any reason, that her father had been killed by terrorists precisely because he was a great landowner and therefore a symbol to be despised by those born to poverty who easily turn their envy to an ideology of political hatred. She desperately needed to get away from it, she could not even think while she was in the country! When she had accumulated enough of her things in the city, she cabled her mother in Paris telling her that she was arriving the following week.

She expected that in due course a lawyer would work out some kind of a release from her wretched marriage, find a buyer for the land, and establish the grounds for a new life for her. For the present, her only desire was to get away and not have to think about anything. All she had known so far had been the torment of a false love—that despicable Matta!—and an existence in which she hated herself even as she perpetrated cruelties on men, knowing while she did so that her behavior was contemptible and that, at the same time, it was the only thing she was capable of doing. If Rafael thought he was suffering, little did the poor idiot know that *she* had been going through hell. She could think now only of the flight across the Atlantic that would deliver her from the blue sky to a new life: as if the flight could also deliver her from the evil she had become engaged in!

8

Madeleine drove the Fiat with considerable flair. Jason was impressed by her judgment in cornering; she had a thrilling way of changing down, always using the correct gear, and precisely steering the car in a faultless line through the curves. The road to Oyarzún's land—once they had come to it after climbing up a mountain and then coming down into another valley—offered breathtaking views and exhilarating driving.

They were alone together, for Violeta had not come. When the three of them had made plans to go to Oyarzún's so that Jason could see that the lost land in search of which he had almost lost his life was only an efficiently run estate, Madeleine's mother, Sylvia, had fallen ill. It was only a slight flu and she really did not need to be looked after, but Violeta had insisted on staying with her. Sylvia, she argued, could not run the household from her bed; and if, God forbid, she got worse, then it would be awful if there was no one there to take care of her. She felt it was her duty to stay. In fact, Sylvia's illness was a convenient excuse for Violeta not to go.

She and Madeleine had been together with Jason for some months now, and it was clear to her that the young man was attracted to both of them. She had wondered to herself if she had fallen in love with him, but could not be certain; and although she had not asked Madeleine what her feelings were, she was sure that Madeleine, too, must experience a mixture of certainty and doubt of being in love with him. Of this there could be no doubt, however: they were both enormously attached to the young man, and should he but give a hint of his preference the matter would be settled. She knew that she

266

would willingly transform the love she felt to a sisterly affection should Jason prefer Madeleine and was convinced that Madeleine would do the same should he prefer herself. Therefore, the opportunity to let Jason enjoy the company of only one of them for several days would be a good test. And she could be certain that Madeleine would never allow him to seduce her, for Madeleine was a person who adhered absolutely to her principles and promises: there was a bond between them—no man could make love to either of them unless he made love to the other first. So, rather than be sorry not to be going on the jaunt, Violeta was glad to have manipulated their going alone, for she had created the opportunity to bring this idyllic and platonic triangular affair down to a practical, carnal level.

Madeleine told Jason more about Oyarzún as she drove. His death had been quite a mystery. It had led to a number of terrorists being arrested, but no real facts had come to light. How could they, she asked, when the people they usually managed to arrest were little more than hired hands? Or youths who sold themselves to a cause because there was nothing else for them to do? They, the youths, had no idea what the real revolutionaries were plotting, only that this way they could have a life. Poor Oyarzún! He had built such a perfect life for himself. Jason would see, she said, glancing brightly at him as she accelerated down a straight stretch, what a wonderful order he had created on his land, as perfect an example of successful and benevolent feudalism as he would wish to see.

It was not entirely so when they arrived at the land. There was only one servant at the house. The furniture in the living room had been covered with sheets which were themselves covered with dust. There were cobwebs in the corners of the dining room. Magazines from five years before lay scattered on a table in the library, their pages gone yellow and brittle. Dust rose from the carpet in the hall as they stepped on it. They went up to the gallery. The paint on some of the pictures had cracked and the floor had not been swept for years. Madeleine was appalled and wondered what all this neglect meant.

When they went down, Rafael had just come in for lunch. Hearing his voice in the dining room, Madeleine hurried to it and entering said, "Why, there you are, Alberto!"

Alberto? he wondered, but the name triggered off a recollection in his memory and although she was no longer the frail girl he had embraced, he remembered her. He was about to tell her that he was really called Rafael but decided that it would be too tedious to go into an explanation which would involve describing the whims and lunacies of Oliva.

"Remember me," she asked, "Madeleine?"

"Yes, of course," he said, rising to greet her, "how could I forget?"

That was gallant of him, she thought, smiling at him. He looked sad; his cheeks had hollowed somewhat and his eyes appeared to be melancholy; but there seemed to be a strength in him, as though some power resided inside him and surfaced in his slow, deliberate gestures. Whatever he had suffered, the passage of years, bringing him to maturity, certainly made him look more striking.

"Oh," she said, "meet my friend Jason." And while the two men were shaking hands, she went on, "Alberto, you'll never guess that Jason crossed Amazonas all by himself. And do you know why? In order to find *this* land!"

Rafael invited them to join him for lunch during which Madeleine prompted Jason to tell his amazing story. Rafael was impressed by the young man's adventures and, with Madeleine's cheerful voice, which interpolated comments creating such a pleasant sound, reminding him how much he had missed a female voice in the house, he began to enjoy the company of his visitors. They must stay. Jason should make a good study of the lost land now that he had found it!

"But, Alberto, what has happened to this place?" Madeleine asked. "Where is . . . ?"

"Oliva?"

Madeleine nodded.

"Let's go to the garden," Rafael said. "It's cleaner there, and cooler too with the breeze coming over the lake."

They sat under a tree on the lawn where the servant brought

268

them coffee. "I'm sorry," Rafael said, "that you had to find the house in such a mess. You see, I've had no reason to keep it up. One gets dispirited living alone and suffers from a terrible loss of will. Sometimes I'm surprised that I don't let the entire estate run to seed. Only the fact that the workers would otherwise starve to death keeps me going."

He told them sketchily, and with no show of emotion, his story. The place had cast a spell on him the first day he arrived. He had not perceived anything clearly. The beauty, even Oliva's beauty, had been false, drawing him blindly into a world of self-deception. He had been such a fool, marrying her!

Madeleine could not help feeling an inner satisfaction on hearing him abuse Oliva. His first real happiness, he was saying, was when he discovered that she had taken off for Paris, deserting him just as her mother had deserted her father. At least the continuing earthquake that attended her presence had finally stopped sending tremors through his body, and he could step out on the earth with some confidence that it was not going to open before him.

Madeleine was filled with pity as he told his wretched story. "You simply cannot go on like this," she announced when he had finished.

"What can I do? It takes all my strength just to go through the motions of running the land."

"First of all, we shall make the house habitable," she declared. "You take Jason on a tour of the land. Send me three servants and we'll see what we can do."

Determined to eliminate the filth that covered everything in the house, she took the three servants marching through the rooms, uttering a stream of orders as she walked. Those curtains must be pulled down and washed. The windows must be cleaned. All the brass and silver things must be taken down and polished. The rugs must be taken out and dusted. The floors must be mopped with wet cloths and then waxed. Having given the orders she herself joined the servants in the work, beginning with the task of cleaning the cobwebs in the dining room and then polishing the furniture.

Meanwhile, Jason was enchanted by what he saw as Rafael drove him to different parts of the land. Seeing a group of Indians making pottery in a hut rekindled Jason's interest in anthropology, and he thought in passing that if he stayed at the place for any length of time he could possibly do an interesting study of this group of civilized Indians who worked at an occupation exactly as their primitive counterparts did. The Indians looked wearily at the stranger, and Jason suddenly had the idea of uttering a phrase in the language he had used in the interior. Astonished at what they heard, the Indians smiled broadly, and Jason resolved to come back to them, realizing that in spite of everything he was quite homesick for their sort of company. It was an odd phenomenon, he told Rafael as they proceeded on their tour.

The lake fascinated Jason, reminding him of the legend on the map his uncle had given him. He wondered what the history of this land was. If it existed on rare old maps and had acquired a myth about it, then surely something must have existed here which made explorers wish to discover it. Or was it only a coincidence that a land existed whose features were precisely those that the memory of the human race had dreamed of as paradise? Or could a poetry have preserved it in a seemingly incredible imagery and, as with Troy, it took a prosaic persistence to discover it, proving a myth to be a reality? If he were an archaeologist, he would be interested in looking deeper into this land.

Keats, on first looking into Chapman's Homer, could not have felt more wonder than Jason did when he stood in the courtyard on the island and found himself staring at the golden sheep. It almost frightened him that the coincidences he had been thinking about should include this kind of particular detail. Rafael told him how the golden sheep came to be fashioned, and Jason thought of the curious ways in which chance worked; the sculptor could as easily have decided to make a bullock or anything else with the materials with which he worked. What impulse was it that led him to make the very thing that a legend of some centuries earlier had stated was to be found in the heart of the lake?

270

By the time they returned to the house, Madeleine had transformed the living room from its earlier dust and gloom to a spacious room brightly lit from the just-cleaned windows with the curtains taken away for washing. The little mahogany tables were polished and had vases of freshly cut flowers on them. Rafael was filled with pleasure when he saw her, in an elegant dark-blue dress into which she had changed from the jeans in which she had traveled, for she presented a welcoming sight, smiling and offering to bring the men gin and tonic, a kind of welcome he had never had from Oliva. Madeleine was thoughtful and precise; most of all, she did not concern herself exclusively with her own vanity. She was observant, saw what needed to be done, and went ahead and did it. And while the two men sat drinking and talking, she went to the kitchen. Normally, Rafael would have had the leftovers from the lunch, but since there had been unexpected visitors, there was nothing that was left over, and the cook had only a chicken in her larder. When she suggested that she could broil it, Madeleine looked at her severely and said that there was to be no more insipid cooking in the house. "Where are the spices and the herbs?" she asked.

The cook brought out a number of jars, and Madeleine found that they were all crawling with what looked like worms.

"Throw all this out," she said, tightening each jar after examining it. "Make a list of what you throw out and get a new supply next time someone goes to the city."

The cook said that she did not know how to write.

"All right," Madeleine said impatiently, "I'll see to it. But throw all this out!"

All that was left was salt and black pepper. "You should have a little herb garden growing outside," Madeleine told the cook. "It's the easiest thing in the world, and you can do wonderful things with herbs."

The cook felt thoroughly humiliated and Madeleine said, "Well, let's see what we can do. Chop up an onion and fry it, will you? And then cut up the chicken and rub it with garlic."

While the cook did so, Madeleine found where the wine was

271

kept. She took out a bottle and uncorked it. It happened to be a 1947 Volnay Santenots, one of the late Oyarzún's stock of rare wines, but Madeleine, having no idea of its quality, simply poured half the bottle over the chicken pieces once they had turned golden in the chopped, frying onion. She added the salt and some freshly ground black pepper, and, covering the pan, said to the cook, "Let that simmer for forty minutes. We'll make do with that for today, but you'll have to do better from tomorrow. I'll tell the young master to send for a fresh supply of spices first thing in the morning and to get his gardener to prepare an area for a herb garden."

She then instructed the cook to make some rice and a dish of whatever vegetable she had. When she had left, the cook thought that if only the house had a mistress like her . . . but she left the idea at that, realizing that her own life under such a mistress would be unbearable. She sniffed at the wine that remained in the bottle and put the cork back on it, deciding to take the bottle to her husband when she went home.

When they had dinner, Rafael declared that he had not eaten so well in five years. He had more memorable meals during the next six days and found a pleasure, too, in entering rooms which he had not gone into for years. For Madeleine spent her days getting the servants to clean more of the rooms, doing as much work herself as any of the servants did, and organizing the meals in the kitchen. The servants admired her for her tremendous energy and for her capacity to get things done quickly but hoped that she would not take up permanent residence at the house; and Rafael began to understand what life could be like if he only had a companion like Madeleine to share it with him.

Jason spent his days with the Indian potters, having convinced himself that he needed to study them. He found it intriguing that the Indians worked with their hands without thinking of what they were doing, for it was the memory of their race which dictated the shapes they made; and yet they appeared to have wiped out other aspects of the same memory from the rest of their existence. From this observation he formulated a hypothesis: that any human tribe, however advanced, was governed by a buried memory of its past; even when, in its advanced civilized state, it had the analytical capacity to determine why it did what it did, it was still engaged in the performance of unaccountable feats. The fact that a rational society believed that it knew what it did, and why, was in itself an item of knowledge which depended upon nearly a mystical belief, for the conviction of knowing was itself a trick nature played on the mind. It was an infinitesimally fractional part of the larger deception one was continually involved in: one's certainties came from a psychological necessity for self-esteem. Jason was impressed by the way his mind was working toward a paradox of universal application, and he was so thrilled to be making an intellectual discovery that he was determined to concentrate on the Indian potters to obtain the evidence he sought.

Rafael began to find reasons to keep returning to the house several times during the day and on the fourth day of Madeleine's presence in it he even fell ill. Only a slight fever which debilitated him, he said when she expressed her concern, it was just a matter of lying in bed for a day and taking it easy. But she insisted that, living as he was on the edge of the vast jungle, not even the slightest fever should be taken for granted, for it was well known that fatal illness began in such a fashion, appearing at first to be nothing more than a passing headache. She brought him aspirins, made him a broth for his lunch, sat beside him looking at him with what seemed to be the kindest eyes he had ever seen.

Her concern was genuine, although she could never forget that this was the man who had slighted her five years before. He would try to sleep while she sat watching him, but continued to see her with his eyes closed. She was such a perfect young woman, so practical and so kind, and so extraordinarily beautiful! Not like that viper he had married. And when he opened his eyes, her wonderful green eyes would be staring at him in pity and tenderness, almost as though she loved him! He put out a hand to hold hers, saying, "See how cold my hand is, the fever has surely passed." And it thrilled him when she did not let go of his hand.

He remained in bed a second day and when she sat with him in the midmorning, he said, "I'm sorry."

"What for?"

"I was blind five years ago. If I could have seen you then as I see you now . . . "

"How do you see me now?"

"You are the most beautiful and perfect woman I've ever seen."

"Perhaps I should get you some more broth," she said. "Your illness has made you weak."

"I'm better," he said, sitting up in bed. "I should be up by this afternoon, at least by dinnertime. But believe me, Madeleine, if I had not been so stupid I would never have desired anyone but you."

"Desired?"

"Forgive me," he said. "But my life has been quite without meaning the last few years. And then you came a few days ago and I realized what I had lost. The torment of my life is not that I married Oliva but that I did not marry you."

"Alberto, I don't believe you know what you're talking about."

He was again amused by his recollection of that name but said nothing.

Later that afternoon, he felt strong enough to rise from his bed and to spend a couple of hours with her in the garden. The next day he was fully recovered but had no desire to go to work, telling her that he was going to take a holiday as long as she was on the land, adding that he hoped she would stay a long time. They went rowing on the lake in the morning and horseback riding in the early evening, and were together at the house for much of the day. When she went to the kitchen to tell the cook what to make for lunch, he went there, too, to choose the wine; when she wanted to have a siesta in the afternoon, he suggested hammocks in the garden so that he could watch her as she slept.

"Did you deliberately hang my hammock from this tree?" she asked.

"I wasn't sure you remembered," he said.

It was the tree on the lawn between the house and the lake where they had embraced, and she said, "There are some things I never forget."

"When we were rowing on the lake this morning," he said, "did you think—"

"Yes, I did."

The next day she wanted him to accompany her to the cottage where she had stayed during the party five years ago. She remembered how charming it was with the water in the stream behind the bedroom window making a lovely sound. It had a small, narrow hall, a sitting room with rustic furniture, and the comfortable little bedroom.

"The dust!" she cried, entering the cottage. "I'll have to clean my poor little cottage, you can't let it go like this."

"This place was created at a happier time," Rafael said, "when Oyarzún had expectations of a large family. He was a very bitter man during the short time I knew him."

"Ah, my poor bed!" Madeleine made a dramatic gesture when she entered the bedroom. "Alberto, you have no idea how much I thought of you as I lay on that bed in the darkness."

He touched her arm. "Did you really?"

She turned round and raised a hand to his shoulder. "You have no idea how much," she repeated. "I thought I was falling in love."

He was just about to embrace her, but she turned away and walked toward the window, saying, "Imagine that! Falling in love. I was only fourteen then!"

There was a climbing rose tree outside the window and rosebushes growing wild in the area before the stream. "This cottage must have been made for lovers," Madeleine said, coming away from the window. "Pity it's gotten run down. We must clean it. Who knows," she added, glancing brightly at Rafael, "what ghosts of lovers are longing to return to this bed?"

At dinner that evening, Jason talked excitedly about the Indian potters, having brought with him a jar one of them had made especially for him. "It's incredible," Jason was saying, "the woman who made this was born on this land and yet she makes a jar exactly like the ones I saw in a village on the Rio Napo."

He went on to talk animatedly about his theory of submerged instinct patterns. Did they not think that was a clever phrase? Rafael and Madeleine listened sympathetically and occasionally made a comment or asked a question but they were not listening to him seriously. Their emotions were in a state of delicious turbulence. After sending a servant to clean the cottage, they had gone rowing on the lake and Madeleine had steered the boat into the green cave where the trees arched over from the bank to the water. They had gone up the bank on the same spot where they had five years earlier.

"You don't forget anything, do you?" he asked laughing.

"It was you who rowed the boat," she said smiling brightly at him. "You are the sentimentalist."

"No," he said sadly. "I'm merely blind."

She held his arms and looked concernedly into his eyes. "Don't say that," she said. "One cannot spend one's life regretting the past."

He embraced her then, hugging her tightly, and would have sobbed had her lips not closed upon his.

What if they *had* fallen in love five years ago? she asked. She was only fourteen then and no one would have taken her seriously. Her parents would certainly have counseled her to wait. Everyone had a crush on the first handsome man they met when they were that young. But she had been so mature even then, he recalled, and he foolish. He had never known what love was. She had given him more love with one kiss than he had ever experienced before or since. That scorpion Oliva had only known how to sting him.

After dinner, Jason went to the library to put his notes together and to start drafting his article on the potters. Madeleine had been thinking about love during much of the dinner and had walked out to the lawn to stroll under the bright stars. No, she was convinced, she had not fallen in love. What was this feeling then? she wondered. She had been drawn to him at first because of the enormous pity she felt for him, and then her emotion had been one of sympathy, an affectionate sort of admiration for the man who could bear his suffering so stoically and continue to do his duty to the people on the land. She knew that he saw her as the alternative that would have brought him happiness had he not made the mistake of choosing the wrong road five years ago. The happiness he now experienced with her was in fact a subtle form of torment, and there was something within her which was eager to heighten that torment. She had drawn him to her arms and by offering him her lips she had given him a taste of the happiness he could have had; but was she sure it was only that? Did she not want to give him more? For she sensed a deeper desire within her which was more than the game-playing she had been engaged in so far.

She heard his footsteps. He had followed her out to the lawn. She walked back toward him and held his hand. Neither of them spoke. They began to walk across the lawn, under the trees, to the grassy bank just above where the water lapped in a gentle waving motion. They sat down and leaned back, looking at the water. He turned his head to look at her. Her eyes were wide open like a cat's in the darkness and gleamed brightly as she looked back at him. He reached for her face and she let her head fall back to the grass, her hand at his neck, holding his face close to hers.

As she lay there, holding him close to her, receiving his kisses, there was a part of her which detached itself from the embrace. Whether I am in love or not, this part of her was saying, I am enjoying making love. She remembered her talks with Violeta about love and sexuality, and feeling Rafael's hard member pressed against her thigh and receiving, in spite of all the clothes, a peculiar sensation, she decided that she was going to live up to all the words about not caring about chastity that she had spoken so arrogantly to Violeta. She decided, pushing back his tongue with her own, that she was going to sleep with this man. She had an idea just as he began to become more importunate and demonstrative and had his hand at her blouse. She pushed him back and said, "No, not now."

277

Not *now*. The phrase gave him hope, and he said, "Then when?"

She had quickly thought out what she must do and said, "Come tomorrow night to the cottage. You will find your real bride there."

She gave him a long kiss and stood up. As they walked back to the house, she gave more instructions. He must come to the cottage at eight, after dinner, when it was quite dark. She would not be at dinner and he must remember to tell Jason that she had a headache and had already gone to sleep. Nor would he see her earlier during the day. They would continue in the next day's darkness what they had begun this night. The sunny part of tomorrow was not to exist for them. And while he would need a torch to find his way to the cottage, he must come to the room without a light and not switch on the light when he was there. They would be two bodies in the darkness melting into one. And he must go away before it began to be light. He thought her extraordinarily imaginative but the fantasy suggested by her idea was so strong in his mind that he accepted every detail which she stipulated. She was wonderful. She could turn any reality into an elaborately mysterious performance. She was an enchantress who knew how to raise pleasure to a pitch of ecstasy. Oh, how he loved her!

9

Sylvia recovered from her flu three days after Madeleine and Jason had left for Oyarzún's land. Violeta continued to fuss over her for another day to make sure that she did not overstrain herself. And then she began to miss her friends, and wondered whether they had begun a closer attachment. The thought of Madeleine and Jason in each other's arms made Violeta slightly dizzy, and she was surprised at herself: could she be jealous? No, she decided, she could never be jealous of Madeleine; besides, she knew her strong-willed friend, and she thought with considerable amusement what would happen if Madeleine, who had talked so often of despising the idea of chastity since it was an invention of male vanity, decided that Jason was the man who should deflower her. By the compact she had herself insisted upon, she would be obliged to ask Violeta to enjoy the honor first. Several amusing fantasies attended this thought but there was a limit to daydreaming and by the next day Violeta began to be bored and wished her friends would return. It was a relief, therefore, when Luis Rejano came to the house in the afternoon and said that some of his friends were giving an impromptu party that very evening and he hoped that she and Madeleine could come. She told him that Madeleine was away but that she herself would be glad to go.

She enjoyed herself and at one point when she was dancing with a young man named Bartolomé she found herself clinging close to him. She felt a fine pleasure in the way he passed a hand across her back and slowly bringing it round her waist raised his palm to her breast. She pressed her cheek to his and

279

felt him squeeze her breast. She pulled herself back and began to dance in a movement which was closer to the fast rhythm of the music. The room was dimly lit and was crowded with couples dancing but she was startled by what she had let Bartolomé do. She made an excuse not to be with him after the dance, for she feared the desire that had been aroused in her. But an hour later they were dancing together again, and she found that she did not mind it at all when he had both his hands at her buttocks and was pressing her tightly toward him. It was the way some other couples were dancing, too. Later on, they were together on the wide terrace, against the wall behind some flowering bush growing in a large pot. He was kissing her and fondling her with the urgency of one who expected their privacy in a public place to be disturbed at any moment. He had managed to get his hand through the opening of her blouse and with his other hand drew one of hers and placed it between his thighs across the stiff fly. He was kissing and squeezing her and beating against her with his thighs with a desperate urgency. Then suddenly he stopped and stood back and soon guided her back to the room.

When she thought of her experience the next day, Violeta was surprised at the thought that came to her: had there been an opportunity, she would have gone to bed with Bartolomé. She wondered if she had been influenced by Madeleine's views on the subject or whether it was simply a natural thing that a woman of twenty-four should desire a man. The next two or three days when her friends still did not return she spent in considerable mental agitation, and on one evening even walked to the square with the hope almost of being picked up, and it was only when she looked at the young men in the square and did not see Bartolomé that she realized that without thinking about it she had come looking for him. And now that she looked for him, she could not precisely remember his face. It had not been particularly attractive, she recalled, and she did not seriously think he was the kind of man she wanted to give herself to. His behavior had really been vulgar when she thought of it objectively, and there was something perverse about the way in which he had beaten his thighs against her and then stopped. She understood what that indicated and thought that she ought to feel revolted. But her real feelings remained obscure and she walked back to the house, deciding that it was foolish to be loitering in the square, but feeling nevertheless that her mental agitation of the last three days came from a deep-seated desire.

Madeleine arrived in the morning when they had just finished breakfast and Antúnez had left for his office.

"I'm glad to see you're well again, Mother," she said, kissing her mother on the cheek.

"Where is Jason?" Violeta asked.

"Still at Oyarzún's. He's totally immersed in a study of some Indians who work as potters. I've hardly seen him for a week."

"Are you going to leave him there?" the mother asked.

"No," Madeleine said. "We're going to have a party and I've come to take Violeta."

"How long is all this going to continue?" the mother asked.

"Oh, three or four more days. Perhaps a week at most."

"You should be meeting people in good society," the mother said, "instead of running about in the wilds."

"Of course we will, Mother, we will!"

"That Otero girl is going to marry Labarca's son," the mother said.

"Oh, well, another eligible bachelor gone!" Madeleine said with ironical playfulness. "But don't worry, Mother, there are plenty more."

When the two girls were alone, Violeta said, "What kind of a party is it?"

"You will see," Madeleine said with a merry twinkle in her eyes.

She helped Violeta pack and after taking a midmorning cup of coffee, when she reassured her mother that she would make her proud of her daughter one day, drove off with Violeta. She talked about Alberto while she drove, at first painting a picture of him as a most wonderful and handsome young man.

"I think you've fallen in love with him," Violeta said.

281

"I don't know, but I decided last night that I was going to go to sleep with him."

Violeta gave a start when she added, "You don't know, Violeta, but I suddenly realized that I badly wanted to." It was precisely what Violeta herself had felt when she had found herself loitering in the square.

"Do you remember what we agreed upon?" Madeleine asked her.

"No, I cannot do that!" Violeta said, suddenly frightened.

"Violeta, you're not going to go back on your word now, are you?"

"My dear, dear Madeleine," Violeta said, turning to her and touching her shoulder. "How can I bring myself to do that to *you*?"

"I would do it to you for the simple reason that I promised that I would. I would be most offended if I discovered that you'd been doing it behind my back."

Violeta felt a pang of conscience thinking that she had in fact come close, as Madeleine coarsely put it, to doing it behind her back; and she was filled with admiration and increased affection for her friend, for here she was, having taken the trouble to drive all this way and keep her own emotions in suspense in order to live up to an idle promise.

"But, Madeleine, we were joking when we talked about this."

"I don't remember it being a joke." Madeleine slowed down and looked at Violeta. Touching her face, she said, "In a peculiar way, I love you more than anyone else. That is why we made this compact. We can never be jealous of each other, and we can be close only by complete sharing. God, it would be a whole lot easier if we were lesbians, but we are not! I long to sleep with a man."

"I do, too." The words slipped out of Violeta's lips.

"Then please do tonight," Madeleine said, speeding up, "so that *I* can tomorrow!"

It was twilight and Violeta stood apprehensively in the bedroom of the cottage. Madeleine had given her elaborate instructions, as she had to Rafael. Not a word was to be spoken, not a sigh was to escape their lips. He would leave his torch in the sitting room. The shutters would be closed on the window, there would be all but total darkness. He would be greeted by the perfume of roses. She would be naked in bed and he would drop his clothes at the foot of the bed before coming to her.

A dozen bowls and vases filled with roses were placed about the room. A faint light still came through the shutters. A clean white sheet covered the bed. Madeleine had sprinkled some perfume on the white pillows. Violeta slowly removed her clothes and found that her hands were shaking. Her mind was in a state of confusion; there was an intense excitement within her and at the same time something of despair. She was about to do what she longed to do, she was about to receive what her body craved for, and yet she felt she ought not to do it. Was it simply the old morality that raised an objection? Or was there something wrong with the kind of compact she and Madeleine had made?

She folded her clothes and put them down at the foot of the bed. Her hands were still shaking. She found herself seizing the roses from their bowls and vases and squeezing bunches of them in her hands, letting the petals drop upon the bed. The activity calmed her nerves. Then a thought occurred to her. What if Alberto were only a mask Madeleine was using and the real lover was Jason? Madeleine had been particularly evasive about Jason, almost as if she deliberately avoided talking about him for fear that some secret might slip out. Somehow the idea of receiving Jason as her lover did not seem so reprehensible. She could imagine Madeleine marrying him and it did not seem wrong at all that if she was going to be a kind of a sister to him after he married Madeleine, she should be his mistress before he did. The thought calmed her, even made her impatient for the young man to come. The window was now a black rectangle; it had grown completely dark outside. She fell into the bed among the rose petals and lay there hearing her heart beat.

Rafael walked up to the cottage, throwing a beam of light

283

from the torch in front of him. He had thought of nothing else all day but of the time when he would enter the bedroom. And there he was now, placing the torch beside the door before opening it. He stood there for a minute trying to get used to the darkness. He opened the door and stepped in and closing it behind him stood for a moment, breathing in the perfumed air. The wonderful enchantress! he thought. He knew the bed was to his right and looked there. God, how pitch dark it was! There was a slight rustling made by a body moving in the bed. He slowly removed his clothes, dropping them where he stood and took one short step at a time in the direction of the bed. He almost gave a little cry when his big toe hit some obstacle; he stretched out his hand, expecting to touch the sheet. He found himself clutching a handful of rose petals.

A little later he had climbed into the bed and, his senses quite overcome by the perfume and the drama that had been contrived for him, was kissing the girl who lay there: he was, in his mind, beginning to possess the beautiful and marvelously cunning Madeleine. And she, who had heard him in the darkness with a beating heart, grateful now that her pent-up tensions had suddenly found a release, answered his pleasure at her body with an equal ardor. She could have cried aloud as his mouth crushed her breasts, now one and now the other, his teeth sharp at the nipples. But no more than a whispering sigh escaped from her lips. She was astonished at the extent of her desire and from her breasts she was pulling up his head to drive her tongue into his wet mouth and then pushing his head down to her breasts again. She could have moaned in her pleasure but she uttered nothing more identifiable than a prolonged, but suppressed, *ah*! And from her breasts she pushed his head down to between her thighs. He was breathing hard when he pulled his head up again. Penetration was slightly difficult but their dumb bodies knew the language of accommodating each other and when it was accomplished she at first felt a little pain and thought that some blood flowed from her, but a moment later experienced only pleasure.

Rafael had never known such pleasure and it was with the consciousness of having achieved a great happiness that he left the bedroom very early in the morning when it was still dark outside. Left alone, Violeta lay touching her thighs and her breasts and passing her tongue over her lips, renewing in her mind the sensations she had experienced, until she fell asleep.

Jason was the first to come down to breakfast in the morning. He was anxious to tell Madeleine and Rafael that he had finished the first draft of his article, but neither was about as yet. The cook had only just put on the coffee, and so he wandered out of the house since his agitated state would not let him sit patiently in the dining room. He could hardly believe his eyes. There was Violeta walking in the direction of the house!

She had woken three hours after she had fallen asleep and when she saw daylight outside she found it impossible to remain in bed. She blushed, getting out of bed, seeing all the. rose petals, so many of which had been strewn on the ground. And now she blushed again, seeing Jason from a distance.

"When did you get here?" he asked when she was near him.

"Yesterday, well, last night. I wanted to surprise you." She hoped he did not ask for any explanation, but thought to herself that his surprise was so genuine that he could not have been the one . . . But, the thought occurred to her that, like her, he too was walking about the grounds, unable to sleep. And of course he was not going to tell her anything about how he had spent *his* night!

Suddenly, he said, "I could hardly sleep all night, I was so excited."

It was not, she thought, the kind of confidence a man would want to give if he had spent the night with a woman. But then Jason was so boyish, almost naïve when it came to sharing his enthusiasms.

They returned to the house where Madeleine had just come down.

"I see that some people find it impossible to sleep," she said ambiguously, giving Violeta a meaningful look, her eyes twinkling with merriment.

They were waiting for the cook to bring out the rolls from

the oven and Violeta, needing to go to the bathroom, walked out of the dining room and down the hall where Madeleine had said the toilet was. She remained there for a few minutes and thought to herself that it must have been Jason. The poor boy's eyes were swollen with sleeplessness. How she had kissed his eyes! She was going to have a word with Madeleine, she thought, laughing to herself, and ask her to change their compact to a permanent sharing, for having enjoyed him for one night it was cruel that now she was to be deprived of him forever!

As she was walking down the hall from the toilet, the door to the elevator opened and Rafael walked out. The two stood frozen for a second, staring incredulously at each other, and then rushed to meet in an embrace. A hundred expressions of surprise and astonishment seemed to emanate from their throats in a minute and, laughing and holding each other by the waist, they entered the dining room.

Madeleine raised her eyebrows seeing them enter thus. So, they had not followed her instructions but had made each other known during the night, she thought. And what's more, holding each other in so shamelessly intimate a manner and laughing as they looked at each other, they were plainly informing her that having met in the dark they had no intention of separating in the daylight. Why, he was even hugging her and kissing her on the cheek! But she suppressed the flickering of anger within her, suppressing also the thought that her Alberto who, until yesterday, she had assumed had fallen in love with her was behaving precisely as he had done when he had Oliva to turn to, and putting on a merry air said, "Why, Alberto, you do look terribly pleased with yourself."

Rafael laughed, walking toward the table with Violeta, and began to say, "Who would have thought that my long-lost sister should suddenly be walking down . . ." but became conscious of the fact that Violeta had suddenly stopped, dropping her hand from his waist, and was saying, "*Alberto?* What are you talking about, Madeleine?"

Madeleine had not heard Rafael's incomplete statement and looked questioningly at Violeta who, suddenly understanding everything, cried aloud, "Oh, my God, *what have you done, Madeleine?* This is my brother, *Rafael!*"

Her voice was so loud and so charged with meaning that Rafael understood the implication of his sister's question, and he too cried aloud, "Oh, my God, *no!*"

Madeleine was stunned and looked desperately at Rafael and said, "But you are *Alberto!* You've never said you're not Alberto."

"That was the name that tarantula Oliva gave me. It was her brother's name. Oh, my God, *what have you done!*"

"*Madeleine!*" Violeta cried in a loud scream and ran out of the open french window. Madeleine followed her. Rafael collapsed in a chair and began to weep. It was Oliva's doing, he half thought to himself, all his sorrows stemmed from her. If she had not given him that name, this horror would not have happened. Jason, having no idea of what was going on, tried to console Rafael, telling him to take a sip of the glass of orange juice he held. "The damn bitch!" Rafael cried aloud. "The damn, damn bitch, she brought me nothing but a curse!"

Madeleine returned to the room. Violeta, whom she had tried to comfort, had called her a terrible name and she had decided to leave the poor girl alone for a while. Let her at least partially get over her terrible shock. She had thought, leaving Violeta under a tree where she sat crying and tearing at her hair, she would be more accessible to consolatory sentiments later when the worst of the shock was over.

Alone, Violeta stood up, her tears having frozen and a fixed, mad look having come to her eyes. She began to walk eagerly toward the lake.

Madeleine and Jason sat drinking coffee. Rafael stood up and slowly walked out of the french window; he came back five minutes later and said in a weak voice, "Where's Vio . . . where's my poor sister?"

"She was sitting under a tree," Madeleine said.

"I don't see her anywhere."

The three went out and searched the more obscure areas around the lawn. It was Jason who, glancing idly up at the lake, saw her and let out a cry. Both Jason and Rafael immediately removed their shirts and trousers and swam out. She was already dead when they reached her

Two days later, when they had buried Violeta, Rafael said in a quiet voice, "This land has been nothing but a curse on my life. It has brought me the worst unhappiness a man can know in this world."

And he walked out of the house. It was not till later in the day that Jason and Madeleine realized that he had gone away from the land. At first they feared that he might have followed his sister's example and began to search anxiously for him; but one of the workers told them that he had seen Rafael drive away in the Jeep.

It was time for them to leave this sad place, but Jason and Madeleine sat for a while in the drawing room. Madeleine blamed herself for some of what had happened; she was certain that Violeta's death would forever be on her conscience. Unable to share the growing guilt within her with Jason, she sat crying softly. Touched by what he saw to be her great sorrow, he sat beside her, his arm around her. "Oh, Jason!" she burst out suddenly and hid her face in his bosom and began to cry loudly and uncontrollably. He held her there as tenderly as he could and when she had calmed somewhat he kissed her wet cheeks, and said, "There, my precious darling, we will learn to live with our sorrow."

She raised her face and looked at him with shining, wet, but wide-open eyes; and then she flung her head to his shoulder, hugged him tightly, and began to cry again.

10

She was walking slowly along the edge of the pasture where there was scarcely any grass and the cattle, collapsed under the shade of the trees, caught one's pitying attention for their conspicuous bones. There had been so little rain in five years! Occasionally, dark clouds would blow across from the east, bringing a hope that the drought would end, but it was always a tantalizing hope; little more than a few scattered drops ever fell. The bad time had to end, Manuela thought; she had seen trouble before—it was no novelty in the history of her people — and knew that nothing ever lasted; there would be rich pastures before long. The cattle would again fatten and the cows give milk, for, unless nature had decided to reduce the entire planet to a desert, which was unlikely, all states of disorder were temporary. It was only within the miserably short life span of a human being that bad spells appeared to be catastrophes. When she thought of it, time was important only to young women whose matrimonial prospects diminished with the passing of each year. The only other significance of time that she could think of was that it made the lives of office workers and shop assistants bearable, giving them the sacred hour of closing-time to look forward to each day and their annual two-week vacation to dream about.

In her own life, time had meant nothing; had she not just spent five years as if she lay in a coffin for a rebirth? And did she not imagine sometimes, or see in a dream, that she had already lived a life on earth, that events had occurred which had to occur, and if not precisely those then some others which—even when they were radically different—were not

289

really seen to be different, for one had the experience one did and that was all? Yes. *That was all!* On some days she was quite content to believe that she was only a butterfly; on others that she was a pot of geraniums to which the butterfly was drawn all day long. She had the idea, too, that she was one of her own ancestors in some village in Spain on the edge of the Mediterranean five or six hundred years ago and that this life was simply a reenactment in another setting. Another place, another time: *that was all!*

Her poor Jorge, how foolish he had been to believe that he was master over this one life! She had given him two beautiful children, as women had done for their husbands since creation, and would have had more if he had wanted more. But the poor man had not understood life, having been distracted by the vain idea that he had to obtain rare pleasures in order to sustain a belief in his existence. His kind had the fanatic belief that time was real and that it was important. It was an inability, really, to perceive that the immediate moment was essentially empty; that the search for increasingly refined pleasures was self-defeating as could be seen in the case of any drug addict. Nothing guaranteed a satisfying vision of the self as a real and a whole identity, for consciousness was a kind of corruption of history. The more one knew of oneself the more one saw all the other people one really was.

She arrived at the house which she had not entered for five years. Her round face had acquired wrinkles and the fat little body which had so infuriated Rojas was no longer fat. During her involuntary exile, she had known exactly what was happening in her house, for a maid who worked there kept her informed. The young mistress whom Rojas had brought to the house had begun by tearing down the curtains and throwing out the furniture. Over the years, Manuela had interpreted the information she received. She felt sad for poor Jorge. It was obvious that his mistress had not brought him happiness. But he had to suffer: he who thought he was so individualistic could not know that his experience was a common, and a rather vulgar, cliché. At last it was over now, Manuela sighed with relief as she entered the house. She had a sense of the suffering and humiliation that Rojas must have gone through; but she knew, too, that he would have suffered any pain to keep the mistress, for the illusions her presence created, even when the illusions were diabolical, were preferable to the man, because they sustained his vanity, to the violent hurt that resulted from her irrevocable rejection. A man thought nothing of throwing a woman out but he was completely beaten if the woman declared she had had enough and abandoned him.

She was not surprised by what she saw when she entered the house. The maid's descriptions of the changes that had taken place—they sometimes bordered on the fantastic—had prepared her. Manuela had seen pictures in magazines of the kind of furniture she was now looking at in the living room. A lot of chrome and glass and tubular steel; some rattan; recessed spotlights where lamps had hung from the ceiling; colored plastic venetian blinds had replaced the curtains; Oriental rugs on polished wooden floors where there had been wall-to-wall carpeting. The effect was rather pretty, Manuela was willing to concede, if you were prepared to delude yourself that you would spend the rest of your life at the wonderful age of twenty-five, dressed up in the latest fashions, waiting each afternoon for the photographers to come and take a series of pictures for the next issue of the magazine in which people like that lived.

Well, it was over now, and perhaps she could learn to live with this artificial setting. It would be up to Jorge, when he returned. She was certain he would; that, too, was part of his destiny, though, of course, he would believe to the rest of his days that everything he did was the result of careful thought. He might not want all this nonsense that his mistress had imposed on him.

There had been times when Rojas—looking at Margarita across the room as she sat diagonally across the rattan love seat in a white cotton shirt and white slacks, a narrow dark brown belt at her waist, her right arm arching casually over

291

her head and a half-filled glass of red wine in her other hand, perfectly comfortable on the cushions with their white fringes of lace, or when she stepped out of the car when returning from a trip to the city, wearing a burgundy-colored angora sweater above a pink satin skirt, a beret on her head matching her sweater, and a thousand such moments—when Rojas had been filled with pleasure and pride. The way she carried herself in the fashionable clothes she wore to go to the city was thrilling to watch; a cosmopolitan sort of sophistication came naturally to her: a firmness of step that drew attention to the perfect line of the calf, or a sudden turning of her head which drew attention to a haughtiness of spirit, for her profile, when she raised her chin in a suggestion of disdain, was expressive of an innate superiority. An aristocratic bearing came naturally to her though ironically her family had been destroyed by the military junta because her father and brothers had been considered dangerous Socialists. Rojas enjoyed, too, seeing her bring fresh-cut flowers from the garden and change the atmosphere of the living room with a simple arrangement. He did not understand the abstract paintings and prints that she had hung on the walls but in certain moments, especially when she was in one of her calmer moods and he experienced the illusion of blissful serenity, he thought he saw a startling beauty in the splashes of color on the canvases.

But these moments when he admired her as herself being a work of art were rare; and the contentment he had felt in the fashionably modern living room would give way to a resentment that the peculiar homely charm that his house had earlier contained had vanished. Sometimes, climbing the stairs, he even missed the amateurish watercolors of the Andean peaks. It was a peaceful day when Margarita did not feel disposed to listen to her stereo; she had purchased an expensive system—he could have bought a new car with that much money!—with huge speakers; for the music, which *had* to be played loudly, she insisted, and which so excited her, was abominable to his ears. But on some days he wished she would play the music; on these days the terrible din from the speakers was preferable to her voice. "You've made me a whore, that's what you've done" was the statement that came readily to her lips, spoken harshly and vindictively, whenever she felt compelled to assert her independence. It was no use his insisting, as he had done in the first months, that she was free to do as she pleased for that only made her say, "So, you'd like to get rid of me, would you?" And when he replied, "No, that's not what I meant," she would repeat, "Of course, you can do what you want when you think of me as no better than a whore."

He found it impossible to reason with her. If he said that he was motivated only by love for her and a desire for her happiness, she would taunt him with, "How can you be such a hypocrite, having thrown out your wife and children? What am I supposed to make of that, I'd like to know! That no bonds are sacred to you?"

"Why do you insist on seeing everything in such a way that it casts a bad light on me?" he would ask. And she would answer, "All you think of is how things reflect back on you. You have no concern at all for other people. Jorge, you have no idea how *selfish* you are!"

He would refuse to argue beyond that point. It was too absurd. They were talking different languages. Could this be possible, he would wonder, that he had less in common with this girl than he had had with Manuela? In that case, he could never hope for happiness with any woman. The embittered and confused emotions that prompted his thoughts deflected him from understanding an aspect of reality: that what he had been looking for was a woman who served his pleasure, threw herself into attractive poses for his delight but never expressed a will of her own. Margarita had made him feel sore when she had called him selfish; in his resentment he had not perceived how accurate her assessment was.

His bitterness only led him to think, again entirely ego-centrically, of himself as a tragic figure. Why that idea of himself answered all questions, he could not have said. His stoic forbearance annoyed Margarita, driving her to further excesses: for there was within her an impulse to perform the outrageous in order to bring him, as she saw it, to his senses.

293

She wished that he should give her a life which was more interesting than lounging around all day in the house listening to music or reading one more trashy paperback. But he invited no one to the house and was usually too exhausted by his labors on the land to do anything more than to gobble down the fine dinner she had prepared, without appreciating its excellence, and to want to make love to her and go to sleep. That to her was a bestial existence, and the least she could do was to refuse him her body, for she had no interest in animalistic couplings. If there were no refinement to existence, there was no point to sex. She was not a peasant.

Her first attempt to seek recompense for herself had been to drive to the city and spend his money. She began to buy expensive paintings when there was no more furniture she needed to buy for the house. She frequented, too, the most fashionable shops and bought herself clothes that she would never have occasion to wear in the country. And then, almost as if to justify the enormous expenditure on clothes, she began to have affairs in the city with men who were flattered to be seen in restaurants and nightclubs with such a sophisticated young woman who dressed like a model in the pages of the latest *Vogue*.

After two years of this life of deception, during which time she sincerely wanted to exist happily with Rojas if only he would make the concessions she wanted, she realized that she had no future with him. She decided that she would need to be ready for her independence when the time came, and rather than take a legal course, which was available to her, she began putting away some of the money she took from him. If a new dress she bought cost a hundred, she said it cost two hundred, and put away the extra money. It did not occur to her that by doing so she was putting herself in a position of inevitably fulfilling her own prophecy. The more money she accumulated the more she found reasons for picking quarrels with Rojas so that it would seem perfectly inevitable that they separated when they did.

For his part, he was glad when she went away to the city, for at least the wretched stereo would be silent during that time.

At first, he did not begrudge her what money she asked for, but gradually, as conditions on the land deteriorated, he began to find it hard to keep up with her demands. A quarter of his herd of cattle had been killed by vampire bats; the continuing drought had made much of the land worthless; he could not go on cutting down the pine forests that now offered the only real income. In the fourth year of his life with Margarita he found that for the first year since he had possessed the land his expenditures far exceeded his income. There was no relief and early in the fifth year he was obliged to raise money by mortgaging his land. He had fallen so low that he had been unable to say anything when he had run into Margarita on the arm of a banker in a restaurant in the city and she had brazenly come right up to him and said, "How good to see you in a civilized place, Jorge. I'm sure you know Marcos Poliziano—he is the manager of your own bank."

They had quite a scene when she had returned to the land a day after him. "You said so yourself," he shouted at her, "you're nothing but a whore!"

"Careful now, Jorge," she said in a coquettish voice. "I understood that you wanted a sizable loan from the bank. Do you think you could have got that without my help?"

"*Help?* Is that what you call your low, degraded life?"

"Don't be so offensive," she said coldly. "Marcos wouldn't have given you a penny without my help."

"Without your cunt is what you mean," he said harshly.

"Now that is terribly cheap. I really ought to slap you for such awful language."

"But it's the truth, isn't it?" he shouted.

"The truth is that you're broke," she answered, speaking very calmly. "The truth is that you came to me with all sorts of promises and all you've given me is a terribly boring life and little money with which I could do anything."

"Little money?" he cried, amazed. "But let's not divert attention from the real issue."

"And what, my dear Jorge, is that?"

"You've been fucking around, haven't you?"

"As it happens, you describe perfectly what *you* were doing when you still lived with your wife some years ago. But please, do you have to use the language of the peasants? I know you spend the best part of your life with them and cannot help acquiring their habits. At least try to show a little consideration in your dealings with people who, although you may not know it, possess a slightly more refined sensibility."

It was no use, he realized. He could shout and abuse her as much as he liked; she would always have an answer, spoken in tones either of outrage or irony, which would in the end make him appear unrealistic or utterly in the wrong.

She left him a few days after that, having quietly in the previous months transferred many of her personal belongings to an apartment one of her lovers had given her in the city. Except for the loan, Rojas was financially ruined, and he did not know that great though the loan was, Margarita had a larger sum which she had invested on the advice of the same banker who, in his enthusiasm at winning her favors, had given the loan to Rojas and added a sum of money of his own to her investment in order to make it into a neat round number.

Rojas had gone to the city on the day Manuela returned to the house. She set about cleaning the bedroom. She removed the sheets from the bed and beat the dust out of the mattress. She cleaned the skirting with a wet sponge and vacuumed the carpet. There was an odor which hung in the room and she was determined to eliminate it.

Rafael arrived the next day. It did not surprise Manuela that he had returned almost as if she had sent him a message saying that it was all right now, he could come back. And nor was she surprised to see him alone. He did not have to tell her why Violeta had not come, for she could divine the reason from his sad face. She went away and sat alone for some time and silently mourned for her daughter. When some days later Rafael described how Violeta had died in a drowning accident, she knew that he was telling only a half-truth to spare her feelings; for five years she had carried the awful knowledge within her contained in the words *the daughter's blood* and knew that, one way or another, her pure, innocent

Violeta must have shed her blood. But there was more to the sadness in Rafael's eyes, she thought, more than sadness at the loss of his sister. The poor boy looked as though he had come face to face with the kind of suffering that human beings are rarely called upon to endure. It seemed as though he had returned with memories that would never cease to torment him. That was something that he would have to live with. She could only pray.

Rafael was appalled to see the condition of the cattle. Where there had been lush pastures the land was dry and dusty. He asked Emilio how such a disaster could have occurred. Emilio himself looked as fleshless as the cattle; he seemed to have aged by more than the five years since Rafael had last seen him: wide hollows appeared round his eyes and his cheeks were sucked in as if he were toothless.

Emilio scratched the bristle on his chin and looked up at the sky. "It will have to rain soon," he said. "It cannot stay dry forever."

But the rivers were not dry since they drew their water from the melting ice far away in the high Andes. Rafael decided that as soon as his father returned he was going to talk to him about constructing canals to bring water to the pastures. It was no use hoping that the next day would bring rain. It very well might, but they should not depend upon the unpredictable elements when they had the resources to keep the land fertile.

11

The sun fell through the open window on the lump of black clay in her hands. Matarainha, the oldest of the Indian women on Oyarzún's land, was making one more pot. Her hands had known the shape of the vessel long before she came to the land with the remnants of a tribe; and her fingers had a memory of those lines which represented the snake or the jaguar or the little *pacu* fish from long before she could remember. The younger women in the shed had learned from her. As they worked, they talked about the young man who had spent so many days with them recently, for the thousandth time expressing their astonishment at his speaking their language and knowing the stories they had learned as children—how the fish came to have the different colors they do, how certain stones can reveal secrets. The women exchanged bright glances as they talked, their hands working deftly at the clay or the beads and macaw feathers with which some were making necklaces.

Matarainha was the first to notice the shadow that fell on the lump of clay in her hands. She turned her head and looked through the window. A dark cloud had overtaken the sun. She gave a little start. The cloud was advancing rapidly and she was convinced in her imagination that it had the shape of a jaguar. The other women came hurrying to the window. There was a general chattering and nervous expressions of some unstated fear. The cloud grew larger but did not change its shape, advancing with great strides. The women began to scatter, rushing out of the shed and running to their own huts. Matarainha was the last to leave; too old to run, she walked ponderously, a poncho thrown over her shoulders, her thin little body bent forward. The wind had risen and large drops of rain had begun to fall. She looked up at the sky, past the commotion in the higher branches of the trees from where flocks of birds were rising and flying out with the wind, and was suddenly reminded of an event in her childhood and it was as if all the intervening years had been wiped out and she stood there, on the bank of the river with the other children of the tribe, an event which had long ceased to exist as a memory. But it returned now as present terror, the great cloud dragging her past across the sky. A black jaguar had eaten the sun and slept in the sky for seven nights and the river had become a great snake which wound its enormous body through the village, swallowing all the huts in its huge belly. The tribe had fled. Nothing remained of it now but herself, and the children who had been born on this land. The rain was falling hard by the time she reached her hut; the wind was roaring through the trees; the sound of distant thunder indicated that the worst was still to come.

At that time of the year, tropical depressions, which sometimes developed into hurricanes, normally took a westerly or northwesterly course from their origin in the Caribbean, striking Central America across Honduras or Mexico or making for the Gulf and ripping into the coast anywhere between Florida and Texas. It was rare, almost a freak occurrence in meteorological records, but instances of it did exist, for a tropical depression to begin off the coast of Venezuela and proceed southwest across continental South America. Such a storm, uprooting trees and producing floods, invariably went unnoticed for the reason that its path was through uninhabited areas where no cities were threatened. Only animals and isolated human tribes had to flee from it.

It was some weeks after Rafael had left Oyarzún's land that just such a depression brought heavy rain to that area. That in itself would not have been so destructive but another meteorological phenomenon combined with it to produce a devastating effect. A storm system off the Andes with high winds proceeded eastward just when the tropical depression from the Caribbean hung over the land. The result was an unprecedented combination of rain and wind that continued unabated for seven days.

The wind tore a tree from its roots just outside the courtyard on the island on Oyarzún's land and threw it across the golden sheep, covering it completely. More trees fell on the courtyard, a pyramid of tree trunks and branches formed itself and slowly settled over the metal sculptures. The roof of the building that housed the antique cars collapsed under the weight of seven days of rain. The water level of the lake rose until it was halfway up the royal palms that grew on the edge of the island. More vegetation blew onto the island and remained there when the storm had finished, covering the fallen roof of the building.

The workers and the peasants, who had been without a master for several weeks and who had begun to be puzzled by their situation, were terrified. The storm blew away a number of the huts; a few people suffered severe injuries. Even before the storm hit, they were beginning to have a sense of mystery about their existence: there was no one on the land to tell them what to do, and they had a foreboding that something had gone wrong; a few of them stole some liquor from the house and lay about drunk; others, fearing chaos when they saw the drunks, took to prayer; and a group of young men drove away in the pickup with the idea of getting jobs in the city. The majority, however, stayed on the land; and although they began to be apprehensive about their situation they continued to go through the motions of the work they had been used to perform. Gradually their actions lost meaning: they seemed to be performing a mime rather than working. The unprecedented severity of the storm brought a great fear to them, and instead of doing the commonsensical thing—taking shelter in the main house whose granite construction made it a fortress—they began to panic, for their fear brought out superstitions that had long—perhaps for several generations— remained buried. They had never experienced a storm of such incredible power before and therefore it had to be a portent of profounder disasters than what it was showing them with its physical force; it was terrible to see the great trees being uprooted, but their superstitions informed the people that the subsequent calm, when at last it came, would show them something far worse. And in their panic, many of them began to leave.

Matarainha and the other Indian women and their men sat in the pottery shed hearing the oldest man tell a story. A ladder had come down from the sky and he had seen a very old man climb up the ladder. Matarainha looked at him in disbelief; the poor man was not telling the story as she knew it. Perhaps only she knew the real dreams of her tribe. But she did not contradict the confused imagery of the man's half-forgotten memory, for she understood that he spoke with a good heart. Most of all, she agreed with his conclusion of what the story meant for them: they must leave this land and return to the land which they had once lost to the jaguar and the snake. They all dispersed to prepare for the departure. Matarainha, coming out of the shed with a young girl, stopped when she saw the broken trunk of a tree near the path. Another memory came to her. It was as if the trunk had been placed there so that she might notice it and do what had to be done.

"What are you looking at?" the young girl asked when she saw Matarainha staring at the ground in what appeared to be either disbelief or alarm.

"Help me to carry that log," Matarainha said.

The trunk was about two meters long and the width of a human body.

"What are you going to do with it?" the girl asked when the two carried the trunk to the shed.

Matarainha did not answer; but when they had placed the trunk on the ground, she fetched the paints they had used to decorate the pots. She painted a small triangle on the curving bark at the top and below it she made two lines about a quarter of a meter apart and between these two lines she made a pattern of diagonal stripes and vertical lines, the entire pattern covering the top third of the log. She went to where one of the women used to make necklaces of palm-nut beads and macaw feathers and picked up a handful of the feathers. These she

301

attached to the two sides of the log next to the top line which contained the pattern.

"Those are like arms," the girl said, recognizing in the image a figure she had seen in a dream. "And the pattern is like a face."

"Now help me to take it to the water," Matarainha said.

"What is it?" the girl asked. "Why are we doing this?"

"It is a *kuarup*," Matarainha said, placing the log down in a pool of water.

"A *kuarup*? What is that?"

"The body of a dead person who will come back to life," Matarainha said, walking away with the young girl.

"Who?"

"The man whose land this is."

But afterward, when she was leaving with the other Indians to enter the jungle on their journey east to their own land, she wondered whether her memory had not failed her. Should the *kuarup* have been placed in water or in the underbrush of the forest? It was too late now; they were already out of the land.

Now only a few workers were left on the land and although they realized that they could eat all the meat they wished and drink wines every day, they found the life of easy indulgence completely senseless; and, perhaps also fearing that such an excess of pleasures was bound to provoke a retributive act by whatever force had wreaked the terrible changes on the land, they began to leave.

When they came to one of the principal rivers that formed the western boundary of the land they saw that the bridge there had fallen. They managed to cross in makeshift rafts and then discovered that about thirty meters of the road just past where the bridge had been had collapsed in a landslide. They realized then that anyone coming on the old road and stopping where it suddenly ended would have to turn back and would never know that a land was to be found across the river which had been as perfect and as beautiful as any paradise dreamed of by man. They imagined, however, that by the time the next traveler came to that region, Oyarzún's land would already be claimed by the jungle. They had noticed in recent days that

302

weeds had begun to overtake the lawns and when going into the house to fetch wine they had observed that creepers were already sprouting out of the cement that held the granite blocks together. Fallen trees had smashed into huts and pavilions on the grounds. Someone had seen a leopard running across a field with a duck in its mouth.

With the passing of another year or two, Oyarzún's land would become impossible to discover; and if anyone, coming with precise cartographical instructions and a description of the paradise that he could expect to discover, did actually cross the river and stand in front of the great mound where the house had been, he would, arriving there, be convinced that there had been an error somewhere, for surely this was not the land that his exploratory instincts had driven him to go in search of with an inexplicably compulsive longing to recover that landscape seen so clearly in his memory. Here dreams, and the divinity that resided in them, were only silent shadows.